THE STAG BROTHERS SERIES

LAINEY DAVIS

The Stag Brothers Box Set

By Lainey Davis
© 2018 Lainey Davis
Join my mailing list and never miss a new release!
Visit laineydavis.com

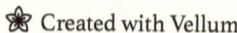 Created with Vellum

SWEET DISTRACTION

1

TIM

I'm not sure why I keep trying to get things accomplished in the office. When I'm here, I'm interrupted constantly. Everyone has questions and apparently I'm the only one with any answers. I'm trying to review the notes from our top clients, but my email chimes every few seconds and I've already had to put my cell on silent because my family evidently needs me to manage them, too.

When my intercom buzzes, I'm in the middle of re-reading a sentence I've started about ten times, so I'm impatient with my admin. "What, Donna? What??"

"I apologize, Mr. Stag. It can wait."

I exhale. Inhale again, exhale. What did that corporate meditation expert tell me I should do? Three long deep breaths before speaking? Who has time?? "No, I'm the one who should apologize for my tone, Donna. What's up?"

"It's just that Ms. Peterson is here to meet with you."

"Peterson?" A glance at my calendar shows only "busy" for the next half hour. It's not like Donna to be vague when scheduling. Who the hell is Ms. Peterson?

I hate feeling caught off guard. This never happens, and I don't tolerate it. But I have no idea what Donna is talking about, and that makes me nervous. I'm always prepared for meetings. That's what I do. I prepare for things, explore every possible avenue, make a plan for each contingency. That's how I steered my family through crisis and how I managed to run my own multi-million dollar company before I hit 30.

"Remember, Mr. Stag?" Donna's voice is calm. "Your grandmother suggested we bring on a chef and when I asked at the culinary school, they said--"

"Oh! The chef! Ms. Peterson is the chef. Right." As usual, my grandmother has been inserting herself into my affairs and, as usual, she's probably right. But I can't have her interfering with my work. I make a mental note to speak with my grandmother about making arrangements with Donna without my consent. "Donna, can you take her for some coffee or something while I prepare for our discussion?"

"She says that she's already had coffee today and that--"

"Give me five minutes, Donna. Then send her in."

"Yes, sir."

What kinds of questions should I even be asking a chef? I should have just left this interview up to Donna. My grandmother took one look at me last weekend and decided I'm pale because I don't eat properly. She's not wrong--I work 18-hour days and usually don't remember to eat until every place is closed. When I get here in the morning, nothing is open yet. I know my staff works hard for me, too, and I actually really like my grandmother's idea to have a chef come in so they can feel appreciated at lunch and maybe eat something good in the afternoon. I click through my research. A lot of big companies are bringing in a chef, having lunch together as a team every day. My competitors aren't--it's mostly tech companies. But the research seems sound. A small investment toward food and the chef's salary for greater retention and improved morale. Who says you can't buy loyalty with pie?

When Donna knocks at my office door, I look up from my monitor and, for the second time today, I'm caught totally off guard.

Standing beside my secretary is the most striking woman I've ever seen in my life. In an office full of power suits and smooth hair, Ms.

Peterson stands out like a star in the night sky. Her blonde curls are unruly, messily held back with what looks like a pen. Maybe it's a chopstick? She can't be more than 5'2", even in black clogs, which she wears with chef whites and a hot pink scarf. The shapeless jacket pulls taut across what I can tell is a full bust, and suddenly all I can think about is peeling her out of that double-breasted coat so I can massage the creamy, white globes it hides.

"And this is Mr. Stag, of course, head of the company. Mr. Stag, this is Alice Peterson." She sticks out a hand and I meet her eyes, pleasantly surprised by her firm grasp as she pumps my hand.

"It's a pleasure to be here, Mr. Stag," she says, and smiles. She has one of those smiles that reaches her entire face, and I'm mesmerized by her violet eyes as Donna excuses herself and backs from the room. The click of the closing door shakes me back to the present and I gesture for her to take a seat.

Suddenly my mahogany desk is too big and too wide; the space between us seems too far. *This isn't going to work at all,* I decide. I can't have someone like this distracting me at work. I sigh, thinking of how I'll explain to Donna that she has to find someone less...tempting. I realize as I'm thinking these thoughts that I absolutely cannot *not* hire her because she turns me on. I should know. I'm a lawyer and we specialize in injury and wrongful termination cases.

I realize the silence has become uncomfortably long when she asks me, hesitantly, "So...what would you like to ask me?"

I meet those violet eyes again and tell myself to go into work mode. This is just another puzzle for me to solve. How to overcome the lust I'm feeling for this woman. Just another obstacle. "Well, I've never hired a chef before, to be honest, but it's something a lot of companies are doing these days."

She nods. "Oh for sure. It's definitely something companies are using to differentiate themselves and attract top talent. Everyone seems to have a 'thing,' you know? Fancy milkshakes or an all-day cereal buffet..."

When I don't say anything, she continues, rambling a bit. "I took a look around your lunch room before I signed in with your admin.

You don't have a ton of space down there, but I was definitely thinking we can work on power bowls. Protein packed, quick meals. Nothing heavy on the garlic."

My wit fails me and I can't think of a response, so I say nothing. *She must think I'm an idiot or an asshole,* I tell myself as I sit there, speechless. I sigh. "It sounds like you have the right idea. Hiring a chef was actually suggested to me by someone who noticed we work long hours. My attorneys are very dedicated and by the time they remember they haven't refueled, most delivery places are closed. None of us wants to rely on fast food."

She nods. "Quick, nutritious meals, ready to eat. You guys need protein and fat if you're cranking out hours like that. Lots of fresh fruit. Nothing that will stain your dress shirt." And then she winks, causing me to glance at my chest. I'm relieved to discover there is no stain.

I clear my throat. "So Donna tells me you did very well in culinary school?"

Alice Peterson perks right up at this. I can tell she's proud of her accomplishments. "I finished top of my class," she says. "My family worked *really* hard to get me there, so I wanted to honor that by doing my best. I've always wanted to be a chef!" She beams. "I even got to intern with Kevin Souza before he closed Salt of the Earth," she says, referencing what had been my favorite restaurant to take clients before the chef/owner closed it to focus on a new concept a few towns over.

"Well," I say, impressed, "Why don't you tell me what I should be asking you."

She nods and stands. "I think we should go look at the space and talk about what's missing."

"Oh," I say, rising. "I hadn't considered that you might need different equipment." My firm occupies the top two floors of one of the skyscrapers in downtown Pittsburgh. When we leased the space five years ago, I knew the former occupants had also been a law firm. As we walk toward the break room, I realize that of course she would need ovens and stoves and an industrial refrigerator if she's going to prepare multiple meals for us every day.

Alice begins talking about her favorite appliance vendor and I lose myself in her speech, which seems to come so easily to her. Her words aren't measured or calculated. When she tells me that Don's is the best appliance dealer for a Viking range, I can tell she really feels this way, and not because she has a reciprocal deal with him.

"What would your ideal meal look like here at work, Mr. Stag," she asks, frowning and pulling out a notebook from the pocket of that bulky coat.

I squint, looking around the small break room. Right now, it's got a standard fridge and sink and electric range. It resembles the kitchen of a college dorm...with a few circular tables scattered around. "I really liked what I read about one of the tech companies in East Liberty," I say. "They have a large space where they all eat lunch together every day, even the CEO. The chef rings a dinner bell when it's time to eat." I remember reading that and thinking of family dinners at my childhood home, before everything turned sour.

My mother used to ring an old ship's bell to summon my brothers and me in from the back yard as soon as she saw my father's car approaching our driveway. Lost in the memory, I'm jolted again when Alice touches my arm.

2

ALICE

I finally couldn't resist touching him, not another second. I just had to feel what would happen. Even through the layers of his suit coat and shirt, I can feel a surge of electricity when my fingers make contact with the rock-hard arm of Tim Stag.

If I didn't need this job so badly, I'd say screw it and shove him against the wall right here in the break room. His grey eyes seem to shift with his mood, looking out from a sweep of short, chestnut hair. Right now, I want to brush that hair back from his skin and shove my tongue down his throat. But, duty calls, and so I pull myself together and decide I'm going to land this job with this brooding, handsome man as my boss.

"Mr. Stag," I say, and his wide eyes meet mine, impossible to read. I pull back my hand and gesture around me. "You're going to have to knock down a wall and put in a serving line." He nods, but doesn't say anything, so I continue. "We can put glass-front coolers over here where I can keep grab-n-go meals and snacks ready. A long row of tables down the middle should be nice. With the wall gone, you'll get natural light and a view of the Point," I say, nodding toward where the city's three rivers converge outside our office.

"We can even do some booths along that wall, if you ever wanted to have clients here for lunch. Or just want more private conversation space."

"And are you able to oversee that renovation? Manage everything you need to get started?" His voice is so deep. I long to put my hand against his chest and feel it reverberate.

My eyes go wide at his question, though. I mean, yeah. I can figure all that stuff out. My dad works construction and my brother sells industrial kitchen appliances. I just can't believe I might *get* to do something like that. I was sure my first cooking gig would be frying burgers at one of the sports stadiums. When my favorite instructor told me her best friend's boss was looking for a corporate chef, I read absolutely everything I could find about this place.

Tim Stag is a hotshot lawyer. Stone cold. He's never lost a case and managed to land the players associations for the professional hockey, football, *and* baseball teams here in Pittsburgh. He finished college *and* law school early, nailed the bar exam, and thinks he needs a corporate chef to help his company stand out. Maybe he doesn't know how much he stands out? His photos online did him no justice. The man is a fox. I realize he's still waiting for me to answer. "I mean, do you have the budget for that sort of project?"

He waves his hand as if that's irrelevant. *Must be nice*, I think. He leans past me to grab a bottle of water from the counter and I smell him--some sort of sporty deodorant mixed with the clean smell of nice soap and...something uniquely male. There's a power scent that's 100% Tim Stag. I watch his Adam's apple move as he swallows a sip of the water. "What I don't have, Ms. Peterson, is time. You can work with Donna to start the renovation. The job is yours if you want it."

"Really? You didn't even really ask me anything. Don't you want to know, I don't know, what my philosophy is? Or if I'm a vegan or something?"

He raises one dark eyebrow at me, his eyes questioning. "Are you a vegan?"

I laugh. "You think I'd be shaped like this if I never ate cheese?" I immediately regret drawing his attention to my body, which is thankfully masked in my chef whites. I flush. "No," I quickly correct myself. "I'm definitely an omnivore." I hold my hand out for a shake, saying, "I'd love to join Stag Law. When can I start?"

I brace myself for the jolt I know is coming when he returns my handshake. I feel the sizzle right through to my core when our skin makes contact, just like I felt when I first walked into his office. I hold his dark gaze and smile, imagining what it will be like to see him every day, lost in a fantasy where I feed him something delectable and he groans with pleasure.

He frowns, looking around. "Can you start right away? I guess you can't do anything with what's here now?"

I can't help but laugh, because I cook meals for my family most days in a space half this size. "What time do you want me to serve lunch?"

He walks me down the hall and leaves me with Donna, who sets me up with a corporate credit card. Two hours later, I'm plating tiny sandwiches with fruit skewers, dishes of hummus with sliced veggies and pita wedges. I've got several carafes of cucumber water scattered around the room just as the first curious employees start poking in their heads. "Help yourself," I tell them.

Soon I'm chatting with everyone, asking them for their favorite snacks and taking notes about their eating habits, things to consider about their work day. I hit it off with a woman named Juniper, who says she's new here, too. "I'm not quite sure what to make of the boss man," I confide in Juniper, smiling as she takes a hearty portion of the various sandwiches.

She nods. "I know. He's sort of hard to read. I was offered this position after a phone interview, so I wasn't sure what to expect, but he is assigning me to represent his brother, so he must trust me!"

I see Donna enter the room and I pat Juniper's arm, which is surprisingly firm. "Hey I gotta go talk to Donna, but I'll talk to you later, ok? Nice biceps by the way."

Juniper laughs. "I row crew," she tells me. "You should check it out sometime. You could be our coxswain."

Vowing to google that later, I head off with Donna to make a plan for the renovation, as well my ideas to feed everyone while that's taking place. I tell Donna that I think we should order biodegradable plates and cutlery until we can get a dishwasher set up. She just nods and tells me to do whatever I think is best. How amazing is that? Three hours ago I was just a jobless graduate from the shabby part of Highland Park. Now, I have my very own office. I can hardly believe my luck. I'm 24 years old and the week I finish culinary school, I land my first full-time job with total autonomy and an unlimited budget. I definitely owe my instructor a flower delivery for recommending me!

My first order of business is to call up my dad--who else would I hire for a construction project? I decide to use the office phone to see if I can surprise my father. When he answers with a chipper, "This is Bob. How can I help you?" I respond with, "Yes, this is Stag Law calling. We're looking for Robert Peterson."

There's a pause on the line and Dad says, "Alice? Sweetie is that you?"

I share the great news with my dad. I know I'm talking fast, but I can't help it. I tell him that I got the job (at the top of the salary range for corporate chefs, too) and free reign over the renovation to get their kitchen up to snuff. "We are going to hire you to do the project for us, Dad! Can you come take a look?"

"Well, Pumpkin, that is fantastic," he says. "You know, we just finished a renovation in that building, too. Some insurance company redid their layout. Why don't I bump my first estimate tomorrow and drive you in to work and take a gander at it?"

Dad asks some basic questions about the project and jokes that I should just make everyone garlic wings with extra ranch to drip all over their designer suits. "Very funny, Dad. But I can make those for you tonight if you want. We could celebrate, get some growlers from Grist House."

"Anything you want, Pumpkin. You know, your mother would be so proud of you." His voice cracks a little and I can tell he's tearing up. My mom passed away from breast cancer 8 years ago. Things have been rough for us since then. Medical bills almost crushed us and we lost Mom anyway. I don't know how my dad managed to scrape together tuition for me to go to culinary school. I kept my job waiting tables and went part-time for years until I finally finished.

I think about my mom's words during our last conversation. She told me to go after my dreams, even if it felt difficult. "I know she'd be proud, Dad, but thanks. I want to get things set up here for tomorrow, but I should be home around 5:30 I think." We hang up, and I get to work stocking the Stag Law break room with snacks and muffins for the morning. I've started stacking all my new equipment in my office, both because there's nowhere else to put it and because I still can't believe it's all mine. I was dancing through the aisles at Restaurant Depot outfitting the basic kitchen, placing my order for spices and bulk produce. Soon, I'll go meet with one of the local farms and set up an account for herbs and eggs. Oh, and dairy.

I'm so lost in my plans I don't notice Tim Stag watching me. When I look up, realizing I've been singing out loud, his intense expression freezes me in my tracks.

3

TIM

"Sorry if I frightened you," I say, realizing she looks alarmed. "I shouldn't have stood here staring. I just...everything smells so good."

Her face lights up behind the mountain of mixing bowls. "These muffins are for tomorrow morning," she says. "I'm just about to slide in the last batch."

Since I saw her last, she's tamed her curls back into a tight braid and tied the pink scarf around her head. Despite having made a lunch my associates won't stop talking about and what looks to be several hundred muffins, she still looks pristine in her white coat. And too fucking modest. Her pink tongue slips out as she hoists a pan into the oven, and I long to taste it, to lose my fingers in that nest of blond curls. Shaking my head, I realize that coat might not be modest enough. I have to pull myself together and remember that this woman is now my employee. She distracts me, and I don't like that.

I might need to go out and find someone looking for a quick release. How long has it been since I've been with a woman? I try to run the calculations, but Alice walks around the table with a muffin. "Here," she says, her face eager. "Taste!"

I raise an eyebrow, but accept the muffin from her and venture a bite. What hits my mouth is the most delicious flavor combination I think I've ever experienced. The muffin is moist and citrusy, but somehow light and hearty all at once. And there's an aftertaste I can't put my finger on. Alice must see me struggling to identify the flavor, because she begins talking in that carefree, delighted voice.

"They're lemon lavender," she tells me, "but I added flax for protein and used sour cream for texture. I also did a banana muffin with whole wheat and...oh. Am I rambling? I tend to get excited. I've been tweaking these recipes for awhile now. I am going to do some smoothies for the morning, too!"

A timer begins to beep and she bends to pull another tray of muffins from the oven. I stare, open-mouthed, at her perfect ass. It's round and tight, and I'm pretty sure each cheek would fill one of my hands. I swallow the rest of the muffin, trying not to think about slapping her backside as I pound into her from behind, right here in the break room. "Alice, they're delicious," I manage to say.

She moves quickly and expertly, wrapping the food in plastic and making piles to wash up at the sink. "I'm already glad we brought you on board. Donna got you everything you need, I presume?"

She laughs then, a hearty sound that explodes out of her. "*Presume*," she says in a mock-low voice, then claps her hand over her mouth. I feel the side of my face pull up in a grin. *She's making fun of me. How long has it been since anyone other than my brothers has made fun of me?* "Fuck," she says. "I'm so sorry. Shit, now I said fuck at work."

"Welcome aboard," I say, laughing quietly. "I always appreciate it when someone calls me out on my bullshit." She still looks horrified, so I try to reassure her I'm not upset. "I've spent my whole career in litigation or talking with judges. I guess I do sound a little pompous sometimes. It's hard to turn that off."

Alice is easy to talk to, and I make note of that. She's someone who might cause me to let my guard down, and if there's one thing I've learned, it's that I can never, ever stop being vigilant. "Well anyway," she says, "Donna's been great and I have a contractor coming tomorrow to give an estimate on the renovation. I hope you don't mind that I called my father's company for that. He's very well known for commercial construction throughout Pittsburgh."

"I don't see why that would be a problem," I say. "You've already impressed me with what you accomplished in one day, and I *presume* he taught you your work ethic. I trust your judgment." My personal cell begins to ring and a glance tells me it's my brother calling. "Excuse me," I say to Alice. "I have to take this. Thank you for your efforts today." I hurry into the hall to take the call as I walk back to my office. "Ty. What's up?"

"What, did I interrupt you with a woman, asshole? You sound so flustered."

"Nice to hear from you, too, little brother."

He busts my balls for awhile before he reminds me that tonight is his welcome home dinner. My kid brother is a professional hockey player. He's been playing in Vancouver for the past few years, and then got sent to marinate in the minors. He was traded to the Pittsburgh Fury this year. Of course he hired my firm to handle his contract. It took some finesse to get him called back up from the minor leagues in time for playoffs, because my brother has a bit of a temper on the ice. We're all thrilled to have him back home where he belongs.

I'm the oldest of 3 brothers, and we're all about 18 months apart, so we've always been tight. When our mom died, we had to stick together. Our father never recovered from the shock of losing her, so it's really been the 3 of us Stag brothers. Having Ty so far away for 3 years has made everything feel off-kilter.

"Listen, dick wad, Gran says I'm supposed to tell you to be on time. I'm a client AND family, so that makes me double important now. She's got drinks starting at 6:30."

"Yeah, yeah, I got it." I look at my watch. "I've got to finish up some paperwork and I'll head over. You still staying with her until you find a place?"

"Fuck yeah I'm staying with Gran. She treats me like a god. Plus then I'm not tempted to bring home any puck bunnies." Ty proceeds to describe his most recent evening with some fan he met in a club, and I have to tune him out before his play-by-play leads me toward inappropriate thoughts about Alice.

I hang up with my brother and open my laptop. I love it here at the office when nobody else is around. No distractions. Just me and my files. I start reading through the case briefing for one of our athletes who is entering contract negotiations, but even with nobody here to call me with questions, I still can't concentrate. My mind keeps slipping back to Alice Peterson and her violet eyes. And her perfect ass in those awful pants.

After 20 minutes or so, I realize it's a lost cause trying to get anything done today. The thought of Alice stirring that muffin batter keeps taking over my thoughts. I decide that maybe if I rub one out, it'll clear my head, and so I lock my office door and sit on my leather couch.

I close my eyes and it takes less than a second before I'm rock hard, imagining her full lips and that sweet tongue latching on to my cock as if it's one of her delicious confections. I begin to stroke my rod, picturing her firm grip on my base as those blond curls bob up and down. Faster than I would have thought, I feel my balls tighten and I cum, spraying forcefully onto my chest. A groan escapes my lips and I feel myself spurt again and again until I'm breathless.

"Fuck," I mutter, seeing that I've spoiled my tie. I didn't even have time to grab the tissues. I'm like a teenage boy ripping open my pants to beat off at work. What the hell has happened to my self control? I rip the tie from my neck and open my bottom drawer where I keep my backup wardrobe. I never risk having to appear before a judge, or even a client for that matter, looking less than my best.

Using the mirror in the corner of my office, I slip on the clean tie and straighten my hair. I text my car service and exhale, walking toward the elevator. As I pass the break room, I see Alice has set everything up for breakfast tomorrow, and I smile. She's good at what she does. The entire car ride to my grandmother's house, I'm distracted by thoughts of my new corporate chef, her curls, and her curves.

I decide to ask my brother Thatcher to introduce me to someone. I'm too wound up lately. He knows tons of artsy women. I'm sure he can find me someone discrete, looking for what I am seeking, too: dinner and a fast fuck, back to the office by 6am. *Yes,* I nod. *That's exactly what I need.*

4

ALICE

I parallel park my tiny Honda Civic in the space in front of our house, leaving the driveway for my sister Amy's minivan. These days, it's pretty unusual for adult children to stay living with their parents like this, but the Peterson family loves being together. The four of us kids have stuck together even more since Mom died.

My Dad still owns the giant house where we grew up. He converted the third floor into an apartment when my sister got married and told them to stay until they got their feet under them. They've got a separate entrance and everything. She and her husband have pretty good jobs--she's a nurse and he's a teacher like our mother was--but it's hard to let go of having family so close.

I spend a *lot* of time watching her kids while she's at work. Between me and my brother Dan, my sister never has to use daycare. I guess that's going to change now that I've landed myself such a cool job. I pull my arms to my chest and hug myself, reminding myself that this *is* all real and not some fantasy I dreamed up.

I grab the bags of groceries from the back and pick up the growlers of beer. I practically dance inside and shout to Dan that I'm home and I'm making wings.

"Sweet! That must mean you got the gig, hey sis?" Dan is a year older than me, but he still lives with Dad, too. He sells commercial appliances, and he really knows his stuff. As I cook, I fill him in on the renovation and assure him I'll be placing an order as soon as Dad gets the bid sent over. Between our dad working in construction, my brother Ryan working as a mechanic, and my sister working as a nurse, there isn't much we need to look for outside our immediate family. Dad's brother's an electrician, and one of his sons is a plumber, so we've got our bases covered. My family all looks out for each other, and I wouldn't have it any other way.

Amy comes floating in the door with my nephews. She pecks my cheek as she pours a glass of beer. She takes a sip and her eyes go wide. "This is really good, Al. What is this?"

"Undead Unicorn," I tell her. "It'll go great with the wings if you can wait ten minutes and not drink it all." I flick her with a dishtowel I've got slung over my shoulder and tell my siblings about my new job. "I have complete independence over all of it," I gush. "Whatever I want to cook. I'm my own boss. Sort of. I mean I guess Mr. Stag is my boss-boss, but he told me to do what I think is best."

"Mr. Stag?" My brother teases me, but my sister raises an eyebrow.

"Which Stag?" she asks. "We went to high school with them."

I shake my head. "I never went to school with anyone named Stag. I'd remember them, trust me. But my boss is Tim."

She sighs. "Ah, Tim Stag. Do you know his full name is Timber?"

She runs for the bookshelves in the living room where my dad has kept every book we've ever owned. She slides out her old yearbook. Amy is the oldest, so I guess that would put her around my boss's age. "Here," she says, sliding the book across the counter.

There he is glaring up from the page, looking as intense then as he did today. Dark hair, unreadable grey eyes. Chiseled jaw line. "That's him," I say.

"Timber Stag," my brother chimes in. "Who names their kid Timber?"

Amy flips the pages and we find Thatcher Stag in my brother

Ryan's year. "I swear there was another one," she says. "Maybe he went to a magnet school or something? Anyway, spill it, Al. Does he still look this good?"

I nod and tell her about wanting to jump his bones in the kitchen. "Gross, Alice. Come on!" my brother feigns disgust and leaves the room with his beer, but Amy leans across the counter while I finish making dinner.

"And Aim, he smells ah-maze-ing. Not that I spent all day sniffing him, but I caught a whiff. And it was nice."

She nods, looking dreamily at the picture. "He was always sort of standoffish in school. Super serious. I remember him just always being...intense."

"He'd have to be, to build such a successful law practice at his age. Everyone at the office is super driven." I start to tell her about meeting the staff at lunch. "Oh! The third brother is Ty. He plays hockey. My new friend Juniper is going to be his attorney. She was telling me how she was excited that Tim assigned her to be his brother's new lawyer."

My sister laughs when I tell her Juniper suggested I try crew. She pulls out her phone and looks up the rowing team here in Pittsburgh. "Look how fit everyone is," Amy says. "Maybe you should sign up to make them lunch after their workout."

"Very funny, Aim. I'll have you know I keep in shape chasing your sons around." I pause then, remembering that I'm not going to be able to watch them during the day anymore. "Speaking of, we're going to have to talk about my schedule." I start to carry the platters of food to the table as the back door opens and my dad walks in to the kitchen.

"There's my pumpkin patch," says Dad as my nephews swarm around his legs. He plants a kiss on each of us. Amy texts her husband, Doug, to come down for dinner. The seven of us dig in and I smile, thinking how fortunate I am.

Dad and I talk about the renovation and how something like that should only take a few weeks if he lights the right fire under his crew. "Which I will, Pumpkin, don't you worry about that." He tells me that as soon as he can get permits in place, he can get started. "If budget really is no issue, that is," he winks.

My brother and my nephews begin bickering about the newest Ninjago movie and I just feel so content looking around at my family. Our lives are so different now than they might have been if my mother hadn't gotten sick. But even as she was dying, she always told us we needed to stick together, to help each other.

I'm reminded again how I'm leaving my sister high and dry for childcare. I hadn't been expecting the job to begin right away, and I know it's not so easy to just find two daycare spaces with no notice. "Hey Aim," I say, whispering across the table. "What will you do with Ethan and Eli? Mr. Stag was pretty serious about me starting right away."

She furrows her brow. "Well, I don't work again until Friday. That gives me a few days to make calls. Honestly, Al, I don't want you to worry about it. I knew you'd be job hunting when you finished school. I really should have had a plan in place by now." Her husband, Doug, starts helping us brainstorm stopgap childcare options until they can find a place for the boys. They wonder aloud if he should cancel his commitment to teach summer school, but Amy shakes her head.

"Really, it's only for a few more months," she says. "Ethan starts kindergarten in the fall. God, I can't believe he's going to school already."

As they all start to reminisce about my precocious older nephew, my mind slips back to my new job and all the recipes I want to put in place. If I really work hard this week, I'm pretty sure I can get to where I'll be mostly in my office on Friday except for serving and cleaning up lunch. "Hey, Aim, I bet I can bring the boys with me on Friday," I tell her. "I'll just be doing admin stuff by then and they can play in my office when I'm serving lunch."

She looks at me with a severe sort of scowl.

"What?" I say. "They were desperate to have me there. I'll just let someone know I might have the boys this one time."

She frowns, and says, "I somehow can't see Tim Stag feeling excited about a pair of rambunctious boys running around his law firm, Alice. How about we save that for a last resort."

Nodding, I start to clean up, thoughts of meals for the staff racing through my mind.

5

TIM

The rest of the week proves just as distracting as Monday, and it sets me into a foul mood. I'd subjected myself to my brothers' merciless taunting when I asked Thatcher to set me up with someone this week, and after all of that, he still hasn't found anyone. I'm starting to think I'm going to rub my dick raw trying to find release every morning in the shower, since I'm waking up hard as steel after dreaming about *her* each night.

I've never met a woman who leaves me so beside myself. I'm not sure what it is about her, especially since I've been deliberate about keeping my distance. She's wild and fearless, joyful and light. I've always craved order and predictability. I operate from a place of reason. I interpret the law very rigidly, and I bring my clients a lot of satisfaction. When I date, it's always for a very specific reason. And I don't bother very often.

I maintain my family's finances, manage their real estate deals, even track their preventative healthcare for them so nothing is in disarray. That is how I keep everyone safe. Except my father, but I learned long ago that you can't help someone determined to destroy himself.

Rifling through a folder on my desk, I can't seem to find what I'm looking for and I buzz Donna. I shout her name and realize, again, I need to get a grip on my tone. "What can I do for you, Mr. Stag?"

I take a deep breath. "Donna, I can't find the briefing on the Jergensmater case."

"All the briefs for this week's priority cases are in the red folder on your desk, Mr. Stag. I compiled everything that needed your immediate attention."

Of course she's right. Everything I need for this case is right in front of me, along with the notes for our other contract negotiations, an injury dispute, and leads on new business that some of my top associates have brought in. "Donna, I'm not sure what I'd do without you," I tell her.

"That's what I'm here for, sir! Would you like me to schedule you for a massage next week? You seem a little worked up." I thank her and tell her to go for it as I make a mental note to give her a raise.

I scan the files I need, but I feel restless. I look at the clock and realize I haven't eaten anything today. Shit. It's eleven. If I go to the break room now, Alice Peterson will be prepping for the lunch rush and I'll have to avoid inhaling her scent as I walk close to her to take some of the food that's destined to be the best thing I've ever eaten.

I weigh the effects of asking Donna to grab me something and feel guilty at the thought of interrupting her work because I'm worried I can't control my dick near the new chef. I pull out my phone and text my brother. *No leads for me for tonight I guess?*

Sorry, T-dog. Can't find anyone desperate enough. You know, Timber, there's this thing called Tinder...

Yeah, yeah. Thanks for nothing.

Little Bro says you've got a new lady lawyer on your staff. Maybe I should test drive her for you?

Stay the fuck away from my employees, Thatcher. That goes double for Ty.

I start to walk to the kitchen, even more pissed off that I can't find a fucking date for myself. Then I start to wonder why this suddenly bothers me so much, since I have never really sought a woman for...I don't know if I'm looking for comfort or if I just want to get laid. The whole situation has me unnerved. I keep walking, and I hear something very unsettling.

Why the hell are there children in my office? Lying on the floor over some sort of tablet device, a pair of tow-headed boys laughs at some animated show with burping slugs.

"What is the meaning of this?" My voice is loud and stern. The kids gasp and look up at me like they might cry. I've put on my courtroom voice before thinking twice. "This is absolutely unacceptable. Who brought these children here?"

Alice Peterson's head appears behind a stack of food trays. "Oh, gosh, Mr. Stag, you scared me. Are they in your way?"

"What they are is in my *office*," I reply. I can feel a vein starting to bulge in my neck. "What if a client were to come in here? And they're lying on the *floor*. This is utterly inappropriate. Are these your children?" Before I can stop myself, I'm laying into her about her inconsiderate choice to burden us in our professional workplace. By the time I finish, my hands are clenched into fists and Alice Peterson looks like she's going to either cry or murder me.

Juniper Jones, my new associate, steps into the break room, frowning. "What's the commotion?"

I hold up a hand to her. "This doesn't concern you, Ms. Jones. I was discussing Miss Peterson's decision to bring children into our place of business without consulting me."

"Excuse me, but I talked to Donna about it--"

"Donna? Is Donna your boss? Does Donna sign your paychecks?"

Juniper steps in between Alice and me, as the kids run behind the counter toward Alice. "Woah. Tim. Enough. You're out of line here with your tone." She's right, of course. My chest is heaving, I'm so worked up over this, and the worst part is that I can't quite put a finger on why this is so upsetting for me.

Juniper walks toward Alice and draws her in for a hug. "You ok, Al?" I see Alice nod and hear them murmuring together. I hear Alice mutter the word "asshole" and I know she's right.

I take a few deep breaths and say, "I apologize that my tone got heated. Miss Peterson, may I see you in my office after you serve lunch?"

She nods, and I add, "Please see that the children find somewhere else to spend the afternoon." I stride toward the new, glass-front coolers and grab two random containers from inside and storm back to my office.

I pull up the folder of notes on Alice Peterson. I read her resume and quickly determine that she's about 24 years old. As I gulp down an amazing--*of course it's amazing, Alice made it*--fruit smoothie with some sort of zesty aftertaste, I realize what enrages me about this situation. *Alice has a family,* I think. Some man has been inside her and she has carried his children. She belongs to someone else, and that means she can't ever be mine.

This won't do at all. I do not respond very well to limits. I buzz Donna and ask her to come into my office.

She glides into the space she helped me design. The corner office with two sides of vast windows, lush carpet. I might be the fire and the brain behind this organization, but Donna is the thread that ties it together. "Hey, Donna," I ask. "Did you give Miss Peterson permission to bring children into the office today?"

She nods. "I did. Alice asked me about it on Wednesday, told me she had been working all week to get the renovation to a stopping place and map out all the menus and ordering. She seemed to have a handle on things, and I said I didn't see the harm if they stayed in her office, especially since we hired her on such short notice. Did something happen?"

I exhale and put my hands behind my head, staring out my window at the confluence of the rivers below. I can see families walking around in the park on this warm summer day, and I wonder whether Alice has called the children's father--*her man,* I think, bitterly--to come fetch the boys. "No, nothing like that. I just came upon them and wasn't expecting to see them. I might have lost my temper. You know I don't like surprises, Donna."

Donna sucks in air through her teeth. "Did you raise your voice at that sweet girl, Timber Stag? The poor dear has only been here a week. You know, she doesn't realize you're actually a big softie."

"I am certainly not a 'softie,' Donna," I retort, turning back around in my chair to face her. "But yes. As I said, my tone was out of line. Thankfully, Ms. Jones witnessed my behavior and put a stop to my tirade before I went into closing-argument-mode." I pause, remembering my new associate standing up to me, which was the right call in the moment. "Remind me later to give Juniper Jones my compliments." Donna nods. "How would you recommend I proceed with Ms. Peterson?"

I raise an eyebrow at her, anticipating. I almost never ask for her advice. She generally offers it before I need to. If only all of my employees took the initiative she takes. Juniper Jones takes initiative. She and Donna are the employees I'd take with me anywhere.

"Mr. Stag. Tim. You need to apologize to Alice for losing your temper. And you need to make it count. Sir." Donna raises her eyebrows and nods to me with finality before leaving me alone in my office.

I unwrap the package I grabbed from the cooler with the smoothie. Some sort of nut bar that tastes lightly sweet and chewy. It's miraculously not sticky or crumbly. The perfect texture. From down the hall, I hear the gentle chime of a dinner bell. It sounds almost exactly like the ship's bell my mother had at our house in Highland Park. Before my mother died and my father fell into despair, before my grandmother moved in to save us from becoming destitute as my father drank away his career and my parents' savings. Before I had to manage my brothers and keep us all in school earning top grades to ensure we could all move on to university. That chiming bell takes me back to when I was a different person, and the pain that threatens to surface at these memories is too great. Too much risk here right now.

I dump the wrapper into the trash and grab my bag. Stopping by Donna's desk, I tell her, "I'm going over to the hockey arena to meet with my brother and some of the other players. I'll be gone the rest of the day. Please clear my calendar and reschedule my appointments."

She gives me a disappointed look, but nods. "Will we see you on Sunday?"

"Wouldn't miss it, Donna. See you in the suite."

6

TIM

Sunday mornings at the office are my sanctuary. Nobody comes in on Sunday, and I'm totally alone. Granted, I could be working alone from my apartment, but I do my best work in this space I've carved for myself. Something about the view combined with the desk. It opens my thoughts, lets me unpack the depositions, find the key to winning my clients the funds they deserve.

I spent the weekend helping my grandmother around the house. Manual labor helps me work through my frustrations even more than sex. I brushed aside Gran's remarks that she pays people to mow her lawn and change the light bulbs. I remembered my days in high school, mowing lawns around our neighborhood for extra cash toward Ty's hockey fees. Friday night I'd written an email to Alice, apologizing for the way I'd spoken to her and asking her to please make me aware of any future unorthodox arrangements for the office. I thought I'd done a pretty good job, making sure to praise her work so far and reminding her that I valued her contributions to my staff. She really is remarkable. She's done so much in the short time she's been with Stag Law.

Now, after an entire week of distracted work, I feel like I can prepare to crush the coming week. Sundays are a constant promise of a fresh start. A new week. A new chance to seize order. Or something like that. I went for a six-mile run this morning and now I feel really good as I spread out my work along the smooth grain of my desk.

I look at my watch and see I have a few hours of blissful peace before I need to head over to the arena to meet Donna and the rest of the staff in the luxury suite. I dive into the Hawkins file--a contract renegotiation for one of my NFL players--and prepare the entire brief myself. I make a note to take Dawson off this case. It feels good to get my hands dirty with this one. These days, I generally tried to pass off the cut-and-dry cases to my junior associates, but I feel like getting my hands dirty with this one. It might help me regain focus.

I work until I realize I feel ravenous. I forgot to eat after my run. *Shit.* I wonder if Alice left anything around the break room or if she got rid of all the uneaten food for the weekend. As I walk toward the construction zone, I hear a sound that halts me in my tracks.

Alice Peterson is here.

I can hear her singing to herself again. Her voice is clear and strong as she belts out an old Madonna song. I stop in the entrance to the break room, peering around the construction plastic. The contractors had demo-ed the wall and the hall appears transformed just by adding more natural light. There, behind a gleaming stainless steel counter, is Alice. Her wild curls are totally free, splayed around her head like springs. Gone are the shapeless chef whites and clogs she normally wears to work.

Instead, Alice wears black running tights that end just below her knee. Her perfect, round ass is accentuated by the blue light of the open refrigerator as she bends at the waist, taking notes on the contents. I see the white cords of her headphones contrasted against the sheer material of a baggy tank top, the arm holes of which hang open nearly to her trim waist. I suck in my breath at the sight of Alice's sports bra, realizing that the black spandex material is all that keeps Alice's breasts from spilling into my sight. Her pale skin appears nearly white in contrast to the dark material. I long to slide my fingers along the lines of her tiny body, to feel her curves pressed against me.

The room feels devoid of oxygen as I struggle to breathe. She is magnificent. She is every fantasy I've ever had and more and it takes all that I have not to sprint across the room and plunge my cock into her depths. *Jesus, she's fucking gorgeous,* I think. I watch her as she takes inventory. She spins, singing, taking notes, checking everything. She's preparing to crush the week ahead, too. God, she's somehow able to organize everything and manage a thousand little details but still keep this lighthearted attitude about her. I smile as I watch her examine new appliances. This is her realm and, given complete control over it, she has pulled it into order. I like this very, very much.

I'm not sure how long I watch her from the doorway, but suddenly, she stops mid-song and sees me. Alice screams, dropping her clipboard with a clatter. She knocks over a stack of takeout cartons in her haste to pick it up. I dash across the room to help her as her hair tangles with the cord of her headphones.

"I'm so sorry, sir," she mutters. "I didn't realize anyone else was here. Donna gave me a key." At the sound of her mouth calling me "sir," my cock springs to life in my jeans. *Holy fuck* I think. Instead of saying anything, I reach around Alice to gather the food containers. Brushing against her, I feel the smooth skin of her arm begging to be stroked.

I shake my head. She smells lightly of sweat, but also like the earth and sunshine. I smell a thousand different herbs and spices wafting from her and I want so badly to taste her, to dip my tongue into her mouth and sample the flavor of Alice Peterson. "You didn't do anything wrong," I say, standing and putting the containers back on the counter. "I shouldn't have stood spying in the doorway."

She bites her bottom lip and looks away. She finally succeeds at untangling the headphones from her hair and she sets her phone on the counter with her rescued clipboard. I cough uncomfortably and fiddle with the stack of containers, straightening them. "I hope you received my email of apology, Alice."

She snorts, and I'm taken aback. *Was it not a good enough apology?* I try to recall what exactly I'd said to her when I saw her children here in the break room. "Yes, well, I did mean it. I'm truly sorry for the way I spoke to you." I cough again as she nods and doesn't meet my eye.

"Ok, well, I think everything here is set, so I'll see you Monday, Mr. Stag." She grabs her shoulder bag and moves to walk past me. I'm not ready to be away from her just yet. Panicked, I reach for her.

"Wait," I say, trying to keep my voice calm. "Who is with your children today?"

"*My* children?" She raises an eyebrow and then begins to laugh. I could listen to the sound of her laughter for hours, even if it's at my expense. "You know those are my sister's kids, right? Well, Donna knows that. Because I cleared it with her before I brought them in." She pauses and laughs a bit more. "Woo, that's funny. *My* children. I'll have to tell Amy."

"Your sister's children." I've behaved deplorably. Jumped to conclusions. Badgered the witness. What the fuck is happening to me? I rake my hands through my hair and along my jaw. "Look, Alice, I think we got off on the wrong foot. I want to tell you how impressed I am with what you've done here so far." I gesture around and begin to explain how she's altered the atmosphere at work in just one week. "You're very driven and you're good at what you do," I finish. "We need you here."

She laughs again. "Did you think I was going to quit just because you had a temper tantrum?" She puts her hands on her hips and her violet eyes darken. She's not nervous around me--quite the contrary. "Did you upset me on Friday? Yes. Was I pissed off? Definitely. But this is a good job and I'd be a fool to walk away just because my boss is a blow hard." She claps a hand over her mouth. "Shit. I didn't mean to say that to you." Her pale skin flames red, from her chest to the tips of her ears, which poke out from among the nest of curls.

"Tell me how you really feel, Alice," I say, smiling. People don't usually speak frankly to me, outside of my family. I'm used to people measuring their words, either because I intimidate them or because they're speaking to me very carefully in a courtroom. "Maybe we are even now?" I suggest, leaning closer to her and boxing her in against the steel counter.

I'm close enough now that I could lean in and kiss her. I could dip my head in toward her plump lips. I'm barely controlling my urge to do just that when she shakes her head. "Nope. Not even. Your tantrum was in front of my nephews, and I had to explain to them why I work with an angry man who yells."

I'm overcome by this woman. I lean in. *She's not taken, which means she can still be mine.* I know I shouldn't kiss her and I don't think I'm going to. My mouth is an inch from her ear, so I whisper, "I'm sorry I yelled, Alice. I find it very hard to be rational when I'm near you."

I see her eyes scan my body. She meets my gaze and I know she is attracted to me, too. I see her pupils dilate and the pink tip of her tongue licks her teeth before she speaks. "Mr. Stag," she says, "I..." She stares into my eyes and I can feel my chest rising with each breath. I watch her chest rise and fall as she stands inches away from me. I know this is wrong; she's my employee, but she's also the most amazing woman I've ever met. Not only is she fucking gorgeous, but she's a breath of fresh air in this place, and I didn't even realize I was choking until she got here. I start to lean closer. I'm so close to kissing her now, I can feel her warm breath on my face. And then my stomach rumbles, audibly. The mood shifts instantly, the tension melting away as Alice smiles at me.

"You're hungry! Awesome. Let me get you something."

7

ALICE

Holy mother of god, I think as I turn away from my boss to grab some stuff from the new coolers. I was a few seconds away from jumping into his arms. If his stomach hadn't rumbled just now, I probably would have just peeled myself out of my workout clothes and spread myself open here on the counter.

Shit, he looks even hotter in jeans and a hockey jersey than he does in his designer suits. He's still pretty stiff in his weekend getup. His posture. Maybe his dick, too? I put my knuckle in my mouth, telling myself I can't be thinking about his dick. Ever. Maybe I should get him to yell at me again so I stop thinking with my clit and maintain my professional dignity.

"Let me guess," I say. "You forgot to eat breakfast again."

Tim grins and hops up on the counter, sitting beside me as I lay out ingredients. I like this side of him much more than uptight, yelling Tim. "Guilty," he says. "I'm meeting everyone at the arena at one, but I don't think I can make it until then."

I decide I can whip him up a quick omelet since my dad's guys haven't disconnected the old stove. I set to work quickly chopping up some veggies while the butter melts in the pan. "What's going on at the arena today?"

His eyebrows shoot up and I can tell I've said something off. "Shit. Alice, didn't Donna get you a ticket? Fuck."

I shake my head. "Ticket for what?"

He leans in and plucks a bell pepper from my pile as I dump the veggies into the butter to soften. I watch his long fingers bring the food to his mouth and I have to look away from the sight of his lips wrapping around the pepper. He bites and says, with his mouth full, "Today is the first game of the Stanley Cup playoffs. We have a suite for the staff since we represent the--"

"The players union," I finish for him, nodding. "I knew that. I googled you before my interview. My family doesn't really follow hockey. Hey, will your brother play today?" I ask him about the Fury as I whisk the eggs and begin scrambling them in the pan with the veggies. He says his brother Ty will be starting his first game with the Pittsburgh team. I guess that means Juniper will be at the game.

Tim watches me as I make the omelet and says, "I'm truly sorry that you weren't included in the celebration today, Alice. Do you have plans? Can you join us?"

I slide his eggs onto a plate and frown. "I smell like a gym sock and I'm wearing a tank top. I think I'd be pretty cold in a hockey arena," I say, handing him a fork.

I cross my arms in anticipation as Tim takes a bite. His face seems to melt and he says, "Good God, Alice, this is the best omelet I've ever had. What did you do to these eggs?"

I tell him how I used fresh Amish butter from a farm about an hour away and ordered eggs from them, too. "See the color? The yolks are almost saffron. You don't get anything like that at the grocery store." I smile.

I see a vein tick in Tim's neck as he eats, and I'm surprised by how delighted I am that he likes my food. He finishes chewing and says, "I'd really love for you to come with me to the arena, Alice. I'm pretty sure I've got a turtleneck in my office. You could wear that and I'd be happy to get you one of my brother's jerseys. You should probably have a Stag jersey for work purposes, anyway, since he *is* a client."

Holy shit, he's offering to let me wear one of his shirts, I think, wondering if he can see the wet spot I'm sure is appearing in my pants at the thought of slipping his shirt over my head. It would be nice to see everyone from work in a social atmosphere. *What the hell,* I decide, and nod. "As long as you buy me a whisky to warm me up if my legs get cold." And then I feel breathless, because Tim Stag smiles at me.

8

TIM

I try not to think about sitting with Alice Peterson for three hours, knowing she's wearing my shirt. I run to get a black turtleneck from my emergency drawer as she quickly washes the dishes. When I hand her the shirt, I realize it will be comically large on her small body. At six feet, I'm the shortest Stag brother, but I'm still about a foot taller than Alice and a great deal bigger than her all around.

I may not be a professional hockey player like my brother, but I run five miles most days and hit the gym with a merciless trainer whenever I'm not pounding the pavement. I hand Alice the shirt and she laughs. We walk down the hall to the bathroom and I know she's in there changing her shirt. Slipping my shirt onto her smooth skin. I shiver a bit at the thought, but Alice walks out of the door toward me.

She stuffs the tank into her messenger bag and looks around the kitchen, turning off the light. "Should we head over? Are we walking to the arena?"

Dazed, I shake my head and text my car service. "My driver will take us to the VIP entrance," I tell her. "We can stop and buy a jersey for you when we get to the arena." Before I can stop myself, I place my hand on the center of her back to guide her down the hall toward the elevator. I swallow and close my eyes as she stands in front of me, asking questions about the game. When she gives her hair a shake, I'm hit again with the exotic combination of smells that must seep from her pores.

"I'm just going to text my dad and tell him not to expect me later," she says, tapping out a message on her phone. She laughs. "He'll have to fend for himself for dinner. Someone else is going to feed *me* for a change!"

By the time we reach the curb, she's told me about her father and brothers and plumber uncle, all of whom were expecting her to cook them Sunday dinner. I don't feel the slightest bit bad for them, though. I'm about to slide into a car beside her, the smell of limes and ginger--*that's what was in the smoothie,* I think, *fresh ginger!*--hovering around her like an aura of light.

My driver, Joe, looks shocked to see me emerge from the building with a woman. I quickly introduce her as our newest employee, but he gives me a look as he opens the door for her. Joe knows I'm thinking unprofessional thoughts about my corporate chef. I curse the comfortable width of the back seat as Alice slides to the opposite window, which she opens to cheer along with a group of drunken tailgaters as we stop at a red light. "I thought you didn't follow hockey," I say when she finishes shouting 'Let's go, Fury!' like a seasoned pro.

"I might not follow hockey, but I know how Pittsburghers support their home teams," she says. "I'm a Pittsburgh girl, born and raised."

"What neighborhood?" I ask her, curious.

"My family lives on North St. Clair in Highland Park," Alice replies. "I think I told you--or maybe I only started to--you went to high school with my sister, Amy. And one of your brothers graduated with my brother Ryan. From Peabody."

I stare at her, open-mouthed, remembering. I whisper, "The Peterson house. I mowed your lawn for awhile when your mother was sick."

She nods and her face lights with recognition. "Well, I don't actually remember *you* per se, but I do remember my dad hired neighborhood kids to help out for awhile so he and Ry and Dan could spend as much time with mom as we could."

How could I have spent most of my life living a half mile away from this glorious, wild creature and only met her now? We pull in front of the VIP entrance and Joe opens Alice's door. He grins at me as he catches me staring while Alice walks toward the arena, handing her bag to the security guard to search. "I could get used to this," she says, gesturing around the deserted entry. "No lines! I guess it pays to have a brother on the team," she says.

I shrug and laugh, telling her it's more lucrative to be the team's legal counsel. I try to remember the last time I laughed. The sound takes me by surprise, actually. This woman stirs reactions in me that I haven't felt in years. I've smiled more this week than I can remember smiling...maybe ever. I escort Alice into the pro shop, where we do have to wait in line. I see her notice the price tag on the Stag jersey I grab from the closest rack, but I wave away her protests. "No worries, Alice. This is a work uniform requirement." I smile again. "It'll be a tax write-off, I promise." I slide my Black Card across the sales counter, wondering if Alice will notice it and feel impressed. When she doesn't seem to respond, I am surprised to feel relieved. *Not a gold digger, then.*

The women I usually take out are very much in tune with the Black Card and what it means I can buy for them. Expensive champagne. Dinners that come one, tiny portion at a time on plates drizzled with sauce they won't eat. Alice grabs my arm after sliding the jersey over her head and gasps, pointing across the concourse. "There's a Nakama in the arena! Can I get sushi?"

I assure her she can get whatever she wants in the executive suite and try not to think about how she will look enjoying her food. She swims in the jersey, but I definitely like seeing her with my last name on her back. As we enter the suite, a chorus of cheers rings out. My staff is excited to see her, and I feel a sense of pride mingled with jealousy as she slips away into easy conversation with Juniper and some of the other associates. I chose all of them because they're good at their job, but I almost never interact with them socially. Alice slides among them as easily as if she'd known them for years. I hear her ask about their spouses, and they ask her questions about her siblings. This type of interaction is always so foreign for me. I try to avoid it, so I stand at the back of the room and just watch her. I see Donna looking at me with a raised eyebrow and then I feel myself flush. *What is going on with me?*

I pull aside one of the wait staff and ask them to bring me a sampler platter from Nakama. Then I wait, anticipating the look on Alice's face when I hand her the tray of sushi.

9

ALICE

I wonder if Juniper can tell that I'm a mess inside. I had to sit as far away from Tim as I could in the car so I would stop throbbing with desire for him. The way he put his hand on my back in the elevator left me breathless, and then walking into the arena on his arm? I need to get it together and remember that I work for him. The kind of women who date Timber Stag are the women who can afford the annual fees on the Black Card I saw him pull out to buy me this jersey.

The announcer lists the starting players, and my co-workers all find seats in the box. Everyone got there before us and already picked the buffet clean, but just as I'm about to ask where I can grab a burger, I feel someone tap my shoulder. My boss is standing behind me holding a tray of what looks like every kind of sushi Nakama makes. I feel my jaw drop and he grins. "Your raw fish and rice, madam," he says.

"You are my hero," I blurt out before I pop a piece of sashimi into my mouth. "I'm starving." I close my eyes--this is delicious. "Mmmm, that's soooo good! I can't believe you bought me sushi. At a hockey arena." Tim nods his head toward two seats in the back row of the box. The seats are amazing--we are looking down right over the middle of the ice and even though we are high up, the glass front of the box retracts until it feels like we are just above the players. "Is that your brother," I ask, pointing to the tall player with shaggy hair and eyes like Tim's. He nods and I can see his pride in his brother as Ty skates a lap around the ice, enjoying the cheers as his name is announced.

And then Tim's arm touches mine on the armrest between our seats and I can't think straight. The blood is pounding in my ears. I keep my head facing the ice, trying to concentrate on the game, wondering if I imagined the heated moment we shared in the kitchen earlier. My skin burns where it's pressed against his and I squirm in my seat as my desire shifts south in my body. And suddenly, the arena erupts as Ty Stag scores a goal just a few minutes into the game.

Everyone around us jumps to their feet, cheering and hugging. I get swept away in the excitement, giving out high fives, and turning to hug the nearest person to me. Who is, of course, Tim. I pull back from the hug and I can barely breathe. I want so badly to be pressed against his body again. His grey eyes are molten and I see him swallow, his Adam's apple rising and falling. I know I'm not the only one feeling the heat.

We sit back down as the game resumes, but Tim keeps his eyes locked on me. I feel his hand move to my knee, those long, strong fingers gently stroking my leg until I whimper, my desire for him magnified by the fact that we are here at his brother's hockey game and there's no way we can do anything. *Can we?*

The light above the goal signals a television timeout, and he leans in. "Come with me," he says. It's not a question, and I nod, following him to a private elevator outside the executive suite. He pulls a key card from his wallet and pushes the button for the conference room. Once we are inside the elevator, I gasp as he pushes me against the wall, pressing his body against mine.

"I want you, Alice," he says, his voice ragged, arms on either side of my face. I can't even get words out, I want him so much. "But I can't do anything about it, because you are my employee." My mind is racing, because I want this so much, and I also know that this would change everything at work.

Or would it? Maybe we just need to do this, savor the experience, get it out of our system. "What if this is just...what if just once..."

"Just once."

I nod and he crashes his lips against mine. I moan into his mouth, finally digging my fingers into his hair. I feel him bite my lower lip and as the elevator door opens, his hands slide under my ass and he lifts me against his body.

I wrap my legs around his waist as he walks us into the conference room, slamming the door behind us by kicking it shut. I can taste his urgency as he kisses me hungrily. The rough stubble on his cheeks rasps against the skin of my neck as he dips his head, kissing and biting his way down my body and placing me on the edge of the huge conference table.

I start to worry about what this will mean for my job, how I'll ever look at him the same way again at work. But then his hands find my nipples beneath his turtleneck and I stop caring. Tim's thumbs rub my sensitive nubs until they are hard as cherry pits, poking through my sports bra. I moan, loving his ministrations while he continues to kiss the skin along the side of my neck.

I run my hands along his abs, surprised at the rock-hard muscle I feel beneath his shirt. How did I not notice that my boss has the body of an Adonis beneath those tailored suits he wears every day to work? I begin to pull his shirt over his head, desperate to feast my eyes on him. I lick one of his nipples and his eyes fly wide open, meeting mine. He looks wild, unmoored, and I love that I've gotten him to this state.

I pull away from him and begin to peel off my own clothes as he unsnaps his jeans. They slide to the floor and I can see his erection tenting his black boxer briefs. I reach out a hand to touch the impossibly-large bulge and grin, saying, "What have you got for me, Mr. Stag?"

"Jesus, Alice," he hisses, ripping down my running tights and panties in one tug. "Say that again." He pulls my legs so that I'm on the very edge of the table and I lean back on my elbows as he spreads my knees wide.

I am totally bared for him and as I watch him slide down his briefs I see the stiff rod of his cock and I groan. It's huge, and a drop of pre-cum glistens on the tip as he strokes himself. "Fuck me, Mr. Stag," I whisper.

10

TIM

I have never heard anything as sexy in my entire life as Alice fucking Peterson asking me to fuck her. And she called me Mr. Stag. I hate that this turns me on even more, but my dick has taken total control of my brain by this point.

"Are you on the pill, Alice," I ask as I dip my hand to her sweet center. Her blond curls are as wild below as they are on her head, and I think it's the hottest fucking thing I've ever seen until I look at her face while my fingers spread her slick folds.

She's so fucking wet and her eyes have gone a deep violet as her pupils dilate huge and black. I slide one finger inside her tight, pulsing tunnel and I can barely stand to wait for her answer. "Are you, Alice?"

I stop stroking her and she nods. "Yes. Please, Tim."

Sliding in a second finger, I press the pad of my thumb against her clit. I have to watch her come. I have to see her face when I send her over the edge. She starts to groan and her hips buck up against my hand. Her shirt and bra are rolled up around her shoulders and her bare breasts heave as I stroke her clit. Her head drops back and she screams when I take a taut nipple in my mouth as I start circling her clit faster. I suck on her breasts, which are every bit as soft and round as I imagined. I move between them, using my left hand to heft their weight and press them together while I pump my right hand in and out of her body. I feel her start to squeeze my finger with her pussy and I know she's close. I lift my head from her chest so I can watch her face.

"Come for me, Alice. I want to see you." I never talk this way during sex. I don't know where this is coming from, but as I finish my sentence, Alice erupts. I feel her pussy contract around my fingers and she moans my name again and again.

"Yes! Tim, yes. I'm coming. I'm coming!"

The sound is almost enough to take me over the edge without even sliding inside her, but I have to feel her, and as she finishes the waves of her orgasm, I line up at the entrance to her body and slide inside. Alice gasps as I fill her, but I am beyond consciousness at this point. I'm mad with lust for her and I begin to thrust in and out. Her pussy is liquid velvet against my skin. I've never been inside a woman without a condom before. Never. But fuck, this feels incredible. I lean my weight on my hands, on either side of her head, kissing her sweet mouth again as I set a furious pace.

I hear the sounds of our bodies slamming together and Alice starts moving her hips along with mine. She clings to my shoulders with her soft skin pressed against my chest. I lose myself in the scent of her, the feel of her. As she moans my name again and again I know I'm not going to last. "Alice," I gasp. "Come with me!"

I slide a hand between us, right above the place our bodies are joined, and begin to circle her clit. Then I feel it. Alice's orgasm has her almost convulsing around my dick, and as her tight muscles milk my shaft, I moan her name. "Holy fuck, I'm coming." I feel jets of my heated release fire into her and when it ends, I collapse on top of her on the table, spent.

Panting together, we lie on the table where I've signed multi-million dollar contracts for my clients. A conference room where I'll never again be able to work without seeing Alice Peterson's face as she lost herself and I gave control over to something larger than myself. Whatever happened here was so much more than just fucking.

When I can finally breathe again, I roll off of Alice's body to lie beside her on the table, one hand playing with those amazing breasts. I try to figure out what comes next, because one thing is for damn sure. Fucking Alice once did not get her out of my system.

I already need to make her come again, to watch the pleasure move across her face and throughout her body. There's so much more of her I haven't yet tasted. No--this cannot happen again, and yet I know I need to have her. All of her.

She rolls onto one side and lifts her head onto her bent arm. She smiles at me and says, "That was pretty incredible." I nod and reach behind her head, pulling on her hair tie until her curls fall loose around her face, wild and unkempt and smelling amazing. Her words are muffled through the curtain of hair. "We should probably go back down, though, don't you think? And watch your brother play?" She bites her lower lip and I know she's right, but damn if I'm not already hard again.

Reluctantly, I climb off the table and help her down. We manage to get dressed and into the elevator. When the door opens, I look around, but everyone is back in their seats. I motion for Alice to go ahead of me and I tell her I'll bring her a drink. The reason for our absence will be obvious to everyone if we re-enter together. I hang back at the door to the suite and watch her sit. All I can think about is that Alice has my cum dripping out of her pussy.

11

TIM

"You're in a good mood," Donna says when she gets to the office on Monday. I'm not sure how she can tell from across the room until she tells me she heard me whistling from the hallway.

She's not wrong. I feel fantastic. After the game, I asked Joe to drive Alice home since I was meeting my family for the after-party. She, of course, refused the offer and said she was going out with Juniper to celebrate a Fury win. I felt so relaxed after the game that I even agreed to do a shot with my brothers--I rarely drink liquor. I spent too many nights in high school mopping up bourbon-scented vomit when my father stumbled in the door wasted. The smell of it turns my stomach.

But my little brother scored two goals in a Stanley Cup final and I screwed the most beautiful woman I've ever seen in my life. I didn't even get angry when Dad showed up at the club wanting to congratulate Ty. I did have security send him away, though. Fuck him. If he can't be there for our lows, he doesn't get to enjoy the highs.

Donna slides me the folder with this week's priority cases and starts to debrief me, but I cut her off. I'm suddenly starving, both for food and another chance to be near Alice. "Donna, let's put this on hold for a half hour. I'm going to get a muffin."

She smiles and nods. I clap her on the back, adjust my suit jacket, and walk down the hall, feeling only mildly foolish as I check myself in the mirror. *This isn't a date. She works for you. This is...an infatuation.*

I find Alice passing a tray of muffins and juice to a group of construction workers in the kitchen. I feel my inner Neanderthal rising when I notice the way they look at her. One of them is talking to her so familiarly that I want to punch his smug face, until Alice sees me. She smiles and the whole world stops. It's like one of those television moments, where everything else in the room fades away.

Bob the Builder sees me glaring and quickly returns to his work. *Good. Fuck off,* I think.

I walk toward her and she offers me the tray. "Fresh squeezed OJ and bran muffins today," she says. I am dying to know if she thinks about what we did yesterday. If it kept her up all night like it did me. If she is also hopelessly in over her head. Her face doesn't answer any questions, though. Her smile is just the same smile as always.

"Only for you will I taste a *bran* muffin, Ms. Peterson," I say, letting my fingers touch hers when I accept the muffin. I feel that familiar sizzle where our skin meets and she blushes. *I am in trouble,* I decide.

Her eyes hold mine, questioning, and it seems like she's about to say something when I hear a familiar voice say my name. "Tim, yo! This place looks totally different."

I turn around to greet my brother Ty, who is standing in the doorway with our grandmother. My body tenses and I feel my vein tick in my neck. I hate surprises. They know this. "Gran," I say, trying to make my voice sound normal. "What are you two doing here?"

She pushes into the room, touching the stainless steel counters and looking around. "Oh relax, Timber Stag. We're just here for a few minutes." Alice has retreated to her new work area and seems to be busily stirring a fragrant concoction of grains and vegetables. My grandmother takes in the new space and smiles. "I see you took my advice."

Ty has a mouthful of muffin and chews as he looks around. "What the hell did you do here, bro?"

Annoyed, I hand him a napkin and tell them how I've hired a corporate chef, who recommended a kitchen renovation. "Alice Peterson, this is my grandmother, Anna Stag, and I suppose you have yet to meet my brother Tyrion."

He winks and shakes her hand, waggling his eyebrows suggestively. "Call me Ty, sweetheart." I feel my blood boil and I stare daggers at him, but my grandmother hits him with her purse.

"Stop it, Tyrion. Behave yourself right this instant." He winces and rubs his shoulder as he finishes the muffin. My grandmother beams at Alice. "I'm counting on you to fatten up my grandson," she says. "He doesn't eat enough. He works too hard."

Alice smiles at her and nods, saying, "They all do here! But don't you worry. I've got them all stopping for lunch every day at noon and eating breakfast and afternoon snacks, too."

Alice starts to show my family around the new kitchen, talking about the quinoa salad she's working on for lunch, but I clear my throat. "Gran, Alice has a lot of work to do. I've given her quite a lot of responsibility."

"Well, *Sir,*" my brother says, mocking me, "We're just heading down the hall to sign the forms my new attorney has for my playoff bonus." He grabs another muffin and flashes Alice his most flirtatious smile, and I want to punch him in his smug face as he says, "It was real nice meeting you, Alice Peterson, muffin magician."

She laughs at his joke, and I find myself swimming with feelings, ranging from rage that another guy made her laugh...to pride that she gets along well with my family...back to jealous anger that my sleazy brother is clearly trying to hit on Alice. I'm literally shoving him out of the room and he says, "Ok, ok. Hey, you want to grab dinner with me and Thatcher later? Mad Mex is dark enough that I shouldn't be mobbed by fans on a Monday."

"If I say yes, will you get the hell out of my office?"

"Timber Stag! You watch that mouth, young man," my grandmother scolds, and I mutter an apology. Some things never change.

12

TIM

Ty is, predictably, late for dinner, but I'm actually glad to get some time alone with my middle brother. He's friendly and outgoing like Ty, only Thatcher is an artist. He's got his own glass studio just north of the city, and he's making a pretty good name for himself in the art world. From what I understand, he's also making good on his goal to screw every single woman in the city. Or at least all the ones who will swoon for his long hair and hipster beard.

Thatcher and I snag a booth in a dark corner and order drinks while we wait for Ty. Thatcher can always tell when something's off with me, and right away he says, "What's got you all messed up, bro? You look like you're about to lose in court."

I exhale, trying to decide how much to tell him. But this is more than a week I've been off my game, unable to focus. Distracted. I was so sure fucking Alice would just get it out of my system, but as the day wore on, and I kept thinking of her with those construction workers, I was more distracted than ever. Not just the idea of them staring at her, but the idea of her bossing them around, making plans. Organizing her space. She's in total control in there, even if her lighthearted demeanor suggests otherwise. "Thatcher...I'm in a predicament."

He laughs and drains his beer, signaling to the waiter to bring us another round. "What's her name, Tim?"

"What makes you think it's a woman?"

"If it was related to work, you'd say, 'this fucking case, man,' and if it was about the family, I'd already have heard about it from Gran." He reaches for the chips and salsa and settles back into the bench. "So tell me about this girl."

"She...distracts me." Thatcher laughs again, and I wish I hadn't said anything. "Fuck you, man. I don't know if a woman has ever gotten in my head like this before." I decide not to tell him her name, that she grew up in the neighborhood, or that she works for me. Instead, I settle on just describing her as someone, professionally speaking, I should not get involved with.

He nods and taps his chips on the table, meeting my eyes. All three of us have the same gray eyes. We got them from our mother. "So you went and got involved anyway, hm?"

"Something like that." I look over my shoulder to make sure Ty hasn't gotten here yet. If he caught wind of my situation, I just know he'd make the association with Alice from earlier. He has a sixth sense for about these things. "It's not just that she's sexy. She's responsible and organized and--"

"Woah." He puts a hand up. "Organized is like porn for you, Tim-bo."

I shake my head. "Thatch, I thought if I slept with her, I'd get her out of my system. You know? Just succumb to the sexual energy and be able to move on with my life?"

"But now you just want her more?"

I exhale deeply. "Yes. Shit, Thatcher, I didn't even use a condom. You know me! I've never in my life slept with a woman without a condom." His eyes go wide at this revelation, because that was something I drilled into all my brothers' heads all through our teenage years. *Do not, under any circumstances, get a girl pregnant. Always cover it up, always. No exceptions.*

"You were like a broken record about that," Thatcher says. "You know, Ty and I used to joke that you were going to become a health teacher and spend your days scaring teenagers away from sex." I drag my hands through my hair, not feeling a bit better after this discussion with my brother. He grins, then, and asks, "So what are you going to do?"

My eyes go wide at this. "I thought you were going to give me advice! What the hell am I telling you any of this for?"

He shrugs, and then kicks my foot, because Ty comes slinking into the booth, looking guilty as sin. Thatcher laughs and throws his arms around both of us. "Ty," he says, grabbing our youngest brother by the chin. "Tell me you at least used a condom?" And all of us break out laughing.

13

ALICE

Finally, I collapse into the couch when I make it home from the office. It's been two weeks since I slept with my boss, and I've barely had time to think about it. A few days after it happened, one of the baseball players Stag Law represents was arrested for drunk driving with a prostitute in his car. The office has been a mess for ten days--constant frenzied meetings behind closed doors. Everyone is tense. Tim even had to miss his trip to the Stanley Cup final because of a court date.

I've been working long hours, not just to make sure there's food for the Stag Law staff, but Donna explained that we'd be hosting prosecuting attorneys and even city officials, not to mention MLB executives. I've kept the sophisticated fare flowing.

My sister brings me a mug of tea and snuggles up next to me on the couch. I rest my head on her shoulder and sigh as she turns on the *Great British Baking Show.* My favorite. "Did he talk to you today," she asks.

Of course I told my sister what happened during the hockey game. I shake my head. "I didn't even lay eyes on him. I never see him. So it's not like he sees me and acts weird...he's just neck deep in this baseball scandal."

"And how are you feeling about it all?"

"Honestly, I don't know! I still think he's hot as hell, Aim. That was the best sex of my life. Easily. No comparison. But what are we going to do? Fuck once a month and then go about our business? He works around the clock, and he missed his brother's world hockey final...whatever it's called. You know family is the most important thing to me. The *most* important thing." I give her shoulder a squeeze.

"Is Ty upset that he couldn't be there? I mean...when you play sports for a living, maybe it means less if your family can't come to a game. And weren't you a willing participant the last time he missed some of his brother's game? Something about sneaking off and doing the nasty in the conference room in the arena?" She nudges my shoulder and I blush.

I slurp my tea and watch the show, hoping to change the subject. My sister asks me about my menus, and I smile, proud of what I've come up with this week. I did three meals a day for the general staff while offering pastries, herbal tea, and--as Donna requested--calming, comfort food for the big wigs. I'd made everything from savory crepes to strawberry-rhubarb tartlets this week, highlighting local produce. I made simple quiche with ramps, cucumber sandwiches. Fruit salads with mulberries I picked right here in the neighborhood. "Aim, I know you don't know a ton about this stuff, but I did all the ordering, timed it all perfectly, took delivery of the eggs from the Amish farmer for God's sake."

I sigh and she says, "When you talk about your day, you look so happy. I want you to be happy, Al."

"I am happy! I had no idea it would feel this good to fully control a kitchen like this. Maybe I wish things would slow down a little bit."

THREE MORE DAYS pass and I only see Tim when I walk into the conference room to deliver the trays of lunch. He doesn't look up at first, because he's so focused on the paperwork he's reviewing with one of the Stag Law attorneys. Something catches his eye, though, because his head turns to where I'm setting out plates. I smile at him, shyly, and feel myself blush when he returns the smile. He doesn't miss a beat, though, and resumes analyzing the paperwork.

I stop back two hours later to clear everything away and find most of the suits have gone. Tim and his staffer are still at the head of the table, and a man I recognize as one of the MLB executives is seated across from them. I smile and lean in to grab the empty tray and I freeze when I feel a hand on my back.

"Are you the sweet thing who brought us these sweet things?" The MLB suit winks at me, his hand lingering. I freeze. Anywhere apart from work, I'd punch him and tell him off, but I'm very aware that I could jeopardize the company's professional relationship with the professional baseball league. *What a fucking prick,* I think, sliding away from his hand. I'm about to force a smile and duck out of the room when I hear a crash.

I look up to see Tim bursting from his chair, the impact sending it flying into the radiator behind him. "Mitch," his voice is dark and menacing. "Get your hands off--"

Mitch throws his hands up, a smarmy grin on his face. "Woah, woah, easy there. It's been a long day, fellas."

My eyes dart to Tim, who is breathing heavily through his nose, lips pinched into a tight line. Mitch rises and gathers his things, saying, "I think we did all we're going to do for this anyway. I thank you boys and I'll see you tomorrow morning at the courthouse to file the motion."

As he leaves the room, I let out a breath I hadn't realized I was holding. I grab what's left of the trays and head back to the kitchen to clean up. By six o'clock, I can hear the halls are quiet. I'm sitting in my office, bent over my notebook jotting down my thoughts for next week. I'm pretty engrossed in developing a new recipe, because I need to get my mind off that creep. That definitely wasn't the first time some asshole put his hands on me in the restaurant industry. I'm sure it's nowhere near the last, either. But it was the first time I felt like the choice to react to it wasn't my own.

When I worked in the neighborhood restaurant, the owners

didn't tolerate that sort of behavior and didn't mind losing a customer if he got handsy and I gave him a piece of my mind. This was a totally different power dynamic. I make a note to talk to Donna about having someone else deliver the food for the conference meetings. Surely there's an intern or something. I don't want to be near those jerks.

I feel my brow furrowed as I try to concentrate. My notes are all over the place. I bury my fingers into my hair, twisting absent-mindedly. I hear someone open my office door, and it startles me. I forgot anyone else was here.

I look up to see Tim, glassy-eyed and disheveled. His tie is loose, and his hair tousled. He leans against the doorframe and just stares at me.

"Tim. Do you want to...come in? Can I get you some water or something?"

He shakes his head slowly but doesn't move. "Alice Peterson," he says, hooking his thumbs into his pants pockets. "I've been...celebrating...our latest victory."

I snort as the fumes reach my desk. It's a small office and he reeks of alcohol. "I can tell." I reach beneath my desk where I've got a case of bottled water. I walk to the door and hand it to him and his fingers linger on mine as the bottle changes hands.

He drops my hand and takes a long pull on the water, leaning his head back against the doorframe. "I fucking hated seeing that fucker's hands on you, Alice. Did you know that?" I nod. He continues. "But then the whole time I was 'celebrating,' I kept thinking. I'm no different from him. I'm not better than him. I'm just some slimeball who fucks his employees."

"Tim, no--"

He scoffs. "I have lost all my control, Alice. All my discipline." He starts tapping his temple with the neck of the water bottle. "I'm distracted. You know what happens when people get distracted?"

I shake my head, starting to worry about him. He must be really drunk. Should I call one of his brothers, maybe? I wonder if he'd give me his phone...

Tim's voice drops to a whisper and he leans close, stroking my cheek. "People get hurt when I get distracted." He swallows and leans his forehead against mine. I've wanted to be close to him like this for weeks, but now I'm not thinking about sex. I'm worried about him. I wrap my arms around him and pull him down into a hug.

"It's ok, Tim."

He shakes his head, but wraps his arms around me. I hear him inhale deeply, feel his hands in my hair as he folds his body down into my arms.

14

TIM

My head is pounding. I crack one eye open and regret it immediately as the room begins to spin. Blinding white light streams through the blinds in my bedroom. *Is this my bedroom?* I take stock of my surroundings. It feels like my bed. Smells like my sheets. *How the fuck did I get home last night?*

This is why I don't drink liquor. I can't be losing entire chunks of my day. I close my eyes again and try to retrace the afternoon. We reached a plea deal and an arrangement with the DA. Then I had that meeting with Mitch from the MLB and he put his fucking hands on Alice.

"Shit. Alice." I clap my hand to my forehead, remembering how I'd gone into her office after I drank most of a bottle of tequila with Ben. The two of us put something like 250 hours into that damn DUI incident over the past two weeks, trying to clear that hotshot pitcher's name as best we could.

I try and dig and can remember nothing after I opened her office door. I take a deep breath and start easing myself out of bed.

There's a glass of water on my nightstand, so I gratefully chug that down, wondering how I thought to leave that there for myself when I got home last night. I see I managed to strip down to my t-shirt and briefs, too. My suit is draped neatly over the clothes rack by my dresser. *What the fuck?*

I stumble into the bathroom and groan as I take the longest piss of my life. And then I freeze mid-stream, my hand leaning against the wall behind the toilet. I hear the sound of footsteps in the living room. Someone is in my apartment.

Panic sets in. Nobody comes up here except my brothers and my grandmother.

What day is it? Is the fucking housekeeper here?

"Tim?" A familiar voice floats down the hall. I shake off my dick and hurriedly stuff it back in my drawers as the bathroom door slowly opens. Alice Peterson is in my apartment, wearing my sweat-pants and one of my University of Pittsburgh hoodies.

"Alice? Um, I don't know...I can't--"

She smiles. "Are you feeling ok? I was really worried about you last night." She reaches for my hand and I just stare down at her fingers rubbing mine reassuringly.

"I'm a little hazy on the details." She laughs and tugs on my hand, pulling me into my own kitchen. I settle into a bar stool and Alice gets me another glass of water, explaining that she walked me home.

"Walked? I never walk home," I interject.

"Well, you did last night!" Apparently the doorman took pity on her and let us into my penthouse, since Alice couldn't find my keys and I wouldn't give her my phone. She penguin marched me into the bedroom, got me out of my suit, and made sure I passed out on my side.

"I hope you don't mind, I borrowed some clothes," she says, gesturing to my gear. *As if I can ever wear them again and not think about her white skin inside them.* Outwardly, I just shake my head. "I crashed in your guest room," she says. For the first time, I'm glad my realtor convinced me to get a two bedroom. And for the millionth time, I'm relieved my housekeeper keeps everything magazine-spread-ready at all times. Alice starts to walk down the hall, saying something about how she will strip the sheets and get them started in the washer, but I move, as quickly as I'm able with my aching head, to stop her.

"Alice, don't even think about it." Her eyes meet mine, questioning. "Thank you. Thank you for taking care of me." I pause. "This isn't...usual for me. I don't ever..." I give up and run my hands through my hair again. "Can I buy you breakfast? It's the least I can do."

She shakes her head, looks at her watch. "I really should get back home before my family wakes up," she says. "It's only 7 now, so I might make it if my nephews don't come crashing downstairs." She laughs, and I decide that's the only sound in the world that doesn't hurt my head.

She agrees to let Joe drive her home, at least. I don't think I am sober enough to drive yet. *Jesus.* I can't be doing shit like this, letting myself lose control. After I call the car for Alice, I crawl back in bed and don't emerge until it's nearly dark.

THE NEXT DAY, my brothers and I all meet to go for a jog in Highland Park before brunch with our grandmother. The three of us don't say much, but it's nice to run together with them. We strip our shirts after the first lap around the path and Ty picks up the pace. He knows we can't fully keep up with him, but the rest of us aren't too shabby considering he's a pro athlete. He throws a grin over his shoulder and tears off, and we scramble to chase after him as he shouts "I thought you fuckers were out for a run today? This is like mall walking!" Before long, we are sprinting through the park, trading obscenity-laced digs at each other depending on who's able to pull ahead. After five miles or so, we stop for a drink at the fountain by the reservoir. Our chests are heaving, but my brothers are ok. I like us like this, together, and I like seeing our family tattoo--we all have a stag etched onto our chest, leaping over a field of laurel. That was our mother. Laurel. Thatcher designed the tattoo and we all went together on Ty's eighteenth birthday. Of course, Thatcher now has about a hundred more tattoos since he's an artist and all.

Ty spits a mouth-full of water at me, and that tips off a three-way wrestling match. Suddenly, we are all kids again, just rolling in the grass until we don't feel like fighting anymore. I give my younger brother's shoulder a final punch, saying, "It's good to have you back, baby brother."

"Wasn't such a baby when I was kicking your ass a few minutes ago, was I, big brother?"

Thatcher's stomach rumbles and reminds us all that we're starving after that workout. Arm in arm, we walk down the hill toward our childhood home. My thoughts drift, as usual, to Alice. The way she took care of me like that, without being asked, like it was no big deal. She's always taking care of her family. She works her ass off and then goes home and takes care of her dad and nephews. I never met anyone as caring and kind as her. It all just comes to her naturally, not an act or with an ulterior motive. What would it be like, I wonder, to have her waiting for me with breakfast. I try to stop myself from imagining her in my kitchen again, cooking for me and only me. Naked. *God, I've never even seen her fully naked.*

Gran has pancakes and bacon ready for us when we finally walk in the door. Ty opens the fridge and begins chugging orange juice right from the carton, and the rest of us berate him as my Gran smacks him with her spatula. I grab my youngest brother in a head-lock and pull him down, rubbing a knuckle playfully into his hair. Again, though, my mind shifts to Alice Peterson and her pink, plump lips. What I wouldn't give to twist my fingers through her hair again.

We sit down to eat, and nobody speaks for the first few bites while we inhale Gran's perfect pancakes. Thatcher pauses, though, and says, "These taste a little different, Gran. Did you do something new?"

She nods, smiling wide at his observation. "I knew you would be the one to notice," she says, pinching his cheek like he's still ten years old. "I added almond extract and a dash of cinnamon." We all moan appreciatively, shoving more of the pancakes in our mouths. "Alice was giving me pointers."

I nearly choke on my food and Thatcher starts pounding on my back. "Who the hell is Alice?"

Gran rolls her eyes and he apologizes for swearing. "She's the chef I told Timber to hire," Gran says.

Ty just nods knowingly. "The muffin girl. Right on." I don't like the way he grins at me. He knows something.

Feeling worried they can read my thoughts, I take a deep breath and remind myself there's just been the one indiscretion. Well...and the fact that she took me home blackout drunk Friday night. Which they would have no way of knowing. I take a long drink of OJ and ask my grandmother when she was trading cooking secrets with Alice. Gran starts cleaning up, and I rise to help her as she talks. "Well, I thought she looked awfully familiar when I saw her at your office the other day, and then I remembered! The Peterson family lives over on St. Clair. Timber, don't you remember? You mowed their lawn for awhile when her mother was sick, the poor dear." My grandmother hands me plates as I silently load the dishwasher. "Well wasn't I out for a walk the other evening and saw her playing with her nephews in the park? She recognized me right away and we got to talking. That's all."

Thatcher catches me staring slack-jawed as Gran walks out of the room, muttering about what a nice girl Alice is and how good neighbors make the best friends. He furrows his brow and says, "Your face right now leads me to believe that this Alice chick might be the 'distraction' you mentioned." He looks at me, expectantly.

I choose not to say anything to my brother, but I toss on my t-shirt and walk out the back door, heading through the alley toward St. Clair Street.

15

ALICE

"Whose birthday is it again, Aunt Alice," my nephew Eli asks, his mouth full of cake batter.

I wipe a stray drop of the chocolate batter from his cheek and tell him, "June 30 is Linda Day. My mom--your mom's mom, too--was Linda, and we celebrate her birthday every year to remember her and talk about how much we love her, even though she's not here with us." It's hard for a five year old to grasp, but today is a big day for my family.

My brothers are both here, wearing nice pants and clean shirts for a change. We all get takeout from Mom's favorite barbecue place and every year, I bake her favorite cake. Rich, flourless chocolate cake pairs nicely with fresh raspberries this time of year. My sister took the boys out wandering to pick some in the wild along the trails in Highland Park yesterday.

I'm about to slide the cake into the oven when I hear a knock at the front door. "Ry!" I shout to my brother. "Can you get the door? I think that's the food."

He walks to the front door with my nephew Ethan slung over one shoulder and I hear him fling the door open. As I shut the oven, I look up to see the dour face of my boss standing on the front mat.

I freeze, and Ryan crumples his face. "You're not the guy from Showcase." He pauses a beat, assessing Tim, who looks like he's just come from an intense sweat session. "Can I help you?"

Eli runs over to his brother and uncle and points at Tim. "That's the angry man from Aunt Alice's work! The one who yells!" Tim's cheeks flush and I walk over to try to salvage the situation.

"Ry, this is my boss. Do you remember Tim Stag? Aim said he went to school with you all. Grew up in the neighborhood."

Ryan nods as he lowers my nephew to the ground. "Stag. I think so. What's up, man? You need something?"

I've never seen Tim at a loss for words. At work he's always so confident. In total control. Except when he was yelling at my nephews I guess. *And when he dragged me off into the conference room for sex...*at the memory, my own face flushes. "Tim," I say, "Come inside for a drink of water?"

He seems mortified and lingers in the doorway. "I don't know what I was thinking," he says, quietly. "I was at my grandmother's house for pancakes and she said she saw you and..."

He drifts off, looking around at my extended family. Dad, Dan, and Doug are watching the baseball game on TV and my sister is flitting around setting out plates and napkins. The actual delivery guy starts climbing the porch steps, and Ryan sort of shoves Tim into the house as he squeezes past to pay for the food. Tim looks into my eyes. "I'm interrupting something here. I'll just see you tomorrow, Alice."

"Wait!" I shout, before thinking twice. "Please stay."

He looks as if I've asked him to lend me a kidney, but he enters the house. "Everyone," I shout above the normal family chaos. "This is Tim and he's here for ribs."

My brother and brother-in-law don't turn from the TV, but my dad glances up. "Stag!" he says, waving. "Good to see you again, son. You still over there on Euclid Ave?"

Tim nods. "Yes, sir. My grandmother lives there, although I own it now." He pauses and looks at me. "I'm not sure why I said that last bit."

I pat his arm and tell him to have a seat on one of the bar stools. I slide him a glass of water, saying, "There's just a few minutes left until the cake comes out of the oven, then we'll eat while it cools." I smile at him. It's good to see him, to be near him, no matter what the circumstances.

He waves around at my family as my nephews start firing Nerf darts at him. "What is all this?"

As I explain Linda Day to Tim, I see his face shifting. His emotions are all over the place as he listens to me explain. I know that his mother is gone, too. I lean closer to ask him, "How does your family remember your mom?"

His face is ashen and stiff. He shakes his head and his mouth moves a bit, but no sound comes out. Finally, he whispers, "we don't speak of her. Ever." Suddenly I'm overcome with sadness for him. For all the pent up grief he must carry. I know his brothers are gregarious and friendly. I'm so sad for them that they don't share their feelings about their lost mother, even to remember what they loved about her. I walk around the counter and wrap my arms around Tim. He melts into my chest and I see my sister Amy looking at me strangely, but I don't feel like worrying about her right now.

Tim is breathing fast and heavy, and I rub his back until the timer beeps on the oven. Reluctantly, I break our embrace to pull out the cake. He props his elbows on the counter, head in his hands. My sister calls everyone to the table to eat and I touch Tim's shoulder. "Come join us," I say. And he does.

16

TIM

The Peterson family goes around the table sharing remembrances of their lost mother. Even the little boys, who never met her, have something to say about things they've learned about Linda. By the time we're done with cake, I feel like I knew her, too, even though all I did was mow their grass as a teenager. When it came to be my turn, I was stunned when Alice's father reached for my hand and thanked me for helping around the yard so they could get more time with Linda in the hospital. I almost lost my shit and wept right there with them.

This family is certainly different from mine. I vacillate between sorrow and rage when I think about how my mother's death is the great taboo at our house, and my father's drunken absence is the elephant in the room. *Why don't we ever just sit and talk about it like this?*

I think Alice can tell that I need to escape, because she dabs her mouth with a napkin and tells the table at large, "I'm going for a walk with Tim. Don't any of you dare use a scouring pad in my springform cake pan when you're washing the dishes." There are groans and laughter and one of her brothers throws a napkin at her as she tugs on my hand and leads me toward the front door.

My dick twitches in my pants as a reminder that no matter what is going on in my world, my lust for Alice Peterson trumps all. We walk in silence for a few blocks until she says, "I'm really glad you came by today."

I clear my throat. Why does she make me so nervous? "I wanted to thank you again for your discretion and your assistance the other night."

She smiles. "You know," she says, playfully tugging on my shirt-sleeve. "You talk in your sleep a bit. At least when you're drunk."

"Not true," I counter, playing it cool while I inwardly panic.

She nods. "You said, and I'm not paraphrasing, 'pretty Alice, hairy curls. Just want to touch them all the time.'" And she laughs. The sound is so warm and delightful I can't help but feel at ease with her.

"Well," I say, "all of that is true." And she flushes. I grab her hand and pull her toward a bench in a nearby bus shelter. We sit, a bit stiffly. My voice is a harsh whisper as I confess, "I'm wild about you, Alice, and I can't seem to stop thinking unprofessional thoughts."

She looks up at me, her violet eyes liquid and warm, and says, "I think terribly unprofessional thoughts about you, too." And I bury my fingers in her curls as she rests her head on my shoulder. We sit in silence for a long time until she asks me about my mother.

Nobody ever asks about my mother. I swallow the bile that rises in my throat when I think about her death, but I remember how much lighter Alice's family seemed in talking about their own worst moments. I choke out, "I missed the bus. I got distracted at the library and missed the bus. I called from the payphone and she dashed out in the rain to come get me." Alice grabs my hand and starts gently rubbing my palm. "We were supposed to have my grandmother over for dinner that night, so she was in a rush to get me and get back to her pot roast."

I pause, and Alice looks up to my eyes. I've never told this to anyone before. She kisses my forehead and I close my eyes. "You can tell me, Tim. I know how it feels."

I shake my head. "Not this. You don't know how this feels. She was t-boned on 5th Ave. Two blocks from the library. Someone was driving the wrong way in the bus lane and she went to turn left as whoever it was kept plowing ahead straight into her." My words catch in my throat, but I keep talking. "After an hour or so passed, I decided just to walk home. Two miles in the rain, I stewed and steamed that she would do this to me. I thought she was teaching me a lesson about missing the bus. I slammed the front door, ready to scream at her. My family sat around the living room in the dark, just staring. My brother Thatcher whispered to me that she'd died instantly in the crash."

I haven't cried for my mother in probably 15 years, but I just begin to release a torrent of years of grief. I'm not sure how long I cry onto Alice's shoulder, but I know she holds me and strokes my back, whispers into my ear to let it out.

"You were a kid, Tim," she soothes. "Kids miss the bus. Adults miss the bus." I'm shaking my head against her shoulder. Alice says, "Tim. The only person at fault here is the jerk driving the wrong way in the bus lane. Not you. Not you, Tim."

I don't know how long she repeats this phrase. When I finally become aware of my surroundings, Alice is gazing into my eyes. Her hands are everywhere on my shoulders and arms and, no matter what I try, I can concentrate on nothing apart from the scent of her. I can tell that she senses the shift in my mood because she gently rubs my jaw with her thumb.

"I like it when you look scruffy like this," she says as the tip of her digit rasps against my two-day stubble. I turn my cheek so it brushes against her palm and when I hear a breathy sigh escape her throat, my dick jumps to attention.

I can't bear to not be kissing her, and I dive into her mouth, tasting the chocolate sweetness of cake as my tongue delves into Alice's warm depths. I move both hands into her wild hair--has it been down and free this entire day?--knotting my fingers into the blonde tendrils. I feel her come alive in my arms, returning the intensity and desperation of my kiss. My mind races--how can I get her to my apartment? Where can I take her to peel her out of those clothes?

Someone clears their throat and Alice leaps from my arms. An old man with a cane is standing near the bus shelter, gesturing. "Mind taking that elsewhere so I can wait for my bus in peace?" he asks, his mood somewhere between amused and irritated.

Alice mumbles an apology and starts down the street back toward her house. I follow, cursing the old man who stole my moment with Alice. When we get to her porch, she moves to enter the house and I reach for her hand. "Wait," I say, and she looks at me expectantly. I am so lost around this woman, unraveled. She's opening up pieces of me I don't understand. "Let me take you out to dinner. To thank you for taking care of me the other night."

Suddenly I feel nervous, like a teenager asking his first crush to the dance, I suppose. For the first time, it matters to me that a woman agrees to my plea. "I'd love to take you somewhere and let someone else do the cooking for you."

Alice breaks into a smile, and I feel my whole body relax. "Thank you, Tim. That sounds really nice." She reaches for my hand and gives it a squeeze before releasing it. My skin vibrates with anticipation and nerves. I run a hand through my sweaty hair, remembering that I'm a mess. An actual mess. God, I walked over to her house and interrupted her family, caked in sweat.

"Saturday night, then, Alice? Where should we go?"

Alice begins babbling in that delightful way she has about her, unfiltered. This was probably the best question I could have asked. "Ooh! Morcilla is supposed to be amazing," she says, "Do you like Spanish food? But Legume is so nice...oh, or could we eat at Spoon? Or Cure! Do we have to wait until 8 to eat? I don't understand why people do that. I get hungry early. Wait." She puts a hand on my arm again as I laugh, enjoying her excitement. "How will you get a reservation any of those places for Saturday?"

Now I can return to my sense of confidence and control. "Alice," I tell her. "I work with sports stars. When a Stag calls a restaurant, we get a table."

"Well look at you," she says, teasing. "In that case, I pick Cure."

17

ALICE

My family all stares at me when I walk back inside the house. They're sitting around watching old movies, and my sister leaps up and pulls my arm. "Alice," she hisses, dragging me into my bedroom. "You tell me everything this instant."

I flop down on the bed and tell her all of it, how Tim opened up to me about his mother and that kiss we shared on the bench. "Amy, it was...I've just never been kissed like that before."

She throws open my closet and puts her hands on her hips. "We have to go buy you something to wear for next weekend, or you won't get kissed like that again."

"Shut up, jerk," I say. But she's right. I've spent the last years waitressing, cooking, or playing with my nephews. I haven't bought a new dress in ages. Tim is always so put together, dressed in killer suits. I think about how young he is, how young he was when he started taking care of his family. He has to look like a shark in a world of salt and pepper suits who've been in the game for decades. Dress for the job you want, I guess they say. Right now, the job I want is Tim Stag's sex goddess. Giggling, Amy and I leave the house and drive to the mall, where she forces me toward the more expensive department stores.

"Alice, you're going out with Tim Stag. You can't look like you're headed to a hockey game this time." She reminds me of my higher-than-expected salary and I agree to try on a beautiful, cobalt blue dress by Kate Spade. My sister pushes me toward the low-cut, slinky dresses, but that's just not my style. She rolls her eyes at me when I tell her I'm going with the sleeveless, boat-neck dress. "I guess he already knows he can get the milk for free," she says. I remind her that it's at least shorter than I feel comfortable with and we find a pair of strappy heels to go with it.

At work the next day, I'm not sure how things will go when I see Tim, but he stops by the kitchen for breakfast and I feel butterflies in my stomach just looking at him. He lets his finger linger on my hand when he takes a muffin from me, and I bite my lip, wondering how I will make it until Saturday before really touching him again.

I think he's very busy with a lot of hockey endorsement contracts now that the season is over, because I don't see him much all week. I hear Juniper talking about him taking his grandmother to some doctor appointments even though Ty is the one who lives with her right now. I really like that Tim makes sure his family is ok, in his own way.

I'm like some teenager in middle school, looking for him every few minutes, unable to speak when I do see him, finding ways to make sure I touch him. I spend the entire week on edge, on fire, constantly aroused and remembering the feel of him inside me, around me, kissing me. Friday afternoon, as I'm cleaning the kitchen up for the weekend, I hear someone approach from behind, and I know it's him before I even turn around.

"I was starting to think you were avoiding me," I say, continuing to wash the dishes. I've got all the food put away and I couldn't stand to be in my chef coat for another minute today, so I'm washing dishes in my tank top. Most people have gone home for the weekend already and it's been a long, hot day in the kitchen. Despite the heat, I shiver when I feel Tim's hands on my skin.

His breath is sweet against my cheek as he says, "I have, Alice. I can't concentrate when I'm near you." I swallow, relieved it's not just me overcome by attraction. Not just me imagining something that's not there. He starts to stroke my arms and I let the dish drop into the soapy water. I lean against the sink, unable to move.

"What's happening, Alice? Why can't I be near you without needing to touch you like this?" He presses his body into my back and I feel the heat of his body radiating through his tailored suit. I let my head drop back against his chest and a small moan escapes my throat when his fingertips graze against my breasts. His voice is barely audible, whispering, "I thought once I fucked you, that I could go back to normal. But I can't get enough of you." His breath is ragged and then his lips gently swipe the skin behind my ear. I shiver against him.

"Tim," I say, my voice shaking, "I want you, too." I suck in a great gulp of air and turn to face him. "But not like this. Not here at work."

He frowns, but keeps his hands on my arms. "Tim, I'm serious." I extract myself from his grasp and immediately miss his warmth, his touch. "What will everyone else think? This job is very important to me. My work as a chef is very important to me."

"Alice, I don't think my staff will like your cooking any less just because we're--" he stops mid-sentence.

"What are we, Tim? What is this?"

His face hardens and he runs a hand through his hair, but doesn't answer.

"You're distant and...and bossy at work, but then you pour your heart out to me. You come to me drunk after a stressful day at work and I just--"

"You make me feel safe." He doesn't look at me, but reaches for my hand. He strokes the skin of my palm. "I don't have to take care of you, Alice. And I want you." He brings my hand to his mouth, gently licks my palm in a way I feel straight through to my core. "Very." Lick. "Very," he licks my wrist. "Badly."

I feel my heart racing when he finally meets my eyes. I remember his grandmother telling me how he's always taken care of his brothers, how his father fell apart when their mother died and Tim became the man of their family, even though he was only a teenager. Tim kept his brother in private school even when he got suspended for fighting--got Ty to focus on hockey where it was safe to let out his aggression. Tim always knew what everyone in his family needed, and now he says I am what *he* needs? "I make you feel safe? Me?"

He nods, still stroking my palm with his thumb, leaning against the steel counter with his other hand. I see that he's loosened his tie, that he needs a shave. I like when he looks disheveled like this. "Come home with me, Alice," he says, tugging me closer. And oh my, but he smells good. And feels good. Our romp in the conference room was so fast...what would it be like to spend the entire night with this man?

And then I remember. "I can't tonight," I tell him. "I told Juniper I'd hang out."

"Juniper *Jones?*" He seems incredulous, but I nod.

"We're friends. She's nice. We're going kayaking." I start babbling again, telling him how Juniper wants me to get as excited as she does about exercising.

Finally, Tim presses a finger to my lips and says, "All right then, Alice. I'll have to wait until tomorrow." I nod. "I'll pick you up at 6," he says, and I don't exhale until I've watched him walk around the corner.

I CHANGE in my office and walk down the bike path to meet Juniper, who has already rented a kayak for us. "You know I'm a total beginner, right?"

She smiles. "I know this isn't the Olympics, Alice. You climb up front."

Juniper steers and we slowly make our way up the river, past the baseball stadium. It's pretty cool to watch the sunset from this vantage point on the river. She starts to tell me all about how she got into rowing, how her dad was even an Olympic champion. "Rowing is basically all I have now," she says, "apart from you of course." She splashes me with her paddle.

"Come on, June. The river water is gross. And of course you have me! You were my first friend at Stag Law." Juniper explains that she caught her boyfriend with another woman and needed a new job, a new place to live. Ben from work is the brother of one of Juniper's teammates from Boston. "That's so cool how the rowers just hook you up like that. They sound like family."

"They're absolutely a family. My only family now that my dad is gone."

I smile, thinking about how I keep surrounding myself with people who understand how important it is to stick together and support your family, no matter how that family is defined. "Hey June?"

"Yeah, Al?"

"I hate this."

She laughs and we head back to the dock. Arm in arm, we walk to get Thai food while I tell her about my ideas for work next week. By the time I get home, I've completely forgotten to be nervous about my date tomorrow. I'm tired out from kayaking, and I drift quickly to sleep, remembering the feel of Tim's touch on my sore arms.

18

TIM

I consider using my driver, but decide I don't want anyone else looking at Alice today. It's been awhile since I've taken my Volvo XC90 for a ride, anyway, and I like the look on Alice's brother's face when I pull up at the Peterson house. "Nice ride, Stag," he says.

"Safest car on the road," I tell him, reaching behind the driver seat to grab the flowers I got for Alice.

"I know that, asshole," he says. I shrug, straighten my collar, and adjust the flowers. Her brother nods, approving, and steps aside as I walk toward the door. I'm about to knock when he grins and shouts through the open porch window.

"Yo, Alice! Your *date* is here!"

I feel very much like I'm picking up a prom date when I see Alice's nephews scramble into the living room and press their faces against the picture window. But then Alice comes outside and all other thoughts slip from my head.

"Shit, Al, you clean up nice." Her brother is the king of the understatement, apparently. Alice is radiant. My eyes follow the blue line of the dress from her collarbones to where it stops mid-thigh, not far enough below her ass. Alice's legs look amazing in the strappy heels she wears that bring her closer to chin-height than her usual stop at my shoulder.

I clear my throat when she catches me staring and offer the flowers. "Dahlias," I say. "To match your eyes." When she smiles I forget her entire family is standing around watching. I feel my cock spring to life in my pants and cross my hands in front of my body as Alice turns to put the flowers in water.

She lets me put an arm around her as we walk toward the car. "Ooh," she says. "Is this one of those Volvos where the front seat can be a baby seat?"

I cock my brow, impressed that she would know that, but she reminds me that her brother works as a mechanic. "Ry wanted my sister to get one of these when my nephew was born," Alice says. "But it was a bit outside their price range."

I smile and open the door for her, letting my eyes linger on her legs as she climbs inside. "Worth every penny if it keeps you safe," I tell her, pleased to see her sink into the white leather interior. Someday, I vow, I will fuck Alice Peterson in this car.

I drive to the restaurant and she tells me about kayaking with Juniper. "My arms are sore today," she says. "Which is surprising because I work with my hands all day, you know?"

"I'll rub them for you later," I tell her, sliding my hand from the gearshift to her knee. When she doesn't resist, I decide to keep my hand there until I need to shift gears at a red light.

"How did you get this car with a manual transmission," she asks, running her hand along the dash.

I shrug. "I imported it."

"You imported a manual transmission Volvo whose front seat converts into a baby seat?" She looks skeptical.

I turn to look at her, returning my hand to her knee and regretting the manual transmission for the first time, since it means I frequently have to move my hand. "It's the safest car in the world, Alice."

She puts her hand on mine and smiles. I'm almost disappointed when we arrive at the restaurant and I have to break contact with her to hand the keys to the valet. The hostess greets us warmly as we enter--she wasn't so friendly on the phone when I said I was coming in with just a few days' notice, but I see that she's guiding Alice toward a private table.

"Welcome to Cure. Mr. Stag informed us that you'd be having the tasting menu," she says to Alice, a bit woodenly, handing Alice a card describing the six courses and their drink pairings. Alice is radiant, and not just because she's dressed to kill. Her joy in reading over the menu is infectious, and soon Alice is explaining pickled pears and violet mustards until I'm actually excited about my food for once.

"You should come with me to all my restaurant meetings," I tell her. "I'm usually so busy persuading the client that I barely pay attention to what I'm eating."

She scoffs. "If you come to places like this and manage not to focus on your food, I'm not sure there's any hope for you in this world."

The server arrives with our first round of drinks and I raise my glass to Alice, saying, "You give me hope for a lot of things, Alice." She tries to hide her flush behind her wine glass. "You must have noticed by now that I don't really trust very many people. I've been so impressed with how you approach your work."

Alice picks up her oyster and tells me to look at it closely. "Food," she says, "is so much more than a group of ingredients hanging out together. It's a family. It functions best *together*." She gently prods the sauce with her finger. "If you leave out a detail, an ingredient, a step in the preparation process, it all falls to pieces. But together..." Alice slides the oyster into her mouth and, watching her swallow, I feel my pants tighten around my growing bulge. "Together, it's perfection." She reaches across the table to feed me *my* oyster and I don't think anyone has ever done anything to turn me on more. "I've always just been able to see how all the details need to come together," she says and shrugs. "It's because my family has always focused so much on working together for the big picture."

19

ALICE

By the time we reach the dessert course, I'm tipsy on the excellent wine and Tim's intense attention. He's so direct as he tells me how much he admires everything from my work ethic to the ways my family gets along with each other...and how much he wants me. If only he knew how much that feeling is mutual! I notice that his cheeks are dark with stubble--he must have to shave twice a day if he has evening meetings--and I can see the vein in his throat pulse above the collar of his button-down shirt.

As he pays the check and calls for the valet, I'm feeling ready to just pull him into a dark alley to have my way with him. He's so confident in this environment, telling people what to do and expecting that they'll respond immediately. Which, of course, they do. I can tell the hostess hates that I'm going home with him. Her jaw is clenched when I smile at her, but her whole face warms when Tim tells her he'll be sure to come again soon with Stag Law's top clients.

The valet pulls up with Tim's Volvo, and Tim's hand lingers along my back as he opens the door and helps me inside. His skin leaves a trail of sparks up my back. "Where to now," I ask him as he slides into the driver's seat.

"Now, Alice, I'm taking you back to my apartment to fuck you properly."

"Oh," I say. Then I nod. I barely breathe the entire car ride. He slides into a spot in the garage and pulls me into the elevator. His mouth claims mine, his rough stubble rasping along my skin as he drags kisses along my collarbone. One hand slams the Penthouse button on the elevator while the other pulls me tight against his body. "I don't want anyone to see," I plead as his fingers sneak up the back of my skirt.

He growls against me, sliding his tongue into my mouth in response and I forget to worry about it. We tumble into his apartment and he picks me up, carrying me down the hall toward the room I last saw when I half dragged him to bed. *God, was that only a week ago?*

He throws my purse on the dresser and starts unbuttoning his shirt. I stand next to the bed, panting, and watching him undress. I am so eager to see all of him. Last time was so frenzied. I felt but couldn't admire the perfection he hides under those tailored, designer suits. Tim's muscles are long and lean and hard. The perfect V of his lower abs is hidden by the waist of the pants he stops unbuttoning. Tim walks toward me and says, "Turn around, Alice."

I immediately comply, and moan softly as his fingers tease the back of my neck. He gathers and lifts my hair, searching for the zipper to the dress. Painfully slowly, he eases it down and I feel the halves of my dress peel open. "God, Alice, you are exquisite," he says, running his hands along my skin. I feel the heat of his body against my back and I gasp as he lowers the dress and my panties in one short tug.

He turns me around and I reach for his pants. My body yearns to be pressed against his, fully naked. He dips his dark head and takes my nipple into his mouth through the material of my bra. His tongue swirls around the needy peak and I think I've never felt anything as nice as this. My hands find purchase in Tim's boxers. I wrap my fist around his hardness, loving the smooth length of him in my hand. He continues his work teasing my nipples until I can't stand any longer.

We tumble backwards onto his bed. He feels so good lying on top of me. So solid. I move my hands to his chest, loving the powerful feel of him. Tim starts to rub his cock against my seam and I cry out. He smiles and holds my gaze, teasing me slowly. Each time I'm on the edge of exploding, he backs off, returns to my nipples. "Tim, let me come. Please!"

I beg him, desperate for release. But he shakes his head. His voice is low and I feel his chest rumble as he says, "I want you to come around my cock, Alice. I want to feel your pleasure." I sigh as he slides into me. "You're so wet, baby."

"You turn me on so much," I tell him, but then I lose my ability to speak. I wrap my legs around his waist and the angle is just right. My clit rubs against Tim as he thrusts deep inside me again and again until I'm tumbling over the edge. My orgasm rolls through my whole body in waves. He teased me for so long, my entire body is on fire. I thrash and claw at his chest, screaming his name for an eternity.

"Fuck, Alice," he says, looking into my eyes. "You are so sexy. This is so hot." He rests his forehead against mine, keeping me still, and after a few more hard thrusts, I feel him spill inside me.

My bones have turned to jelly. I'm practically purring as Tim slides out and pulls me against his body. I hear him murmuring soft words to me as he strokes my arm, but I'm too overstimulated, high in the afterglow of a mindblowing orgasm. I drift off into a deep sleep curled against his body.

20

TIM

I don't want to move. I'm holding perfection here in my arms, in my bed. I've never brought a woman to my apartment before, never wanted to stick around after I've fucked someone. But I don't ever want Alice to leave my bed and I can barely wait to be inside her again, to move with her and give her pleasure. I know that I've completely unraveled for this woman. All my rules are broken. All my composure is gone and somehow, with my fingers twined through her mad hair and my body pressed against her soft curves, I just don't care.

Alice has fallen asleep in my arms and it feels so right. After awhile, I hear her phone chirping inside her purse on my dresser. Some sort of persistent alarm grows louder, and I don't want it to wake her. I slip out of the bed to reach for it. The words "Little blue boys!" flash across her lock screen as the tinkling bells keep chiming. I figure she must have planned to tuck her nephews in or something, so I turn it off and climb back into the bed beside her.

As I wrap my naked body against hers, she stirs. I love the tiny noises she makes, the contented sighs as she wakes. I grow hard as Alice wiggles her bottom. *Time for round two,* I decide. "Hey, you," Alice says when I start kissing her shoulder. I let my hand fall to her breast and am rewarded with a soft moan as I massage her nipple. "How long was I asleep?"

"Just a few minutes," I tell her, continuing my exploration of her creamy skin. She turns her head to kiss me and I'm lost to her. I pull her close against my body, the swell of her ass against my cock. She lifts one leg a bit to give me access to her center, and I slide home. We fit together so perfectly. "Alice," I whisper. "You're so wet. You feel so good."

"Mmmm." She groans into my mouth, moving with me. I know I'm not going to last long. This feels too intense. I drop a hand to her clit and, using the pads of two fingers, find the rhythm that will drive Alice over the cliff. She moves with me, thrusting her hips against my hand.

I'm so close to losing control, but I need Alice to come first. "Now, baby. Let go!" And she does, moaning and thrusting until I can't help but join her. I tumble over the edge. My cock swells inside her and I feel my balls tighten. "Alice! Fuck! Yes!" She feels so good. I want to hold on to this moment, of watching and feeling Alice Peterson come, and then joining her in ecstasy. My breath comes ragged and heavy as I pull her tighter against me.

We must have fallen asleep this way, because the next thing I know, I'm being awakened by Alice kissing my chest. I'm on my back and she's straddling me, her hair tickling my skin as she traces a line of kisses down my stomach. "This is probably the hottest sight I've ever seen," I tell her. She looks up at me, violet eyes twinkling in the streetlight sneaking through the closed blinds. I've never gone three rounds in one evening before, but Alice makes everything easier.

Afterward, she's like putty, molded against my body, boneless. "I don't think I can go home like this," she says, a hint of worry in her voice.

"You're not going anywhere, Alice," I assure her, pulling my arms around her. "We're going to sleep now, and after I wake up beside you, I want to have you again in the shower."

"Mm I like the sound of that," she says, her voice soft as she drifts to sleep.

Some hours later, we wake tangled together in my bed and the sun shines across Alice's golden, wild hair. I pepper her with kisses and carry her into the bathroom, turning on the shower.

When I redid my apartment, I installed an infinity shower with no door. I typically use the seat in the corner as a shelf for a cold beer after a punishing run, but today I get up close and personal kneeling on the subway tile as I lick every inch of Alice, perched on her throne in my bathroom. She tastes like a ripe peach, swollen and slick with wanting. As she cries out in pleasure again and again, I almost cum without even being touched. We stay in the shower until the water turns cold, and then I envelope her in one of my Turkish bath sheets. The thin cotton towel is big enough for us both, and I like the feel of being cocooned against her.

"This has been the best date, Tim," she says. And she sighs. "But I really have to get home." She kisses my cheek, and rubs the thick scruff that's grown to mountain-man lengths since I last shaved. "Next time, I want to shave you before..." She blushes and looks down.

I notice the red, irritated skin at the tops of her thighs. "Oh shit, Alice! God, I'm so sorry."

"It was worth it, Tim," she says. "I like how you look with some scruff. I've just got really sensitive skin. You should see me after I work with habaneros!" Alice talks to me about her tricks for avoiding contact with hot peppers as I hand her a spare toothbrush from the closet and help her find a pair of shorts that won't fall down.

"Those look like pants on you," I joke. "Unfortunately I don't have any shoes that will come close to fitting..."

Alice stuffs her purse, dress, and shoes into a grocery bag and pulls my arm, walking barefoot to the elevator. I offer to carry her so she doesn't cut her foot, and again when we pull up in front of her house, but she declines. "What am I going to cut my foot on, Tim?"

I don't have an answer right away, but I can't shake my worry that she'll get tetanus or something.

Her brother is out front again tossing a ball around with Alice's nephews. He gives me the stinkeye when I get out to open Alice's door, but she doesn't seem to notice. She kisses me softly and says, "I'll see you tomorrow."

I stand and watch as her nephews crash into her for a hug, asking where she's been. She looks so happy here, surrounded by this family. They're all tied up in each other's business, but I can see how much love lives in this house. My apartment, sterile and white, feels very empty in comparison once I get home.

21

ALICE

The next few weeks fly by in a haze. I spend every weekend with Tim, either screwing like rabbits at his house or else eating family dinners at mine. As he dropped me off one morning, my nephews insisted he join us for breakfast. I was surprised that he did, sinking into the couch afterward with my dad and brothers, watching the baseball game on television.

At work, I keep worrying that everyone will be able to tell there's more going on between us, but as per usual, the pace is so hectic we are barely in the same room as one another. I'm pretty sure Juniper caught him kiss me one day when he stopped in for an afternoon snack, but she hasn't said anything.

I'm finishing an inventory order in my office, looking over the schedule for the next week, when my desk phone rings. "Alice Peterson," I say, not looking at the caller ID.

"What are you wearing?" It's Tim. I blush.

"Well, I'm at work, so I'm wearing my chef whites and clogs," I say. "What's up?"

"I've got a big request for you. I'm scheduling an all-day meeting with the Cavs' players union and I'd like to keep them happily well-fed."

"The Cavs? Like from Cleveland? Do we get people from far away like that?"

He laughs. "Well, I certainly hope so, Alice. Stag Law is building quite a reputation. Can you have something together for Monday?"

"Monday?? Tim, it's Friday afternoon. I wish you'd given me more notice!" I start to panic, looking at the clock and wondering how I'll manage to place orders in time.

"Stay at my place this weekend. I'll help you work on it." His voice is smooth, but it doesn't quite sound like a question.

I sigh. "How many people will there be?" We review the details and I've barely hung up the phone before I start poring over menu ideas.

I start organizing my ingredients lists by the different markets I'll have to visit on the weekend. Most likely, I *will* stay with Tim this weekend, just to have easy access to the vendors in the produce terminal. I'm finishing my notes on a pesto for tortellini--*must make a trip to the Italian market for fresh pasta*--when my cell rings. "Shit. Amy, what time is it?"

"Alice, it's 7 at night! Where the hell are you?" My sister is hopping mad. I was supposed to watch the boys for her tonight so she could go on a date.

"Oh god, Amy, I am so sorry. I'm still at work." I sweep everything into my bag and start running toward the elevator. "Is Dan home? When do you need to leave?" It'll be a half hour or more until I can get home. I remember that I took the bus today. "Shit, Amy, I don't have my car at work."

"Dan was supposed to go out tonight, he says." I can hear my brother complaining in the background.

"Ok, but he's home? Tell him to chill out for an hour and I'll be there as soon as I can." I start to jam the elevator buttons. Of course, today it's taking forever. Of course, our office is on the top floor of huge skyscraper.

"What's wrong, Alice?" Tim slips up behind me. I didn't even realize he would still be here. I turn around and quickly blurt out the whole scenario. The elevator finally arrives and I sprint inside, but he calmly follows and pulls out his phone. "I'll have my driver take us to your house," he says. "I'll hang out with your nephews while you pack for your weekend at my apartment." He grins, still not flustered.

"You're going to come with me to babysit my nephews?" I raise an eyebrow at him. He's such a renaissance man. Negotiating contracts with professional sports executives one minute and chasing preschoolers around the next. He nods.

"The town car is downstairs waiting for us." He leans in to kiss me, and I forget about the stress of the last few hours, forget that he's the source of the stress. "Tell me what you're working on," he whispers. "I love to hear you talk about food."

He starts to kiss my neck and I lean against the elevator wall. "Well," I say. "Mmm, that feels good. I'm going to make scones for the morning. Lemon...of course...Tim!" He bites my neck and presses me against the elevator wall.

The door slides open and he stands back, straightening his collar. I'm too flustered to walk, and he grabs my hand. "You were saying...lemon donuts?" He opens the door to the Town Car and I climb inside.

"You think donuts?"

He nods. "I don't think this is the tea and scones crowd, babe."

By the time we pull up to my house, we've tweaked the menu into something masculine enough for Tim's standards--basically various cubes of meat served at regular intervals throughout the day. My brother pulls the door open as we hit the porch and he storms out. "At least one of us is getting some. I was supposed to be at the bar an hour ago, Al, and you waltz in here late because you're out messing around with your damn boyfriend?"

"Dan, I was working late and lost track of time and--"

He scoffs at me and shakes his head. "Sure. Working. Save it, Alice."

"What the hell is that supposed to mean, Dan?" But he's already in his car peeling out down the street. My nephews walk out onto the porch as I stand there, shaken up.

"Aunt Alice, what's a boyfriend?" Elijah hands me a jar of bubbles, and I open it, squatting beside him to help him with the wand.

"Well, it's..." I'm not sure what to say.

Tim squats down next to us. "It's me, buddy. I'm your Aunt Alice's friend, and I'm a boy, but I also like to kiss her." He ruffles my nephew's hair.

"My mom says you're Aunt Alice's boss at work, though. Can you have a boyfriend at work?" Eli's eyes are big, and he pauses to blow a series of bubbles into the humid July evening.

"Well, I guess you're not really supposed to," Tim says. "But your Aunt Alice is just so awesome, I really wasn't happy until I was her boss *and* her boyfriend."

This seems to make sense to Eli, who scampers inside, but my brother's angry insinuation has left me uneasy. This is the main problem with my involvement with Tim Stag. He's my boss. Will anyone ever believe my achievements are earned? Tim leans in to kiss the top of my head, then helps me to my feet.

I head off to my room to change and pack for the weekend. When I come back to the living room, my heart melts to see Tim engrossed in a game of Jenga on our dining room table. My nephews egg him on as he slowly wiggles out a precarious brick and the three of them high-five when he successfully places it on top of the stack. I lean against the banister, just watching. He folds into my family so seamlessly. *Maybe I should look for another job,* I think, but I know I'll never find a position that gives me the same creative freedom and independence as this one. This is my dream job, and I know I'll never give it up without a fight.

My phone alarm sounds, my reminder to take my birth control pill. I walk to the kitchen for a glass of water and kiss each of my men as I pass. I won't give any of them up without a fight, either.

22

TIM

Having Alice with me the entire weekend has been like a dream, a movie about someone else's happy life. I feel like I'm an entirely different person when I can fall asleep beside her, then wake up wanting her just as badly. She has no background in law, but listened to me when I talked about our strategy for wooing the Cavs to sign with us.

Bringing on a big client from Cleveland will mean travel and long hours, but our firm feels ready for growth. Alice is part of that. I know we haven't known each other long, but something just clicks with her. I might have met someone I can really trust.

Sunday night Alice tells me she's going to make the donuts at my apartment so they're ready for the early meeting. I try to manage my discomfort at the huge mess she's made of the kitchen. "Just stay in the bedroom," she tells me as she weighs flour on a scale on my formerly-pristine table.

I'm pretty sure I don't own half the gadgets she keeps pulling out, and frankly I'm fascinated by this process. "I didn't know donuts were something you could just make at home," I say, wringing my hands so I don't reach for the eggshells she's left on the counter.

"Tim, you know I'm going to clean this when I'm done. You know this. You're making me nervous." She's got a streak of flour on her nose. She's baking in one of my t-shirts and, from the looks of things, nothing else. Even with the AC cranked, the kitchen is scorching with the oil heating on the stove. I catch a glimpse of Alice's ass as she turns to grab a set of tongs, and I suddenly care less about the mess.

"How much longer will this take?" I step behind her, not wanting to get in her way, but making sure she can feel my intentions.

Alice is a stone cold pro, though, and barely responds. "Half hour. Then clean up. Go on, scoot."

I don't want to miss my chance to see her ass again, so I pull up the presentation outline and read it at the counter while she finishes. The second I see her turn off the stove, brushing her hair back from her forehead, I tackle her to the kitchen floor. "I love the way you sound when you squeak," I say, reaching up under the t-shirt.

"I do not squeak," she says, indignantly. "Mm, that feels good. But I thought you wanted me to clean up this mess?"

"I found something I want even more," I tell her. "We'll clean it up together in a few minutes."

IN THE MORNING, Alice doesn't look well. Her eyes have dark circles underneath and she moves sluggishly as she gets ready. "Hey," I say, rubbing her shoulders. "What's wrong, sweetheart?" She shakes her head, tells me she didn't sleep well. I chalk it up to nerves and overexertion. "Take tomorrow off, babe. Comp day."

She doesn't respond, though, slowly walking through the motions of packing everything up.

We get ready together, and I think about how easily she fits into my routine. She showers while I shave. We dance around each other to access the mirror and brush our teeth. It feels like *home* with her instead of just a place to live. When we're ready to go, Alice has boxed up the food and tries to balance it with her duffel bag from the weekend. "Babe," I tell her, "don't take that huge bag to work. Come on, we'll get it at the end of the day, ok?"

She nods and lets it drop. She really doesn't look great, but I've never seen her game face before. I figure she might just be focused. We don't talk much in the town car on the way to work, and I peck her cheek after depositing the cardboard boxes for her in the kitchen.

Right on time, the suits from the Cavs enter the lobby of Stag Law, and I hear Donna greet them. I straighten my tie in the mirror. This is it. Time to win a new client, and Tim Stag doesn't lose.

Donna opens the door and I walk confidently toward the six men. "Stag," they say pumping my hand. "Nice place you got here."

"We do our best, Steve. If you could just follow Donna to the conference room we can get started."

Alice must have come in advance to set everything up. She's brought several types of donuts and coffee, procured a fruit tray, and made little dishes of yogurt with granola. Juniper Jones and another of my associates rise to greet our guests. I turn the floor over to Juniper, and I can already tell we've got them eating from our hands. Literally.

Juniper spends the next two hours guiding the conversation. She has read up on this franchise, knows the ins and outs of the players union, and is absolutely flawless describing our strengths representing professional athletes across different sports.

Steve glances over to me at one point, reading some documents, and I jump in, saying, "We represent our athletes through all legal aspects of their careers, from endorsement contracts to workers comp litigation...and we've got a fantastic record when it comes to exploring the morality clause in their contracts."

He laughs and throws the papers back on the table. "In other words, you can make the hookers and blow disappear when you need to." I shrug. *We are in,* I think, but I can't let that show.

The door opens and Alice comes in with lunch. Perfect timing. She sets out the salad and fresh pasta. I can smell the basil and lemon--always lemon with her food--from across the room. I meet her eyes with a smile, but my face quickly falls. Alice looks ashen. She reaches for a pitcher of cucumber water from the cart, and I see her falter.

"Alice," I rise, walking around the table. She looks at me, and as if in slow motion I see her start to fall. "Alice!" Her eyes roll up in her head and she pitches forward. Her temple catches the corner of the table. I reach her as she hits the ground, a stream of blood flowing from her forehead.

"Stag? What's going on here?" The room is on their feet, everyone crowding around Alice.

I develop tunnel vision. I pull her onto my lap. She's still unconscious. "Juniper, call 911," I bark out. Alice groans in pain and brings her hand to her temple. I pull the pocket square from my suit jacket and press it against her cut. I'm not sure if she needs stitches. There's so much blood.

I feel someone's hand on my shoulder, but I won't let go of Alice. I need to know if she's all right. The paramedics arrive and peel me from Alice. Juniper puts her hand on my shoulder again. I hear her this time. "Tim," she's saying. "Tim, she just fainted."

I nod. She's going to be fine. "Because this happened at work, they're going to take Alice to Mercy hospital to get checked out." Juniper keeps talking and I realize we are still in the conference room. The Cavs are still here, retainer contract unsigned. "Would you like me to go to the hospital with Alice or would you like to go?" Juniper pauses. She meets my eye, and I know she knows Alice is more than an employee to me. "Maybe you should go to deal with the paperwork? As her boss?" I nod, and don't look back as I sprint down the hall after the paramedics.

23

ALICE

My head is pounding. I'm going to be sick. I roll onto my side and dry heave--I haven't been able to eat anything all day. I didn't want to tell Tim I felt sick to my stomach. Today was too important. *Oh shit, what have I done?* I remember going into the conference room with lunch, thinking I could go lie down in my office if I could just make it through this one task.

I didn't really think I had a stomach bug. What happened? As I take stock of my surroundings, I realize I'm on a gurney. I open my eyes and see Tim's face, deeply concerned. "What's going on?" I croak.

He kisses my hand. "We're in an ambulance, babe. You fainted. You've got a nasty cut." I hear the siren, realize the jolting feeling is the ambulance rocking as it hurries down the cobbled side streets behind Stag Law.

"Your meeting," I whisper. "I ruined your meeting."

"No, baby. You didn't. Your health is the most important thing. Juniper's got those guys eating from her hand right now."

The paramedic clears her throat. "Ma'am," she says, coming into my eye line. "We're going to take you in for some imaging when we arrive. We need to know if there's any risk you might be pregnant."

I shake my head. "I'm on the pill," I say, putting my hand to the source of the stinging pain on my forehead. I feel a bandage. The paramedic must still be talking. She's looking at me, expectantly. "I'm sorry. Could you repeat the question?"

"I asked whether you're using your contraception as prescribed. Nevermind. We're going to draw some blood from your IV and do a test."

IV? I glance over to Tim, who looks even more deeply concerned. The paramedic explains they've been giving me IV fluids because I showed signs of dehydration. She pulls a vial from one of the shelves in the ambulance and fills it with blood from my IV access.

We arrive at the hospital and are rushed back to a room, where a nurse helps me onto the bed. A crew of people flock around, asking me questions, shining lights in my eyes. They determine that the cut on my head can be closed with glue, and I close my eyes while everyone works around me. I'm just so tired.

"Are you the father?" I hear a voice as I drift back to awareness.

"Excuse me?" Tim sounds upset.

"The father." I open my eyes. A smiling young woman in a lab coat stands at the foot of my bed with a chart. "Of Mrs. Peterson's baby! I'm the resident, Dr. Shaw. My notes tell me she's expecting!" Before I can register what she's saying, she walks toward me. She continues, "Normally we'd like to do a CT scan to rule out concussion, but it's not really advised for the first trimester. Do you know how many weeks you are, Mrs. Peterson?"

I feel like I've been pushed into a dark tunnel. "It's miss," I say, stunned.

"Excuse me?"

"Miss. Miss Peterson. I'm not married. Did you say pregnant? I don't understand."

She looks puzzled, glances over at Tim, then back to me. Tim looks as though someone has slapped him across the face. "Well, *Miss* Peterson, your blood test came back positive. Did you not know you were pregnant?"

"There must be some mistake," I say, shaking my head until the room starts spinning. "I'm on the pill."

Dr. Shaw looks at her notes. "I see you're taking a low dose pill. Those are very sensitive to timing—you have to take it at exactly the same time every d—"

"I know how the fucking pills work," I spit at her. I'm trying to make sense of what's going on but everything seems impossible. "I have an alarm on my phone every evening." I cover my eyes with my hands. This can't be happening.

"Alarm? Fuck!!" Tim pounds on the bed rail with his fist. "Can you give us a minute, Doctor?" Tim's voice quivers. I open my eyes to see Dr. Shaw backing out of the room. Tim grabs my hand. "Alice...the first night you stayed over...you were asleep..."

Tim confesses that he shut off my alarm, thinking my covert secret phrase was about my nephews. That was what it took. One night. I mean sure. We had sex like 4 times that day I missed my pill...Now I'm pregnant? Pregnant by a man I've only known two months.

I groan. "I think I'm going to be sick again," I say and lunge for the pink basin on the table. Tim steps back as I dry heave into the bowl.

"Alice...what do you want to do?"

I pause in my retching to look at him. "I can't really think about that right now, Tim." I flop back against the bed, hoping Dr. Shaw comes back. "Tim, can you call my sister for me? She works in this hospital."

"We need to make some decisions here, Alice. Decisions...shit." He rakes his hands through his hair, cursing and muttering under his breath. "How could I be so stupid?"

I scoff and then sigh. "I'm not going to terminate anything if that's what you're talking about, Tim."

He holds my gaze for a long time. Then he reaches out and strokes my chin. "We're going to have a baby then." His eyes are wide with wonder, and he gazes at me like I'm some foreign creature.

Tim has the nurse page Dr. Shaw and asks them to find my sister, who comes sprinting into my room a few minutes later. Dr. Shaw has come and gone. I'm diagnosed with a bruised head and morning sickness, with instructions to start prenatal care ASAP.

Privacy laws mustn't hold for hospital staff because my sister knows everything when she skids into my room. "Alice what the hell?? Pregnant??" She grabs my hands and looks over to Tim, who is now collapsed in the wooden chair like a deflated scarecrow. "Timber fucking Stag, you knocked up my sister!" Amy helps me out of bed and hands me my bag. "I'm going to send you the number for the midwives. Carol has been there so long she caught us AND my boys."

When Tim sees that we are leaving he scrambles to his feet. Amy keeps talking. "You have to wait to tell Dad until I'm there to watch. Oh. And Ryan. Please wait for Sunday dinner and just blurt it out in front of everyone."

"Aim, I'm so glad my crisis is so amusing to you." She steers us toward the exit as Tim calls for his driver to come pick us up.

My sister pulls us both in for a hug. "It's not a crisis! It's a baby!" She claps her hands. "You're both adults and you have homes and decent jobs. This is going to be amazing. I promise." I wish I could share her confidence. Or even make sense of what I'm feeling right now. I huddle against Tim as we wait for the town car. He's wooden and unyielding, gritting his teeth like he can chew right through this challenge.

When Joe pulls up, I don't even wait for anyone to open the door. I collapse into the back seat and close my eyes until we start moving.

"Wait, where are we going?" Joe is headed west along the Allegheny River, not east toward my house.

Tim looks at me, utterly perplexed. "I'm taking you home. To rest. So we can talk."

"Tim, I want to go to my house, to sleep in my bed and to think."

Tim shakes his head. "Alice, we need to talk this through. This is ...you're not thinking clearly and... Alice! A baby. *Our* baby..."

My head is pounding. I can't think. "Joe, please take me to my house." Tim starts to protest, but I cut him off. "I just really need to be alone right now, Tim."

When we finally pull up to my house, I'm surprised to see both my brothers are home, but then I remember it's late afternoon and we've been at the hospital since lunchtime. When Tim opens the door and I climb out, my brothers leap from the porch and come running to me.

"What the fuck, Alice? Who hurt you?" My brother Ryan balls his hands into fists, glaring daggers at Tim. "Stag, if you so much as laid a finger on her, I swear to Christ I will end you right now."

"Relax, Ry. I just fell at work." Tim's mouth opens, but no sound comes out. I glare at him. "Tim drove me to the hospital and I'm fine. No stitches even. I'll probably have a black eye, though." I'm babbling again. My brothers don't seem quite appeased, but I'm so exhausted and I'm feeling another wave of nausea. "Look, guys, I just want to go to bed. Tim, I'll see you on Wednesday."

"Alice, wait."

"No. I really just need to go to bed." I start to walk into the house.

He moves to follow, but Dan puts his hands on Tim's chest. "She said she's good, dude."

"Alice, I'll bring your things over later. Please call me when you've slept." He looks desperate, and part of me wants to go to him, but if I stay upright another second I'm going to puke and cry all at once. I close the door, hurry up the stairs, and collapse into my bed.

24

TIM

Pregnant.

Alice is pregnant.

I got my girlfriend pregnant, and we haven't even had a conversation yet about whether she *is* my girlfriend.

All through my teens, I expected this to happen to my brothers, probably Thatcher. Part of me waited for this type of phone call in college. And now I'm the idiot who fucked a girl with no protection. And what the hell was I thinking, shutting off her phone alarm and not telling her? I never let myself assume anything...so much for following my own advice.

I don't even recognize who I've become.

Shit. The meeting.

"Joe, can you take me back to the office?"

He looks at me in the mirror. "Are you sure, Mr. Stag? You're not looking so hot."

"Joe. Office. Now." I don't have time for people's assessments. I need to get hold of Juniper Jones.

"Right away, sir." We head west, Joe avoiding the highways and finding a back road to avoid the rush hour traffic. I pull out my cell and breathe a sigh of relief that I've got Juniper's number. Donna must have programmed it in for me.

I punch the screen to call her up and, almost like she was waiting for my call, she answers after one ring. "Tim."

"Juniper. Give me some good news."

"Tim, how is Alice?"

Shit. Of course she's concerned about Alice. Everyone probably is. Alice knows everyone, knows their food preferences and knows the names of their damn grandmas. I breathe deeply. "Just a cut and a shiner. She'll be back on Wednesday."

"Everyone will be so relieved," Juniper says. She covers the phone and shouts this news. "We all have been hanging out waiting to hear an update. I tried calling Mercy, but of course they wouldn't release anything. I even told them I was her attorney, but I was very relieved they insisted on protecting Alice's health information--"

"Juniper! The Cavs! What happened??"

"Oh! Oh, Tim. It was fine. You know they were so impressed with everything this morning. They took the contract with them to review, which is customary, but I'm certain they'll come back with a yes and a retainer check tomorrow."

I exhale the stress of the past few weeks, the part of my mind that focuses on work feeling much needed relief. Juniper continues. "Should we give some thought as to who will service this account? It will mean a lot of travel to Cleveland and our scan of the news lately seems to indicate we'll have our work cut out for us with the hookers and blow, as Steve so delicately put it."

It never occurred to me that anyone other than myself would handle this client. I delegate the less prestigious work, but this has been the prize I've been eyeing ever since I got my brother Ty back and signed. "Juniper, I really appreciate how you handled that meeting today. You were poised and professional and, really, quite excellent--"

She cuts me off. "Tim, if I can be blunt, I'm not interested in taking on this client. The travel would take away from my training time."

Shit. She thought I was buttering her up to give *her* the Cavs. "Of course, Juniper. I plan to work this client personally. I was just making sure to praise your work in getting them here."

"Oh." There's silence on the other end. "Well, thank you, Tim. While I have you, I really want to discuss the ideas I mentioned for the firm."

"Juniper, I'll be at the office in ten."

"You're coming back today?"

"Yes. What do you mean?"

"Well, I just thought...don't you want to stay with Alice?"

"I'm not interested in pursuing this line of conversation right now, Juniper. I'll see you in ten minutes." I hang up on her. Things have never been this complicated for me. Just keep my nose down, work on the plan, account for all potential complications. Even with our dad drifting in and out of the house, I managed to keep our financials together, keep my brother Ty in private school for hockey. I scoff at the memory of forging my father's signature each month to deposit our mother's life insurance payments while he drank away his sorrows in one dive bar or another. At least they had their ducks in a line before she passed so we didn't lose the house.

And here I am about to have a child, unable to even get my shit together at work let alone my personal life. This shouldn't feel so complicated. Haven't I already provided for my family? Haven't I already made sure my brothers found success? Even if my middle brother defined that differently from the rest of us. I shake my head, twist my fisted hands in my eyes to clear the cobwebs. I need to sit at my desk where I can think.

Juniper meets me at the door and we walk and talk. I'm only half paying attention to her ideas. I'm sure they're good ones, and I actually trust her to pursue them, so I don't file that as urgent. Instead, my mind drifts to the Cavs contract and what I need to do to make sure Alice and the baby are safe, protected, and cared for. I settle into my chair and start to work out the logistics of my plan.

25

ALICE

I wake up to my sister rubbing my leg. "Al, babe, let's talk."

I sit up and collapse against her chest. Her strong hands rub my back and she mutters soothing words into my hair. I'm the only one of the Peterson kids to inherit my mother's curls. Unruly and wild, just like Dad always says she was. "Hey," a thought occurs to me. "Do you think the baby will have curly hair?"

Amy laughs and I burst into tears again. It starts sinking in that a real human is growing inside my body right now. A baby our mother will never meet. "Amy, what am I going to do with a baby?"

She laughs. "What do any of us do with babies? You'll do the same thing you did with my babies. He or she will hang out and watch baseball with Dad and the uncles. But shouldn't you also be talking about this with Tim?"

"Oh God, Amy, I am so overwhelmed. I love where things had been going with him. But now everything is going to change. And Tim hates kids. You should have seen how he reacted when the kids were at the office."

"Alice," Amy's hand is firm on my shoulder. "I've seen him with the boys. He's great with kids. It sounds like he just doesn't like surprises. Remember how I told you not to just take the boys to work with you?" She flips on the light and reaches into the pocket of her scrubs.

"Here." She says, handing me a card. "This is the number for the midwives. This is the same practice Mom saw for each of her pregnancies. I wouldn't imagine going anywhere else."

I exhale. This is too much reality for a Monday. "Hey, Aim?"

"What's up, Al?"

"I just want to go to sleep for now, ok?" She kisses my forehead and slips out, turning off the light. I sink into the mattress and sleep until mid-morning.

It's strange being in the house alone during the day. There's no commotion, no noise. Everyone is at work or school. I'm alone with my thoughts and that appointment card for the midwives...and a phone that seems a little too silent. I guess I was expecting Tim to call by now. I make myself a cup of coffee, wonder if I'm allowed to have coffee, and decide to call and ask before I do anything else.

The nurse schedules me for an intake appointment and answers all ten thousand of my questions. I'm relieved to learn there's really nothing in my life that needs to change apart from cutting out craft beer and turning off the now-useless alarm reminding me to take my birth control pills. They email me some information and a recommended book list and I decide to spend the day reading it all and shopping at the bookstore. All in all, I'm feeling much better despite the nasty bruise. With some careful adjustment of my curls and a scarf tied around my hair, I'm able to hide most of that when I head to the bookstore.

I return home an hour later to see Tim sitting on my porch with his head in his hands. He looks...not good. His hair stands on end and he's wearing the same suit as yesterday. "Jesus, Tim, are those spots of my blood from when I fell?" His shirt is stained. I've never seen him look like this.

"Alice! Where the hell have you been? I've called you 100 times."

I look at my phone and notice that it's still set to Do Not Disturb from when I went to sleep last night. "Oh, Tim. I'm sorry. I had it--"

"Let's go, Alice, we need to get your things."

"What are you talking ab--"

He grabs my hand and snatches the keys from me, unlocking the front door. "You need to pack your things. I'll have someone come to get them and move them for you."

"Tim, what the hell?" He looks stunned. "Have you even slept? Tim, I'm concerned about you right now."

He shakes his head. "No, Alice, I haven't, but it's fine. I figured it all out."

He launches into some convoluted explanation that evidently involves me quitting my job, moving into his apartment and--"Wait. Tim, did you just say marriage?"

"Of course." He looks at me like I've got spinach in my teeth. "We have to get married. My child will be a Stag."

"Tim, we don't need to get married for the baby to have your last name. But this is besides the point. Everything you're saying is just...it's too much right now."

"Alice, if you think for one minute that I'm going to live separately from my child and his mother, you are gravely mistaken."

I shake my head. "Tim, just wait."

He looks manic. "I've made some calls. You'll be seeing the best obstetrician in the tri-state area and we'll schedule your delivery the day after the due date. Everything will be safe and controlled, Alice. Especially once you stop working. You can focus on the baby and staying healthy!"

I blink my eyes, not wanting this to be really happening. "Timber Stag, if you think for one minute I'm moving into that sterile waste-land you call a home you are out of your damn mind. And quit my job? Really? To be what? Barefoot and pregnant at your house? What makes you think I even want to be with you if this is how you really feel about raising babies?!"

I didn't really mean to say that, because of course I want to be with Tim. But Tim as he's been the past few weeks. Not this maniacal, safety-obsessed madman with bloodshot eyes. How is he going to respond to late night wakeups if just knowing about the baby has him insisting I quit my job?

My words have cut him. I can tell. "Look, Tim, we both need to cool down and think here."

"You don't want to be with me?" His voice wavers and I can tell this is not something he had considered as part of his "master plan." "But it's my baby, too...it's my baby, Alice. I have to keep the baby safe."

"Tim, you've had a shock and you're exhausted. You need to shower and sleep. I'd like you to leave now and go do those things. We can talk tomorrow." He lunges for me, and I duck past him into the house. I have no idea how he's going to respond right now. "You should call Joe to drive you," I shout through the open window. "You shouldn't drive like this."

"ALICE!" he pounds on the front door. "Let me in right now." I close the window and sit on the couch, clutching my shopping bag to my chest. This is just not how I ever imagined starting a family. This isn't what happened when my sister got pregnant. I screw my eyes shut tight. *She was married and had been with Doug for three years* I remind myself. Tim persists. "Alice! You cannot do this. It's my baby, too, God damn it!"

When I open my eyes, my Dad and brother are standing in the kitchen. They must have come in the back door together. "Alice, pumpkin, want to tell me what's going on before I call the cops on this guy?"

26

TIM

After Alice's brothers chased me off their property and threatened me with a PFA, I wandered the park until dark. And then I couldn't figure out what to do next, so I sat down next to the fountain to watch fireflies. I have no idea what time it is. My phone is in my car, double parked where I screeched to a halt outside the Peterson house.

I hear someone approaching, but don't look up. The massive forms of my brothers come into my line of vision, and I grunt by way of greeting when they sink down into the grass next to me. "Been looking for you, bro," Thatcher says. "Gran is beside herself. You were supposed to take her to dinner today."

Shit. What day is it? "Is today Tuesday?" I look from one brother to the other. "How did you find me?"

Ty slaps a hand on my leg. "Listen, Timber. Juniper told me what happened during the Cavs meeting, and then she told me you holed yourself up in your office covered in blood, and then she told me you tore out of there muttering to yourself about some plan of action."

"Why the hell is Juniper calling you with that information?"

Ty lets out a long breath. "She's my lawyer and she's worried about you and she knows I'm your brother, dude. And we all know you've been fucking Alice Peterson. And I know your car is parked half-assed in front of her driveway because I went over there to move it for them." I close my eyes, but Ty keeps talking. "AND we know her family thinks you're a fucking lunatic. Thatch, does that cover everything?"

Thatcher grabs hold of my other leg. "Almost, baby bro. I believe the Petersons said something about a shotgun, owing to the fact that our brother Timber seems to have gotten Alice Peterson pregnant."

"Right." Ty starts talking again. "So. Talk to us, bro, and then we're taking you home to get cleaned up."

Thatcher hands me a bottle of water, and I suck it down gratefully. And then I tell them all of it, starting with my inability to stay away from Alice since the first second I saw her. I tell them how she has consumed my thoughts, how good it felt to have her at my apartment. How terrified I've felt since the minute the doctor said she was pregnant and I realized it was my fault.

Thatcher puts his arm around my shoulder. "Tim," he says. "You've been on watch for a long time, man."

"On watch?"

"Yeah. On watch. Watching out for us, day and night, around the clock. Since mom died. But from what I've seen and from what you're saying, it sounds like Alice helps you let your guard down." I nod. "It's ok to let your guard down, Tim-bo. You know that, right? You don't have to be the one in control all the time..."

And then we sit in silence for awhile until they help me to my feet. Ty climbs into the driver seat of my car and I start to protest, but they push me into the back seat. I fall asleep and don't wake up until we pull into the garage in my building. My brothers walk me into my apartment. It really is a sterile, empty shell, just like Alice said. Thatcher procures a six-pack and my brothers camp out on my couch while I shower. I don't even like being in my fancy shower without Alice. Nothing feels right. I'm worried I fucked everything up with her and she won't ever come back.

I walk to the living room after I shower. Ty hands me a beer and looks at his watch. "We keeping you from something, Tyrion?" Thatcher doesn't let anything slip by.

Ty shrugs and looks around my apartment. "This place sucks, Tim."

I frown. "What do you mean by that?"

"Do you even live here? There's, like, nothing here. Just furniture."

"I've got pictures of you clowns," I say, pointing to the wall across from us. But he's right. That's the only personal touch in the whole place. I really don't spend much time here, and once I took Alice's bag to her house, all the little things she had set around this weekend were gone, too. I take a long swig of my beer. "I fucked up, guys."

Thatcher doesn't look away from the TV. "We know, bro."

We sit in silence for awhile and eventually I fall asleep. I wake up to the sun streaming in the windows.

Alone.

27

ALICE

After I finish hurling up my breakfast, I take a deep breath and head into work. I try to arrive before everyone, but there's a stream of well-wishers coming into the kitchen. Everyone has heard what happened by now and wants to check on me. I know they care, but it makes me feel a little like a freakshow as they ask about my black eye. The bruise from my forehead has sunk down so my whole cheek is purple and green. There's no hiding it.

So far, Juniper has helped me spread the story that I was so focused about catering the Cavs meeting that I didn't eat or drink anything. It was a really hot day Monday. Nobody has trouble believing I passed out from dehydration. I make sure to keep a huge glass of lemon water nearby at all times. Lemon is about the only thing I can consistently keep down. Whatever else this baby is, he or she most certainly is not interested in food. *Definitely doesn't take after me,* I think.

Once the first big wave of Stag Law employees heads back to their offices, Juniper hangs around in the kitchen. She bites her lip and looks at me. "Want to go get some coffee and talk?" she asks. "I thought about calling you yesterday, but wanted to give you some space."

I exhale deeply and nod. It will feel good to talk to Juniper. We head toward the elevator together. There's a coffee shop across the street, and I try ordering mint tea. Juniper and I grab a table near the back and as soon as we sit, she says, "Look, I know there's something more going on with you and Tim. And I want to be someone you can trust to talk about that." I open my mouth to speak and she holds up a hand. "I want to prove that you can trust me, because I need a friend to talk to about something, too. So I'm just going to tell you-- I'm sleeping with Ty."

My jaw drops. "Ty *Stag?*"

She nods and takes a long sip of her drink. "It started before I even knew him. I needed to move on from...well, I needed to get laid, and I picked him up in a club. I had no idea who he was. You should have seen my face when Tim said he wanted me to represent his brother, and his brother ended up being that nameless guy I fucked in a bar bathroom."

"A bathroom? You? Jeeze, Juniper. This is all...well I'm really surprised."

She raises an eyebrow at me. "You know more than anyone how irresistible the Brothers Stag can be, right?" We share a laugh. "So tell me what's going on. Maybe I can help? Or just be a friend at least. I'm new to this city, and there aren't enough women at work."

She's right about that, which I remember she had planned to speak with Tim about last time I talked to her. "I slept with Tim during one of Ty's hockey games," I tell her and brave a sip of the mint tea. My stomach seems to accept it gratefully.

"Oh my god, Alice! The first playoff game where the whole office came to watch! I remember you snuck off for a 'tour' of the arena!" She laughs. "So this has been going on for awhile."

I tell her how at first we were just infatuated, how we both thought we could get it out of our system. "But then, I don't know. It just started to feel like more. He really opens up to me, and I really like how that feels."

Apparently things are going the same for Juniper and Ty. It sounds like her feelings for him are stronger than she's even admitting. For a brief minute, I let myself fantasize about us being sisters. Then a wave of nausea washes over me and I cram a crumpled napkin against my mouth.

She starts pushing a drink stirrer around in her empty cup, then says, "So look, Alice, I care about you and I care about Tim. He's a good boss and a good guy. I just want you to know that you can talk to me. Because it sure seems like the other day was about more than a bumped head and dehydration."

I bite my lower lip and nod, not trusting myself to talk without crying. I haven't actually said the words myself yet. Even the nurse on the phone at the midwifery practice had access to my medical records from the emergency room when my sister made the referral. But if Juniper is in a relationship with Ty, she's going to find out soon. I'm sure Tim talked to his brothers about what's going on. Or at least I hope that he did. Juniper looks at me expectantly, and I figure everyone is going to know soon enough, anyway. At least I'll have an ally when I have to run off and hurl while I'm serving lunch. My voice is barely above a whisper, and I tell her, "I'm pregnant."

Juniper breaks into a wide smile. "Alice! That's so exciting! I mean, I guess it must be a shock for you. But I was afraid you had cancer or something. Seriously, this is the best news!" And then she's run around the table to hug me. To my surprise, I let her, and it feels really good to have a friend like her around. I tell her a little bit about Tim's breakdown. She doesn't seem surprised, telling me how he wouldn't come out of his office until he stormed out of the building. She apparently called Ty and he came to get Tim's car from outside of my house.

By the time we walk back up to the office I'm feeling ready to forgive Tim for freaking out--he'd had a shock, after all. Now seems as good a time to go talk to him as any, and Donna gives me a warm smile as I approach the executive office. "Is he in, Donna?"

"He is! Do you want me to buzz him for you? He's just reading over some contracts that arrived this morning from Cleveland."

"No, Donna, that's ok. I'm just going to go in and...thank him...for helping me on Monday." She nods and returns to her computer screen as I push open the door.

Tim's desk is covered with papers, and he's turned to face out the window. He stares out at the river below, looking peaceful and contemplative. I gently clear my throat and he spins around to face me. "Alice," he says, his voice quiet and questioning.

"Can we talk?"

28

TIM

Alice offers me an opportunity to explain my behavior, which, given the way I yelled at her and pounded on her door, seems like more than I maybe deserve right away. "I'm so frightened, Alice."

She walks around the desk and reaches for me. I rise to hug her, and as soon as I have my arms around her, I feel so much better. She's solid and real and as I hold her, I begin to think that maybe this can eventually be ok. "I'm here, Tim," she whispers. "I'm scared, too." She starts to cry softly against my chest and I stroke her hair.

We hold each other like this for awhile until Alice says, "I know we have a lot to talk about, but I'd like it if you came with me for my first prenatal appointment later today."

"Of course! Alice, I want to be at every appointment. You need to understand that this is my top priority. You are my top priority. That's why I panicked the other day."

She squeezes my hand. "Tim, I know you panicked. But you have to know that there aren't going to be one-sided decisions here. You're not, like, the king who hands out the laws for me to obey."

"I know that, Alice. I know. God, I'm such a fool." I pound my fist against the desk, stirring the papers. I turn to the window again, looking out at the river. "I don't know what the hell to do, Alice."

"Do you have to decide today? Can you *talk* to me, Tim? What are you thinking about right now?"

I gesture to my desk. "This...Cleveland...the Cavs. I've been chasing this client for almost a year, Alice. A year. This is a signed retainer contract and right now I don't feel like I can accept it." She sits and I explain how I don't want the travel anymore. I don't want to spend half the week heading to Cleveland and miss ultrasounds or birthing classes. I want to assemble the crib and just be present. "Alice, I want to be all in for this."

"Tim, neither of us has to give up our dreams because I'm pregnant. You know it's not just the two of us, right? Like, you understand that my family is going to be very, very involved in this baby's life? That's not negotiable for me. And I'd really like Baby Stag to have some Uncle Stags around, too."

Fuck me. Uncle Stag. I hadn't even thought about my family's response. I try to imagine Thatcher holding a baby and realize I can't even picture *myself* holding a baby. Alice stands up. "One day at a time, ok? Just meet me in the lobby at 2 to head over to my appointment." She walks out of my office and I can tell this round of Deep Discussion is over.

After lunch, where I try not to bother Alice in her element, I call for Joe. I realize I'm not sure where we are heading exactly, so I tell him to hold tight on our destination. She stands by the elevator waiting. I don't even stop to think about it, but I walk right up and kiss her on the cheek. She blushes and looks around to see if anyone is watching. "I don't care who sees, Alice. Things are different now."

We ride down to the lobby in companionable silence and Joe is parked right out front with the town car. "Where to, Miss Peterson?" She smiles at him and fires off an address I don't recognize.

A short ride later, Joe pulls up beside some nondescript building near an industrial complex. There's murals of women painted all over the outside. Alice climbs out of the car and walks toward the door. I follow, skeptical. "Alice, what the hell is this? Did you cancel the appointment I made with the obstetrician?"

She turns to face me. "Tim. First of all, you never graced me with the name of this fancy obstetrician you keep talking about. And second, I told you. No unilateral decisions. I'd like you to come and meet the midwives who worked with my mother and sister."

I follow her up the stairs, past the wall of photographs of babies and their half-naked mothers. *Midwives?* "Tim!" she shouts at me and I catch up to where she's signing in at the registration desk. This isn't going well.

The receptionist smiles at me. "Congratulations, Dad! We've got paperwork for you, too. Just your basic family history stuff." She slides me a clipboard. I start sweating. Alice plunks down on an armchair. This place looks like someone's living room. I walk over to her. "Alice, I really would prefer a *medical* provider."

She doesn't look up at me. She starts scratching away at her forms until a woman comes out the doorway. She has gray hair tied back in a loose ponytail. "Welcome to the Midwife Center, Alice!" *First names?* She's not even wearing scrubs. I really want to drag Alice out of here, but she grabs my arm and pulls me over. "And this must be Timber. Right?"

I grit my teeth, but return her handshake. "Tim."

I try my best to hold an open mind while she chats with Alice about being present for her birth. Ok, so it's obvious this woman has been around awhile. She catches me staring at her and says, "We get a lot of nervous dads here, Tim. What questions can I answer for you today?" I shake my head and stare away toward the wall. "Let me see if I can guess." She puts the clipboard on the desk and stands, rummages through a filing cabinet and sits back down on the padded chair. "You're thinking we're a bunch of witches with cauldrons cackling over herbs and smoke. Am I getting close?"

I scoff at her. "Your words, not mine."

She laughs. "You hate that this isn't some sterile examining room and you're thinking your baby would be better off under the care of a skilled surgeon. Am I there yet?" I shrug. She throws me a pamphlet. *Midwifery 101: A Guide for Nervous Partners*

"Is this a joke?"

She turns serious. "No, Mr. Stag. Prenatal care is serious work. For the record, I, and many of my colleagues, received advanced training from Yale and the University of Pennsylvania. I've caught over 4,000 babies, including your partner. I'm happy to discuss the advantages of midwifery care for healthy women with normal pregnancies. You clearly have reservations about our facility, and I'm offering you an opportunity to discuss them before we begin Alice's examination."

I'm taken aback by her tone, overwhelmed by all of this. I'm not sure what possesses me, but before I've made a conscious decision, I stand and storm out of the office. I stomp down the stairs toward the street, trying not to notice the photographs along the wall.

Until I see it.

Near the middle of the staircase, beaming in a black and white photograph, is my mother. She holds a tiny child, face contorted in its first wail. My mother. My mother was a patient here, too.

29

ALICE

I try not to cry after Tim storms out of the midwife's office. She pulls me into a hug and asks me to talk about how I'm feeling. She has such a warm personality and I love knowing that she's hugged my mother with these same arms. That she knew me as an infant. I might not be able to ask my own mom any questions about pregnancy, but it helps knowing I can ask this woman who cared for my mom during that time. I tell her how this pregnancy was unplanned, that my relationship with Tim is still new and we are clearly on rocky ground.

"Unplanned does not mean unwanted, Alice. I want to make sure you know that." Carol makes some notes in her file. She reviews some of the information with me about the do's and don'ts of a healthy pregnancy and hands me a prescription for some bloodwork. We talk about my cycle and she estimates I'm about six weeks pregnant. We make a plan for my next few visits and then she gets ready to give me a tour of the center.

They've got a number of nature-themed birthing rooms with regular beds, rocking chairs, and whirlpool baths. Carol even shows me the nitrous oxide I can use if I feel like I need pain management.

She takes my arm. "Would you like to see the room where you were born?"

Would I? "I'd love that!" I tell her, and she walks me to the staircase. I'm stunned to see Tim standing there, staring at the wall.

"Mr. Stag?" Carol says, her voice kind and calm. "May we help you with anything?"

He points to a picture of a woman and baby. She's radiant, glowing, smiling down at her precious child. "This is my mother," he says. "Laurel."

Carol smiles and drapes an arm over his shoulder. "It appears your family shares Miss Peterson's history with our practice," she says. "Laurel Stag was one of our first patients here nearly 30 years ago. We were about to show Alice the Desert Room where she was born. Would you like to join us?"

"She's beautiful, Tim," I say to him. "Look how happy she was to be a mother." I reach for his hand, and am glad he accepts mine in his. We walk around the birthing room, with its soft colors and peaceful decorations. Carol shows us how the dresser drawers contain medical equipment for various situations that are unlikely to come up.

"Most likely, your midwife will need little more than a pair of rubber gloves, if your birth goes anything like your mother's or your sister's!" Carol smiles warmly and says we can take all the time we need to explore before we head out. She heads off to greet her next client and leaves me with Tim and all of our baggage.

"Want to sit," I ask him, gesturing toward the upholstered bench in one corner. I lean my head on his shoulder, still feeling the thrill and spark when our skin connects. I have feelings for him. I want to be with him. But I can't let him call all the shots like he's been trying to do.

"I messed up, Alice," he says.

"I know," is my reply. "Want to tell me what you're thinking about?"

He takes a deep breath, and tells me about Sunday pancakes with his grandmother. "She's been adding cinnamon lately, ever since she talked with you about it," he says. And he talks about going running with his brothers, nearly keeping up with Ty even though he's a professional athlete and Tim and Thatcher are just your average fitness fanatics.

"I like hearing about your family, Tim. I'd like to spend more time getting to know them."

He nods. We sit together a while longer, and he asks--his voice apprehensive--"Did I ruin everything, Alice?"

"No, Tim! It's all just...heavy. You know?" I lean in to softly kiss his cheek, relishing the smell of him close by. "Let's just take things slowly, ok? We have 8 months before anything needs to change."

He wraps his arms around me and I can feel him relax as I let him hold me. "What comes next?" His voice is soft, his fingers in my hair. He feels safe and warm and his vulnerability right now, the way he's trusting me to see this soft side of him--I realize this is what I want more than anything else. Just to be open and raw and real with him and to hold each other.

"How about you take me out to buy some prenatal vitamins and we'll go from there."

30

TIM

The next few weeks are probably more stressful than prepping for the bar exam after only 2 years of law school. Every day, I have to drum up the courage to tell Alice what I'm afraid *might* happen and talk with her about how we both think we should respond to everything from breastfeeding to circumcision.

I never imagined I'd enjoy reading about the female reproductive system, but I'm finding all the pregnancy information to be fascinating. Alice and I look at those "pregnancy week by week" websites and she bases each week's menu around whatever food they've said our baby is supposed to be that week. Of course she does. Once it got out at work that we are together, Alice has told anyone who will listen how excited she is to have a nursery here at Stag Law. Alice and Juniper have a plan to make this the most family-friendly workspace in Pittsburgh.

I do like that she's making plans, but I still feel strongly that financial planning is crucial. I've got Alice on board to start a college fund immediately and we've got life insurance policies in place for each of us, but she isn't ready to get married yet and refuses to move into my penthouse with me. I feel like it's reasonable to live five miles from her family, but she says if our child can't walk over to visit

Grandpa, we live too far away. And, she insists, my place is too barren. I've offered to paint and remodel, but she says we need to agree to disagree that the penthouse is an acceptable home.

At least I got her to agree that we should all live together. I can't bear the thought of sleeping apart from her and it kills me to do so now. She's so tired after work that I usually drive her to her family's house and she goes right to bed. The pamphlets say this is normal for the first trimester, that she's working so hard growing a brain and organs for our child that she's exhausted.

I don't have to hold myself back from kissing her when I see her, but I have to say, after a month, I'm wild with desire for her. I can see her body changing subtly and she looks sexier than ever to me. I want to tell every single person I see that this woman is growing *my* child inside of her. And then I want to ravage her.

I glance up at the clock. I've got about a half hour before we need to leave for Alice's next midwife appointment. We're going to try to hear the heartbeat today and I'm so eager for that sound, it feels like the seconds are scraping by. I take a last look at the papers on my desk, comb over everything one final time, and hand the stack to Donna to have them delivered. "Donna, I'll be out the rest of the afternoon. Would you be able to overnight these? I trust you implicitly."

"It took you long enough, Tim Stag," she says, laughing.

"Truly, Donna, you're excellent at your job. I'm thankful to have you by my side." Donna blushes and I rap the side of her desk with my knuckles as I walk down the hall.

Alice's face lights up when she sees me. She hangs her chef coat on a hook and I admire her as she heads toward me. This beautiful woman is mine. Sort of. She's carrying my baby and I intend to keep working until she's mine officially, legally, and all ways there are to belong to someone. "I made a decision about the Cavs account," I tell her as we wait for the elevator.

"Tell me."

"I declined to take the contract. I don't want to do all that travel and Juniper declined it, too. There isn't anyone else at Stag Law I'd want on that specific client and..." I shrug. "It just didn't seem important to the big picture.

Alice stands on tiptoe to kiss me. Her mouth is soft and warm and I take a minute to just savor how she feels. "I'm glad, Tim."

"If I would have known you'd kiss me like that I would have declined clients earlier." Alice punches my shoulder playfully. I really like how things are between us right now.

The whole way to the Midwife Center we talk about how excited we are to hear the baby's heartbeat, but the truth is I am anxious. I think once I hear that sound, I will feel more comfortable that everything is safe. For now. Alice rushes through Carol's questions, eager to get to the finale. She tucks her shirt up and wriggles her pants down her hips just a little. I try to control my dick when I see the creamy white skin of Alice's still-flat stomach. When Carol asks if I want to direct the Doppler I'm terrified, but Alice smiles at me and I squirt the goo on the wand. I aim where Carol suggests, right below Alice's naval. The room fills with a swirling static sound that pulses until...there it is. The steady, strong beat of my child's heart. The ticking music brings me to tears and I drop the wand, overwhelmed by this proof of life in Alice's body.

Here is this tiny force, a piece of me and of Alice, outside my control yet depending on my protection. "Everything sounds perfect, Alice. Just perfect." Carol helps Alice wipe off and sit up. "Baby's heartbeat is strong!" She makes a note in Alice's chart and tells us to take our time leaving.

I crawl up on the table with her and pull her into my arms. "That was magical," I say, kissing each of her knuckles, splaying my hand across her stomach. She nods. She looks so satisfied, so happy. I want to tell her what I've been thinking about this week, but I'm worried she will think I am being too controlling. I really am trying hard, but I have been taking charge for so long. I am not used to consulting someone. "Could I take you somewhere, Alice? I'd like to show you someplace I think you could be happy raising our baby."

"Tim..."

"I haven't signed anything or done anything. I just had this idea the other day and I'd really like to share it with you if you'd let me."

She nods. I leap down from the table and scoop her into my arms. "I was hoping you'd say yes. I've done so much today I never thought I'd do and all of it just feels so right."

"Put me down, you crazy fool." Alice has laughter behind her voice and once again I'm giddy with anticipation of showing her my idea. I help her into the Volvo and head toward the neighborhood where we grew up. Her eyes question my actions as we drive closer until I finally park in front of my grandmother's house. The house where I grew up. "Tim, what is this?" She asks.

Alice has only been here once or twice since we got together, but it occurred to me the other day that it's a lot of house for one old lady to live in alone. "Hear me out." We walk to the front door and I fish for my keys. "You know Ty finally moved out. I was standing in his empty room the other day and I got an idea."

I guide her up the stairs into Ty's room, which faces south. Two huge windows look out upon the neighborhood. Light streams into the room, with its built in bookshelves and beautiful floors original to the house. "I kept imagining a little boy playing cars there in the square of light from the window. Or a girl reading books on a carpet here."

Her eyes are wide as she stares at me, but she doesn't speak. Not yet.

I pull her down the hall to the next room. "This was my room as a kid." My grandmother has been using it as a guest room, so there are twin beds and a dresser in here, but not much else. "There's room here for a king sized bed and there is *just* space for a crib here in the turret. I know you want the baby to sleep in our room for a while because of breastfeeding." I can't get a read on Alice's face. Now it's my turn to babble. "I mentioned to my grandmother that you wanted to raise the baby close enough to your family that he could walk over for a hug."

I walk to the window and beckon Alice to follow. We lean forward. The leaves are just starting to show signs of changing. "Once the leaves fall, we have a clear view of the Peterson house," I tell her.

"But for now you just have to squint a bit and you can see it. Your dad could be waving at us from the window for all I know."

"Tim." Her voice is a whisper. My heart races with anticipation. I want her to want this, to want me. "This is perfect." And then Alice is kissing me the way I've wanted to be kissing her for weeks. Her tongue parts my lips and I accept her gratefully, moaning as I taste her. She leans back against the window for support and I press my weight into her small body, loving the curves and warmth against my chest. "Is your grandmother home now?" I can feel Alice's apprehension mixed with desire. I hope I'm not misreading her desire.

I shake my head. "She's out playing cards this evening. She'll be gone for hours."

Alice is a woman transformed. She places two hands flat on my chest and shoves me across the room until I land on the small bed. I pull her down onto me and just enjoy making out with her, slowly and hungrily, until I feel like I might burst. "Alice, I've missed this so much," I tell her, shifting our bodies so I'm on top of her, nestled between her legs.

"I love that you want us to live here, Tim," she says. "I love *you*." Her words cause my blood to race.

"I love you, too, baby," I say, breathless with emotion. "I've loved you for so long now. I just didn't know what to do with that before now." She smiles and those violet eyes meet mine. Her hands reach for the tails of my shirt, pulling and fumbling. I quickly unbutton it and toss it across the room while Alice lifts her own shirt over her head. "Holy shit, Alice!" Her breasts are huge, heaving as she breathes in the fading light of sunset. "Can I..." she pulls my hand against her chest, and my fingers knead the soft flesh, thumb circling the hard, hard point of her nipple.

I dip my tongue against the other breast, sucking through the thin material of her bra. She arches her back against me and I reach behind her to pull off this barrier between our naked chests. "God, you feel so good," she says, as her hands explore the skin of my back. I've missed the feel of her soft palms against me, her curious fingers that work such magic with food. As I suck each swollen teat, Alice groans and reaches for my waist. I lift my hips so she can slide down my trousers, kicking them off as they get past my knees.

"Your body has changed so much, Alice, already." I pepper kisses all along her stomach, circling her naval, feeling the firm fullness of her lower belly. "You're so fucking beautiful." I ease myself down her body, taking her pants and panties with me until I'm kneeling on the floor at the foot of the bed.

I reach for her ass and tug her toward the edge of the bed, draping each beautiful leg over my shoulders. "Oh, Tim! Please!" she moans as I reach between her legs, parting her soft curls and finding her slick with wanting.

I tease her folds with my fingers, one hand massaging her nipples, enjoying the look of pleasure on her face. She bucks her hips against my hand and begs. "Please, Tim. I need you." I spread her pink center and dip my tongue against her, and she begins to moan like I've never heard her. I love that I brought this out in her, that I can take her to this place. Deep, animal groans escape her mouth as I lave her with my tongue. I don't stop until she's screaming, her pussy pulsing around my fingers, practically pulling me inside her body.

"I love to watch you come, Alice." I hold my hand flat against her center until she stills. Easing out of my boxers, I crawl back onto the bed. She parts her legs for me, wraps them around my hips, and I slide inside her with one smooth thrust.

I have never felt more at home. She reaches for my head, pulling me against her mouth, the taste of her on both our tongues. Slowly, I move with her, sheathed fully inside her beautiful body. I adjust my weight so I'm supported on my forearms and Alice runs her hands along my pecs as she lifts her hips to meet mine. She grinds against my pelvis, circling to find the friction she needs to come again.

"I love you, Tim Stag," she says, breathlessly, and then she erupts. She screams my name again and again until I can't hold back anymore. I burst inside her, groaning, feeling our wet heat combining, and we both sink slowly into blissful silence.

"I love you, Alice." I roll to my side, still joined with her, not ready to separate, and hold her close. "I'm never going to let you go."

EPILOGUE: TIM
8 MONTHS LATER

Alice finally agreed to marry me in early May. Our families gathered in her parents' back yard and one of my friends from law school, now a judge in the city courts, officiated. Alice's wild hair hung long and loose, spilling down her back and around the deep green dress that hugged our baby.

The round form of our son jutted from Alice's front, taut and centered so you'd never know she was pregnant from the back. As I pulled her in to kiss her after our vows, I felt him kick and admired his timing.

A few days after the ceremony, Alice carries the final box into our kitchen. She began sleeping here with me as soon as we finished painting and all the fumes dissipated. We sold my penthouse and have been gradually rearranging so the house is ready for Baby Stag. Gran decided she was more comfortable on the third floor, despite all the stairs, and it seems like every corner of our home has fresh life in it. Alice has added plants, family photographs, and soft rugs. Every room has a quiet place to sit, with a stash of baby supplies.

She's really taken this musty old house, full of sadness and grief, and transformed it into a place of love and life and hope. I take the box from her hands--her cookbooks are far too heavy for someone 40 weeks pregnant--and pull her into my arms. "Mrs. Stag, you should be resting."

"Mr. Stag, I feel restless!" she giggles. "I keep having this feeling there's something else I need to be doing, but I can't figure out what it would be." She shrugs and lets me massage her shoulders. "Mmm that feels nice."

I move so I'm standing behind her, pulling her close against me, massaging her shoulders and rubbing her arms while I kiss her neck. I twist her hair around my fist and lift, blowing gently on the nape of her neck. "I can help you find an outlet for that nervous energy," I tell her. When she groans I let my hand drift lower, lower, meeting the heat of her core.

"Tim." Her tone shifts, her body stiffens under my hands.

"What's up, babe?"

"I'm having a contraction."

My hand shoots instinctively to her belly, where I feel the strong muscles tighten and eventually soften. "It's really happening! Ok, what do we do?"

"Now we just walk and wait," Alice says, pulling my hand. She asks me to text her sister, who of course tells her brothers and they somehow reach *my* brothers. Soon enough, our house is full of aunts and uncles taking turns rubbing Alice's lower back, breathing with her as she walks up and down the stairs.

A few hours later, Alice can no longer talk through her contractions and she tells me it's time to head into the Midwife Center. I freeze, momentarily terrified. I'm not ready. How can anyone ever be ready for this? My brothers squeeze my arms, and I look at them. "You got this, big bro," Thatcher says. "We'll be right behind you in Amy's minivan."

I nod and, breathing slowly through my nose, I help Alice into the back seat of the Volvo. I try to help her with her seatbelt, but Alice shoves my arm out of the way. She isn't talking right now, breathing through pursed lips. She leans backwards over the seat. "You're not going to buckle up? Alice, that's--"

"Tim, just fucking drive." She nestles her head in her hands and I see that there's no getting around this. She groans as I drive through the night, much too fast for neighborhood roads. "Next time I think we should just stay home," she says, in between contractions.

Carol greets us at the door and ushers us quickly inside the Desert Room. As quickly as Alice is able to move, in between groans and long contractions. I ask Carol if she's planning to check Alice's progress, but Carol smiles as Alice moans long and deep. "No need to check anything, Tim. Your wife is about to birth this baby."

The second we cross the threshold, Alice drops to her hands and knees. I move around front of her to meet her eyes. She locks her gaze onto mine and puts her hands on my shoulders. She starts panting and I can see her body squeezing. Her body is pushing a human being to the outside. "Alice, you're so amazing, sweetheart. You humble me right now, baby."

She can't speak. She's not blinking and I don't dare break her gaze until suddenly, she starts breathing easily again. "The head's out," Carol says softly. "Alice, reach down and feel your baby." I'm frozen in awe, looking down to see the dark curls of our son. "One more big push and he'll be here with us." Carol puts a gloved hand on my shoulder. "Tim, why don't you reach down and catch your babe?"

I don't even pause to think that I have no idea what to do. Alice groans one final time and I reach out to lift the slippery, pink, howling child my wife just brought into the world. Sobbing, I hand him to Alice. Because it's a him. A son. I have a son. She gazes down at him, euphoric, kissing him everywhere. Peter Stag is here to change everything. Somewhere in the distance, I hear Carol congratulating us, telling us he's healthy and that Alice is perfectly fine.

Somewhere in the distance, I hear my brothers and Alice's siblings spilling into this room that's no longer a desert but an ocean of love. At the center of it, amid all the cheers, kneels Alice, looking radiant and exhausted. When I meet her eyes again, she is so much more than she was a second ago. My wife, my world, the mother of my son. I lean in to kiss her and wrap my arms around this family that will make me whole and teach me every day to let go and trust. "I love you," I whisper to them both. "I love you."

FILLED POTENTIAL

31

JUNIPER

There's nothing like the pull of the oars on the river at sunrise. I'll never grow tired of this feeling, alone in the water, just me and the current. I was a girl on fire this morning. I pulled out a 10k in record time. Probably because I'm so excited about my job offer. I was fairly certain I'd get offered a position at the firm where I interned my last year of law school, but nothing is ever certain until the ink is dry on the contract.

I feel so proud of myself as I slip back into my sandals on the dock before hoisting my boat above my head, carrying it back into the spot I rent in the boathouse. I pay more to house my beloved scull than I pay Zack for rent. I don't feel too badly about that, though, because his parents have been paying the lease on our apartment for years.

I wonder for the thousandth time why I'm still with Zack. As I walk toward home, I hear my father's concerned voice. *Juniper Jones, I didn't raise you to settle.* All through college, Zack was just...safe. Between my training for crew and trying to graduate early, I didn't have much time to devote to relationships. I fell into an easy rhythm with Zack. He was a year older than me, but we graduated at the same time and moved in together into the apartment along the

Charles a few blocks from his father's investment company where Zack now works.

As I walk home, I think about how I've been wanting to move. Somewhere maybe closer to my new office. We could find a middle ground, a place that's really just ours, now that I won't be living off student loans. My mind is adrift with possibility as I mount the stairs to our townhouse on Sparks Street. A light in the front room is on, which registers as strange this early in the morning, but I throw my keys on the table and head upstairs. I'm quiet so I don't wake Zack. He's not a morning person. Stopping in the bathroom to turn on the shower to warm up, I walk toward our room and strip out of my sweaty clothes, tossing them in the hamper.

I'm not sure what makes me look up, but I do. I look at our bed and see Zack sitting in it. Next to a naked woman with the covers pulled up to hide her breasts. Zack looks stunned. The woman sneers at me and says, "Are you planning to join us then?"

32

TY

I stare at my name on the contract, watching as the black ink dries on the page. The background noise of the restaurant fades out as I look at the papers on the table. My brother Tim sits across from me, grinning from ear to ear. "Welcome home, little brother," he says, rising to fold me into a hug.

Well, he doesn't really *fold* around me. I'm probably twice the size of him now, and I remind him of this. "You can barely get your arms around me these days, dude." But not even a tradition of goofing around can overpower the emotions I'm feeling right now.

After years playing with the Vancouver Blades and then festering back in the minors, I've been signed by Pittsburgh. Hockey has taken me all over the world and now, finally, it's bringing me back home. This time with a hefty raise and a multi-million dollar, air-tight NHL contract. My brother represents the players' union and worked with my agent to fine-tune my contract. My agent Matty, the execs from the Fury, and Tim all took me up on Mt. Washington to sign my contract with their idea of a celebration dinner: fine dining with a sprawling view of the city from the glass windows of Le Monte. "I can't thank you enough for this, Timber," I say, looking into his eyes.

Tim's looked out for me and my brother Thatcher ever since our mom died in a car accident when I was 9. Our dad never got over it and has basically been drunk ever since. Tim took over as our parent. Enforced our curfew, made sure we kept our grades up. All that shit. Now he's making sure I'm treated right, and I'm grateful to him.

I shake hands with the suits from the Pittsburgh Fury before they head out, leaving me with my agent and my brother and our rare steaks.

Matty, my agent, starts talking about arrangements. I got called up pretty late in the season, but career ending injuries for other guys mean life-changing opportunities for me. As my brother reminds me, this is my chance to get my shit together, rein in my temper, and play some fucking hockey. The Fury are in the Stanley Cup playoffs and my contract has me starting practices this coming Monday. I haven't even moved my shit out of my apartment in Canada yet. I'm getting bored already with this meeting. I want to really celebrate. I nod along as Matty explains how he'll send in some professional movers to pack up my personal shit and ship it over here. I'll have to get all new Fury-branded gear anyway, so I don't need much more than the Armani suit I'm wearing. "Matty," I say, clapping my hand on his shoulder. "I'm 100% certain you'll take care of everything and what-ever you miss, my brother here will clean up." I stand up. I need to get out of this place, to celebrate and live a little. "If you'll excuse me, I believe I'm going to find some fans."

I slip off my tie and jacket and hand them to my brother. He shakes his head as I walk out of the fancy-ass restaurant, shouting after me to "wrap it up, Ty! I'm serious!" My brother knows me well. There's only one thing I want on an evening like this, and that's a firm pair of tits in my face while I'm balls-deep in some pussy.

I walk along Liberty Ave until I find a club where the bouncer recognizes me and sends me inside with a nod. I slide up to the bar, order myself a top shelf tequila, and almost immediately, a smoking hot chick winds her way through the crowd, straight toward me.

33

JUNIPER

This is so unlike me. I don't wear short, tight dresses. I don't wear high heels; I don't go to nightclubs. I also don't move 600 miles with two days' notice, accept a job after a phone interview, or put french fries on my sandwiches. And yet, here I am. This is New Juniper. Pittsburgh Juniper. Doesn't-take-shit-or-tolerate-cheaters Juniper.

That morning I found Zack in bed with that woman, I threw on a bathrobe and walked right back out of the house--I didn't even stop for my shoes. One of my crew teammates, Lisa, lives close by the house I used to share with Zack and I crashed at her place while I made frenzied phone calls. She, as it turned out, has a brother who works for a law firm in Pittsburgh. They do sports law, had just landed a contract with the local NHL players union, and needed to bring on new attorneys pronto.

I had an interview with Tim Stag, the owner, over video chat. He offered me the job and actually smiled when I negotiated extra PTO instead of a higher salary than his initial offer. Like I explained to my Boston rowing team, I'll move just about anywhere that's got a river and a boathouse. But I'm not going to give up the regatta circuit and I need plenty of vacation time if I want to race with a women's team.

Lisa and her brother, my new colleague Ben, actually reached out to the rowing club in Pittsburgh for me. He doesn't row, but he knows from his sister that crew is a tight community. They hooked me up with a lead on a furnished apartment down the bike path from their boathouse. I didn't even go back to my townhouse to get anything. Fuck it. I can afford new clothes with the salary Stag is paying me. Everything I really cared about was already stored in the boathouse in Cambridge. I just packed it all up, strapped my boat to my roof rack, and drove to my new home without looking back.

For the first time in years I feel like I'm making the best decision for me. Not the safest. Not by a long shot. But this job feels like it's got growth potential and it felt good to walk away from that cheating slimeball.

There's only one thing left to do to cleanse myself of that entire experience with Zack: I need to fuck someone else.

Zack was my first and only so far. I'm 24 years old. I've always done everything just like I was supposed to do it. Stayed a virgin all through high school. Kept good grades all through undergrad and dated the first guy who asked me out after we met studying at the library. I didn't even sleep with him until we'd been together for a year. I realize now he probably only accepted that because he was probably fucking other women the entire time. Who the hell gets a booty call at 6 in the morning anyway? I try not to think about the logistics of him fucking someone else during my morning row.

Tomorrow, I'll meet my new rowing team and take out my frustrations on the Allegheny River. Tonight, I've decided to get laid. I probably could sleep with any number of guys from the boathouse. But that would get messy and complicated and I'd have to see them again almost daily. I want someone whose name I don't even know. Some cocky, attractive asshole who isn't interested in my number. Sex has never been that great for me anyhow, so I figure anyone will do. I just need for Zack's dirty dick not to be the last one that's been inside me.

I straighten out my too-short skirt, smooth down my short, inverted bob, and walk into the night club. I take a look around until I spot my target. Over by the bar stands a massive man who looks cocky enough that he won't want to talk to me again after tonight. He must be at least 6'3", without an ounce of fat on his firm body. I can see the muscles of his shoulders filling out his shirt and immediately want to run my fingers along his arms. I don't bother to look away when he sees me staring at him. He's got a messy crop of dark hair, but striking, grey eyes. The way his designer clothes hug his body tells me he appreciates nice things. He'll do just fine, I decide, and walk right up to him.

34

TY

This chick moves with absolute confidence. It's like she parts the crowd with her attitude. People seem to move out of her way as she glides straight toward me. I can tell from her toned, tan arms that she's in great shape. She's solid--not skinny, or fragile. I like a girl with meat on her bones, and this girl has it stacked in all the right places.

I sip my drink and watch her walk, noting her defined quads beneath a tight, black tank dress. When she stands in front of me, she's almost as tall as I am, which throws me a bit, because the women I fuck are usually so short it's hard for me to do them standing up. This chick is in heels, but I'd guess she's 5'10" in her bare feet. I run a hand through my hair and decide she will be just the right size for just about anything.

She holds eye contact with me as the bartender asks what she wants. Not moving those liquid brown eyes an inch, she says, "I'll take whatever he's having."

I give her my best smile, the one with two dimples, and tell the guy to stick it on my tab. This is going to be interesting. I raise my glass to her and say, "What should we drink to?"

She frowns, thinking about it, and says, "The Steel City and new adventures." We clink glasses and she downs the shot. No salt, no chaser. Just belts it down and doesn't even cough. She's used to good tequila I guess.

I realize that she's not here with anyone, which is unusual. Chicks usually move around in groups to ward off jerks like me who just want to fuck them. "You're here alone," I say, eyebrow raised.

"No," she says, signaling to the bar tender for another shot. "I'm here with you." And damned if that doesn't make me hard in an instant.

We spend another few minutes in a weird sort of silence that isn't quite awkward, but not quite comfortable, either. This chick doesn't do small talk. She also seems to have no idea who I am, which is unusual in a club like this. A lot of the pro athletes in Pittsburgh come here to unwind. I can see a few football players surrounded by women on the dance floor and over on couches in the VIP area. Hell, a few of my new teammates nod at me as they head off to dark corners with a scantily clad woman on each arm.

"So," I start to ask, touching her arm. She doesn't bristle or move away, but she doesn't lean into me, either. "You wanna dance?"

She shakes her head and grabs my hand. "What I want is for you to take me someplace private and fuck me."

My eyes go wide and I look around. Is this chick for real? I mean, I'm totally down to fuck, but I don't usually get offers like that. I have to work a bit harder, even with the puck bunnies. Most of them want a little dancing first, at least. Some sort of pretense that we're not going to just go screw our brains out and then part ways. There's something really different about this girl, but I don't think she's drunk.

She doesn't seem high. "What gives, sweetheart? Are you for real?"

Her eyes flash and I can tell she's fired up about something. "I'm as real as they come. Now are you going to fuck me or should I find someone else to do the job?"

Hm, so she wants an angry fuck, I think. *Well, if it's got to be some-body, it might as well be me,* I decide. I pull her hand and walk toward the VIP bathrooms. I tip my chin toward the bouncer standing discreetly in the shadows as I push open the door. The bathrooms here are singles, each one a separate room with a door that locks. Habitual chivalry kicks in and I hold the door open for...shit, I don't even know her name.

She walks in ahead of me and as I close the door, she crashes against my chest. Her mouth is on fire against mine, pleading and desperate. I sink my teeth into her plump lower lip and I love the tortured little moan that escapes her throat. I twist the lock on the door and get to work with Jane Doe, sliding one hand along her ass and bringing the other slowly up to cup her tits.

Her body is firm and muscled. I love the feel of her against me, those thick thighs wrapped around my leg. She opens her eyes and I think I see a flicker of doubt, but then I start circling her nipple with my thumb and her face melts into pleasure. "You like that?" I keep my voice low and she nods as I tweak her nipple into a firm peak. I like watching this chick respond to my touch. I dip my head to suck on her breast, my tongue soaking the fabric of her thin dress. She thrusts her hips against me, her hands digging into my shoulders as I go to work on her chest.

God, even her tits are firm. *What the hell does this chick do to work out?* I shake my head a bit to resume focus and then move a hand down her chest, rubbing her pussy through her dress. Everything about her body is so firm, and I fucking love that, but what I really like is how she's so into this. She seemed really angry back at the bar, but I can tell she is as turned on right now as I am. I can feel the heat of her arousal, the damp cloth of her dress as I press my finger against her slit. I can hear her breathing fast as I begin to slowly, slowly circle her clit with my thumb, but I see in her eyes that her mind is wandering. No fucking way is she going to think about something else while she's fucking me. I'm going to be the only thing she can think about. I'm going to take over her mind as I make her body explode with pleasure. I move one hand to lift her skirt. I slide a hand between those hot thighs that she spreads wide, straddling my leg. My fingers reach her slit and--"Holy fuck, baby. No panties?"

She looks me in the eye again, those dark eyes almost black, her pupils are so dilated. She slides her hand down my chest toward my cock and says, "I told you. I came here to fuck." She struggles with my belt, trying to get my pants down in a hurry.

"Easy now, beautiful." I take her wrists in one hand and spin us so she's pressed against the white tile wall. "See that mirror over my shoulder?" She nods and I start to stroke her clit. She is sopping wet, slick with arousal. "I want you to watch yourself come on my hand, and then you're going to come on my cock." I slip a finger inside her, then another. She's into it, and it's making me very, very hard as I pump my hand in and out of her body. But soon I feel her attention drift again. Fuck that. When her eyes lose focus again I kiss her, pulling back to say, "Eyes on me, then. I'm going to watch you come."

35

JUNIPER

hat is he doing to me? Nobody has ever done anything like this to me before. As soon as my thoughts slip away to Zack and how his pitiful ministrations were nothing compared to this, my Romeo grabs my chin and forces me to look him in the eye while he fucks me with his fingers.

He's got my wrists pinned above my head against the wall and I'm totally at his mercy here. And I fucking love it. He's taking charge of this entire situation, so confident. Everything he's doing feels like a custom move designed to drive me wild. He is literally stirring my body into a frenzy with his long, thick fingers. God, if his fingers feel like this, what will his dick be like? Zack always fumbles around in his own rush to climax without much skill at getting me there, so I usually let my mind wander off. But this feels so good. I want to be here, in the moment. This is new to me. I never feel focused like this except when I'm rowing.

Mr. Huge, Dark, and Handsome bites my nipple and I scream. And then he grins this devilish, crooked smile as he slides another finger inside my body. My breath catches and my heart is racing as the pad of his thumb finds some secret rhythm against my clit I didn't know I needed. I'm getting so wet while he touches me. I can feel his hand getting slick with my wanting, and I feel my bones melting away, my legs shaking as something bursts inside me. As I stare deep into his grey eyes, he makes something explode. Something I've never felt before this moment. Something so fucking good that I can't control the sounds escaping my mouth. "Holy shit," I yell.

Who the fuck is this guy and how does he know what to do with my body? This bar trip feels like the best decision I've made in *years*.

He growls and nips at my neck. "That's gorgeous, sweetheart. You're so fucking sexy, coming on my hand." My hips buck against his hand and waves of pleasure rip through my body. I am shameless, rolling my pelvis against him, desperate for more friction, more of everything. He has reached inside me and pulled this orgasm from somewhere deep, yanked it out of me while staring into my eyes. And I know once will never be enough. Except it has to be. This is just a one-time thing to help me forget.

My chest heaves as I gasp for breath. He lets go of my wrists and my arms sink to my sides. I don't notice him unzipping his pants, but from somewhere in my consciousness I hear him rip open a foil packet. He leans close to my ear, whispering, "Are you ready for the next one? Cuz that was just the beginning."

When I open my eyes and look down, I laugh out loud--a single, snorting huff of incredulity. Surely the massive piece of granite in his hand isn't real? "There's no way that fucking thing will fit inside me," I breathe.

His wolfish smile returns and he strokes his giant dick while he massages my thigh with his other hand. "I'm pretty excited to give it a try, babe." He nudges my legs wider and I keep my eyes locked on his as I feel the tip of him pressing against my entrance. I hold my breath as he starts to work his way inside. I'm surprised to realize how much I am looking forward to this. Whatever the hell just happened with his hand, I know his cock is going to bring a new level of heat. He slides inside me slowly, letting my body adjust to his size. And I feel so full, like he's invading every spare inch inside me.

He smiles as he inches deeper and I exhale, feeling myself stretch to accommodate him. "Look down," he says, and I do. I look between our bodies, past the bunched up material of my dress, to see myself fully seated against him, my body pressed against the dark hair of his crotch. And then he starts to move.

Suddenly everything my teammates ever giggled about makes sense. He's got his rock-hard arms wrapped around me, holding me tight against his massive chest while he fucks me, and I'm enveloped in the smell of him, the warm feel of him. Everything smells like pine and mint and tequila. God, I want to see what he has under his suit. I fist his shirt as the pleasure starts to build. My head falls back, and he nips at my throat with his straight, white teeth. My body craves what he is doing, and more. "More," I whisper, and he looks at me with those grey eyes. "Harder," I say, not knowing how I know that's what I need. But he complies, fucking me so that my hips slam against the wall, my ass bouncing from the tile. When I look over his shoulder into the mirror, it's just as he said it would be. I see his hips pistoning into my body and I see my face transformed by pleasure.

And then he slides a hand between our bodies, rubbing his giant thumb knuckle so gently against my needy bud, and I rocket over the top again. I hear myself screaming as my hips thrash against him. I pound my fists against his chest, forgetting myself, and then I bury my face into his neck. I start to suck on his earlobe, run my fingers through his tousled hair, feeling the sweat build along his neck as he works my body. "Yes," he grunts, moving faster and faster. "Fuck, that's so good. Holy fuck, baby." And then he stills as I feel his cock throbbing inside me.

I'm slick with sweat and weak from the exertion of the most intense orgasms I've ever experienced. I heave against the wall, feeling like I just raced a regatta. I slide over a bit, seeking the cool tile behind my back. "That was--"

He kisses me then, a different sort of kiss. Long and deep, sensual. Personal. "That was incredible," he says, and winks.

He walks over to the trash to throw out the condom and starts washing his hands. I stare at him in the mirror above the sink, marveling at his half-hard dick. "I can't believe that thing fit inside me," I say, adjusting my skirt.

He grins and hands me a paper towel. "You know, I never do get tired of hearing that." I wash my hands and dab cool water on my neck, smoothing out my hair while he tucks himself back in. I'm not sure what comes next, because I fulfilled my mission here, but it wasn't at all what I expected. He reaches for my hand, his thumb gently stroking my wrist. The thumb he just used to get me off. "So can I get your name at least? Maybe your number?"

I sigh, letting out a long breath. *Shit.* "Sorry," I say, pulling back my hand. "That's not how this works." And, before I can change my mind, I open the door and march out of the bathroom, out of the club, into a cab toward home.

36

JUNIPER

The next morning I feel sore, but I don't mind. It's the kind of slight ache that makes me smile, remembering how good it felt with that guy in the bathroom. So now I know what passion feels like. Passion for a person, anyway. I've always felt a similar thrill from my sport. Ok, not quite similar. Sure, winning feels good. Whatever the hell that was last night? That felt like lightning struck and jolted me awake. I don't ever want to go back to sex the way it used to be.

But I do miss the water. It's been days since I last rowed! I feel off kilter without the water. I need to visit my scull at the boathouse, make sure she made the trip safely. I drag my sore body out of bed, get dressed, and walk the few short blocks to the boathouse for my first row in my new city.

My boat looks just beautiful, and I'm relieved to see she made the trip just fine. I carry her down to the dock, checking her out, re-assembling my oar locks, when the women's team heads down the ramp carrying their 8-seater propped on their shoulders. Once their boat's in the water, I introduce myself.

One thing I love about rowing is that the community is so friendly. There's not a bit of awkwardness as they welcome me to

Pittsburgh. I even meet their coach, Derrick, and find out the details about practices for the women's team. Before they shove off, they invite me to go out for breakfast with them after practice, and so I spend an hour anticipating the easy conversation among like-minded new friends.

My oars dip into the brown water of the channel between the island and the north bank of the river, and I head up against the current. Once I set an easy pace, my mind drifts back to last night. *What the hell was that,* I wonder again. If that's how sex is supposed to feel, I decide I'm really angry with myself for settling with Zack for so long. *Four fucking years,* I grunt, digging in with my thighs and rowing faster as I think about him.

How could I not know? How could I be so focused on my career, so in tune with my surroundings on the water, but not know the man who said he loved me was playing me for a fool? I reach the dam on the river much faster than I anticipated. I pull toward the side and catch my breath. I see the women's team boat working on their race start technique. Every oar is in perfect unison. All their legs move together. Hell, I know even their breath is connected. They are a unit, a team. They help each other. That's what I need to focus on. Work and rowing. Everything else just winds up a disappointment.

The team meets at a diner nearby after their practice. Derrick claps me on the back and asks about rowing in Boston. He winks and asks me what the men looked like on my team there, and I relax all the more. I'm definitely not in the mood to think about dating anyone, especially after what happened last night, so knowing the male coach doesn't play for that team takes some of the pressure off.

When the table asks me if I've met anyone here, I can't control my blush, but it does feel good to say I had a good time at a club last night. I leave the diner with all their cell numbers, plans to go for a run over my lunch break later this week, and 9 new friends pestering me for more info about my tryst.

"It was just a bar hookup, guys," I say, downing the rest of my cranberry juice.

Tina, the coxswain, laughs. "Well, you'll have to come out with us next weekend and help me find a bar hookup who makes me blush like that."

MONDAY MORNING I meet Ben for coffee before heading into my new office. The area around our building is all cobblestone streets and plate glass buildings. There's a cute little sitting area in the middle of the square, where I'm surprised to see Ben sitting at a two-top with a flat white for me. He grins. "My sister told me your drink." I sink into the chair feeling very welcome in this new city and, for the thousandth time, grateful that I have the rowing community to support me in so many ways. "Lisa told me I'm supposed to say they're useless without you, and you'd better return her call or she's going to come hit you over the head with an oar."

That's Lisa. I make a mental note to call her after work today, tell her about my new job once I get a sense of the place.

"Thank you so much for everything, truly," I tell him. "I'm so glad to finally meet you in real life and not just on FaceTime with your sister! Your whole family really saved my ass."

Ben waves his hand at my thanks. "So," he says, "You ready for what's up there?"

I shake my head. "No! I have no fucking clue what to expect, actually. Tell me everything." Ben describes Stag Law, how in just four years it grew into a multimillion dollar firm under Tim Stag's calculated direction.

"The man is serious as hell, but it's actually a great place to work." The company represents the players unions for the professional football, baseball, *and* hockey teams in Pittsburgh, and so the majority of the work relates to contract negotiations, but there's a fair bit of injury work, termination disputes, and, as Ben explains, a lot of the athletes struggle to keep it in their pants. "We do a *lot* of paternity-custody cases...and then some defense work if they're caught with hookers and blow."

I'm not quite sure how I fit into this high-stakes, masculine world, but Ben explains that Tim really wants to build diversity on his staff. "That starts with you, I guess."

"Wait. I'm the only female attorney? I don't want to be here just to be the diversity."

He shrugs. "Like I said, the business is only four years old. Most of us have only been on staff for two years. I do know Tim was way interested in your resume and talked about you at the staff meeting after your interview. I think you're the only athlete as well. I mean, the rest of us work out. When we have time. But you are involved in team sports. Tim mentioned that your perspective would be really invaluable."

I nod and finish my drink. We walk upstairs and I'm introduced to the executive assistant, Donna. Ben tells me she is the one who really steers the ship. He whispers, "Donna knows everything about every-thing that happens here. Tim is totally fucked without her." *Noted: suck up to Donna*, I think as I shake her hand and give her my best smile.

"Juniper, you let me know if you need help with anything while you're getting settled," she says, squeezing my arm. I like her. I can tell her offer is genuine.

We walk into the corner office, a huge space with 2 walls of windows and a massive desk. Seated behind it is Tim Stag, looking impeccable and handsome in a tailored suit. He smiles to greet us, but I notice his smile doesn't quite reach his eyes. There's something familiar about him, but I can't place it. I decide I must just be recog-nizing him from my video chat interview. "Juniper Jones," he says, pumping my hand. "We meet at last. I hope Ben was filling you in about Stag Law?"

"I only told her the bad stuff," Ben jokes. Ugh. Male posturing.

We all laugh and at a nod from Tim, Ben ducks off to his own office.

Tim goes through his whole spiel again, even asking me about rowing because he seems really interested in this athletic perspective I bring to his team. "I've never had someone negotiate for time off versus increased salary," he says, and I smile.

"I take rowing as seriously as I take my work, Mr. Stag. I'm fast and efficient at both, but I need a lot of Fridays off to travel to competitive regattas."

"As you know, most of our clients are professional athletes," he says, and I nod. "One reason I was eager to hire someone with a team sport background is because I need my employees to understand our clients, but not get starstruck. You're going to be brushing shoulders with a *lot* of famous men, Ms. Jones. I take it you can keep your wits about you?"

This makes me laugh, since I don't really follow sports much outside of rowing. I practically grew up on the water. My dad was an Olympic rower and coached my team in high school. There was no room at the Jones household for drooling over football stars. "I promise to treat our clients like I would anyone else with a strict training regimen," I say. "I'd rather ask them about their anaerobic workouts than their prowess on the field."

Tim seems really pleased with this information and leans to grab a file. "Come on," he says, "Let me show you to your office and tell you about your first client." He walks me into an office a few doors down from his own. We're on the top two floors of one of the skyscrapers downtown, and from my window I have a great view of the confluence of the rivers. I feel a warm sense of anticipation, looking forward to mornings spent out there, days spent in here.

I run my fingers along the polished wood desk. A brand new laptop and extra monitor are angled away from the glare of the window. I vaguely pay attention as Tim tells me someone from IT will be in to get me set up with email and the company wifi.

I hang my bag on a hook and look at him, expectantly.

"May I sit, Juniper? Should I call you Juniper? We mostly do first names here, including clients, but stick with formal titles when pro executives are in..."

"Please sit," I say, sinking into my own leather desk chair, "And absolutely, call me Juniper." I adjust the levers on the side of the seat to accommodate my height and find that it hugs my body perfectly. I'm going to really love it here.

"I'm assigning you to my brother Ty, who plays for the Pittsburgh Fury as of this weekend," he says, and I feel my jaw drop.

"Your *brother* will be my first client? Tim, are you sure that--"

He cuts me off. "I want to review the details of my brother's contract negotiations before he comes in to meet you in a bit. I would ordinarily handle this sort of case myself, but it's a conflict of interest. Him being my brother and all." I nod, and Tim tells me about Ty's transfer from Vancouver. The only thing unusual about the contract is that the Pittsburgh team, the Fury, are in Stanley Cup playoffs and Ty will immediately begin practices. We still need to work out the details of his playoff bonus.

"This seems relatively straightforward," I say to my boss, and I furrow my brow, still trying to place why he seems so familiar to me. "What's with the emphasis on morality and sportsmanship?" Tim coughs.

His face shifts, as he explains that his brother is a hot head who gets himself in trouble for fighting on the ice, and partying off the ice. *Great* I think. *A cocky, impulsive asshole.* Apparently this guy was on timeout in the minor leagues for a while and is getting his shot at redemption because a Fury player tore his ACL right before playoffs.

Tim's phone beeps several times and he stands. "I'll leave you to look it over, and I'll meet you in the conference room in an hour. Ty will be there along with his agent to look over paperwork." I nod as he backs out of the office, taking a call.

When I make my way to the conference room, I feel totally familiar with Tyrion Stag's Pittsburgh Fury contract. Shoulders back, confident, I push open the door ready to impress, and I freeze in my tracks. The blood drains from my face and I have to clutch the doorknob to steady myself. Sitting at the table with my new boss is *him*. The man from the nightclub. The guy I fucked last weekend is my client and, worse, my boss's brother.

37

TY

"There she is!" My brother stands and walks toward the door and I look up. *Holy shit, it's her!* The woman from the nightclub, the broad with the hot thighs and the strong need to angry fuck. What are the fucking chances that she works here with my brother? That she's my new fucking lawyer?

This is going to be fun. I can tell.

She looks like she's seen a ghost. Yeah, she's rattled to see me here. Tim puts an arm lightly on her shoulder and ushers her into the conference room. That grinds my gears a little. I don't want my brother touching this woman. "Juniper Jones, this is my brother, Ty Stag."

She stands stiffly beside him but doesn't speak, and I can tell he's annoyed. He thinks she's starstruck because I'm famous, but I knew she had no idea who I was the other night. Nah. She's spooked because she fucked her client and she has no idea what happens next.

"Juniper, huh?" I stand and walk over to her, sliding my hand into hers for a shake. Her arm twitches when my hand makes contact with her skin. "My brother says you're new to Pittsburgh, too."

She nods and sits. I can see her trying to gather her wits. She looks at me, sort of desperately, and clears her throat. I just give her my best smile until she stammers, "Yes, things worked out quite nicely. Your brother hired me just as I was looking to make a change." And then she just stares at me uncomfortably until Matty clears his throat.

"Ok, well, now that we're all here, Juniper, Tim said you've reviewed the contract. Again, that's really pretty straightforward, but while we have the team together I wanted to talk about our agency's plan to help bolster Ty's image."

She starts chugging a glass of water while Tim glares at her. God, I love making my stiff-ass brother uncomfortable almost as much as I like seeing this woman squirm. I lean back in my chair with my hands clasped behind my head. Because I can. I'm paying these people to put up with shit like this.

Matty frowns at me, but continues, "Our first idea is to get Ty connected with the community back here in Pittsburgh. It's been awhile since he's been home and we're always looking for new opportunities for outreach. An obvious idea is to get him involved with youth sports."

My brother shakes his finger. "No. Sorry, Matty, but I have to disagree with you there. I don't think it's wise to put Ty in front of a bunch of kids until we know for sure he can keep his nose clean. Ty, no offense, but your reputation precedes you."

"None taken, dickwad. What's your next idea?"

Tim smiles and points two index fingers at Juniper. "Juniper is an athlete. I've been thinking about your image ever since I interviewed her. Juniper, what you said about amateur athletes using paid time off to compete, really negotiating to build a life around your sport...that really stuck with me."

Matty looks interested in this line of thought. "What sort of athlete are you then, Juniper?"

She blushes. "I'm a rower." *Fuck yeah, you are,* I think, remembering her firm arms and chest. Those thighs...Jesus. "But I'm new here, so I don't really--"

Tim cuts her off. "I did some research. There are a lot of amateur *adult* sports organizations in our city, ranging from deck hockey to Gaelic football. But I liked what I saw about the rowers." Tim and Matty bow their head over a folder Tim extracts from his briefcase, talking about adaptive rowing for people with disabilities and sponsoring teams so the inner city high schools can afford to participate in rowing.

Matty strokes his chin and claps Tim on the back. "This is why I love partnering with you, man. This shit is great." Juniper just sits with her mouth hanging open. Matty continues. "We'll get Ty on board as a sponsor of the team to the tune of--Juniper, what does it cost for oars or life jackets or whatever?"

"Team boats cost tens of thousands of dollars," she says, and my face falls a little thinking of how much it's going to cost me to polish my reputation. "I think it could be appropriate if Ty were to finance some of the indoor training facility upgrades, though."

"Indoor! Perfect. He can keep showing up to events year-round. I love it. Ty, we're going to reach out to the coach and have you shadow a few practices, wave a flag at the start of a race, or whatever the hell you call it. Juniper, is it a race? Is there a flag?"

She opens her mouth to speak, but Matty cuts her off again. "When's the next team practice?"

Juniper looks like she's seriously regretting ever moving to this city, but her next words wipe the smile off my face pretty quickly. "The women's team practices tomorrow at 6am."

My brother and my agent share a long laugh about this and tell me to get my ass to the dock at 5:45. Matty stands and claps Tim on the back again. "Tim, have Juniper finish up the language regarding Ty's playoff bonus and get a courier to bring that contract to my office later. Ty, baby, good to have you on board." He practically waltzes out of the conference room, but sticks his head back in and points at me. "5:45, dude. Seriously, do not fuck this up."

38

JUNIPER

"So you fucked your client?" Lisa laughs at me when I call and tell her about my arrival in Steel City.

"It's not funny, Lisa! I could lose my job. I have to tell my boss I can't take on this client. Ugh! But then I have to tell him why..."

"Could you say you just don't like the big guy?"

I sigh. "I don't think I can do that. I can't be burning through jobs because of men. Asshole men. I'm off men, Lisa. No more men for me."

She laughs again. "From what you described, I'd say it was worthwhile. Did you say you were limping afterward?"

I roll my eyes and we hang up. She texts me that she thinks everything will work out, but I'm not so certain.

I don't sleep well. When my alarm sounds at 5:30, I groan and consider not getting out of bed. But then I remember that my rowing practice, formerly my sanctuary, my holy place, is now pretty much an extension of my work. I have to meet Ty Stag on the docks and introduce him to the team. *I* have barely even met the fucking team, I mutter as I heat up my oatmeal and slip into my workout clothes.

I brush my teeth, grab my bag, and walk the half mile trail along the river to the boathouse. I'm not sure whether I'm furious or relieved to see Ty leaning against the wall. He looks like a movie star, with his tousled hair and slate grey eyes. He fills out his designer jeans, I'll give him that. I can't help but stare at his forearms and the bulging muscles beneath his t-shirt cuffs. I've always had a thing for forearms. But I can't think things like that. Not about my client. *Why does he have to be so damn good looking?*

He spots me and grins. "Juniper Jones, nice to see you again." He looks at his watch. "Think we have time for a quickie before your coach gets here?" Then the bastard winks at me.

"Listen, Stag, you are never to discuss that night again. You are my client. Do you want me to lose my *job??* It's bad enough you've invaded my personal space and affected my training. I wish I didn't have to ask you not to jeopardize my career as well."

He throws up his hands. "Easy there, tiger. I can behave. I promise. Look, I'm new here, too." I raise an eyebrow at him. "I mean, I grew up here, but I've been gone since high school. It's not like I have a ton of friends outside my brothers and my teammates."

"*These* are *my* teammates, Stag," I hiss at him. Understanding dawns on him, then, and to his credit he does stop clowning around. My coach, Derrick, emerges from the clubhouse and heads down the stairs with a few of the rowers behind him.

"Juniper Jones! Welcome, welcome, welcome, my new meat wagon." I hate that nickname for the center pair of rowers in an 8-seat boat. I'm tall and solid, and I always get placed in the middle of the boat where they need my strength.

But I'm not about to make a stink about it. I want my coach to like me!

"Guilty as charged, I guess." I shake his hand, and smile at the other rowers I met at breakfast the other day. I can see them all ogling Ty, and I remember that he's a big celebrity. Tina is shifting around uncomfortably and I can tell she wants to hug him or make out with him. Or both. I'm glad she refrains. Pittsburghers love their sports stars. Even these amateur athletes are fawning over Ty as Derrick makes small talk and everyone gets ready to get on the water. Derrick turns to Ty and explains how practice will go--we will inspect the boat, set it in the water, warm up, and then he's going to send us on a long row to the confluence of the city's 3 rivers.

Derrick and Ty will follow along in a motor boat with a megaphone, barking out instructions in Derrick's case, and hopefully Ty won't be a distraction or get in the way. Not that Derrick or anyone else resents his presence here. Oh no, everyone is pretty ecstatic to have a source of funding and a little publicity for our program...and a hot guy to stare at, I guess.

Derrick explains that Matty gave him a call and planned out a whole promotional strategy. "Any new commercials and stuff for the Fury that feature Ty will show him at our facilities, talking with our athletes, stuff like that! Plus we get a set of season tickets for next year." Derrick winks at me and says, "It was a lucky day for our team when Juniper Jones landed a job in Pittsburgh!"

I flush, really wishing I'd had a chance to prove myself to them before feeling like I bought my way on the team with my work connections. Derrick snaps into game mode then and tells us to head into the boat house. Ty watches, seemingly fascinated, as we carry the boat to the water. "Dude," he says to Derrick. "Shouldn't we help them carry that thing?"

Derrick just laughs as we ease the boat gently into the water and slide in the oars. Ty has no idea how strong we are, apparently. Derrick clues him in on some of the rowing commands and even lets Ty yell into the megaphone as we warm up. I can't help but look at him in the boat, muscled arms crossed. Firm jaw, piercing stare.

But then we set our pace, heading toward the fountain at Point Park, and all other thoughts slip away. It's just me and the oars, feeling the pull of the water. I match my pace to the other women and together we dig deep and set the boat flying.

39

TY

From where I'm sitting in the motorboat with Derrick, I'm impressed that these women work so hard for their sport and don't get paid for it. They're doing a lot of the same things we do at hockey practice, just for the hell of it. At six in the fucking morning.

My coffee is long gone, but I don't need caffeine to feel the thrill of watching Juniper row. I can't take my eyes off her, loving the determination on her beautiful face as much as the movement of her long muscles. "Why'd you call Juniper a meat wagon?" I ask Derrick, hoping he's not going to say something about her ass that will cause me to punch him in the face.

"What do you notice about her," he asks, not turning his eyes from the boat.

"I mean, that's a pretty loaded question," I shout back, not sure I like where he's going with this. I feel really possessive about this girl, now that I think about it. I know I shouldn't be, and that makes me want her even more. Especially now that I've had a taste.

Derrick rolls his eyes, though. "Juniper is tall and strong as hell," he says. "I stuck her in the 5th seat because she's got a long stroke. She's the biggest and most powerful woman in that boat."

"Didn't you just meet her, like, this week?" I wonder how he can tell all of this.

He doesn't answer, but the longer I watch, even I can tell what he means. We're about a mile from the confluence, and they're moving at a pretty good clip. Some of the other women are sweating, breathing hard. Their faces look strained. It's got to be one hell of a workout. We must be miles from where they started, and they're in this tiny boat.

I let my eyes settle on Juniper. I see the defined muscles in her thighs as she slides her seat back and the long muscles of her arms as she pulls the oars. I think back to how good she felt pressed against me, how I wondered what she did to get her body to look and feel that way. As I watch her move so gracefully, I feel myself getting hard and I want very much to do something about that. With her.

I move past thinking with my dick for a minute to really look at her as an athlete. Derrick calls for the team to pick up the pace--the tiny girl in the front of the boat they call the coxswain is really screaming at them now--and everyone else is struggling. I can tell they're hurting. Then I look at Juniper's face and I notice something. This is easy for her. *She's holding back,* I realize.

The boat reaches the tip of the Point and Derrick yells, "Hold water!" Immediately, the women raise their oars and rest, their chests heaving. Juniper is breathing easy, like this was barely strenuous.

"Hey, Derrick," I say. "My attorney doesn't quite look winded yet. What happens if Juniper really takes it to the max?"

He smiles at me, and I can tell he's glad I saw what he saw. "Ty, my new friend, I am really excited to find out."

He blows a whistle and they turn the boat around, crossing the river in front of the barges and booze cruise boats getting lined up for the baseball game later. Since the team is fighting the current, he takes it easy on them with the pace, but even still, I can tell everyone is spent when they finally climb out on the dock. They all high five each other and head for the showers, asking Juniper if she's got time for breakfast.

She shakes her head and gestures toward me. "I've got to get to work and finish a contract for this guy so he can play in the game this weekend." I ask the team to remind me of all their names and promise to remember them when I come out again Thursday. I would have a whole host of new phone numbers by now if I weren't trying to keep my nose clean, but I realize I don't want any of this random tail anyway. I want what I can't have. I watch her walk up the path, longing to squeeze her ass again.

40

JUNIPER

Wednesday morning, I make time for the worst part of my move. I have to go to the DMV and change my driver's license. Tina tipped me off that the downtown DMV is the worst one, so even though it's further from work, I go to the office in East Liberty. It's in the basement of a gorgeous old building with a glass dome, which I'm busy staring at when someone taps me on the shoulder.

"Do you mind moving? You're blocking the stairs." A shaggy head moves to block my view, and I groan. Of course it's Ty stag.

"What the hell are you doing here??" Ouch. My tone is harsher than I intended, but I'm rattled to see him out in public. "Are you following me?"

He shrugs. "I'm here same as you, babe. Gotta get my PA license. In case you forgot, I've been living in Canadia, the hinterland, driving a bobsled and all that." I wish I weren't staring at his dimple when he smiles after joking around.

"Look, Ty, you *cannot* call me babe. Ever." He shrugs. I sigh and huff down the stairs to get in line. Of course there's a line. I can smell him when he stands a bit too close to me. He's got a hint of cologne today, something like pine with a citrus scent behind it. So subtle.

Maybe it's aftershave. I try not to be obvious as I sniff him behind me. *What am I doing??*

"So hey," he says. I turn sideways, keeping my eye on the line of people, half looking at Ty. "I just wanted to...is thank you the right phrase for this? Anyway, I am really glad I got to see all that at the docks and on the river. I learned a lot."

I have no idea what he means, and I furrow my brow. He keeps talking. "Rowing seems really fucking intense. Can I ask you something? I noticed you weren't even tired from that training, and the rest of them were talking about how their legs feel like jelly."

"Okay..."

"It reminded me of the other night. You know, in the bathroom?"

"Oh my god. No. Ty, just no. We are not discussing that." I turn around. Can this line move any slower? He reaches for my arm. I hate my traitorous body for feeling a spark from his touch. "Juniper, wait." I sigh and turn to look at him again. He runs his hand through his hair like he's not really sure where he's going with this. "I just...why do you hold back?"

"What did you say to me?"

"I said why do you hold back? During sex, while you're rowing...you had more in your tank..."

I can't move. I'm shaking with emotions I can't quite identify, but I need to make sure I heard him correctly. "Are you seriously talking about my sexual performance in relation to my rowing?"

"I mean, I know you were pissed off that night and it took awhile to get you to let loose while we were fucking, but I was just wondering what it takes to really open you up on the water..."

I don't even think about what happens next. I shove him as hard as I can, pressing both hands flat against his chest. Since he wasn't expecting the onslaught, he goes flying backwards, catching his head against the railing, nearly falling down the stairs. Once he regains his feet, he crumples, bent in half at the waist, moaning. "Jesus Christ, Juniper! What the fuck was that for?"

Shit. A security guard approaches. Fuck.

"Sir, is everything all right?"

Ty is doubled over, breathing heavy. He stands up and his nose is bleeding. "I'm fine. It's fine. I just tripped over my shoelace."

The security guard reaches for his radio. "We've got a situation here, Brad."

"Sir, really, I'm his lawyer. This is fine."

He raises an eyebrow at me. "You're going to have to come with me, ma'am."

Another security guard comes running up. Apparently this is Brad, and, now that Ty has wiped the blood off his face with his t-shirt, Brad evidently recognizes him. "Holy shit! This is Ty Stag! Yo, Ty Stag just got hit by some chick!"

The color drains from my face as I remember the morality clause in Ty's contract. He glares at me as a crowd begins to form. But then I see him enter PR mode, and I can tell he's been in this world for a long time.

"Brad, is it? Hey man, you wanna take a selfie with me?" Brad is beside himself, putting an arm around Ty, not caring about the blood staining his shirt. I rummage in my purse to see if I can find some tissues or something, but before I can hand anything to Ty, a woman wearing a hockey sweater comes out from the reception desk, shaking one of those ice packs from a first aid kit. *Of course, the Pittsburgh DMV staff are all hockey fans.*

Soon, he's signing autographs and joking with the staff about whether he looks more authentic for his driver's license with a swollen, red face. "What do you think, gals," he asks the room. "Should I pull out my fake teeth for the picture?" He waits a beat. "That's a joke. These are all real, ladies." They're eating it up. Even the DMV employees are smiling. I decide to slink away, out into the parking lot.

I don't slow down until I'm inside my apartment. I slam and lock the door behind me and turn the hot water all the way up in the shower. While I stand there letting it scald my skin, scrubbing Ty's blood from my arm, I feel myself about to cry. I shake my head, choking back my tears. I'm furious. I'm angry at Zack and angry to have moved here, and above it all, I'm angry at Ty Stag and I'm not even totally sure I know why.

If I'm honest, he's right about the rowing. I'm not tired after team training and that wasn't the hardest I've ever worked out, but what kind of showboat shows up and lets everyone know she's in better shape? I hear my dad again, talking to me about never settling. This isn't the same thing as settling for Zack. But god, Ty was right about the bathroom. I wasn't so much holding back as...shit. I had no idea sex could even be *like* that. The feelings he pulled from my body! I've never felt anything even close. I remember how he looked into my eyes, how his big hands felt on my body, but I can't go there right now.

I have to go to work...and he's my *client*.

Besides, neither Ty nor my dad ever had to know what it feels like to be different and stand out.

It's one thing being a tall woman. I can deal with that, and I don't even slouch like some of the other tall women I know who try to mask their height. Hell no. I wear heels and proudly. But otherwise? Where I grew up...if you stood out you got hurt. Rowing in a team gave me safety, support. Any time I've stood out, alone, that's when you get noticed.

Rowing crew, the whole goal is uniformity. Even if you've got the ability to go faster you need to match pace with your teammates. It's always worked well for me. I'm strong as the powerhouse, and they need me!

I finish my shower and get dressed for work, thinking about how I can possibly convince my boss to move his brother to another lawyer in the firm. Maybe that will be easier now that I punched a Stag in the face? This just isn't going to work well for me.

I text Lisa. *Emergency. Can you talk?*

My phone rings an instant later, and I don't even say hello. "I shoved Ty at the DMV and he fell and got a bloody nose."

"Say what now?"

I relay most of the story to Lisa, saying only that he said something rude and I wasn't thinking.

"Hang on a sec." I hear a rustling in the background, a clicking sound. "Oh shit. June, go to your laptop."

"What? Why?"

"Just pull up TMZ."

It takes a minute to load, but I see a gossip story about Ty, bloody and grinning with the staff at the East Liberty DMV. "Mother fucker."

Lisa is reading aloud. "Pittsburgh hockey hottie gets the hand when he hits on a hometown gal. That's not a bad headline," she says. "It looks like they're making it sound fun. Ty must be really good with the public. Look how even the guard is excited to hug his bloody ass."

"What do I do, Lees?"

There's a long pause and I can tell she's reading and searching the web for more news. "I think you ignore it. Or maybe, like, apologize to him? Send him a bottle of aspirin?"

"You are useless." I shove my feet in my heels and grab my bag.

"At least I'm not guilty of assault! Go take it out on the water later."

I sigh. It's going to be a long day at work.

When I arrive, I grab Tim by the break room for a word. He is more animated than I've seen him so far. He is evidently thrilled with the contract work I've done so far for his brother, loves the campaign to clean up Ty's image, and says Matty called about some good press on the gossip columns.

"Good press?"

Tim grins. "My brother was working the fans. I think he got fresh with some feisty woman and she gave him a bloody nose. I don't know. Matty says it looks great from his perspective. Ty really has matured. A few years ago, this would have been a sex scandal story." My jaw hangs open, and Tim says he wants me to meet with him later about taking on some of the MLB players to my client portfolio.

I sigh and sink into my desk. What is it about this city? Nothing makes sense here. I lose myself in my work, preparing contracts for everyone Tim suggested, and I don't come up for air until well past dark.

41

TY

When I show up to practice with a black eye, coach looks at me like he wants to punch me in the other one. I tell him I was horsing around with my brothers, but I can tell he's not buying it.

"You don't think my people tell me about the gossip, Stag? I fucking read the Internet. What did we talk about? No fights. No chasing tail."

"No, sir." I shake my head, but he puts a meaty hand on my chest.

"Lace up and get out on the ice. Make me happy I signed you."

Great. What the fuck got into Juniper? I mean, yeah, I said something sorta rude, but I wasn't expecting her to check me like that. Hell, she'd give some of these guys a run for their starting spot. I should bring her to practice sometime. I wonder how hot she'd look in hockey pads?

I manage to forget about it and get in a good practice, but while I'm getting iced down later, I decide to call Juniper on her little jab. She picks up after one ring.

"Ty."

"You trying to get *me* fired so you're not my lawyer anymore so I'll fuck you again, baby?"

"I swear to Christ, I'm not even sorry anymore, Ty."

"Easy, easy. I just called you to let you apologize. I'm in an ice bath right now, so I've got time to wait for you to gather up all the humble pie you want to eat."

I hear her snort, but I'm not going to let her off easy. "My face hurts so bad, Ju-jo. I'm worried I will have to get PT. You might have cracked my orbital bone."

"All right, all right. Ty. I am sincerely sorry that I shoved you and that is never ok, no matter what awful thing you said to me."

I settle deeper into the whirlpool tub. This shit feels so good on my aching body, and the sound of Juniper's voice in my ear feels good in a different way. "How are you going to make it up to me?"

"Excuse me?"

"The whole Internet knows I got rejected by an angry girl. They think I'm some scoundrel now. I'm probably going to get a lot of panties thrown at me on the ice."

"Well, then I guess I helped your dating prowess, so that's how I'll make it up to you."

"I'll think of something, Juniper Jones."

She snorts again. I love all these noises she makes. "See you on the dock tomorrow morning?"

"Yes, Ty, I'll see you on the dock."

AGAIN, I watch with Derrick from the motorboat while the team rows. Again, I stare at Juniper the whole time. I ask Derrick some questions about her form, what he looks for when he's coaching. He talks about breath and unity. Everything he says, I see Juniper doing perfectly. Perfectly. She makes me think back on how hockey was for me in junior high. I was so much better than everyone around me, it really stalled my own progress until Tim got me transferred into a different school with a better hockey program. That's when my career really took off. I wonder if Juniper's rowing team in Boston was better than this one, but when I Google it, they seem about evenly matched.

I look at Derrick and wonder if he's the Tim she needs to kickstart her rowing.

ON THE ICE, everything is going so great. I gel with my teammates. I remember some of these guys from junior leagues and we've played against each other before. It's not like we're strangers. I'm starting to get a feel for their pace and energy, but of course you can never really tell until you're in a game with these guys.

I'm ready for a game.

Sunday arrives and I fucking love the butterflies in my stomach. This all just feels so right and so surreal at once. As I'm lacing up, some of the guys pound me on the shoulder. I look down at my gear, stare at my name STAG on a Pittsburgh jersey.

My whole life, I've dreamed of playing with the Fury. My home-town team. Today is the day.

I know my brothers and my grandma are up in the suite above center ice. I am pretty sure Juniper is up there, too. I want her to see me play, and I realize I really want her to be impressed with me as an athlete. That's weird for me. I really never give a shit what women think about me. I mean, most of the ones I sleep with are mostly with me because I'm famous and I have a nice body. That's just plain objective fact. But none of them ever know anything about me as a person. About what it means to be good at a sport like this.

As they announce my name, I skate a lap around the ice, and I feel so grateful. I remember everything about why I play this sport, why I worked so hard my whole life to be out here.

At the face off, some guy from Colorado starts saying some shit to me, but who gives a fuck? "Hear you got beat up by a chick, Stag." What do I care what this asshole thinks? Halfway into the first period, I slam him into the boards, steal the puck from him, and pass to my guy Kingston, who shoots it right into the corner of the net. Fucking swish. That's what I'm talking about. I don't even feel like I need to fight. What the hell was I so angry about playing before, anyway?

Scoring against these assholes feels way better than fighting with them.

All game long, the Colorado guys are trying to bait me, and what do I do? I look over at Coach, and I score two fucking goals, that's what I do. In a playoff game. Everything clicks, I can see where my teammates are going to be, and I connect with them. When we change lines, Coach claps me once on the back and pounds my helmet. Yeah. I'm good here.

I barely recognize myself now, though, getting back pats in the locker room, joking around. When they moved me to the minors to get my shit together, I just felt like that pissed me off more. Hell, I got in more fights playing minor league hockey and spent more time in the sin bin than I ever did in the big leagues.

But I don't know. Sometime in the past year, I got sick of all that shit. I guess maybe I grew up. I'm still a cocky asshole. But damn if it doesn't feel better to win the game than it does to win the fist fight.

The press is waiting outside the locker room, and I decide to talk to them before I shower. I know my eye is still black and blue, but half these guys are bloody and bruised after the game. I know they're going to ask me what changed out on the ice. "The truth is, I'm really glad to be back in my hometown," I tell the guy from ESPN. "Lacing up for the Fury today, with my brothers in the stands, was really a lifelong dream for me."

"Ty, how were you able to keep your temper in check today? That's been an issue for you since you started your pro career."

I work hard not to roll my eyes at this guy. "I started pro when I was still a teenager, right from high school. I've come a long way since then. You know, my coaches here have a strong game plan. My teammates and I play for each other. It's easy to keep my eye on the goal and tune out all the background noise." *That'll shut him up, right?* I can see my coach nodding and Matty gives me a thumbs up.

As the press slowly files out, the other guys talk about how they're going to celebrate. I consider ditching my plans with my brothers to join the guys at the strip club, but I realize that I just don't feel like doing that. The only set of cans I'm interested in seeing was up in the suite with my family today, and I can't exactly go call her up for a celebration fuck. And I hate that.

Who have I become that I'm more excited to go sign my contract update tomorrow than I am about winning the most important hockey game I've ever played? I roll into my house before 11pm, and even my grandma is surprised to see me.

"Tyrion Stag," she yells from her bedroom. "I didn't expect you to come home tonight!"

I sit on the edge of her bed, still wearing my suit and tie. Our coach insists on "number ones" for all the official business after the game. I know I look damn good. Gram acts like she's picking a piece of fuzz off my shoulder, but I think she just wants an excuse to pat my arm. "I'm so glad to have you back home, you know," she says. "It was good to watch you out there, to watch your brothers enjoying you play."

She smiles at me and I pull her close. Gram has basically been the only mother in my life. I was really young when my mom died, not even ten years old. Dad never recovered and drank himself into..."Hey, Gram," I ask her. "Do you even know where Dad is these days?"

She sighs and sits back against her pillows. "I haven't heard from or seen him in months. He's still around...somewhere." She clutches at the locket around her neck, where she's got a picture of the 6 of us. Mom, Dad, Gram and her 3 grandsons. A happy family from a long time ago, who've been scattered for a long time. "I bet he watched your game though, from whatever bar he's holed up in lately."

I nod. She's probably right about that. It's a wonder he hasn't come around to hit us up for money. I'm sure he knows Tim is doing well financially. I don't want to brag, but I'm sort of famous, too. Maybe he's ashamed. I decide not to worry about Dad anymore tonight, though. I keep thinking about whether Juniper was watching, what she thought about when she saw me score. I sigh.

"Hey, Gram, you wanna come with me tomorrow to Tim's office? I'm signing my contract and then we can get lunch. I'll buy!"

"Of course you'll buy, young man. You're living here rent free!" She whacks me with a pillow and I laugh.

"We'll head out around 11. Sound good?"

I check the locks and turn off the lights for Gram, falling into bed still thinking about how I'm more excited to see my lawyer in the morning than I was about scoring 2 goals in a Stanley Cup Playoff game. This chick feels more important to me than hockey right now, and that scares me shitless.

42

JUNIPER

"Here's to hockey!" Alice, the new chef at work, and I decided to go grab a beer after the Fury game. The entire staff of Stag Law was in the luxury suite to watch, and I have to admit it was pretty spectacular to see the game from that perch. I tried not to stare at Ty the entire time, but it's impossible to take your eye off the guy who has 10 shots at the goal.

My mind keeps wandering, thinking about how fierce Ty looked handling the puck. He played aggressively, and I could definitely see how he ran into trouble for fighting throughout his career. The other team kept trying to bait him, but a slap shot from the blue line straight into the goalie's five-hole was definitely a better answer than a punch to the jaw and a ride in the penalty box.

"Earth to Juniper! Hello!?"

"Oh man, I'm sorry Alice. I keep thinking about the game."

She smiles--she looks particularly happy tonight. "Me, too. And I don't even really like hockey!" Alice tells me about her family, how all of her siblings are so close. I love how warm and friendly she is and I'm glad she reached out to ask me for a drink after the game. She tells me that her sister and brother are in a fight over how high up they store the baseball bat, because her sister doesn't want her nephews to get hold of it. But as they were fighting, the boys got the bat and hit their uncle in the shins. I could listen to her stories about family for hours.

"Your house sounds like such a warm place," I say, and she nods. "I never had anything like that." I explain to Alice that it was just me and my dad growing up, but I don't have the energy to tell her the full story. I know that she lost her mom, though, so I tell her how my dad passed away a few years ago when I was in college. "It's just me now," I say, shrugging.

She smiles over her beer and pats my hand. "You and your new Stag Law family! But seriously, just come over sometime. I make way messier food when I'm at home, and I know you'll work it all off rowing anyway."

"Speaking of, I have to be on the water pretty early tomorrow. Sure you won't join us?"

Alice laughs. "I have enough going on. But I'll make you a good recovery shake for when you get to work. Deal?" I shake her hand and then we gather up our things and head home.

Lying in bed, I keep seeing scenes from the hockey game. I gripped the arms of my seat in the front row of the box, oblivious to everything around me, staring at Ty's face as he sped across the ice. The way he took control of the puck and the team around him reminded me of how he took charge that night in the bathroom. How he wouldn't stop until I was putty in his hands. Remembering, I can't help but slide my hand down my panties to feel the pulsing heat still thrumming there. I squirm, telling myself I shouldn't do this, but I can't escape my longing to feel him again. It doesn't take much--just a few flicks and I'm falling over the edge at the mere memory of Ty Stag and his magical body.

MONDAY MORNING I'm consulting with some other attorneys, divvying up some of the baseball contracts, when I hear a commotion in the hallway. I hear my boss scolding someone and then, there it is. The unmistakable voice of my notorious client, his brother. "Why is Ty here today?" I ask the room at large. They all shrug, but gather up their things as Tim opens the door in a huff.

"Juniper," he growls, "Can you come into my office?" *Shit. He doesn't know. This is about something else. Everything is fine.*

I walk in the hall and wait for the Stags to go ahead, but Ty pulls off to the side of the hall. "After you, Ms. Jones." He exaggerates his eye movements, dragging his gaze up and down my body, and I work very hard to maintain my composure.

"Mr. Stag," I say through gritted teeth, "Is there something I can help you with?"

His grandmother smacks him in the head, and I don't hold back the laugh that escapes my throat. "Tyrion, don't be a pig. Apologize right now."

Tim shoves his brother against the wall. "At least have the grace to look smug about getting called out. I told you to behave yourself here."

Ty shoves him back, saying, "You're just crabby because I flirted with your muffin chef."

"I told you to leave her the hell alone, too!"

I leave the Stag brothers to squabble in the hall and take a seat in Tim's office. Eventually they all come in, and Tim sits down.

"Juniper, ordinarily you wouldn't have to be here for Ty to sign his playoff bonus contract, but I wanted to discuss a situation that has come up here with Stag Law."

Ty grabs the contract, scribbles a signature, and gets up as if to leave, but Tim asks him to stick around. "As you know we manage all aspects of our clients' legal needs, and--"

"Tim, spare us the boring part. Gram and I have lunch plans."

Tim frowns. "You'll hear later, I'm sure, that Jason Murdo was caught in a...situation."

Ty's eyebrows shoot up. "The baseball pitcher? What did he do?"

We all sigh, but Tim continues. "I'm going to be spearheading the situation with Murdo until we can resolve everything, and so that means I'm naming Juniper as our point person for all our NHL contracts."

I feel my jaw drop. "Wow, Tim, that's a huge gesture of trust from you."

"I don't anticipate this taking too long, but until it blows over, you'll be traveling with the teams for their away games. Donna can set you up with all the details for the travel account."

"Tim, I negotiated Friday flexibility as part of my salary with Stag Law. I have a regatta coming up and--"

"Juniper, you've got clients in the Stanley Cup finals and your company has another client facing prison. This is an extenuating circumstance, and you'll be awarded comp time, obviously."

Tim keeps talking and eventually shoos us out of his office so he can head down to the courthouse. I'm feeling stunned and disoriented again as I start walking with Ty and Mrs. Stag toward the elevators, not quite conscious of my actions, until Ty winks at me and says, "Don't worry, Junebug. I'll make sure we win each series in 4 games so this won't take very long."

I start to protest him calling me that, but the elevator door slides shut and he's gone.

43

JUNIPER

True to his word, Ty and the Fury are on fire. They sweep their playoff series and are up 3 games to 0 against the Dallas Knights. Some of the players wolf-whistled when I climbed onto their private plane the first time, but Ty stood up and screamed that I was their "fucking legal counsel" and called them a bunch of jagoffs. So that was interesting. Mostly I try to keep to myself on the road, meeting with team executives and hiding in my hotel gym, burning a hole in the treadmill.

I've missed several rowing practices now, and it seems unlikely that I'll be able to compete in the team's next regatta. I keep hoping Tim will finish things up with his baseball hotshot, but he's been wound up in court and bail hearings for weeks.

As a result, work is tense, too, when we're in Pittsburgh. I don't actually have much complicated legal work to do with my new group of NHL clients, but I'm finding there's a lot of communication with agents and legal departments from current or potential sponsors. Ben and Donna have both assured me that I'm catching on fast, and that my work is efficient, accurate, and meets the needs of my clients. So why do I feel so unsettled?

On the road in Denver, I don't get much sleep. After the Fury victory, I lie in bed in my hotel room trying not to think about how hot Ty looks all sweaty and happy, when my room phone and cell begin to ring simultaneously. I pick up the room phone, and a chorus of male voices floods into my ear. "Joooooooooniper! We neeeeeeeeed you!"

"What the hell?"

"Give me the phone. I said give me the fucking phone." I hear Coach's voice above what appears to be a herd of cattle in the background. "Juniper, I apologize."

"What's going on?"

"We need you. In an official capacity."

An hour later, I'm signing Hayden Murphy out of the drunk tank at the Denver police station. The rest of the team is waiting outside on the sidewalk, leaning against sign posts, sloppy drunk to a man. I can't help but notice Ty isn't among them.

Hayden slumps over my shoulder, drunkenly saying, "You don't take any of the shit, do you?"

I shove him off me, and I'm strong enough that I succeed, which surprises him and causes the rest of the players to start cheering. "Listen," I shout at them.

They stop talking and stand straighter. "I'm going to bed. I don't want another one of these calls. Get drunk in your room if you must. Do not piss on other people's property. Is that clear?"

They collapse again in a fit of drunken laughter, and with Coach's help, I usher them into a set of minivan taxis he evidently called while I was in bailing out Murphy. I slump back to my hotel room, not sure whether to be relieved that Ty wasn't out with this gang of drunken fools.

Back in Pittsburgh, my office is filled with roses. My heart skips a beat, and then sinks when I see they're from Hayden. And Coach. Apologizing and thanking me for taking care of the disorderly charge and keeping it out of the press. Rather than enjoying the recognition for what was actually a lot of really delicate legal work, I feel foolish for hoping the flowers were from Ty. I guess this is my work now.

To make matters worse, I've been seeing Ty almost every day at the boat house when he's not on the road. Even with the playoffs, Ty's holding up his end of the image commitments. He hangs out at the boathouse, flirts with the team, and buys everyone new gear. And then, of course, I'm with the hockey team when they *are* on the road, which means I'm seeing a lot of Tyrion Stag these days.

The man is easy on the eyes, and that's a huge problem for me. I keep catching his stare on the plane, or else he'll catch me staring at him when we're in meetings or the team is viewing film before a game. I mostly try to ignore him at practice, which works about as well as when I try to ignore him all the time. I am totally unable to stop myself from behaving this way. I burn for this man. I need to talk to Tina or Alice, find out where I can meet some other men I can actually date. I wonder if Ben knows anyone...

This morning I have nowhere to hide. I came out to the river to row alone--it's an off day from team practices. My heart skips a beat when I see him leaning against the garage door, sipping his coffee and soaking up the early morning sun. I hate that I know he drinks his coffee with just a splash of milk. Two cups a day. I try to walk past him and just get to my workout, but he steps into my path.

"Knew you'd be here even on an off day, Junebug," he drawls, his grey eyes twinkling beneath his hat.

"We've discussed that name before, Stag." I brush past him as I unlock. He follows me inside.

"Yeah, and I decided I'm going to keep calling you that until I think of something better. Like Jonesy."

I snort.

"Nipper?" My face contorts in horror at the thought of that nickname, and Ty laughs. "Nah, not your style. Seriously, though, I had an idea about your training."

"Since when do you have any inside knowledge about rowing?" My voice is harsher than I intended, but I decide to blame the pressure from work.

He doesn't seem bothered by it and forges ahead, saying, "I don't know shit about rowing, but I'm a professional athlete. Surely you've noticed that I work out for a living. I've been talking to Derrick and learning some shit. And anyway, I noticed that nobody here ever records your trainings."

"Records them how?"

"Film, Juniper. Video? I spend hours every week watching myself skate. Someone records everything. Drills. Scrimmages. All of it. Then we sit with the coach and talk about it. Sooooo I thought I could record you rowing."

I pause in my task of lifting my boat from the rack. He's right, of course. Nobody films us. My father used to back in Boston. In high school, when I was making tapes for college teams, he would put together montages of me starting, mid-race, and finishing. But I haven't looked at my form on film in years. "All right," I say. "But you don't have anyone to take you out in the launch to record."

He grins, flashing a set of surprisingly straight teeth. "I thought of all that." He points to the deck of the boathouse. "I borrowed a camera from one of the film guys. If I stand on the deck there, I can record you for a long ways. If you circle the island, I can walk to the point there and catch you coming back around."

He really has given this a lot of thought, which both stuns and angers me for reasons I can't quite figure out. "What's your game here, Stag?" I cross my arms defensively. "Why would you do this for me?"

"No game, Juniper. Honest. I'm spending all this time here with you guys. Might as well help you up your performance, right?" He opens the duffel bag slung over his shoulder. "You going to let me record you?"

"Don't you have to go do a protein binge or carbo-load or something?"

He waves a hand at me. "I drank a shake on the way here," he says. "And before you ask, I have PT *after* practice and yesterday was strength day so no. I don't have to be in the weight room, either. I'm all yours this morning." Why is his grin so fucking irresistible? "We making movies or what?"

I sigh. "I guess I don't really have a choice about it." What I don't say is that I'm scared to see. That I'm so blown away by his offer I can barely think straight. This isn't some flirtatious gimmick. This is Ty offering something truly meaningful to me. *He wants to help me be a better rower.*

I really don't think anyone other than my dad has ever done something like this for me. I realize I've been standing still, just staring at him, so I shake my shoulders and get my boat in the water. I have no idea what my form looks like, haven't had individual coaching in years. He walks up the stairs to the deck and gives me a thumbs up once he's got himself situated. I shove off from the dock, planning to circle the island twice while he records and runs to his alternate viewing perch.

Like usual, I spend the first few minutes angry rowing. I'm pissed that I've missed team practices and might lose my seat to another rower who isn't as good as me, but shows up. I'm mulling over all my frustrations from work, trying to figure out why I'm irritated that Ty Stag seems to know his way around my mind *and* my crotch.

But as I find my rhythm, all those thoughts slip away. It's just me and the water again. I smell the river water, cool and brown in the morning haze. The muscles of my back and legs start to warm up from my efforts and when I enter the channel for my second lap, I decide I can really step up the pace. I glance over my shoulder and the way is clear as far as I can see. Grunting and pulling, I race toward downtown. I make my way around the southern tip of Herr's Island and ease up the oars, gliding back to the dock, gasping for breath.

I'm just pulling the scull from the water when Ty jogs down with his bag, grinning. I don't fully have my breath back yet, and I'm heaving a bit as I walk with the boat, but he follows me, saying, "That was awesome, Juniper. Seriously! Can we go sit inside and watch? My boy showed me how to hook the camera up to a laptop."

He reaches out a hand to steady my boat as I settle it on the rack. "I don't have my computer here with me," I say, frowning. "Can you email me the files?"

He shakes his head. "I don't know how to do that. Didn't you say you live just up the path or something? This won't take long and you can still be at work before my brother cracks the whip."

The thought of Ty Stag in my house sends my heart racing. I run through a mental scan of the townhouse. I haven't really been home enough to make a mess, but I know there's laundry all over my bedroom. He absolutely cannot see my bedroom. Or any space that would make him think about sex. I know it's impossible for me to be near him and not think about sex. He really shouldn't come to my house. But I want to see that film... Finally, I shrug and start walking toward home. Ty follows me, fiddling with the camera.

"This place has a great view," he says, grabbing my laptop from the kitchen counter before I can protest. He looks out the window to the porch, the panoramic view of the river outside, complete with the gentle sound of water lapping the banks. He settles himself onto my couch, spreading his long legs until there's barely any room for me if I don't want to touch him physically.

He spreads everything out on the coffee table, pops a cable into the laptop, and clicks the file that comes up on the screen. I wedge myself against the arm of the couch, trying not to think about how good he smells. Like sunshine and a little sweat. He must have really had to jog quickly between the deck and the lookout, because even though it's June, it's not hot out this early in the morning. Suddenly I feel shy realizing how hard he's working just to do something nice for me, and I'm treating him so suspiciously.

"There you are, Juniper," he says as I come onto the screen. At first it's awkward to watch, but soon I'm leaning forward, staring at myself. He points a thick finger at the screen and says, "Tell me what I should be looking at."

"Me looking," I tell him. Sure enough, I'm looking over my shoulder when the oars catch sometimes, or dipping one hand lower as my head swings back around. I explain to Ty that I should look over my shoulder while I'm driving my legs, to keep the boat stable. I'm describing what should be happening at the turn when I realize I'm totally leaning on Ty's leg with my elbows, as if it were a counter. The muscles are certainly as firm as the faux granite in my kitchen, but as soon as I'm aware of how close I am to his body, I jerk back.

"I really need to get ready for work," I say, my voice quiet.

Ty looks at where I'd been leaning against his leg and his hand slides to his lap. He nods and starts disconnecting the camera.

"Thank you, Ty, for the film. That's going to be really helpful for me."

"Any time, Juniper," he says. I can smell his breath, like mint gum and a very particular Ty-scent I shouldn't be remembering from the club bathroom. Then he says, "I like watching you." The air between us is charged. I can tell he wants to kiss me, and god! I want him. But it can't happen. I can't let it.

I stand up shakily. "Well, you probably need to get this camera back. Can you let yourself out? I'm going to shower before going to the office. Like you said, your brother's in a special mood these days..."

"Sure thing, Junebug," Ty says and winks. I rush into the bedroom and lean against the door with my eyes shut, as if that will help anything, and don't exhale until I hear my front door latch.

44

TY

"Stag! Get in here!" Coach bellows to me as I limp past his office. Practice has been brutal this past week, but we're a few wins away from a Stanley Cup. This is exactly what I've trained for the last 20 years.

"Sure thing, Coach. What's up?"

"Don't give me that smug shit, Stag. Sit down." I can tell this isn't going to be a quick chat. I sigh, because I'd hoped to head to the boat house this afternoon and see if I could stare at Juniper's ass for awhile while she helped coach the high school kids.

Coach swivels his computer monitor toward me, pulling up a video. It's last night's game against St. Louis. Squinting, I see that he's been watching me and their winger, Houser. "I fuckin' hate that guy, Coach."

He frowns. "I know you do, Stag, and so does the rest of the NHL." Houser came up with me in the minors, was drafted the same year, and we've probably had more fights on the ice than anyone else I can think of. "I want to know what the hell you plan to do about it."

I shrug. Last night I managed to ignore him other than a few shoulder checks. "I'm not going to throw the first punch, Coach." I know what's on the line here. I've read my contract. Matty has been very clear. One fight and I'm gone. The Fury were the only team even willing to touch my contract, and that's just because they got a critical injury right before playoffs. Nobody wants a hothead they can't control. "I swear to God, I'll behave."

He scowls at me. "You're a loose cannon, Stag. Guys like you give the other teams power plays with the fighting and the penalties. And now Houser has something up his sleeve. I could smell it last night."

"I scored a hat trick twice so far in the playoffs," I snap back at him. "Look, I know my reputation is shit, but I've been festering in the minors for years now. I learned my lesson, I got the message, and I'm not going to fucking start with Houser. Remember how I wasn't there the night Murphy got arrested?" I shouldn't be smart mouthing to Coach like this, but he's not being fair.

He nods and scratches his chin. " Yeah, yeah. Good. Now get the hell out of my office and ice your hamstring."

I stagger down to the trainers, thinking how little I care about Houser, and how much Juniper is invading my thoughts lately. I've never met a girl who "got it" about sports. I don't have to explain anything to her, because she knows about timing my protein intake and stretching, the mental zone before a game. She does all that, too. It drives me wild. I could sit with her all day, watching her film, and not just because I like to look at her. When we were in her apartment, her face was so concentrated. I could see her analyzing every little thing in that video.

And then she leaned on my leg. Holy fuck, she leaned across my thigh and then told me she was getting into the shower. Naked. I had to go home and immediately take care of business as I remembered the feel of her pressed me.

I practically ran to my room and fell on the bed. I ripped down my shorts, panting, and started stroking myself, imagining it was her hand on my dick. I thought about the expression on her face when I made her come in the bathroom, could still smell her scent clinging to my clothes from sitting so close to her on the couch. In my fantasy, as I rubbed myself furiously, I imagined I actually did lean in to kiss her in her apartment. That she reached for my cock, kissed me back, stripped out of her sweaty clothes and straddled me. With one final tug, I felt the head of my cock swell and a thick stream of cum spurted into the air like the Point Park fountain, all over my clothes and my sheets. With a heaving sigh, I collapsed onto my bed as the last glimpse of my imagination faded--a memory of Juniper smiling, sexually sated.

God, soon, I think. *I have to have her again soon.* As I sink into the massage table, I reach for my phone to shoot her a text. **Can i ask u a favor @ the game 2morrow?**

This had better be related to my legal expertise
Record me so we can watch and talk about my slap shot
Doesn't the NHL pay people to do this for you?
They don't smell as good as u
Good night, Tyrion
So you'll bring your camera tomorrow?

SHE DOESN'T RESPOND, and it takes all my restraint not to text her something crass about my text vibrating in her pocket.

MY BROTHER TIM is still wrapped up in the Murdo scandal, so he's not at the game against St. Louis. It's a home game, for god's sake. He must be really tied up if he can't even come watch a home game. I know he'd rather be here with Thatcher and Gran, but part of me feels glad because I like Juniper sitting up in the box with my family. I know she's only here for work, but I like the look of her in a Stag jersey. I give her a wave when they announce my name, and I must have a shit-eating grin on my face because I can see Houser fucking staring at me across the ice. *Shit.* That's like rule number one. Never give those assholes something to bait you with.

There's no way he can know anything about Juniper, though. She could be anyone sitting up there next to my brother, with the agents and other families.

Every fucking faceoff, though, that asshole lays into me. "Who's your girlfriend, Stag?" "After we're done here, I'm going to show your girlfriend how a real man fucks." I sink a goal into the net right past his fucking skates and ignore him. The arena erupts. We're up 1-0 in the first period.

I can't help myself. I look up at the box again, smiling at my family, and then I lock eyes with Juniper. I see her blush and smile, and I remember why I became a professional athlete to start with. Moments like this. But I'm not just a superstar to her. She gets what it took to be here, how it fucking feels to score like that. She knows how I feel right now. I'm grinning like a lunatic, which is why I don't even see it coming when Houser clocks me from behind.

I don't know how I keep my feet, but I sway, giving him time to toss off his gloves and come at me again. This time, I'm ready and my conscious mind goes dormant. I'm totally in primal mode. I don't even know how many times I hit him. Both our helmets have flown off at this point and I can see blood flying. I land an uppercut under Houser's jaw and he flies backward. The ref comes in to break it up, dragging me over to the penalty box.

When I look over at Coach, he draws a hand across his neck and I know I fucked it all up. After my two minutes is up, the team manager comes to escort me down the tunnel. *Shit, they're not even letting me finish the fucking game,* I think. "Coach, he hit me first. He fucking started it, Coach."

Coach turns away from me, which pisses me off. Murphy and Kingston stare down at their skates. This isn't fair and they all know it. I've done my part. I reined it in. All I've done wrong is lust after my lawyer, and I'm pretty sure none of them know that. I think. Now I'm not being allowed to play hockey, and I'm wild with rage. I see red and start kicking the wall with my skate on. Fuck that guy. Shit. My whole body hurts from that fight.

I see Matty come charging down the tunnel and he pulls me aside. "Ty, baby, Houser says he's pressing charges for assault."

I actually laugh, because the thought is so ridiculous. But Matty tells me the entire thing is under review, and I can't be on the ice until they reach a decision. "Where's your attorney, Ty?"

"You know where she is, Matty. Why do I need a fucking attorney for this? It's a god damned hockey fight that I didn't even start."

"You didn't drop your stick when Houser hit you the first time," he explains. I can't even remember. It came out of nowhere. When did I drop the stick? Is he seriously trying to claim I used my stick as an assault weapon? Matty's long face tells me this is really happening. My jaw drops and for the first time, I'm worried they're going to end my career over some stupid technicality after I got sucker punched.

45

JUNIPER

"What the hell is happening?" I lean over to Thatcher Stag as I see some officials hauling Ty out of the arena. He shrugs. "Surely this isn't typical after a fight?"

I hear the door slam and through the windows of the box, I see Matty running down the hall. I sigh and reach for my bag. I do a quick mental scan through Ty's contract, remembering he has a morality clause in there and specific language about instigating a fight. They're replaying the whole thing on the jumbo screen again, so I can see quite plainly that Ty was sucker punched by the St. Louis player.

My phone starts to vibrate and I see that it's Ty's agent. "Matty, what's going on?" He shouts some nonsense about a dropped stick and tells me to get down to the locker room.

By the time I reach Ty, the press is swirling around trying to get a comment. I can barely push my way through and Matty yanks me into the room and slams the door on the reporters.

"This is clearly an intimidation tactic by a bunch of sore losers," Matty declares. I'm sure he's right. St. Louis is about to lose their third game in a row and the Fury are basically clinching the Cup...but I'm only concerned about my client right now.

"So what do we do about it?"

It turns out we just sit around and wait until the officials can all agree that Houser's claims are utterly bogus. Meanwhile, the game has continued and St. Louis has enjoyed 25 minutes of ice time without the Fury's leading goal scorer. It's a pretty brilliant strategy on their part, I guess. Bait and attack the notorious hothead. Get him out of the way. If you can't win with talent, I guess you have to resort to this kind of thing.

"This is bullshit," I say. "Where is Ty?"

Matty waves over in the direction of the training room. I'm desperate to see him, and I can't tell where my professional obligation to him ends and my personal care for him begins, but when I walk in the room and see him wincing in pain as the trainer treats a cut, I just about lose it.

His face is swollen and bruised, his lip cut. His knuckles look like raw meat. He must have gotten Houser in the teeth with his fist. I reach out a tentative hand to touch his cheek, thinking to comfort him I guess, but he stiffens beneath my touch. The trainer looks at me with a raised eyebrow.

I clear my throat. "I'm the lawyer. And this is ridiculous. We should charge *him* with assault. Don't think I won't do it."

Ty puts his good hand on my arm. "Juniper. It's a hockey fight. We aren't pressing charges. I just want to fucking play in the game. I don't even want to take revenge." The trainer looks concerned again. "I swear! I just want to fucking play."

I pat his arm and look him right in the grey, swollen eyes. "I'm going to make sure that happens, Ty. I promise." I set my jaw and run through my options. I straighten up to my full height and Ty smiles.

"Matty!" I yell and march back across the locker room. "Show me where these assholes are making decisions."

Matty grabs security to walk me back into the arena. The game has restarted. "This is unacceptable," I mutter. Now the lawyer in me is fired up. This is injustice. I'm pissed.

Even though I have no idea what's going on, I shove my way past all the security guards back in the arena, over to the off-ice officials. "Excuse me, I'm the legal representation for Tyrion Stag. I demand to know what's going on and why the game is being allowed to continue while his status is in limbo."

Six heads whip in my direction and I can see a group of suits approaching. I don't care that I'm wearing a hockey jersey with jeans. My client is being treated unfairly, and this is why I'm here. I demand that the video judge run back the footage of the incident, and within a few minutes, I've threatened to sue the management of the St. Louis team. Not for assault. For fixing the game. That shuts them up real fast.

Ty is reinstated, and I'm still on an adrenaline rush when I return to the locker room to tell him so. Everyone around me cheers and starts patting me on the back, but Tyrion Stag picks me up and kisses me.

My heart stops. My body longs to respond. I want to melt into his soft lips, plunge my tongue into his mouth. He's so passionate, and I fully admit it was a huge turn on when he smiled at me after scoring his goal. But I'm here at work, and my senses all fire warning signals. I squirm out of his arms and slap him.

He seems stunned and looks around the room, where everyone is staring, slack-jawed. "I'm sorry, Juniper. I got carried away." His voice shakes.

I can't find words, but Matty laughs nervously and says, "We're all a little over excited here, Ty. No worries, baby. Get your ass back out there."

I spend the rest of the night praying that Tim will be done with his baseball scandal in time for the next game. The Fury win 4-1 with Ty scoring another goal in the third period. I'm terrified to think what will happen if I have to travel with the team and find myself in the same hotel as him after another victory. My lips still tingle from his kiss long after the arena is empty.

· · ·

MATTY CALLS the next day to report that Ty is getting benched for the next game. "Matty, that's ridiculous. He was sucker punched!" I protest, but Matty explains that they can't afford to have something like that happen again or play short-handed.

"They'd rather play a full roster than risk Ty in the sin-bin for extended time periods and lose because of power plays," Matty says. This is a team decision, and I can't do a thing about it, legally, and I hate that.

After work, I take out all my frustrations on the water. I've missed so many team practices now that I told Derrick I was withdrawing myself from the women's boat. I'm just rowing solo when I can fit it in. I'm surprised to see Ty standing on the dock when I get back from my row.

"Hey," he says, sitting down.

"Hey yourself," I reply. "I'm so sorry, Ty. I did everything I could to fight this."

He nods. "I know you did, Junebug. The whole NHL is talking about what a stone-cold demon you were with those officials." He grins at me and I feel slightly better. But his smile isn't a fully happy smile. He sighs and asks, "Want to watch the game with me on TV somewhere?"

I nod. "Can you wait while I change?"

"Can you just throw on a jersey and watch some hockey all sweaty?" I roll my eyes at him, but when he hands me a Stag jersey I toss it on and follow him up the bike path to one of the bars that is broadcasting the playoff game on the big screen on the deck. Ty pulls his hat low over his eyes and keeps his sunglasses on, trying to avoid being recognized.

Should I ask him about the kiss? I can't read his face. I've never seen him like this before. My heart aches for him. I see him nervously drumming his fingers on the table.

"Ty." He looks over at me. His expression breaks my heart and I can't help myself. I reach out and squeeze his hand. He doesn't let go, just holds it while the game plays on without him.

We sit in silence and watch as the Fury lose 1-0.

46

JUNIPER

A week and a Fury comeback later, of course, Tim is still neck deep in his cocaine case and I have to fly to St. Louis for the final game.

I have Lisa on video chat, filling her in on everything that's happened with Ty as I figure out what to pack. "So you held hands? For like an hour? Then what happened?"

"Then he walked me home and patted me on the back like I was a teammate. He turned away and jumped in his car and took off. Hey, do you think I need anything dressy?"

She nods and reminds me there might be some sort of victory party I need to attend. Shit.

"Juniper, I don't even know this guy, but I already like him so much better than Zack. Like, before I even knew that Zack was screwing around on you, that guy gave me the creeps."

This is news to me. "Wouldn't have killed you to say something to me about it," I say.

"Girl, you know you can't tell your friends you don't like their partner. Then I'd turn into the bitch who didn't like your spouse and you'd stop talking to me. But it doesn't matter because I like *this* guy. He filmed you rowing, Juney. He *helped* you."

"Well it doesn't matter because I can't be with him unless I figure out a way to get Tim to reassign him to another lawyer. Which I can't do if I don't ever get to talk to him--he's neck deep in this court case w the damn baseball player." I sigh. "I wish your brother and I could just swap clients."

"Tell my brother I approve of this plan," Lisa says. "Whatever gets my Juniper laid."

I hang up with Lisa and drive to the airport, where I get to go through a special security line and off to the terminal for the Fury's private flight. This will never get old. I'll admit, I am still pretty starstruck by the whole process. This whole being treated like royalty bit? I could get used to this. The players are all taking selfies with the flight crew, signing autographs. I check in with Coach and the executive team, briefly review the legal needs for the trip: none unless the guys get drunk and piss on someone's porch again. I slide my tablet into my bag and get ready to board the plane. I don't even make eye contact with Ty.

He's got his hat pulled low, his headphones on. I can tell he's deep in concentration, getting ready for game mode. I don't want to interfere with this. He's coming back from an emotional hit, his hand still looks a mess, and this game could clinch the cup if they win. No pressure, right? Ha. The air is full of it. It smells of anxiety and confidence and testosterone. I can actually smell it.

I sit way up front and spend the whole flight reading a romance novel. At least someone is getting a happily ever after.

ON GAME NIGHT I head up to the executive suite with Matty and the Stag family. Well, all of them but Tim. Thatcher seems to have brought a date, who is not wearing enough clothing to keep warm in an ice cold arena, but that doesn't seem to be the point.

Anna Stag smiles and waves me over. "Mrs. Stag," I say, shaking her hand. "How was your flight? Are you in the team hotel?"

"Fine, fine. Timmy put me up in a fancy room. They put a mint on my pillow. Did you ever have that?"

I shake my head. "I got a bag of popcorn on the night stand, though." This friendly rapport with Ty's grandmother seems oddly inappropriate, but she's nice so I try to roll with it. She gives a harsh look to Thatcher, who shrugs and puts his arm around his date. Mrs. Stag says, "I wish they'd just get started already. I really want to watch Tyrion win this thing!"

"Me, too. Trust me!" I've had about enough of meeting with stuffy NHL officials who all think I'm a heinous bitch. Every time one of them catches my eye, I see them twitch. At all our pre-game meetings, when I bring up unsavory and questionable player discipline procedures, they wince. Good. They've all behaved like assholes. Let them think what they want about me. My client is playing tonight.

I waffle about texting Ty before the game. I don't want to distract him when he's doing his mental prep, but I feel a deep yearning to connect with him. He hasn't spoken to me since he walked me home after we watched the game together. I sigh and pull out my phone, typing **Just wanted to let you know I gave STL legal counsel the full Juniper treatment. There shouldn't be any funny business tonight.**

Glad u got my back. He adds an emoji of a dragon. I smile.

This is what you pay me for. Good luck out there, Ty.

Thanks for being here, JJ.

God, *I'm blushing like a teenager,* I think. Eventually, the anthems and the speeches end and the puck drops. I only have eyes for Ty. He's everywhere on the ice, and I'm sure he's moving so fast his blades are melting the surface. It's hard not to get caught up in the excitement of being here. Is it the high profile game or is it just Ty?

I spend the next three hours pressed against the glass of the suite, rapt. My body yearns for Ty as I watch him on the ice. He moves so gracefully, with such precision and purpose. He is aggressive and confident, and I hear him shouting out calls to his teammates, intercepting passes I didn't even see coming.

I can see exactly why the Fury sought him out despite his reputation for fighting. He brings the Fury together, acts like the spark they all need to function as a unit. He's passionate and animated, shouting to his teammates as he glides by, calling out plays. He doesn't score in this game, but gets 2 assists, and when the final buzzer sounds, the Fury win 3-2. The best in the league. They won the cup. I actually tear up, I'm so excited for him. I know he's worked for this since he was 3 years old and started bruising through junior hockey leagues.

And I know I don't just feel happy for him as his lawyer. I want *him*. I want this man who cares enough about me to help me with my athletic performance. I want the funny guy who tries to think up annoying nicknames for me. I want the man who smells like mint and pine and citrus. I want him and he's off limits.

This is his moment, but when they start the awards ceremony for the Stanley Cup, I know I can't bear to watch as he starts partying with his teammates. I don't want to think about him slurping champagne from the cup with some bimbo.

Amidst the chaos of celebration in the suite, I slip away back to the hotel to be alone with my thoughts. My feelings for Ty aren't appropriate. He's my client at the job I need...I cannot leave two jobs in one year, and especially not because of men. I don't even know what's going on with Ty. Infatuation? Is it just lust because I've never had a sexual experience like I had with him?

I feel terribly alone as I sink into my bed, wishing I had someone I could confide in about this. I can't call Lisa at this hour--she has a regatta in the morning. She'll have gone to bed hours ago. My feelings about Ty are so much more than just a lustful romp in a bar bathroom. We've gotten so close at rowing practices and elsewhere, and I can talk to him about "clean eating" and interval training. I'm desperate to be around him, to make him smile, to hear his thoughts. My tears are on the verge of falling, the knot in my throat about to give way to sobs, when I hear a knock at the door of my hotel room.

47

TY

I didn't even have to work hard to get the girl at the desk to give me Juniper's room number. It's not like I flirted with her. I just asked nice. Sometimes you have to swing your celebrity status around. Eye on the prize. Juniper is the ultimate prize. I need her, right now, or I'm going to lose my mind.

I loosen my tie as I wait for Juniper to come to the door. I hear her shuffle up and see her eye look through the peephole, hear her little intake of breath when she sees that it's me.

"Juniper, open up," I whisper, not even sure why I'm bothering to keep my voice down.

She opens the door and she looks a mess, and I love it. She's still wearing a jersey with my name on the back, but she took off her jeans, so all I'm seeing are those long legs sticking out from the black and gold fabric. "Fuck, Juniper, you look so good right now."

"Ty, what are you doing here?" her face looks concerned, upset.

I shrug. "Do you want me to leave?"

She hesitates, then shakes her head no. "Shouldn't you be out celebrating with your team?"

I push my way into the room and close the door behind me, not taking my eyes off her. "Juniper Jones, you're the only one I want to be with tonight." I close the gap between us so I'm standing an inch away from her, breathing in the scent of her arousal, looking into her eyes as her pupils dilate. She bites her lip. I lean in to whisper right against her ear. "And I want to celebrate by licking every inch of your body and fucking you while you're wearing my jersey."

She gasps, and I press my mouth against hers. I pull back and ask, "Do you want that, Jonesy? Do you want me to fuck you tonight?"

Her mouth works up and down like she's thinking about it, and I hesitate, but she finally whispers, "Yes." All bets are off now. I don't care about hockey or my brother or anything except tasting this woman. Her mouth opens and I slip my tongue inside, running it slowly against her teeth while my hands explore that beautiful body.

Her tits are so firm in my hands and I feel her nipples pebble through the jersey material. *No bra,* I realize, and I feel my dick swell in my pants. I hook a hand under her knee and back her up until we tumble onto her bed. God, it feels good to lie on top of her.

She's kissing me back in earnest now, and it's so hot when I feel her get excited by what we're doing. Her hands are fumbling with my shirt and tie, so I pull up onto my knees to shed as many layers as I can while Juniper sits halfway up to watch. "You like what you see," I tease, moving more slowly as I unbutton the dress shirt I had to stick on for press interviews after the match.

She grabs me by the tie and pulls me back down to kiss her as her hands dip to open my pants. I moan when she finds what she's looking for and wraps her fist around my cock. "That feels so good, babe." I kick my pants the rest of the way off and climb back between her legs, fully naked now against her silky skin.

I want to touch and taste all of her, and I waste no time getting started. She moves to take the jersey off and I shake my head. I take her wrist in my hand and bring it to my mouth, planting soft kisses on the sensitive skin at the base of her palm until she gasps. "Keep the jersey on." I make my way down her body, sliding my tongue along each curve, each firm muscle. Juniper lifts her hips as I slide off her little black panties and then I hear her suck in her breath as I toss her legs over my shoulders.

I settle on my knees at the foot of the bed and slowly, gently spread legs her open. "So beautiful," I say, my voice a rumble. Juniper is quivering and I grin at her. "You want me to touch you there, don't you?"

She nods. I run the pads of my fingers gently along her upper thighs, teasing, growing closer and closer to her center, but never quite touching her. I want to make this last. I want to see her let go, to make her fall apart, and then I'll be there to pick up the pieces. Finally, she throws her head back and bucks her hips up toward my hand. "Jesus, Ty, will you fucking touch me?" Her voice is guttural and I can see she's going nuts with want.

"I am touching you, baby," I tease, grazing my nails along her stomach, the tops of her thighs again. "Did you want me to touch you somewhere specific?"

She pulls my hair. I'm still in no hurry. And fuck, I want to hear her mouth say exactly what she wants from me.

"Ty! Please. Touch my clit. Please."

"There now, Junebug. Was that so hard?" I circle her clit gently with one finger, adjusting my weight, getting ready to taste her.

When I bend to kiss her pussy, she screams as my tongue finds home on her neat little bud. I work her clit with my tongue gently, savoring the taste and feel of her. I've finally got her body beneath me and trembling. For me. I fucking love this. I turn my head to gently lick her inner thighs where the skin is soft and so, so sensitive. She tremors, muttering and saying my name again and again, begging me to return to her clit, but I want to draw this out. I've waited so long to be here. As I make my way up her legs with my tongue, so slowly, I gradually put my hands under her ass, slowly kneading her cheeks. I love how each cheek fills my hands, and I have big fucking hands. I start licking her everywhere except her clit, but every so often I thrust my tongue inside her as deep as I can. Juniper moans and gasps and I feel her legs reacting as the super sensitive skin makes contact with the stubble on my cheeks. She's wide open for me, so wet, and I slide a finger inside, crooking it toward me while I lap at her with my tongue.

I can feel my dick weeping pre-cum as the sight of Juniper losing her mind turns me on. I love that I'm able to do this to her, make her let go, bring her this pleasure. I can tell Juniper is close. "Please, Ty. Please. Fucking touch me. Make me come, Ty!"

I growl at the sound of her begging this way, and start to gently suck on her clit, holding it so gently between my teeth. I know this is working for her because she slams her knees against my head, holding me in place with those iron thighs of hers. I feel her hands in my hair and hear her screaming, "Fuck, fuck, fuck! Ty! Yes!!!" I lick her harder, pumping my hand faster, and when I can tell she's almost there, I suck on her clit just that much harder. I pull back just a little to blow cool air on her clit while I speed up the finger that's pumping in and out of her center. I feel her whole body tense and she grasps the sheets, thrashing around like wild.

"Ty!" She yells. "Ty, I'm going to come. Oh God!!!" And I feel her contracting around my hand. I rock back on my heels, just watching her, enjoying her ecstasy. I slide my hands to her thighs and I feel her pulse racing, see her chest heaving as she tries to regain her composure. Finally, she opens her eyes and smiles at me, and I realize I'm not just lusting after this woman. I'm falling for her.

48

JUNIPER

He broke me. I'm sure of it. I just crumpled into a thousand pieces and I will never be able to move again. I'm not even sure what just happened there, because nobody has ever done anything like that to me before. Ever.

I feel Ty gently placing my legs back on the bed, kissing his way back up my body until he's lying between my legs again, chest hovering above mine with his weight on his forearms. I love the feel of him on top of me, big and heavy and firm. He's got about five inches of height on me, but lying this way, our foreheads line up and I stare into his eyes. As his hand gently strokes my side, I feel goose-bumps raise on my skin. I also feel like I want more. "I want you inside me," I say.

He nods and reaches for his pants on the floor next to the bed. He pulls out a strip of condoms and I laugh. "Did you stop at the drugstore on the way over here?"

He grins until his dimples appear. He slowly and carefully opens the wrapper and rolls the condom onto his massive cock. "They were in all our lockers after the game," he says. He nestles back on top of me, his sheathed tip at the entrance to my heat. "I'm going to use all of them tonight, Juniper."

"Mmm, yes, please."

He kisses me as he slides inside and I groan into his mouth. He tastes like champagne and...oh shit. He tastes like me. I can taste myself on his mouth and it turns me on. He begins to move inside me and I lift my hips to meet each of his thrusts. Oh God, this feels exquisite. Fucking him in the bathroom was hot and fierce. But this is something else entirely. As we move together, it's hot and needy and so personal. His big cock fills every inch of me, but even more than that I feel him connecting with me mentally. This big hockey guy who knows what makes me tick as a rower, who always has a smile for me and makes me come until my eyes roll back into my head. I feel how much he wants this. With me. I feel how he has longed for this, maybe as much as I have. "That's it, Juniper. Wrap those long fucking legs around me, baby." I comply, eagerly, pinning him against me so tightly, grinding against his pelvic bone to find the friction I need.

Suddenly, he freezes. "What's wrong?" I gasp.

But he shakes his head, looking around the room. "I want to watch," he says. He pulls out and stands up and, before I know what's happening, he lifts me and carries me to the dresser by the mirror. He places me at the very edge and stands between my legs, sliding into me again. *Oh, yes.* I lock my legs around his back and cling to his shoulders, the wooden edge of the dresser digging into my thighs as he fucks me. My nails press into the muscles of his back, trail along to his chest as he groans. Looking up into his face, I follow his gaze to the wall mirror, where the sight of us fucking is enough to send me over the edge again.

We look amazing together. His rippling muscles gleam with a sheen of sweat and the jersey with his name on it is bunched up so he has access to my breasts, to all of me. I'm clinging to him to stay upright and I can see my muscles shake with the force of him thrusting into me.

"Ty!" I shout his name, groaning and moving against him. I wrap my arms around his neck for support and his hands brace his weight on either side of me. The dresser slams into the wall--we are being so loud--but I can't even care about that as wave after wave of electricity shocks through my body. I'm so wet. I can feel my desire coating his cock. He slips in and out of me and it feels so damn good.

Ty speeds up his pace, pummeling into me, and I love to watch his muscles flex and move. I should have been fucking athletes years ago. This is amazing. And just like that, he grabs my chin and turns my head so I'm staring into his eyes. I fear he can see right inside me. His grey eyes are fierce and I feel him redouble his efforts. I can't believe he's able to go faster, harder. I squeeze my own muscles, trying to draw him into me and hold him as tightly as I can. "Fuck, Juniper, that's hot," he growls. "You're so fucking wet." He pulls out again and quickly twists my body around so I'm bending over the dresser.

Ty stands behind me and lifts the hem of his jersey, his big hands massaging the globes of my ass. When he slams back into me, the impact makes my tits jiggle. He holds me tight with one forearm, pressing his chest against my back while he pounds into me, and I love it. I love every thrust. From this angle, his cock rubs against some secret spot inside me that makes me erupt. My eyes roll up in my head as I scream and when his other hand moves from my ass to rub my clit, I lose whatever control and consciousness I had left. I feel my hips bucking back against his until he shudders and shouts "Yes! Juniper I'm fucking cumming. I'm cumming so hard, baby."

I can feel his cock swelling inside me. I feel him emptying himself into the condom. I gasp for breath, exhausted, and collapse against the dresser.

He kisses my neck while we both catch our breath, then steps away from me. Immediately, I miss the heat of his body. I feel like my knees are going to give, and a few seconds later, I see Ty toss the condom in the garbage. Then he tugs me down onto the bed beside him and touches me so gently, stroking my arm, my hair, my cheek. I've never felt so satisfied, so safe. We just fucked like beasts, and yet it felt so personal and so much more real than anything else I've ever done with a man.

"What are you thinking about," he asks as he gently tickles the skin of my back, up inside the jersey. I shake my head, but he insists. "If you don't tell me, I won't fuck you again, Juniper."

I can't help but laugh, and when he rolls me to face him, I bite my lower lip and take a deep breath. "I was just thinking I didn't know it could be like that."

His hand stills. "Like what?"

I shrug. "Like whatever the hell that was."

Now his eyes light up and he puts his thumb against my lower lip. Instinctively, I draw it into my mouth, sucking on his massive digit. He smiles, and I could stare into his eyes all day like this. He asks, "Are you saying I gave you the best sex of your life," twisting his other hand into my hair. I nod and keep sucking his thumb, and even though we just finished having sex a moment ago, I feel him stiffen against my hip.

"Well, shit, Juniper. If I knew the bar was so low, I wouldn't have worked so hard." I love the feel of his laugh echoing through his chest. He begins stroking my hair and I close my eyes, feeling safe and secure in an unfamiliar way I don't want to end.

We lie still for a few minutes. I start to fall asleep, but hear him say something. "Tell me your story, Juniper Jones," he whispers.

"What do you mean?"

"Like how did you get into rowing? Start there."

I explain that my dad was an Olympic rower, that rowing wasn't optional at my house, but he wants to know about the first time, the way I knew I loved it, all of that. I sigh. "I've never talked about this part before," I tell him, and he looks into my eyes, expectantly.

"Well you said you never came like that before, either, right?" His steel grey eyes focus on mine and I'm mesmerized by him, drawn in as always. I feel myself spilling my deepest secrets, telling Ty that I don't actually know who my birth parents are, that all my conscious memories begin in foster care and group homes around Boston. "I have no history," I tell him, choking back a tear.

"But you have a dad, you said..."

I nod. "When I was 12, my school took a field trip to the boat house. Who even knows if it was just a stop along the day or what.

Anyway, my dad was there volunteering. He saw the other students picking on me." I tell Ty how I was fascinated by the oars, by the rowers we saw on the water. I raised my hand to ask question after question, making myself stand out. "Anyone who stood out for whatever reason...that's who got hurt. It didn't matter if you had a toy the others wanted, or if you were more beautiful than the other girls so the house father gave you special attention..." I have to pause here and gather my wits. Special attention from the foster fathers was the worst part of it. I'd do anything to avoid that. Anything. "Or the house mother beat you for her own lost ambitions. If you cared too much about whatever you were learning in school. Anything, Ty. Anything that made you stand out got you hurt."

I feel him grit his teeth when I describe growing up like that, but he presses me to tell him more about the day I discovered rowing, about that field trip to the boat house.

The kids bided their time and didn't realize anyone was watching. "They shoved me into the river, and my dad grabbed an oar and knocked their legs out from under them, then used the oar to haul me in," I tell Ty, smiling. We both laugh at this mental image.

"He must have been one tough son of a bitch," Ty says. I nod.

"Dad was in his 60s when he adopted me. He took me into the boat house to dry off, found out I was an orphan, and started the process to adopt me that day. Said he saw a fire in me that he admired."

"What happened to him?"

I roll away from Ty, facing the wall to hide my tears. It's still raw to talk about. "He died a few years ago," I manage to choke out. "I only got him for ten years."

49

TY

"God, Juniper, I'm sorry," I tell her, kissing her neck and rubbing her shoulders. "You know, I know how it is to lose a parent. That shit will fuck with your head for years. What you described? Being in all those houses? That could have been me and my brothers if Tim hadn't stepped up and gotten my grandmother to move in with us." She doesn't say anything then and I just hold her close, telling her stories about my family. How Tim basically raised us while my dad drank away his grief and our income.

"And all I did was give Tim shit, too," I say. "He will tell you he fought to get me into schools that had good hockey programs, but the truth is I would have gotten kicked out of all the other schools. Hockey was the only way I could beat the shit out of people and not wind up in juvie." I sigh. "Hey, Juniper?"

"Mmm?"

"I'm glad you wound up in Pittsburgh and found me in the bar that night." I hadn't meant to exploit this moment, seeing as both of us just spilled the beans about our dead parents, but I'm totally overcome by my feelings for this woman right now. There's never been anyone who could relate to me about this stuff before, on top of understanding all the other things that make me tick.

But I can't help what my cock is doing, and right now it's growing hard nestled between Juniper's ass cheeks. I'm prepared to walk away and hop into a cold shower, but she wiggles her hips around, nudging against me in a way that shows me she's down for some distraction sex.

I roll onto my back, and Juniper sits up. She takes off the jersey then and holy shit, her tits are amazing. I pull her against my chest and roll on top of her, rubbing the silken expanse of her front, letting my rough hands tease along her skin. I love how solid she is beneath me. She's firm and perfect. I don't have to worry that I'm going to break her. I can just lose myself in the moment. She starts to moan in pleasure and when she reaches down to palm my length, I groan right along with her.

I reach for the strip of condoms on the nightstand and tear open the next one in the line. "We've still got a lot of work to do, baby," I whisper, wrapping myself in latex. Then she shoves me back on the bed and straddles me. I look up to see all of Juniper rising above me, like a goddess, before she slides down onto me with her warm, waiting folds.

In this position, locked together face to face with her on top, I just have to rock my hips slowly and it feels so tight, so deep, so good. Juniper sways her hips along with my mine and I smile. "We're moving together like rowers," I say, laughing.

She plants a kiss on my mouth, then bites my lip. "No crew jokes until you make me come again, Stag."

"Yes, ma'am," I tell her, and waste no time getting us both across the finish line.

AFTER, I'm feeling pretty spent, what with having played a Stanley Cup Final and fucking my attorney ten ways to Tuesday. I lie on my back with my hands laced together under my head, hoping to catch some shuteye, but I feel Juniper staring at me. "What?" I ask, cracking open one eye.

Her short hair is tousled and messy. Her lips are swollen from my kisses and her eyes are glassy, like she's stoned on post-orgasmic fumes. She says, "Are you actually going to stay?"

This takes me by surprise. "Babe, I have no intention of moving."

"You're going to spend the night? I didn't think Tyrion Stag did things like that." She looks skeptical.

"Tonight was a first for me in a few ways." I laugh. It feels good to laugh with a woman. I guess we're getting ready to have a conversation again, because she starts tracing the tattoo on my chest.

"A stag?" She touches the leaping stag above my heart. My brothers and I all have the same tattoo. Thatcher designed it and the day I turned 18, we all went together to get it.

"He's leaping over laurel," I tell her. "That was my mom's name. Laurel." I bring her hand to my lips and kiss her fingers. She strokes my cheek with her other hand, and instead of recoiling from this intimacy, I want to soak it in. With her.

I reach over her again and turn off the light so we're immersed in darkness. I pull her close against me and adjust the blankets to fight off the chill from the hotel air conditioning. "We still have one more condom to use later," I whisper into her ear. "Now get some rest."

I feel her smile even though I can't see her face, and as we are drifting off it occurs to me that Juniper doesn't have to be up early tomorrow...because she's here for my athletic event and missing hers as a consequence. "Hey," I ask her. "What's up with your crew team? Don't you have a big regatta this week?"

I feel her stiffen. "Well, I've had to miss a lot of practice," she says. "I ceded my seat to Jamie after Tim told me about the Murdo situation. I've been rowing alone to stay in shape but I'm not going to be able to compete tomorrow."

"Aw Juniper, you can't miss your race for me."

She scoffs. "I'm not. I'm missing my race for my boss." In a rush, the reality of us comes crashing down on me. She can get fired for being here with me. What was the phrase she used? Ethics violation?

Juniper can get disbarred, I guess, which means she can't be a lawyer anymore. Hell, more than missing a race for me, she could lose her entire career for taking a risk with me tonight.

"There has to be a way," I say. "Let me talk to my brother."

"Ty, you must not, under any circumstances, tell your brother that we slept together. Do I make myself clear?"

I nod, seeing the glint in her eyes even in the sliver of light that creeps into her hotel room from under the door. She's my secret then, I guess. She feels like one worth keeping.

She rolls over, putting a little distance between us in the bed, but she doesn't kick me out of her room. I think about how much her career means to her, how she doesn't have any family left and really, all she cares about is her job and her rowing. Now both of those things are at risk because of me. I want to do something nice for her, to let her know she can count on me. Not just for sex. I let my fingers trace lines down her spine, feeling the strong muscles of her back, and I get an idea.

50

TY

As soon as the light of dawn slips through the crack in Juniper's curtains, I start waking her up the best way I know how: morning sex. God, I love how tall she is. She fits right up against me, so solid. I slide into her from behind, lying on our sides, where I can kiss her neck and suck on her ear lobe until she practically purrs. Once we've used the last of the condoms, I tell her to get cleaned up and put on her workout clothes.

"I don't really feel like going to the gym right now, Ty," she says, but I roll her out of bed. I need to make a call, and I need her out of the room if I'm going to surprise her.

While Juniper gets herself ready in the bathroom, I call up the number listed on the website for the St. Louis rowing club. I swing my celebrity status around again and offer them a very generous donation if they can find a single boat for Juniper to borrow for an hour this morning to get in her workout.

Once she's ready to go, I tell her to go ahead and check out and meet me back at my room. "You can stash your stuff there until your flight," I tell her, and when she looks concerned, I've got that figured out, too. "I've got to meet a sponsor for lunch, and I'd really like my attorney to accompany me and make sure they're not trying to fuck me. Contractually."

She laughs, but I can tell she's still nervous about getting caught with me. "Just give me your bag, go check out, and I'll meet you in the lobby in ten minutes," I say, and this seems to sit better with her.

I put on my suit pants and undershirt, not caring a bit that anyone who sees me in the hall knows exactly how I spent my night. Most of the hotel guests are with the Fury anyway. Up in my room, I brush my teeth and change, tossing J's bag in the corner, and grabbing my wallet.

I pull on some dark shades and a ball cap, hoping to be at least a little incognito while the lobby is still buzzing after last night's game. Word seems to have leaked out that the Fury are staying here, and the place is crawling with photographers--both professional and iPhone paparazzi. I see Juniper sort of hiding behind a plant and I sidle up behind her, whispering "you should pick a taller fern if you're looking for camouflage."

She shakes out of my grip, looking angry or terrified or both. "Come on," I tell her. I move to take her hand but she looks like she's going to hit me again. I throw my hands up, "woah, babe. I called a car service. We can go out the back door, ok?"

She doesn't ease up until we're in the back seat of the car. I had given the guy the address over the phone, and I take quite a bit of pleasure in watching Juniper try to figure out where we're headed. As we pull up to the boathouse along the lake, her eyes go huge. "Ty," she says, "What are we doing *here?*"

I hop out of the car and hold the door open for her. She lets me pull her hand as we walk to the door, where my man is waiting. I clap him on the back and slap some bills into his shirt pocket, saying, "Dude, thanks for setting this up for us. This is Juniper Jones, and she'd like to borrow a scull."

Juniper looks back and forth between us like she doesn't know what to say, which is likely a first for her. I give her a million-dollar grin, and tell Rick the boat guy, "Juniper had to miss training because she was out here for work. I'd really like it if she could stick with her workout before New Haven."

Rick looks skeptical as he pulls open the garage door. "You her coach?"

"Nah. Just a devoted fan, you might say." I pat his chest pocket again and say, "I'm a great supporter of the rowing community."

He blows air out of his cheeks and looks around, like he's not sure what to make of all this, but he walks Juniper over to a rack of boats and they pick one out that she likes. Rick walks with her to the dock, talking about her route and what she wants to do. He finally seems satisfied that she knows what she's talking about, and he comes to sit beside me as Juniper shoves off.

I settle in to watching her, mesmerized as always by her power and grace. Once she picks up speed, I remember that Rick is sitting next to me because I hear him whistle through his teeth. "Shit, dude. She's good." I nod, but it's nice to keep hearing in-the-know confirmation of what I can plainly see. "She's, like, really good," he tells me, and he pulls out his phone, opening up a timer app.

Rick tells me she's on par to place at nationals.

"Really? When's that race?"

He shakes his head. "Dude, it's like right now. Today. She'll have to wait for next year to compete there."

I exhale through my nose and watch as Juniper turns the boat and heads back toward us. I vow right there to make sure I'm watching *her* compete for the big cup next year instead of the other way around.

51

JUNIPER

This is the nicest thing someone has done for me since my dad adopted me, and I don't know what to say to him as we drive back to the hotel. It's too much. Sex is one thing, but this? Finding what makes me happiest and making it happen? First the filming and now this effort to make up for me missing my race. He knows me, and I realize how good it feels to be seen like this. And that makes it sting worse, because I can't be with him, and I hate that. He drapes an arm over my shoulders and plays with my hair, tucking and untucking it from behind my ear. I'm unsettled by how comfortable this feels, and know that I can't let anyone see. I whisper to him, "What if the driver puts something on social media?"

Ty drops a kiss on my cheek and pulls out his wallet. "I've got his business card, and I tipped him well not to. No worries, babe. I've been indiscreet with women before, you know."

I nod. "Yes, Tyrion, I do know. That's how you wound up with such a specific contract."

He laughs, but doesn't move away and eventually I let myself sink into his body like a warm blanket.

"I thought today was just a regular race you were missing, JJ. And that was bad enough. Why didn't you tell me you were missing nationals," he asks after a long silence. The truth is that I don't know. I never considered competing at nationals solo...and Derrick knew that I couldn't travel with the team, even as an alternate, because I had to be here with the Fury. I've been very disappointed that Murdo's recklessness cost me something I care about so deeply. I think about how I'll be flying back to a lonely apartment while the team will be out celebrating together, regardless of today's race outcome.

"I haven't finished deciding how I feel about it," I tell him by way of response. When he kisses me, turning my cheek up toward his mouth with his big hand, it's passionate and soft, pleading and apologetic all at once.

"Juniper," he whispers against my face. As the car pulls into the hotel drive, I stiffen. There are people everywhere, most with cameras. I leap from the car before it has a chance to come to a complete stop, willing Ty not to shout after me from the open window.

I manage to rush to his room and grab my bag. I can't do this. I can't risk being seen. I've been foolish. I scrawl *I'm sorry* on the hotel notepad on the desk in Ty's room and scurry out the front door without passing him in the hall. I grab a taxi straight for the airport, texting Matty that I won't be at the meeting and to send me any documents electronically. Matty can handle it, whatever it is. I spend the entire flight home trying to figure out how I'll deal with all the feelings I shouldn't have about Tyrion Stag, and then I push all that down inside and pull up other client contracts until I'm bleary-eyed from work.

MONDAY, Tim calls me into his office. He's worked out a deal for the baseball pitcher and can jump back in as point person with the NHL contracts. "Well that's shitty timing," I tell him, not bothering to hide the frustration in my voice.

"Juniper, I know this has been a lot to dump on you, especially when you are so new. That's partly why I wanted to talk with you today." He slides a folder across the desk, and I open it, raising an eyebrow at him in confusion. "I have a meeting with the Cavs," he says, grinning.

"The Cavs? Like in *Cleveland?*" He nods. "Tim, that's two hours away from here. How are we going to service those clients?"

He seems to brush aside my remarks, telling me what an opportunity this is for the firm and what an honor it should be to get considered for such an important contract. "We're going to have to really stretch ourselves to land this fish, Juniper." He asks me to help him prepare for a meeting with their executives next week.

I can't believe he's missing the point like this. Talk about no work-life balance. This is a nightmare. "I will help you prepare for the meeting, but I need you to know that I can't be involved in case work that takes me to Cleveland. As I said before, I value my free time more than a higher salary--"

"Juniper." Tim's voice is sharp. "This is the direction the company is heading. We are expanding. Rapidly. In no small part because of your work here this month! Now get the hell out of here and help me prepare the brief."

I raise both brows at him and stand. I move to walk out and he spins around in his desk chair. "One other thing."

Fuck. Does he know? He would have led with it if he knew I was sleeping with his brother...right? I decide to stick with my irritated demeanor. "What now? Wooing a team in Tennessee perhaps?"

"Don't be a smart-ass, Juniper. That's not your style. No. The Fury's post-season gala is this Friday. Would you like to go as our representative? You did the bulk of the work, after all."

I consider this for a moment. A fancy party does sound nice, especially after the stress I've been under, but how can I go to a gala and simultaneously prepare for a meeting with a client I don't want our firm to take on? I open my mouth to decline, but Tim starts talking first.

"I'll have Donna send you the details. It's black tie. Bring a date." Tim walks me out of his office and closes the door. I hear him yell through the closed wood, "I want an update on the Cavs strategy tomorrow morning!"

A black tie formal and a major client pitch all in one week. Good thing I don't have a life outside of work. I pull my phone from my pocket and see a series of missed calls from Ty and two texts.

I wish u would talk 2 me

I miss u JJ

I lean against the wall and take some deep breaths. Nothing in my life is recognizable. College and law school were so orderly, if hectic. Rowing practice, studying, chill with Zack. I always knew what to expect. Not one thing has been predictable since that morning I walked in on my live-in boyfriend cheating on me. I don't know if I'm cut out for all this.

On my way back to my office, I pass the kitchen and see my friend Alice in there preparing lunch for the staff. She looks up and I guess she can tell my emotional state from my face, because she rushes into the hall. "Juniper, you look a mess," she says. I don't respond, but she tosses her chef coat onto a table. "Come on. Let's go downstairs for a coffee."

I can't tell her about the situation with Ty, but I am able to open up to Alice about my hesitation with this Cleveland deal and convince her to come shopping with me for a formal dress in one of the department stores downtown. "Alice, this isn't how I imagined my career in law," I tell her as we wander the aisles of gowns in the formalwear section.

"I always thought I'd be defending the disenfranchised...not bailing out superstar athletes caught with cocaine."

Alice laughs. "Technically, you didn't even do that. You're just following around hockey players and watching them get into fights!"

"Very funny. Do you think this one will make me look too tall?" I explained to her that I thought I'd ask Ben from work to be my date to the gala. He knows a lot of the players and NHL staff from being with the firm, and I'm pretty sure he's a safe date in terms of not trying anything romantic with me. His sister would have told me if he was into me that way. Ben is about the same height as me, though, so I'll have to wear flats or risk looking ridiculous at his side.

Alice urges me into a fitting room, and coos when I emerge in a champagne-colored, halter-top dress with a plunging v neckline. "Oh, Juniper! That looks amazing with your hair and your skin tone. That's the one!" The dress is sateen and shimmers when I move.

"You don't think the neckline is inappropriate for a work event?" I don't like how low it plunges. It's not my style, but Alice clucks her tongue at my concerns. "All right, then. Let's get out of here so I can finish that damn brief for the client I don't want so I have time to go to the damn gala."

52

TY

Usually I spend the off season pretty drunk, in the company of a revolving string of women whose names I forget as fast as I churn them out of my apartment. This year, none of that appeals to me. All I can think about is Juniper. I know she is feeling something for me, because she keeps running away from me when things get too intense. I know she's not used to this, but fuck. I'm not, either. I wish I could just go to the club, pick up some random woman and fuck her until I feel like myself again. But the thing is...I haven't been myself since I moved back home. I've been a different person. I actually like helping that rowing team with their publicity stuff. I like spending time with Juniper, damn it. All I've done for years is hang out with my brothers, hunt for tail, and play hockey. Now the hockey part is on hold for the off-season and my brothers are all busy with work.

I still show up at the arena every morning to work out for a few hours, but then I face long stretches of free time I'd rather be spending with my girl. If she'd ever let herself be my girl.

Juniper stopped responding to my flirty texts and doesn't pick up when I call. Something's up with her and I need to get her to tell me about it. Trying to distract myself, I've tightened every screw in my grandma's house, mowed every blade of her grass to perfection. Hell, I even hung out with my brother Thatcher at his damn glass studio in the heat of June, watching him make giant flower vases and shit. And all the while, I think of how I want to be taking Juniper to dinner, asking her about her training, watching her row. And then I remember I can't do any of those things because she's off limits.

The rowing teams are on hiatus after their big regatta, so I haven't even been hanging around the boat house. I had a few phone calls with Derrick about a television spot, but that's not even happening until fall. I think we've done just about all we're going to do with them in terms of my image strategy or whatever the hell Matty is calling it. The press loves me. Coach is in a good mood now that we've won the Cup. I'm supposed to be living it up, but I just feel like I'm drifting.

After about a week of me sulking around, my grandma whacks me in the head with a newspaper while we're eating lunch.

"What the hell, Gram?"

"You're a mope, Tyrion Stag. What are you doing with yourself?"

"Jesus, that hurt. I'm trying to relax a bit is all." I try to go back to eating my sandwich, but Gram is relentless.

"Get out of here and go do something. Go to the library. Visit kids at a hospital. I don't want to see your mopey face back here today."

I decide to go for a long run and take Gram up on the idea to visit kids at the children's hospital. I spend hours there, giving each kid a photo op and signing everything they hand me. Their moms swoon and all the dads pat me on the back and ask when it's my turn for a day with the Cup. I feel good, but it doesn't last. After all that, I'm alone with my thoughts again. Only one thing feels right to me, and I decide I'm just going to go for it.

Before I can reconsider, I'm knocking on the door of Juniper's townhouse.

She answers and I watch her face drop in fear. "What are you doing here?" she hisses, pulling me inside and slamming the door. "Someone is going to recognize you, Ty. People use the bike path all the time."

I pull her into my arms and just inhale her scent. I haven't seen her in almost a week. Too long. "I just had to see you, Juniper." And then I claim her mouth with mine. I feel her struggling with her doubts, and then give in to wanting me.

She sighs, says my name like a whispered prayer. "Ty." It doesn't take long for me to strip her out of her work clothes, wrestle out of my jeans, and work our way over to the couch.

We don't say a word, but she grabs the condom from my jeans on the floor, rips it open with her teeth, and rolls it onto my shaft. I pull her onto my lap and she straddles my waist with those long, thick thighs of hers. I can't help but moan as she sinks home.

Juniper braces her hands on my chest and rides me like she's taking out all her anger at the world. It's fierce and it's fast and intense. I don't let her look away, keeping my eyes locked on hers while I knead her ass cheeks and drive up into her as she slams against me. "Yes, baby. Fuck me just like that." She finds the friction she needs and tilts her hips, bouncing up and down on my dick until her tits are shaking and I feel her clench around me. I let go right along with her.

This is what I want. I want to make love to this woman and just melt into her. I think back to the hotel and how good I felt *after* we finished, when I just got to hold her and talk with her about life. She's collapsed against me on my lap now, and I just want to sit here with her until we grow old and creaky.

Eventually, she rolls off my lap and lies on her back on the couch with her legs sprawled across me. "Why Tyrion?" she says.

"Huh?"

"Why Tyrion and not Tyler or something? For Ty?"

"Oh." I get up to throw away the condom, and tell her, "My mom was really into reading *Game of Thrones* when she was pregnant with me. Then it became sort of a joke--I was the youngest, but I was always the biggest. I'd tell you I was the smartest, too, but we all know that's Tim." She laughs and I nestle in beside her, stroking her arm and just lavishing the chance to be close to her. I love that she's letting me in. "How come you're not on the pill, Juniper?"

She doesn't answer for a while, so long that I wonder if she fell asleep, but she finally explains that it just never felt like a good idea. "And in the end, Zack was cheating on me. Who knows what disease I might have caught if I'd been on the pill and stopped using condoms. I guess I'm nervous to trust anyone that much again." The thought of him betraying her like that makes me draw my hands into fists. I want to tell her she'd never have to worry about that with me, that she can always trust me to keep her safe, but the words don't seem to come to me. I realize some of the fan-girls I slept with might have had boyfriends or husbands. A wave of shame rolls over me at how I used to behave. Now that I've found someone, found Juniper, I realize what I was missing out on.

"I hate that that fucker abused your trust, Juniper," I breathe into her hair.

She turns her head to look up at me. "We can't keep doing this or I'll get fired."

"Juniper," I say, my voice serious, "I'm going to figure something out. I want to be with you, baby. For real with you."

She looks away and eventually starts to put her clothes back on. "Hey," I say, tugging on her arm. "You've got to stop running away from me when things get real."

She lets out a "humph," but I keep going. "I'm serious, Juniper. You've been avoiding me for a week since we made love at the hotel. I fucking miss you. Let's work on this thing together."

"There's nothing, Ty. There's no way out of this. You should leave."

I pull her back onto the couch beside me, half dressed. I don't give a fuck what she is wearing. Or preferably not wearing. "I'm. Not. Leaving." I punctuate each word with a kiss on her neck and shoulder. I feel her melt into me and I know, for a little at least, that I got her to forget about work shit and just be with me.

We turn on the television and just hang out until I realize I'm half starved. "You got any food, JJ?"

She wrinkles her brow and shakes her head. "I might have some protein bars..."

"Nah. I need a full meal. We'll have to order in."

I can see her hesitate about this, but there's nothing to be done. "I'm staying overnight, Junebug, so you'd better feed me something. I'll hide in the bedroom and you can answer the door for the delivery guy, ok?"

Except that when the food arrives, Juniper is in the shower, so it's me answering the door for a young kid in a Fury jersey. A fan. Of course. "Holy shit! Ty Stag!" the kid practically drops my food, which I grab from him before disaster strikes.

"In the flesh," I say, looking over my shoulder to make sure Juniper doesn't hear any of this. "I'll sign anything you want and snap a pic with you if you promise to forget my friend's address here. What do you say?"

The kid's jaw drops, so I grab his phone and snap a selfie of us together. Then I sign a receipt for him, scribbling his name from his nametag while he just stands there mute. I stuff an extra twenty in his fist and usher him out the door just as Juniper comes out of the bedroom with a towel wrapped around her head.

"You didn't answer the door, did you, Ty?" She looks worried.

"Never fear, babe. The kid had no idea who I was and I paid cash."

53

JUNIPER

In the morning, it's hard to go to the office. I woke up in bed entwined with Ty, showered with him, ate breakfast with him, and told him how much I hated working on this Cleveland briefing. It felt like a fantasy of how life could be if I were in a real relationship instead of unethically fucking my famous client. Then I had to leave him, sneak out of my own house like a fugitive while this man I care about so much slinked away in a hoodie like some sort of cat burglar.

He called Donna at work to set up a meeting with me for official business, but that doesn't brighten my day. I have to pretend like he's just a regular client, like he wasn't inside my body or listening to me bare my soul, talking about the loss of my dad and what that's meant for my life.

At lunch, when we're looking over his endorsement contracts, I notice that he's supposed to pose with the captain of the local women's hockey team for a promotional campaign. "We have a women's hockey team in Pittsburgh?" I never heard of them.

Ty shrugs. "I mean, it's not like they're the pros, but yeah. I've met some of them. They're nice."

We go over all his paperwork, but I can't get the women's hockey team out of my mind.

After he leaves, I call the team contact, Alicia, who turns out to be the team captain, coach, and business manager. They've got no funding, no legal representation, and are beyond thrilled for this advertising opportunity because they're going to put the funds toward their rink time. The whole team has day jobs, and everything they do is grass-roots, hard work, gritty. I explain to Alicia that I totally get it as a rower, and the experience gives me an idea.

For the rest of the week, I give only cursory attention to the Cavs meeting and dive into my new theory for how I can enjoy my work more while helping Tim expand the firm. Alice actually has to drag me from my office on Friday to get ready for the gala. I can tell she's hiding something from me when she's helping me with my makeup in the women's room, but I don't press her about it, because then I'd be tempted to spill my own secrets. I try to just enjoy spending time with a friend, a real friend, and probably the first one I've made outside of rowing in years.

"Ugh," I tell her, sliding my dress over my head where Alice has topped off my smoothed hair with a glittering pin. "This freaking meeting with Cleveland."

She nods. "I just found out about it, actually. I mean that it's Monday and I have to cook for it. I wish Tim had given me more of a heads up. I'll be doing the menu the entire weekend."

I whip my head around. "You didn't know? Gosh, Alice. I feel like a jerk. I should have told you they were coming Monday! Want me to help you?"

She shakes her head, smiles a small smile. "Juniper, you look perfect. Go have an amazing time, and make sure to text me and describe the food in detail when you get home."

"Do they serve actual food at these things? I thought it would just be tiny bites with sauce drizzled in a pattern." I laugh, but promise to tell her all the details about the menu.

I had told Ben I'd meet him in the lobby of our office building, and I burst out laughing when I see him emerge from his office in his tux. "Working late like me, I see!" Apparently everyone in this place burns the candle at both ends. Not tonight. I'm determined to cut loose and enjoy myself.

"Juniper, you look radiant," he says, offering me an elbow. We share a cab over to the art museum. Along the way, Ben catches me up on Lisa's week, making me feel sheepish for not keeping in better touch, but he also tells me about the barista downstairs whom he's head over heels in love with, but too shy to make a move.

"Well now I know why you're always greeting me with a flat white," I say, laughing and really enjoying his revelation. I feel myself relax fully, knowing I can just be myself and not worry that he's going to make a move. We make a plan for him to slide her his number on Monday. The thought of his budding relationship takes my mind, of course, right back to work and my own personal tangle.

"Hey, Ben, I know we're supposed to relax tonight, but can I ask you something about work?"

"Sure. What's up?"

"Do you want this Cleveland thing to work out?"

He sighs. "Ah, I don't know, Juniper. I already feel like we're working pretty hard here. All of us! I mean, Tim's had you all over the country with the hockey team and I've had to step up with the NFL guys. Maybe Tim will hire new people if we land the Cavs?"

"Maybe." We pull up outside the building. Ben opens the door for me, lends me his elbow, and we joke about walking in on the red carpet. Of course, we aren't the celebrities the crowds are here to see.

Tonight is all about the Fury, and the press is here in force. Everyone is congratulating the team, the team staff. The atmosphere is so joyous.

I'm not sure why it didn't occur to me that I'd be walking into a hockey celebration where Tyrion Stag was sure to be a focal point. It just wasn't something I was thinking about when he was over the other day, and I haven't talked to him in a few days. It's not like he called me to ask if I'd be here, either. But the moment Ben and I walk into the atrium I feel his gaze upon me, dark and furious as Ben places a hand on my waist to usher me toward the bar.

"I feel like an idiot," I tell Ben as we wait for a drink. "I didn't stop to think that I'd be seeing the players tonight."

He laughs. "Why do you think I was so eager to say yes when you invited me? I gave up a good night to stare at my coffee gal so I can brush shoulders with the Fury! I love these guys."

He orders us each a drink, telling me how he's taking the liberty to go full fan-geek tonight. One of the guys walks up to us then, and Ben starts tugging on my elbow. It's Hayden Murphy, one of the guys I had to bail out for public urination.

Murphy smiles and hugs me, casually. "Juniper! Glad you could join us!"

"Hayden. Glad you stayed out of trouble so I could be here." I punch his arm playfully. "This is my colleague Ben. He's a big fan." I mouth "huge" and Hayden laughs. The guys take a selfie and start to talk about the last game.

When Hayden excuses himself, Ben pulls me into an excited hug and shows me the pictures. He's so excited I can't help but smile and lean into his hug. "Just don't let Tim know you're so star struck for the clients, Ben!"

"Never, Juniper. I'm all game face at work. Game face and golf puns."

He starts to chatter about the other Fury players here and my mind wanders as I sip my mojito.

Suddenly I feel my phone start to vibrate in my clutch. Repeatedly. A peek inside reveals a string of texts from Ty.

What the duck r u doing here?

Who is that asshole w u?

Why is he touching u, Juniper?

My face flushes, and I quickly zip my bag as Ben looks at me, concerned. "Everything ok?"

"It's fine. I just forgot to tell Ty that I was coming here to represent Stag Law." I gesture across the room, where Ty is still smoldering amongst a group of his teammates. Ben smiles and waves, but I know Ty doesn't know who he is. Why would he bother to remember some other random lawyer from his brother's firm? I'm the only one who has been traveling with them, joking around on their flights, bailing them out when groups of them get a little rowdy at the strip clubs. Ty shoots a look at Ben that would melt ice, and I can't decide if I should go over and try to calm him down.

Ben and I make our way toward the executives we are supposed to be thanking and get busy with the small talk and sucking up portion of our evening. I finish complimenting the team owner on his decision to sign Ty before playoffs as my phone begins to vibrate again. I'm able to glance at the new text, which reads **meet me in the stairwell.**

Now, JJ.

I glance around, but don't see Ty. "Would you excuse me," I say to Ben and the gang of suits. "I have a client with an urgent need I have to address." I walk away to the sound of them admiring my dedication as a lawyer and I hear Ben steering the conversation back to the playoff game where I intervened on Ty's behalf.

When I enter the stairwell, it's eerily silent. I see Ty standing down a level, staring at me. I've never seen him look like this before. I can feel his intense mix of emotions from ten feet above him. "Ty," I start, but as I approach him he pulls me in to a rough kiss. I pull back my head. "Are you drunk?"

"Who is that guy, Juniper?" I can smell the whiskey on him, but can tell that while he's been drinking, he's not drunk. He's angry and jealous.

"It's Ben. From the firm, Ty. A colleague. He got me this job with your brother and--"

"You're mine, Juniper. Don't you know that?" His voice is barely above a whisper as he boxes me in with his arms against the wall. "I should be able to tell Murphy to keep his filthy hands off you, too, but I fucking can't." I feel the heat of his body as he presses against me, and I want him. I know I shouldn't feel a thrill that I've stirred this emotion in him, that the thought of me here with another man has made him react this way. And yet I've never been more turned on in my life. I want so very badly to be his, in every way.

"I can't be yours, Tyrion." I fight back a tear. "I can't."

But then he's kissing me again and I respond. I need him, and I kiss him with all my power, burying my fingers in his unruly mane, pulling his face into mine as he crushes my lips with his need. I gasp for breath when he breaks the kiss and stares into my eyes. "You're mine," he says again. I nod. He hisses, "I want you," and I nod again.

"I need you, Ty," I say, and then I yelp. He spins me around so I'm facing the wall and I feel him inching up my gown. I drop my forehead against the cool concrete blocks in the stairwell as Ty slides down my panties.

He runs his fingers down each of my calves slowly as he pulls the panties off, then stands. I hear him pull down his zipper, and I gasp when I feel the smooth, bare tip of his cock nudging me open.

"Ty! Don't you have a condom?"

54

TY

"I need you so much, Juniper." I start kissing her neck, tucking that smooth, chestnut hair behind her ear. "I need you, now, with nothing between us."

"Oh god, Ty. I trust you. I trust you. But you have to pull out." She looks over her shoulder at me and I nod. She tilts her hips back, opening herself a little more for me to slide in. I've never been with a woman like this before, bare. Just me and her. "Jesus Christ, this feels so good, Juniper." Her pussy glides against my cock, the warm honey of her arousal coating us both as I slide in and out.

"There's nobody but you for me," I tell her, pistoning into her body, not caring who comes into the stairwell at this moment. Nothing exists except the warm, moist heat of Juniper Jones swallowing me body and soul. "Who makes you come, baby?"

She doesn't answer, just moans as I pick up the pace and reach around to massage that magical place that brings her over the edge. Desperate, she rocks her hips against my fingers. I pull back my hand. "Say it, Juniper. Who makes you come?"

"Christ, Ty. You do. Only you. Please." And at that, I press a knuckle against her clit in the way I know drives her wild. I feel her pussy contracting against my cock inside her as she comes.

"You make me cum so hard, Juniper," I groan, slamming into her once, twice more before I pull out. I cum right on her back, hot jets spraying out of me, marking her as mine. I feel savage and raw, and I lean my head against her shoulder, both of us breathing heavy. I massage her shoulders and start to ease her gown back down, but I don't wipe up the mess. I just kiss every inch of her I can reach. As I zip my fly, I think about her going back up to that party with my cum dripping out of her dress. The caveman in me rears up again and I remember the jealousy that brought me into this stairwell. "Juniper."

She turns to look at me, but neither of us says anything. What is there to say after what we just did? It was hot and intimate and primal. I stoop down and pocket her panties, which draws a short laugh from her. She smooths out her hair and opens her mouth to say something when I hear the door to the stairwell open above me. Juniper gasps and we look up to see Matty standing on the landing.

I lean back against the wall and don't say anything. Juniper walks up the stairs and past Matty, eyes wide, and goes back out to the party.

He starts to walk down the stairs after the door shuts and he stands next to me on the landing. "How long have you been fucking her, Stag?"

"It's not like that, Matty."

He holds a hand up to stop me. "Don't pull that shit with me, Ty. How long?"

I exhale. *Fuck it,* I decide. "Since the day I met her," I tell him. "I'm in love with her, Matty."

This makes his jaw drop. I didn't know I was going to say that, but once it falls out of my mouth I know it's true. I fucking love that woman. I've rendered him speechless, and that's saying something for a sports agent. He's seen a lot of shit in his day. "You *love* her? You?" I nod. He whistles. "Well that's unexpected. I thought you were just screwing her to get back at your brother or something."

"Come on, man. I can screw anyone I want. I don't need to do my brother dirty that way."

"All right, all right." He leans against the wall. "She the one who gave you the bloody nose at the DMV?"

I nod, and he laughs. "I ought to take self-defense lessons from her. Seems like she knows what she's doing."

He has no fucking idea how strong my girl is, but I'm not about to go into all that right now.

"This entire stairwell reeks of sex, Ty. You know that, right?" I nod. He claps me on the back. "Let's get back up there and we'll figure something out."

BY THE TIME I get back to the party, Juniper is gone. I call her, but she doesn't answer. **At least let me know u got home safe,** I text her, but I don't even see that she reads my message. That Ben fucker is gone, so I'm hoping he got her home. Every fucking time, that woman runs out when shit gets intense. I sigh and head for home, promising myself I'll find her in the morning.

MATTY CALLS ME BEFORE DAWN. I'm half hungover, slumped sideways across my bed and I only reached over to pick up the phone because I thought it'd be Juniper. "We've got a problem, buddy. Pull up TMZ. I'll wait." I roll sideways and pull up the website on my phone. I see pictures of myself coming out of Juniper's townhouse--grainy, far-off shots of me kissing her goodbye, walking away toward my car. The headline reads LUSTING FOR LAWYER and there's some puff piece bullshit about how I'm boning my lawyer in secret.

"That fucking delivery guy," I say to Matty. "I tipped him, gave him an autograph, and took a damn selfie with him and he still ratted me out to the paparazzi. How did they find out Juniper's name?"

Matty prattles on about data aggregate sites and how much information is public if you feel motivated to search. I can feel my blood start to boil as fast as the whiskey hangover sends my head throbbing.

"Look, what are the chances that your brother is aware of this?"

I wait for a beat and say, "Ordinarily, I think he'd be on top of this shit immediately. But I know he meets with the Cavs on Monday and I think he's holed up with his secret girlfriend preparing all weekend."

"Your brother has a girlfriend, too?"

"Some chick my grandma knows from when we were growing up," I tell him. "She's a muffin chef. Or something. He doesn't think we know, but he's been seeing her on the sly for weeks."

"All right, Ty. Give me until Monday and I'll figure something out. Luckily this doesn't seem too scandalous and I don't think it'll stick much to the top of the gossip sites. You better hope one of your teammates pees in the Stanley Cup or something this weekend."

55

JUNIPER

I can't bear to stay at the gala after Matty nearly caught us in the hallway. What happened with Ty was too intense for me to just go back up there and make small talk. I tell Ben and the execs I need to focus on a client, remind everyone how much time I spend bailing the Fury out of the drunk tank, and I leave to high fives and martini salutes. Ben and I share a cab back to Stag Law and work on the Cavs presentation for awhile.

"I'm sorry I took you from your celebrity hockey party," I say.

He shrugs. "Plenty more where that came from. What do you think about these numbers for workers comp claims?" We work for a few more hours and eventually I take a cab home, worn out. I feel empty inside and barely sleep.

WHEN I FINALLY DRIFT OFF AROUND dawn, I wake to the sound of my phone buzzing on the nightstand. Another set of texts from Ty.

U up? Need 2 talk

. . .

ALSO THIS. He sent a link to a series of studies about birth control and performance in female athletes. Something about fewer knee injuries.

I roll my eyes and send back, **ok ok I get it. You like it bareback.** I flush thinking about what happened between us last night. How raw his want for me was and how much I responded to him. I was out of my mind with passion. It was a totally new level for me, even with Ty.

Just looking out for ur rowing, babe. Call me, though. Important.

Is this a thing I do now? Call up Ty and let him call me babe over text message? I sigh and dial his number. He answers on the first ring, like he's sitting there waiting for me to call. "Good morning, gorgeous. Did you shower yet?"

"What? Why?"

"Just wondering if you've still got me all over your beautiful backside."

"Jesus, Ty. You're disgusting. You're lucky you didn't stain my gown." I blush again, remembering his finale in the stairwell.

"I would buy you a new one. It was worth it. Anyway, listen. Something happened."

I remember that Matty had walked into the stairwell just after we had finished fucking, but I feel pretty sure he hadn't seen anything definitive. "What?" My voice is hesitant, but doesn't shake as much as my hands.

"I mean, you know Matty knows. But he's not the problem."

"What are you talking about, Ty?"

"We're on TMZ."

I FEEL like my insides are turning out. I start to hyperventilate. *I'm going to lose my job and I'm going to get disbarred.* "Juniper!" I realize Ty must have been calling out to me.

"I'm here. What are we going to do? There's going to be a fucking ethics review, Ty."

"We're going to talk with Tim. Matty says he thinks it'll be ok. Listen, since everyone knows about us anyway, do you want to come have breakfast with me and my grandma? She can meet you as my girlfriend."

"Ty, this is all really fast for me. I don't share your confidence that Tim is going to be ok with this and--"

"Just come over for pancakes. Tim is holed up with Alice getting ready for the Cavs on Monday. I promise he's not looking at the celebrity gossip."

I snort. Tim is a maniac about that contract with Cleveland. I want to tell Ty that I need to be working on it, too, but I don't want that client. I don't want to work this weekend. I want to go eat pancakes with my boyfriend and his grandmother, and I start crying into the phone from all the stress of the whole situation.

"Hey, Junebug. Hey. Don't shut me out this time. Don't run away from me. Do you want me to come get you? Let me take care of you today."

When he talks to me, his voice as smooth as maple syrup, I feel safe. He makes me think it can somehow all be ok. That I can be a person who eats weekend pancakes with my lover and his grandma. Some sort of fantasy orphan chicks don't even dare to utter out loud. And yet he's right there on the other end of the phone assuring me it's all real. "No, I'll be ok," I sniffle. "When should I come over?"

"I smell bacon, Junebug. You better hurry before I eat it all."

A HALF HOUR LATER, I find myself parked outside the Stag family home, still on the verge of hyperventilating. As I ring the doorbell, I realize I shouldn't be officially meeting his grandmother wearing sweatpants. Why didn't I stop to change? Or buy flowers? The door opens.

"Juniper! Dear! Come inside." Anna Stag ushers me into the house before I can apologize for my informality. "When Tyrion told me he wanted to introduce me to the woman who makes him mopey, I was hoping it would be you!"

"Mopey?" *Does everyone in this family speak in code*, I wonder. She pulls me into the kitchen and hands me a mug of coffee, hollering for Ty to come down and greet his "own damn girlfriend."

He pulls me in for a kiss and I stiffen instinctively, forgetting that I'm here to discuss a plan to go public with our relationship. He rubs my back and I relax into his arm, clutching the caffeinated brew. Once I finish the coffee, I feel like I can concentrate enough to ask questions. "Did you say Tim was with Alice this weekend? Why would they be together preparing for the meeting? Unless..."

Mrs. Stag smiles as she flips pancakes into the air. Ty nods. "Oh, big time. He thinks we don't know, but Gram saw him over at her house a bunch of times playing with her nephews."

"I can't..." I try to imagine my stern boss playing with children and come up at a loss. "That sounds so unlike him. But you know, Alice has been on the verge of telling me something for a month now. Huh. Tim and Alice."

"Try these, dear," Mrs. Stag says, sliding me a plate of pancakes. "I know Tyrion said you worry about your food, too, so I added flax and buckwheat to these."

I taste a forkful of the pancakes, and I melt into my stool at the counter. "These are amazing, Mrs. Stag."

She pats my hand. "You should have been calling me Anna a long time ago, dear. And I got these recipe ideas from Alice."

As I eat, Ty and his grandma talk about how they think we should use Tim's secret relationship to our advantage. I'm not really comfortable with the idea of capitalizing on something like this, but Ty says we're not going to blackmail him. "No way, JJ. I'm going to explain that I couldn't help but fall for you, like he couldn't help but fall in love with Alice. Like a--what's that called, Gram?"

"It's an analogy, dear," she says, smiling.

I shake my head. "I think you're both being naive about this." I can't stop eating the delicious pancakes and Ty's grandma slides me a plate of bacon. "But I do think you're right that he won't notice this happened until at least after the meeting on Monday."

Ty and his grandmother both start to talk about how much they hate the idea of him expanding the firm too fast, too big. Ty gets especially angry when I mention that Tim implied I might have to do some travel to service the new clients if we land the deal. I sit in the kitchen with them for hours, talking and eating, until I realize I've nearly missed my morning opportunity to row before all the beer cruise boaters get reckless on the river. I excuse myself to go train, and allow myself to savor the comfortable, familiar feeling of kissing Ty by my car before driving away. *Could this be my future,* I wonder. It feels too good to be true.

I STAY UP LATE Sunday preparing for Monday's meeting, and enter it with a heavy heart. I don't want it to be successful, and yet I can't allow myself to perform poorly on purpose. The morning of, I climb into my best power suit, complete with heels. I like to look as tall as possible when I'm presenting for a crowd. I am at eye level with the suits when we shake hands in the hall at work. Tim seems delighted. I feel distracted throughout the budget presentation and when Tim takes the lead to discuss numbers, individual athlete contracts, and injury clauses, I notice that Alice looks practically grey as she passes out trays of food in the conference room.

I try to catch her attention to ask if she's ok, when I see her start to faint. Then, all hell breaks loose at the office.

56

TY

"Thatcher, pick up the damn phone." I yell into his voicemail as I barrel down the highway toward his studio. "Fuck!" When he doesn't answer I keep driving. To hell with him if he has some woman squirreled away in his studio today. I knew something was wrong when I didn't hear from Tim or Juniper on Monday after their meeting, and then she called me this morning with the news. I screech to a halt in the gravel lot outside Stag Glass and throw open the door.

My brother is bent over his workbench, blaring music and banging away at some red-hot piece of molten glass. I shut off his radio, but don't get too close because I don't want that fucker to burn me. "Thatcher. We have a problem, man."

He frowns, plunges his work into a bucket of water, and raises his eyebrows--my permission to explain myself. "Juniper just called."

"Your lawyer?"

I wave away that question. "Listen, she said Alice fainted during their big meeting at the law firm and cut her head. Tim rode with her to the hospital and then went insane, holed himself up in his office, and just rushed out of there all bloody and wild-eyed."

Thatcher just stares at me.

"Dude, Tim has been fucking Alice."

"Our brother Tim? Mr. stern Stag? And one of his *employees*?"

I nod. "I know, man, but he's freaking out. Apparently he drove over to Alice's house spewing some insane scheme. Juniper said he was holed up in his office ever since he got back, muttering."

Thatcher scratches his beard, thinking. "He told me he was banging some chick without a condom. A few weeks ago. He said she drove him to distraction." Thatcher shrugs. "Where is he now?"

"Let's go, man, he's probably over at the Peterson house causing a scene."

We drive in search of our brother and I fill Thatcher in on my TMZ situation. Thatcher laughs when I tell him I'd been planning to use Tim's distraction at work as a screen to convince him it's cool that Juniper and I are together. "His situation sure trumps yours, baby bro."

I grit my teeth and head to our neighborhood, where the Petersons live just a few streets away from me and Gram.

Only Tim isn't at the Peterson house anymore.

When we pull up, Alice's brothers are sitting on the porch with a metal baseball bat. Thatcher laughs. "This doesn't look great, Ty."

I see Tim's car parked half in the street, blocking their driveway. "Thatch, let's go up there together."

"I'm not going anywhere near this shit-show, baby brother," he says, tugging on his damn beard. "Listen, you go talk to them and tell them you'll move Tim's car."

I shake my head at my brother and climb out of my Tesla. "Hey, Petersons," I call, walking toward them with my hands up. "We just came to find our brother. We don't want to cause any trouble here."

One of the Peterson brothers stands up. The one with the bat. I can handle a bat. "It's me, Ty Stag. You guys went to school with my brothers?"

"You mean your crazy ass brother who knocked up our sister and showed up here trying to kidnap her?"

"What?"

"You heard me, Stag. Get the fuck out of here. Move that fucking car of his while you're at it."

I freeze in my tracks. I feel my face contorting. Did he say pregnant? My brother Tim got his girlfriend pregnant? "Hey, guys, what do you say you put the bat down and I sign some autographs for the kids and you tell me exactly what my dickhead brother did so I can make amends."

THATCHER and I park Tim's car at Gram's house and walk the neighborhood, until we eventually find him in the park. He's slumped over by the fountain looking like he's been in a fight with Satan himself. We sit on either side of him and pat his leg, which is bro-speak for "everything is going to be ok, dude."

I give him an exaggerated sniff. He's obviously been wearing the same clothes for a few days. I have never seen him disheveled like this, even when he was cramming for law school exams. "Bro, I hate to tell you this, but your shirt is untucked," I say. Thatcher cracks up and starts plucking blades of grass off the shoulders of Tim's suit.

Tim has been our rock for over ten years. Nobody asks to be responsible for their snot-nosed brothers, but Tim stepped up as soon as it was obvious our dad wasn't going to be around to parent us. I realize, looking at him falling apart like this, that it's all been really one-way. Even once we became adults, Thatcher and I never reached out to him or offered any sort of support. "Tim, you know you can talk to me about stuff, right? I mean...shit. I'm here for you no matter what. God knows you've been there for me." Thatcher nods.

"We're going to be amazing uncles," I say. "And from the looks of things, Baby Stag's got some other uncles who'll look out for him, too."

Thatcher lets out a huff, muttering about a shotgun wedding until I punch him in the shoulder. I wish I were better at talking about this stuff. Tim's still staring off into space, blood on his shirt, stubble on his face for the first time I've ever seen. "All those times you bailed me out, talked to teachers when I got in fights, made sure I was allowed to stay in school. Tim, you've been a dad to me for a long time, bro. You've been *our* dad. You're already good at this, is what I'm trying to say."

He looks over at me then, like he finally hears me. His eyes are all watery, and I choke up. Thatcher pipes in, saying, "It's true, Tim-bo. You're already good at being everybody's dad." Tim closes his eyes and his body seems to relax a bit more.

"Come on," I say, giving him a lift to his feet. "Let's get you home before Alice's brothers come after us with their hunting rifle."

57

JUNIPER

Things have been crazy at work since Alice passed out. As soon as we got her off in the ambulance, I snapped into action mode with the executives from the Cavs. I managed to spin Tim's panicked departure into a description of him as a devoted and dedicated leader, which is all true. But everything about the presentation sat wrong with me.

Since I came here, I compromised almost everything that's important to me. I'm sleeping with a client, which is unethical no matter how strong my feelings might have grown for Ty. I'm slacking on my rowing, I took a leave from the women's rowing team, I missed watching tryouts for nationals...there is almost nothing left I recognize about myself.

While I try to settle my mind, there's nothing I can think to do other than escape to the boathouse. I reach for the phone to call Lisa in Boston, but saying all this stuff out loud feels too overwhelming. I can't really call Alice, because she's got enough going on with her drama. And Ty. I just can't call him right now, either. Everything is a mess.

I've got nothing on my plate at work right now anyhow. All my NHL clients are behaving themselves and I'm pretty sure I unwittingly bagged the Cavs contract. Might as well take to the river while I still can.

I hoist my scull out of the garage, running my hand along the hull. I get her onto the water and take my time adjusting my shoes once I'm seated inside. She's in fantastic shape despite her neglect of late, and as I shove off the dock, I feel like I'm slipping back into my own skin for the first time in a few weeks.

I have no plan in mind, but I just need to row. I head up river toward the dam, the island passing by my periphery in a blur of green leaves. I see people standing along the shore sometimes, but I don't want to break form to wave back at them. I've got too much negative energy to burn off.

Later--I'm not even sure how long I was out, to be honest--I pull up to the dock and am surprised to see Derrick waiting there. He helps me out of my boat and remains quiet while we get everything put away. I start to chug from my water bottle as he leans on the wall and says, "So. Juniper."

I just raise my eyebrows but keep drinking. I'm exhausted. I was really going hard there at the end. Derrick isn't usually around in the afternoon since he coaches all morning. "I was up filing some paper-work in the boathouse office and I saw you heading up river," he says. "I came out on the deck to watch, and then I couldn't look away." I'm not really sure what to say to him, so I fidget while I wait for him to continue. I still feel bad about pulling out of the women's team with so little notice.

"Juniper, you know you're the best rower I've ever seen come through here. You have to know that."

My jaw just drops open, and I can feel my eyes go wide. *The best ever?* Derrick strokes his chin, thinking, and then says, "Putting you in the middle of an 8-seat boat would be wasting your talents. I know you missed qualifiers for nationals--hear me out!" I am about to inter-ject something about work, but I close my lips. "I made a call. The staff for the women's national team is willing to come to New Haven this weekend and whatever time you get for the singles races there can qualify you for a spot on the Olympic team, Juniper."

"Are you serious, Derrick? The Olympics? Quit messing around with me." I figure he must be pissed that I ditched his team. I know they didn't do well last weekend. But this seems a bit far-fetched. The Olympics! I haven't even been training carefully.

"Juniper! Your dad was an Olympic rower. Your form is textbook perfect when you're not focused on it. Your stamina is unparalleled and if you can put out the kind of speed I just saw while navigating around coal barges, I'm pretty sure you're going to do fine on the water in Tokyo!"

I start walking away from him, toward my townhouse. I'm not even sure why I'm so angry. His words bring up all sorts of feelings about my childhood, about my dad. I row to drown out the anger inside, to keep me focused on work. I'm not trying to be some Olympian. "Juniper! Wait up." Derrick chases me down, doesn't back away when I freak out. This surprises me, too. I'm just not used to people sticking around with me when shit gets hard. He says, "I'd like to help you train...you know, after you qualify next weekend."

"You're serious about all this? Me? I just...I blend in better in the team boat, Derrick. I've never raced solo before."

Derrick breaks into a grin. "Then we are all in for a fucking treat this weekend, Juniper Jones. I'm serious as a heart attack. Go home and start getting your shit ready for New Haven this weekend. We leave Friday at 7am."

58

TY

Juniper isn't answering her phone and when I swing by her townhouse, it doesn't seem like she is home ignoring me, either. This is the longest I've gone without talking to her since...well, ever. I spent a lot of time with Tim this week talking him through all his anxiety about Alice and the pregnancy. And then I spent a ton of time trying to find Juniper and not succeeding.

As my Gram would say, I've been a mope. I did the whole circuit, everything I'm supposed to do. Nothing is right without Juniper. All of it feels empty and shallow. There is nothing my trainer can do to work me hard enough to forget how empty I'm feeling without the sound of her voice.

I have no idea why she's avoiding me since she called to tell me the news about Tim and Alice, but I can only assume something happened at work with Tim going off the rails. And so I do the thing she told me not to do: I drive downtown and barge into her office.

And she's not there. Her laptop isn't on the desk, her purse isn't hanging on the door. *What the fuck?* She's not at home and she's not at work? Something isn't right here. I start to panic that she told my brother about us and he fired her already. But where would she have gone even if that happened?

Raking my fingers through my hair, I can't even think straight. I stomp down the hall and past Donna, right into my brother's corner office.

He's sitting behind his desk, his chair turned so he's staring out the window at the river. I can't tell if he's still panicking, or just pensive, or what. "Tim, we need to talk, brother."

He doesn't turn around. I see him sigh. "What's going on now, Ty? Please tell me how I have fucked up your life, too. Maybe take a number, though. The list is getting long."

I sit down in one of the chairs at his desk. It's too small for me. "Jesus, Tim, if you're going to represent athletes, you need to get some bigger fucking chairs in your office."

He swivels around at that and sees me trying to wedge myself out from between the unforgiving arm rests. I slump over to the couch instead. "I just need to say that you can't fire Juniper."

"Fire her? Why would I do that?"

Oh. So he doesn't know after all. Then where the fuck is she? I'm starting to try to piece together where she might be when Tim presses me for more. "Ty, why would I fire her? Why would you storm in here worried that I'd fire Juniper Jones?"

I clear my throat uncomfortably, and say, "Well, I can't find her, so I assumed you fired her."

"Why would you be looking for her? All your business is settled for the next few months at least. She's at some damn boat race. Left this morning. Wait a minute--"

His eyes spark and he stands up, starts pacing. "She called *you* to tell you about Alice."

"Yeah, because she was worried about you. With reason!"

"No. This is different." He squints at me. "I can't fucking believe you, Ty. You're sleeping with her."

I pause a second too long, and Tim continues railing into me. "You can't leave one thing alone without dipping your dick in it, can you? Not my study group in law school. Not the fucking cheerleaders from the high school hockey team. And not my best employee. I really don't need this right now from you."

"Tim, it's not like that."

"Get the hell out of my office."

"No way, man. Not until you talk to me about this."

"This is seriously the last thing I need right now when I'm trying to figure out how to support a fucking family now with Alice and Juniper both telling me I'm an idiot. Jesus, I just passed on the Cleveland deal, Ty. Do you know how that makes me look? I went after them and then told them no thank you and--"

"Tim, I'm in love with her."

"What?"

"Juniper. I'm not just sleeping with her. I'm in love with her. I want to be with her. Like, forever. I think."

"What are you even talking about?"

"I'm telling you I didn't just come into your office and fuck your employees to be an asshole like when I was younger. I met Juniper before she started here. And I'm in love with her."

"She'd been sleeping with you and still took you on as a client? Jesus Christ. This is an ethics nightmare. Does your agent know about this?"

"I mean, she didn't know who I was then...it's just...it's complicated."

"You're damn right it's complicated, Tyrion! God, get out of here so I can get to work trying to fix this."

"You of all people should know about falling in love with someone you maybe shouldn't. Or was that not you rutting on the conference table in the hockey arena with your corporate chef?"

"You need to shut your mouth and get out of here, brother."

"I saw the damn security footage, Tim. So don't tell me you don't know what it's like to get carried away. And now you and Alice are having a baby. And Juniper and I are in love." I stand up and start walking toward him, not sure what I'm going to do but not feeling particularly civil. It's been awhile since we Stag brothers had a brawl.

"You're so in love you didn't know she was off competing in a boat race this weekend? Spare me, Ty."

I freeze. He's right about that. Why didn't she tell me she was going to race? I sigh, take a deep breath, and continue. "Look, just reassign me to Ben or whatever his name is. Can you do that? And don't fire Juniper?"

He starts laughing, but it's a sort of crazed laugh. "I can't fire her. She's a fucking genius. She could be fucking my entire client list and I couldn't fire her. I wonder if she knows that..."

Tim starts muttering something about return on investment, but I stopped listening to him after he said he couldn't fire my girl. I don't even say goodbye, but I brush past him and head down the hall. I have to figure out where the hell she went.

Suddenly, I remember that Ben guy has a sister who rows. Juniper knew her from Boston. I bet he knows where she is this weekend. But where the hell will I find *him*? I'm stomping around like an idiot when I stumble across the kitchen. "Alice!"

She screams and drops a pan of food. "Oh shit, Alice, I'm sorry I scared you. Are you ok?" I rush over and help her pick everything up. "I'm really sorry."

"Ty, it's ok. You just startled me."

"Hey, so, can I say congratulations? About growing my niece or nephew in there?"

Her face lightens up and I can tell not too many people have been happy for her about this. She throws her arms around me--as much as she can. Alice is a really tiny person--and thanks me.

"Oh come on, Alice. Don't thank me--of course I'm excited about a baby. Anything you need, you let me know. Even if that's just to beat some sense into my brother." I pop one of the dropped pastries into my mouth, and of course it tastes amazing. She smiles at me. "Hey, you wouldn't know where Juniper is this weekend, would you?"

Alice looks puzzled. "She didn't tell you?" I shake my head. "She's at the regatta in New Haven."

"New Haven! I remember that that was her upcoming race. Awesome."

"But there's more! The rowing coach guy saw her training earlier this week."

I listen as Alice tells me everything about Juniper's big opportunity. I can't fucking believe she shut me out from this, but I'm not missing it. I'm going to support her no matter what, in person. I rush out of the Stag Law building to catch the first flight I can find.

59

JUNIPER

"All right, ladies, I want all of you in bed by 9," Derrick says as he slides his credit card to the server at the restaurant. "Tomorrow is a big day for some of us, and a huge day for Juniper."

I blush immediately and look down as he draws attention to the fact that I'm here as a separate entity. A sort of tag along with the team. "Cheers to that," says Ashley, one of the rowers from the team boat. The women on either side of me clap me on the shoulders. They wish me luck. I'm stunned by their support for me, which I don't feel like I've earned, but all they care about is that the Pittsburgh team gets mentioned when they put out the list of rowers for Tokyo. "Our city is going to be known for producing Olympic-caliber crew," Ashley says, winking.

We all walk back to our hotel rooms and start our pre-race rituals. I'm not even sure what to do for mine, since I'm not going to be on a team tomorrow. I've got my uniform laid out, my sunglasses and sunscreen. We're all checked in at the docks already. There's not much to do but sleep and show up at this point.

Nobody chats much as we get ready for bed. There's one thing you can count on with rowers, and that's an eager, early bedtime. Years of getting up at 5am means we're all ready for sleep practically as soon as it gets dark, if not before.

I lie in my bed and think about the past week, about the Stag brothers. When I went to talk with Tim about taking off on Friday for the race, I reiterated that I wouldn't consider traveling to support the Cleveland account. He surprised me by telling me he decided not to go after that client. I know he's worried about the reputation of the firm, since he wooed them hard core, but I'm pretty sure it'll be ok in the end. Ultimately it's better not to expand too rapidly, too wide.

While I was in his office, I talked to him about my idea about the women's hockey team from Ty's promo shoot. Tim was surprised to learn about all the pay inequities with women's sports. A huge smile spreads across my face as I think about our new agreement. I convinced Tim to let me represent the women's hockey team pro bono in their case seeking equal treatment. Tim had no idea these women weren't even offered disability insurance to compete for our country, let alone were being crammed in coach when they flew to away games. The US men's team gets private jets! The next winter Olympics, I vowed to Tim that I'd make sure our national women's teams received equal funding to represent our country. "Think of the publicity opportunities for Stag Law surrounding the Olympics," I'd told him. A few hours later, Tim had emailed me to ask about women's basketball and soon, we had mapped out a plan of Title IX opportunities that would keep me busy for the next few years.

Of course, these cases will never bring in a fraction of the income even something simple like Ty's endorsement contracts can swing, but I told Tim that profit can't always be the bottom line. I got really fired up, telling him how much diversity and inclusion matters to communities, and how proud I would be to help shepherd Stag Law through these endeavors. Pittsburgh and Stag Law will be famous for defending women's rights and athletic equality. I get chills just thinking about it.

I headed off to Connecticut today feeling confident in my work at least. I decide to put off thinking about Ty until I have more energy to focus. I need to make sure I get enough rest so I can perform well, make it worth it for the national team staff to have traveled here for my own Olympic dreams. I drift off to sleep thinking about the rhythm of the oars, the pull of the current, and the slip of my boat in the water.

60

TY

A few minutes with Google is all I need to find my way to the regatta early Saturday morning. According to the schedule, Juniper's race starts around 8am, but I want to get there early enough to see if I can find her coach and find the best place to watch.

Some of the women milling around start calling my name, and I recognize them from the Pittsburgh team. "Ty! You made it up here to watch us! That's so nice of you." The short girl named Tina grabs my arm and pulls me to the Pittsburgh team. I immediately relax as I head over to them and get the scoop.

Apparently Juniper is in the zone getting ready for her race, and I'm not going to mess with that, so they show me where I can sit in the bleachers near the finish area. I settle in with them, waiting for her heat. I can see the officials and the men with clipboards on the floating dock, and I know those are the guys determining Juniper's rowing future.

There are four lanes set up for the race, and I see four women getting their boats set up way up river. Ashley hands me binoculars and points out Derrick at the start area. He's hanging onto the ball on Juniper's bow, I guess so her boat doesn't drift over the start line. I try to fight back my jealousy that it's not me there whispering encouragement to her before the race. I try not to remember that she didn't even call me before she left. We've both had a really intense week.

I steal Ashley's binoculars so I can see every second. She only half protests until the gun goes off. Then she and everyone else around me starts screaming for Juniper. I wish I could see her face, but her back is toward me as she races down the water. Juniper is two lengths ahead of the field within a minute of shoving off. I can see the muscles of her back working, can tell she's clenching her jaw in concentration. *Relax, baby,* I think, and as if she heard me, I see her shoulders drop and her body tension eases. Now she's really flying down the water.

The beads of water off the end of her oars glisten like diamonds in the sunshine. Every person here is on their feet screaming for her. It's not even a race anymore, but an opportunity to see just how fast my girl can get here. I look at the judges, and they're all either grinning like fools or have their jaws dropped in shock. My girl is fast as fuck, and now everyone knows it.

A few strokes to go and she'll be here. I'm flying out of my seat and down the bleachers. I want mine to be the face Juniper sees when she crosses the line and pulls up her oars. I get as close to the water as I can. Bam! She's past. Her chest heaves as she pulls up and just leans back, gliding to a stop.

But then our eyes lock and we are the only people in the world. She makes her way to the dock to climb out of her boat, and I'm stumbling over to her. I crouch down and lift her out of the seat and into my arms. My lips crash into hers as she melts into my arms. This is all I want. Right here. This moment, this woman.

"You came to see my race," she whispers against my chest.

"Baby, you're going to have to do more than not tell me about it if you plan to keep me away." I start laughing and kiss her some more. I can never get enough of how she tastes, and the salty musk of her sweat just adds to her appeal for me right now. Finally, I pull back and cup her chin in my hand. "Juniper Jones, I love you," I say. I can't hold it in anymore. "I love you."

She starts crying then, which I was not expecting, but I also know how emotional I get when I'm competing. She buries her face in my chest and, with a muffled voice, she says, "I never thought I would have any of this."

"Any of what, JJ?"

She waves her hand around. "All of this. Love. Success. Rowing. Just all of it."

"Of course you have all these things, baby. You earned all these things." I'm starting to freak out a little that she hasn't said anything specifically about loving me back, when she bites my neck.

"I love you, Tyrion Stag." And then she kisses me, soft and tender, hungry and longing. Eventually I realize some of the cheering and wolf-whistling I hear is Ashley and Tina and the other rowers standing around waiting to congratulate Juniper. Guess the cat is out of the bag about us being together. *Good,* I think, and kiss her even harder.

Derrick has to peel Juniper out of my arms for the award ceremony and I cheer louder than anyone when they slip that medal around her neck. Some old codger takes the microphone and announces that Juniper's time was the fastest on record for that race length, and he's thrilled to offer her a spot on the women's national team. "I'll have you know I raced with your father in Montreal in 1976," he says, pumping her hand. "It will be my honor and my pleasure to serve on your coaching staff as we prepare for Tokyo next year."

When Juniper finishes hugging everyone and crying, I tug her over to my rental car. I've had about all I can stand of looking at her in spandex race gear. I need to get her naked, pronto.

She sits back in her seat, looking so content as I speed to my hotel. I park in a screech of tires. She squeaks when I jump out, pull her door open, and lift her out of the car. I toss her over one shoulder and she starts smacking my ass while I walk to my room. "Ty, put me down. People can see!"

"Baby, I don't give a shit who can see. I need you and I need you now."

I slide the key card into the slot and see the green light I've been waiting for. I stride over to the bed and ease Juniper onto it as I'm peeling off my shorts.

She shakes her head at me, laughing. "We don't have to hide anymore, baby," I say, stepping out of my boxers. I'm naked in front of her, and she's still fully dressed in her uniform.

"What do you mean we don't have to hide? What did you do?" She crawls back, like she's trying to get away from me.

"I talked to my brother and I told him I love you and you're not my lawyer anymore," I say, crawling onto the bed after her. My dick is so hard it's lying up against my stomach, and I see her look at it, licking those luscious lips of hers.

"I was going to talk to him on Monday," she whispers. When I finally reach her, I start licking the hollow of her throat, kissing her shoulder.

"Mmmhmm," I moan. "More kissing, less talking about my brother." This gets a giggle from her, and she starts to peel off her spandex tank top. I help her out with the little shorts and ease her down so she's lying back on the bed.

"Ty, I'm all sweaty and gross," she says, but doesn't really make an effort to move.

"You taste amazing," I say, licking the salty skin of one collarbone. Just thinking of her working so hard today, that determined look on her face, is enough to drive me wild with want.

I nestle in between her legs, tickling her stomach with the medal she left on. I brush the cool metal across a pert nipple, flicking the other one with my tongue until Juniper begins to moan. "I've missed you, baby," I say, dragging my tongue around each nipple while she starts to writhe beneath my chest. Her nipples feel so good against my skin.

She reaches down and finds my cock, and a groan escapes my throat. Her hand feels so good wrapped around my shaft. I'm lost in the sensation and I don't fully notice what Juniper is doing until I realize she has me lined up against her hot entrance. Bare.

I raise an eyebrow at her, questioning.

She pulls me down by the shoulders. "I read those articles you sent me," she says, now licking my chest in all the ways I'd been licking her a few minutes ago. "I'm on the pill."

My animal brain takes over with those words, and I waste no time sinking inside her. "Holy fuck this feels good," I practically grunt. Her pussy is so wet, so tight and smooth against my skin. "Juniper!"

She wraps those long legs around me, her heels driving me deeper into her body, pressed into my ass cheeks. I'm about to lose control, but not before I get her there first. I brace myself on my forearms, angling my hips so my body rubs right up against her clit. I find the friction I know she needs when she drops her head back and starts screaming my name.

I fucking love how loud she is right now as I drive into her, nothing between us. Just me and Juniper Jones. I can feel it when her orgasm rips through her. She starts to spasm around my cock, her hips bucking wildly off the bed. "Fuck, baby, yes," I shout, and then I'm with her.

I feel it start to spiral inside me and then my balls draw up tight. My release fires inside of her again and again, thick ropes of ecstasy. My dick twitches and finally rests, and I collapse on top of my lady, both of us heaving and gasping for breath.

"Ty, that was amazing," she whispers.

"Mmm you're telling me," I say, tracing letters on her back as I pull her against my chest. "I'm never letting you go, you know."

She nods. "I'm ok with that."

EPILOGUE: TY
TOKYO, SUMMER 2020

"Ty, baby, everyone here is flipping the fuck out," Matty yells into my cell. I'm about to hang up on him, but Juniper's race start is delayed for wind so I figure I'll let him blow off some steam. The Fury made it to the Stanley Cup playoffs again, and I'm missing a whole slew of television appearances and parades and shit, to be here with Juniper.

Matty is talking up a blue streak and eventually I cut him off. "Look, if you think I'm going to miss watching my girl compete in the Olympics you're crazy. Take it up with my lawyer." He gasps, inhaling for another tirade, but I hang up on him. Ben will sort it all out. So what if I have to pay a penalty. Being here for Juniper is worth way more than any bonus pay.

My phone rings again, and I see it's my sister-in-law. "Hey, Alice, what's up?" I can hear the baby crying in the background and it sounds like she's pacing and trying to shush him to get him to calm down.

"Tim said it looks like Juniper's race is delayed. Just wondering if you knew how long? It's past bedtime here, but we all stayed up..."

"It looks like they're getting everything set up. I think the wind died down."

I can hear my brother shout in the background. "Did he say it's soon?"

"Yes, Timber, it's soon!" I shout so loud that the other husbands and boyfriends all turn around to look at me. "Ok, fam, I gotta go. The Dutch are annoyed that I'm on the phone." I roll my eyes and slide my phone into my pocket. I'm ready to behave, until the race starts anyway.

I try to sit calmly. Juniper has trained so hard for this moment. Everything at work is so rewarding for her now that she won all sorts of money and regulations for the women hockey players, and I got the Fury to all pose for some solidarity promo shots with their team. It's been pretty amazing.

But Juniper is so disciplined with her sport, too. For me, the best thing about her training is how it helps me with my own game. I moved out of my grandma's house soon after Juniper and I went public with our relationship. We got a bigger townhouse together, near where her old one was, so she would still be close enough to the boathouse to row before work.

It's easy to keep up a good diet and conditioning routine when you're doing it with the person you love and live with. She even comes to the weight room with me sometimes. Derrick might be sleeping with one of my trainers, but I'm not entirely sure. Anyway, Juniper and I are both fit as hell and peaking at just the right time. We push each other to be better. I need her, and I want to be there for her in every way she needs me.

A hush rolls over the crowd as the race finally gets started. It's a long course and there's no way to see the start from here, so they've got the race broadcasted on a giant screen. I know this won't be another New Haven where Juniper wins by like five boat lengths. These women are the best in the world, but they've never raced my Junebug. I wish her father could see her now as she sits at the start line, face determined. The camera zooms in on her in her USA gear and my heart swells with pride.

I hear the gun and I hear the crowd around me, but I don't look away from Juniper on the monitor. The camera stays close with her, because she holds the lead from the very beginning. I can see the French boat creeping up on her, and I start to scream for her to dig deep, even though she is too far away to hear me. And dig she does. Juniper Jones comes into view almost a full length ahead of her next competitors.

When she finally glides across the finish, I can see all the happiness in the world streaming from her face with her tears. My girl just won an Olympic gold medal.

"Yes!" I jump in the air and start trying to give high fives to my European seat mates, who must not celebrate that way because they have no idea what I'm doing.

I start to climb down the bleachers and make my way toward Juniper. I know in my heart I'm going to marry this woman. I'm not going to ask her today, though. This is about her. About her victory, her moment. I'm here to support her.

She finds me up in the crowd and we make our way toward each other. She lays a kiss on me that just about knocks me back, and I know there's no other place in the world I'd rather be than right here with her.

FRAGILE ILLUSION

61

THATCHER

I realize the second I finish that I have no idea what this chick's name is. Did we talk about names? Or did we just walk back to her apartment last night? I don't usually stay over, but I was completely exhausted after our acrobatic routine in her living room, her hallway, and her bed. And then she was down for an encore this morning...so here I am.

"Fuck," I shout, looking at her clock radio. "Is that the right time?"

She rolls over, pushing the curtain of her blonde hair out of her eyes. "Mmmm. I guess so." She runs her fingers lightly along my chest, letting her head flop back down on the pillow.

"Fuck. I'm so fucking late. Shit." I'm out of the bed in a flash, scrambling around her apartment looking for my clothes. I'm going to have to go wearing the same stuff I had on last night. I run my fingers through my long hair, trying to tame it a little. My family is going to kill me.

"Thatcher, wait." I hear her padding down the hall, still naked. Fuck me, she's hot. A tall, leggy blonde with big eyes and full lips. Do I want to get her number? Fuck it.

"Babe, I'm sorry. I have to get out of here." I find my wallet under the couch near my jeans. My keys...aha! They're on the floor inside the front door. When I stand up with them I see her standing with her arms crossed.

She raises an eyebrow. "You're just going to run out of here like this? Literally run out?"

"It's my nephew's birthday party. I'm sorry. I didn't mean to--"

"Give me five minutes and I'll come with you."

Woah. "What?" My tone is harsh, but is she serious right now?

"Bring me with you. To the party. I love kids!"

I hold my hands out, palms up. "Look, doll, we just met last night. I don't want you to take this the wrong way, but I can't bring you with me to my nephew's birthday party with my family."

"Doll? Babe? You don't even know my name do you?"

I open my mouth and then close it again. Fuck it. I wasn't coming back for more anyway.

"Fuck you, Thatcher Stag. Fuck you!" She starts throwing magazines at me from the shelf in the hall. I duck as a huge bridal catalogue comes flying at my head and then I remember. "Amber!" I look at the address label from one of the projectiles. Fuck. "Tiffany, come on. You seemed like you had a good time..."

She shakes her head. "You are unbelievable."

I don't have time to talk about this more. My brother is going to tear me a new one if I'm not there for this party. I pull the door open and then shut, jogging a bit to find my beat up old Ford Ranger parked outside. I slam the truck into gear and screech out of the parking lot just as I see Tiffany stick her head out the apartment window. I don't even hear what she's shouting at me.

I take stock of myself. My hair and beard are a mess. There's definitely lipstick on the collar of my polo. I'll have to go in just my undershirt. I wonder if my brother will buy it if I say I got hung up in my work this morning and lost track of time.

Luckily I have my nephew's gift with me. I can tell them I was putting the finishing touches on it, even though I've had it done for months. I had picked it up from the engraver last night before I hit the club, which was why I had it along, tucked safely in the glove box.

I pull up outside my brother's house in Highland Park. It's the house we all grew up in, where Tim took care of us after my mom died and my dad took off. Now Tim lives here with his wife, Alice, and their baby. Tim's always been hard on us, insisting that we keep our shit together. And with good reason. It's not like it rained money for our family. We had to be careful, couldn't afford any missteps. But I'm an adult now, and Tim's become even more of a hard ass since he married Alice. At least with me.

Our other brother, Ty, can do no wrong as far as Tim's concerned. Ty is a professional hockey star and his fiancé, Juniper, is a lawyer at my brother's firm. She used to be Ty's lawyer until they got together. Tim acts like the sun shines out of Juniper's ass and Ty is basically another sunbeam, between all his community service and the way he helped Juniper train for an Olympic gold medal in rowing.

I'm left to bear the brunt of all of them judging me. They think I'm some dirty, deadbeat, wanna-be artist. They think I'm a selfish womanizer, and maybe that part is true. I breathe slowly in and out through my nose. *Yeah. That part is true.*

I climb out of the truck and head inside, wondering how much I've missed and how long Tim is going to yell at me about it later.

62

THATCHER

"Happy birthday, dear Peter, happy birthday to you!" I walk in the door in time to join the chorus singing to my nephew. I slide over to the dining room, where my family and Alice's family are all clapping and cooing at my nephew. He's strapped in his high chair wearing just a diaper as my sister-in-law slides him a giant cupcake. She's a chef, so I'm sure she made it for him from scratch. Knowing Alice, it's probably made of carrot flour with lemon zest and extra protein or some shit...but tastes amazing anyway.

I pull out my phone and take a picture as Petey smacks the chocolate frosting, then rubs his hand on his belly. He's a cute kid, with his mom's tight, blond ringlets but the grey eyes all us Stag men inherited from our mother, Laurel. Petey sticks a hand in his mouth, tentative, and then the sugary icing blows his little mind. He dives in, face first. We all laugh, but when I look up, I see my brother Tim scowling at me.

I raise both my eyebrows at Tim, but don't keep his eye. I look back at Petey. He's got, like, 15 adults staring at him and his cousins-- Alice's sister has 2 boys--are running around screaming. The poor kid must be going crazy with all the stimulation, plus his first experience with sugar.

"All right, Petey, let's get you cleaned up and we can open your presents!" Alice swoops in and lifts him out of the chair, not even flinching at the mess. She's like that. Doesn't care about stuff like frosting on her shirt. She holds Petey on her hip, trying to keep most of the mess at bay. He reaches for her face and she kisses his choco-laty hand. I take a picture of that, too. Alice has brought a lot of light into our family.

Things were really rocky with Tim and her for a bit there. She got pregnant pretty early in their relationship and insisted she had to raise the baby within walking distance of her family. Tim wanted them to live in the fancy downtown penthouse he owned at the time. Alice would have none of it. Family is the most important thing to her, and I appreciate that. I mean, my brothers are pains in the ass, but they're all I've got. The Petersons are way up in each other's business--a few of them still live at home with their dad and Alice's older brother just bought a house in the neighborhood. I laugh a little at how nicely things worked out now that Alice and Tim live in Stag HQ. Alice grew up just a few blocks away from us. We're all one, giant Stag-Peterson group now for Sunday dinners and shit. It's nice. At least Alice's brothers don't judge me for my piercings and ink.

I meet Tim's eye again as Alice and her sister get Peter started opening presents. Yep. Tim is pissed. I shift uncomfortably, grabbing a plate of snacks off the table while Petey opens toy cars and a tricy-cle. Of course, Ty bought him a hockey stick and Juniper got him a life jacket.

I crouch down next to Alice and Peter to give him my gift. Alice sniffs and makes a face at me. *Shit.* How bad do I stink? I need to start keeping deodorant in the truck, at least. I slide the wooden box out of my back jeans pocket and hand it to Alice. "I made something for you, dude." Peter smiles at me and tugs at my beard. He's the only one I'll let do that. I know it's wild and unruly, but that doesn't give anyone free reign to yank it. Except Petey.

"Thatcher, this box is gorgeous," Alice says, rubbing the smooth finish.

"My buddy made that for me, and engraved it. See?" I point out where Property of Peter Stag is etched into the wood. She hands me the box and I show her how to slide the lid open. The glass marbles I made glisten in the light.

"Marbles, Thatcher? For a baby?" My brother is angry. He's about to blow his shit, I can tell. He storms over and snatches them from Alice's hand.

"Chill, dude. I used the silicon blend for the base material." I take a marble from him and bounce it on the hardwood floor. "It won't shatter. He can't break it. I promise."

"It's a fucking choking hazard, Thatcher." Tim takes the box and moves to put it up on top of the bookshelf, but I grab his arm.

"Give me a little more credit than that, would you?" I hold up one of the marbles. "Alice told me nothing smaller than a toilet paper roll. I made sure these were *just* bigger." I look back and forth between Tim and Alice. She smiles at me warmly, but my brother clenches his teeth. I see a vein ticking in his neck and he walks through to the kitchen.

"Thatcher, they're just beautiful," Alice says. She holds one of the marbles up to the light. I swirled in black and gold on that one, for our Pittsburgh sports teams. The other marble I made with grey, like our eyes. And a few streaks of purple, for Alice's. I'm pretty pleased with how they turned out. Perfectly spherical. Lightweight enough that I don't worry Petey will hurt himself with them. I know I'm an asshole to women and I show up late to birthday parties, but I would never give my nephew a gift that would hurt him. My family is everything to me.

Alice kisses me on the cheek. "Go talk to him," she urges. "He's just being cranky, I think."

I nod and grab a cupcake before the kids and Ty eat them all. I sigh and walk to the kitchen, where Tim is gripping the counter and staring out the window into the backyard. "Hey, Timber," I say, my mouth full of cupcake.

"You're a real piece of work, you know that, Thatcher?"

"Dude, I was a half hour late for a baby's birthday party. Can you cut me a break?" I wipe my mouth with the back of my hand. "And at least turn around to look at me if you're going to give me shit."

Tim whips around and crosses his arms, talking to me like I'm some little kid. "You still smell like pussy. Do you know that? And fucking liquor, too. Did you even shower after?"

I don't say anything, but I don't think it can be true that I reek that badly of sex...although I did go down on what's-her-name in my truck before we headed to her apartment.

"What do you care what I did last night?"

"I care when you show up hungover and dripping with STDs to my son's fucking birthday party, Thatcher. You're late for every family dinner. You're always out at bars. What the fuck are you doing with your life?"

I throw the rest of the cupcake into the sink. "You have a lot of fucking nerve, Tim, judging my life. I go to functions promoting my god damn artwork and it's really none of your fucking business who I bring home."

"It is my business, brother." He steps right into my face. "It is my business when you bring some bimbo to the family suite to watch Ty's hockey games and then you piss her the fuck off and she slanders the family name on social media. It is my business when you screw over some executive's daughter and I start losing business to other firms. Are you sensing a pattern here?" He holds up his phone and I see Tiffany has been bashing me online already. That didn't take long.

"Her father represents the football team, Thatcher," Tim snarls at me. "I've already gotten calls." He grinds his teeth together and I can tell he wants to deck me or sue me. Maybe both.

The thing about Tim is that he's 100% correct about me pissing off all these women. Yeah, I go to my brother Ty's pro hockey games and seduce the glamorous women there, and yeah, I forget their names, sneak out of their beds in the middle of the night, or wind up fucking their roommates the next weekend. But they all know this going in. They all know that Thatcher Stag isn't in it for the long haul. One great night. I make it worth their while.

The other thing about Tim is that he's 100% an asshole right now, and I just can't stand it another fucking second. He's always harping on me for how I do business, because it's not how *he* does business at Stag Law. Fuck him and his uptight, designer suits. He has no idea how successful I am, the kinds of negotiations my agent makes for my glass. Could I be a bit more discreet about how I unwind after work? Ok, maybe.

But my whole life, he's just treated me like his whipping boy, taking out all his frustrations on me because Ty's the youngest and I'm always just *there*. But I'm sick of him thinking of me as a loser, which is why I respond to him by saying, "I don't know where you get your information from, Tim, but it's outdated. And that chick is delusional. I'll have you know I'm engaged."

I hear a gasp from behind me. Alice and Juniper had walked into the kitchen to see what the commotion was as Tim and I were shouting. Juniper claps her hands. "Engaged? Thatcher, really?? Why didn't you say anything?"

"Yeah, brother. Why didn't you tell us anything about this fiancé of yours?" Tim raises an eyebrow at me and I can tell he knows I'm lying. Fuck him.

I run a finger through my long hair, trying to smooth it down. "I didn't want to take away from your wedding plans, Juniper. This summer is about you and Ty and I don't want to steal your limelight is all."

"Aww, Thatcher, you are so sweet to consider me that way. You know you getting engaged wouldn't take anything from my wedding, though."

I give her a 2-dimple smile. Not that she can see them behind the beard. "I just know you don't have any family, Juniper, so *our* family should dote on you. This is a big deal for you. You guys can all meet her soon. I promise."

Tim is looking at me like he still wants to murder me. "Why didn't you bring her with you today, then, if she's your fiancé?"

I shrug, stalling. "She's working." Shit. I need to start keeping track of the lies before I get myself in trouble. I just want to get my brother off my back for a minute so I can regroup.

"Well!" Alice throws her arms around me in a hug. "I insist that you bring her over for family dinner next Sunday. No--Thatcher, don't you look at me that way. She has to come. Tell her to ask off now if she works weekends."

My mouth drops open. I look at Tim and he's smiling like the Cheshire cat. "Great idea, Alice. I need to meet this mystery woman so I can call Tiffany's father and assure him his daughter must have been thinking of a different hipster artist who fucked her and forgot her name."

I'm seething right now, angry...and panicking, I guess. I can't fucking bear to let him be right about this. "We will be here, brother. Count on it."

I guess I have a week to find myself a fake fiancé.

63

EMMA

I smooth out my jeans and tie my hair up in a high ponytail to get it out of my face. I've been summoned to the editor's office, but I'm wearing my "thinking clothes" and I look a mess. I tap on Phil's door frame hesitantly. "You wanted to see me, boss?" He gestures for me to come in, so I sit in the chair by his desk while he types furiously. Hopefully those aren't comments on my latest draft. He has high standards, and I want to improve my writing, but it's still hard to get a file back that's more red ink than black.

Phil stops typing, sighs, and leans back in his chair. "Emma. I need you to do something for me."

"Sure, Phil. Anything for the Post!"

He sighs again. "Davis quit and, frankly, I'm screwed. I need you to cover an art opening."

Art? I frown. "Hm. Well, Phil, you know I don't really know anything about art..."

He waves a hand, dismissing this concern. "I'm emailing you all the press release stuff. You can pick up lingo, highlights, whatever from the PR people. Thatcher Stag is debuting some series of glass botanicals in the conservatory. It's supposed to be hot shit. We need to cover it." He looks at me over his monitor, face stern. "Consider it

an advertorial--think positive copy, Cheswick. Ben will go photograph
the event. You just need to interview the artist, get some quotes about
his process and his vision for our city. Blah, blah. You realize I'm
giving you *permission* to write a puff piece here, Cheswick."

My frown deepens. This job as a general reporter at the Pittsburgh Post is a dream for me. Only because I pushed myself so hard
in college did I have a strong enough portfolio to land a job here at
all, and then I got promoted to reporter. For the past six months I've
been writing whatever Phil tells me to write, whether that's meant
interviewing city council or watching kids race robots around the
science center. But art? I'm not an artsy gal.

"Davis really quit? Can we just expand our coverage of local
science initiatives?"

"Emma, we've got investors. Surely you've noticed that we have an
arts and culture section? I'm assuming you read every issue cover to
cover?" I blush. He smiles. "You will write me 2,000 words on
Thatcher Stag's glass show, and you will submit your copy by end of
work day tomorrow." I open my mouth to protest, but he holds up his
hand. "Go home, change into something more presentable, and be at
the conservatory by 5."

He throws me my press credentials and a parking pass he knows I
don't need, because I don't drive. *Fifteen years of uncontrolled seizures
took away that opportunity,* I think, letting myself feel angry for just a
moment before I shake it off. I've been healthy for over four years. I'm
in a good place now. I pick at the medical alert bracelet on my wrist as
I head back to my cubicle and grab my things from my desk.

I walk the few short blocks home, thankful as always that I got a
job in such a walkable neighborhood. I cut through the park, trying
to plan out questions to ask an artist about his work. God, I really
know *nothing* about art. I smile despite it all when I reach my apartment. I'm able to afford the first floor of an airy duplex on the north
side of the city, where I got a good deal by promising to help the land-
lord write ads for her vacant apartments. Now she doesn't have any
vacancies, and I've got cheap rent in an amazing space. The beautiful
brick building was lovingly restored with gorgeous woodwork, wide

plank hardwood floors throughout, and large windows that let in tons of sunlight. I put two huge planters of lavender and sage on my stoop, since they do so well in the direct sun, and the place looks inviting. Like a real adult lives here. *I am an independent adult, and I'm doing great,* I remind myself. It still takes me by surprise sometimes.

My parents won't even come visit. They insist this neighborhood is "unsuitable" and I can tell they disapprove of my job as a reporter. I'm sure they'd be much happier if I had pursued political science like my perfect sister Veronica. I shake my head, trying not to think too much about my parents, and investigate my wardrobe options.

I ordinarily wear all black when I'm working, but it's a hot day and Phil didn't specify whether the exhibit would be indoors or out. I settle on black slacks with a lightweight grey top with a boatneck cut and 3/4 sleeves. It's a bit more snug than my typical reporting getup, but I remind myself that just because something fits doesn't mean it's inappropriate. My mother's rules about modesty and proper dress always baffled me. I spent years with her cramming me into pencil skirts and "respectable nude pumps." I cringe just thinking about it as I slide my feet into my favorite flats.

Since college, I've relied on my friend Nicole to coach me through most decisions that don't involve pearls and formal dinners. If Nicole said this top was ok for work, it must be true. She's working for a tech startup, but always looks like she could be featured in our Lifestyles section in the Post.

When I arrive at the venue, my breath catches. The gardens are so lush, so serene. I can't believe I haven't come here since I was a kid. I giggle, imagining my mother here for a fancy hat party, and I flash my press pass at the entrance. As I walk up the main stairs, I almost trip while staring up at the glass chandelier. Brilliant curls of glass in green, blue, and yellow intertwine, catching the light of the glass dome entryway. When the automatic doors slide open to reveal the exhibit, I am thrilled by the floral scent, the dazzling green plants, and the fiery shoots of glass I see peeking out from among the leaves. Maybe this won't be so bad of an assignment.

Spotting someone wearing a lanyard, I step into his path. "Excuse me," I say. "I'm Emma Cheswick from the *Pittsburgh Post*. I'm here to talk to Thatcher Stag. Would you be able to point him out to me?"

The man grins. He waggles his eyebrows, which seems strange to me, and he yells across the room toward a long-haired man squatting by an orange piece of glass. "Yo, Thatch. This chick is here to talk to you." My face twists in confused anger at this misrepresentation, but before I can elaborate, the strange guy brushes past and the man who must be Thatcher walks over.

He's wearing stained jeans that hang from his hips in such a way that I can see he has a perfect, round ass. His ripped t-shirt barely hides the black ink twined around his muscular arms. Shit, he's hot. *Remember, he's a subject. Not a conquest.* Thatcher leans on a column and crosses his arms, smiling at me. "The show opens in about an hour, sweetheart, but we've probably got time for a decent *conversation.*"

Is he hitting on me? I hold out a hand for a shake. "Emma Cheswick. *Pittsburgh Post.* I'm actually--"

"Emma. I like that. Follow me and we can *talk* back in one of the offices." He winks, and walks in front of me, holding back a palm frond for me as we head through a side door in the conservatory. "So how'd you get in early, Emma? The ladies usually come find me *after* the show..."

I'm feeling less and less interested in this guy the more he talks. "I just waved my press pass. It hadn't occurred to me to look for you afterward. I guess that makes sense--what the hell??"

Thatcher spins me around so my back presses against a wall in the hall. Boxing me in with both arms, he leans in close. He smells like sweat and fire. And he definitely is hitting on me. I stiffen. "What, baby? You shy about being in the hallway?" He raises a hand to, I think, stroke my cheek, but I duck out from under his arm.

"You know what? I can get what I need from the conservatory PR people. Have a good show, Mr. Stag." I rush back out the door and into the atrium before he can formulate a response.

64

EMMA

I walk away from him as quickly as I can, digging in my bag for my phone. I text Phil. **Thatcher Stag is a sleazeball. He just made a pass at me.**

My editor responds almost immediately. *All men are assholes. Find someone from the conservatory to help you. Get this interview, Cheswick.*

Unbelievable. I bite my lip and tap my foot, trying to figure out what to do next. I decide to just start wandering the space before the crowd arrives. As I walk through the purple and pink orchids, I see more of what must be Thatcher's art. His glass is delicate and ferocious at once. The contrast to the green surrounding it is stark, and yet I can tell each piece was placed intentionally, thoughtfully. His work is not so different from the flowers in the room. Some of the orchids sprout seemingly from nothing--no roots or dirt to be seen. His glass seems more natural here than those delicate, outlandish blooms. How can one man create something so beautiful and also be such a jerk?

When I've made a full lap of the inside, I've sufficiently calmed down to go searching for the PR staff from the conservatory. A smiling woman named Linda shakes my hand warmly and hands me a whole packet of information about the exhibit, the flowers that accompany it, and the conservatory's vision in hiring a glass artist to embellish their space.

"Anything else I can help you with, Emma? You know we're always thrilled for page space in the Post."

"Well," I say. "Actually...about Thatcher..."

Her face falls. "Yes. About Thatcher."

"I need to get a few quotes from him, but he seemed...distracted when I tried to speak with him earlier."

Linda rolls her eyes. "Will you be here for awhile? Do you want to give me your questions and I can make sure he answers them? I've got an intern who can record him talking while he...finishes setting up."

"Oh! That's a perfect solution." I mean, it's not. Third-hand interviews are a terrible idea, but Phil did say it was a puff piece, and I did tell him the source was a dick. So I tear my question list from my notebook and hand it to Linda. "I'll just interview some of the guests about their feelings when they experience the exhibit and I'll make sure I find you before I leave?"

Linda nods and marches off. I see her hand over the slip of paper before embracing someone from Pittsburgh Magazine. I wander through the garden, chatting with people about the glass and the flowers. An hour or so later, I've almost forgotten that Thatcher Stag lured me into a hallway and tried to make out with me. Almost.

I finish up my conversation with a middle-aged woman named Marge, who drove in from south of the city to enjoy the show. She's got me answering questions about growing up in the same suburban town where she lives, and when I see Thatcher approaching us, it takes me a real minute to figure out which scenario is less annoying.

He sidles up to us, snagging two glasses of champagne from a server standing nearby. "May I offer you ladies a drink?" he says, smiling a crooked grin that only raises one side of his mouth. Why am I looking at his straight, white teeth? Maybe because I want to punch them out, I decide.

I shake my head at his offer. "No, thank you. I'm on the clock. Marge was telling me how much she's enjoying your art, though."

Marge is delighted. "Oh are *you* Thatcher Stag?? This Stag Glass show is simply superb." She flutters a hand to her chest and takes a flute of champagne from Thatcher. I smirk at him and duck away. Seeing Linda glide past, I rush over to her.

"I see you've got him distracted," she says as she hands me a thumb drive and my question sheet, where the intern has scribbled a few mono-syllabic answers to my carefully crafted questions. "Anyway. I think we've got about seven or eight words from him...his contact information is in the packet I gave you if your fact checker wants to verify any quotes you can garner from that file."

"Thanks for trying, Linda. I appreciate you looking out for me." I assure her that I will talk to Phil and come back sometime to write an in-depth piece on the conservatory and their efforts to revitalize and attract more guests. "Phil loves when I find him good tourism leads," I assure her.

I head for home, frustrated and pissed off at my editor, Thatcher Stag, and anyone else I happen to encounter as I go. I send Nicole a series of furious texts and she sends me angry GIFs. *I can't believe your boss still wanted you to interview that scumbag after you told him he hit on you. I'll never buy Stag's bullshit tchotchkes.*

Thank you! You're a true friend.

IN THE MORNING, I sulk my way into work and bang out the meanest review I can tactfully write about the show and submit it to my editor before he leaves for lunch. Not ten minutes later, his admin pokes her head over my cubicle wall.

"Hey, Emma," she says, grimacing.

"That bad?" I sigh and start to stand.

"Phil wants to see you right away."

65

THATCHER

After my installation opening, I decide to just go home. I can't get my fight with my brother out of my head and I'm very aware the clock is ticking for me to find someone to agree to fool my family for a few weeks until after Ty's wedding. There has to be someone who isn't mad at me after we hooked up...

My assistant, Cody, comes back with me for a few beers. I decide to let him know what's going on to see if he knows anyone who can play a role for a while.

"Dude, you rolled up to your nephew's birthday party right from a one-night stand? That's crude, man." Cody takes a deep pull on his beer. "Hm. I honestly can't think of a woman you haven't already fucked. You even fuck all their roommates...you're pretty prolific."

I throw my beer cap at him. "There has to be someone. Someone left from art school? One of the new grad students at the Pittsburgh Glass Center?"

Cody rubs a hand across his chin, thinking. "Hey, what about that reporter chick from tonight?"

"What reporter?"

Cody's eyes go wide. "The redhead chick who came early to interview you."

"That fucking girl was a reporter? You made her sound like some groupie." I stand up and my stool tips over backward. "Fuck, Cody, I made a move on her. What paper was she with?" *Don't say the Post.*

Cody thinks for a minute and my heart sinks when he says, "She was there from the Post. You hit on her? Really?"

"You called her a 'chick' and said she was there to talk to me."

"Yeah. For the paper." Cody swigs down the rest of his beer and throws his bottle into the bin by the workbench. "Look, Thatch, it's late. I'm going to get on out of here. I'll be in--what? Thursday morning?"

I'm so pissed off I can only nod. What the fuck is wrong with me? I don't even ask first anymore. I mean, to be fair, 90 per cent of the women who want to talk to me are using 'talk' as a euphemism. It's just my luck that the one woman who actually wanted to talk was a fucking reporter.

That opening was a really big deal for me. I never did anything like that before, partnering with a conservatory. I worked for months with them, talking about the different plants that would be in bloom when the show opened, discussing different pieces to highlight at different times of day to catch the light. One day I was in there at sunrise taking pictures, sketching out my ideas. It kills me to think the work won't even get a fair review because I can't turn off...whatever it is that makes me do that shit with women.

I'll just have to kiss her ass before she turns in her draft. I look around my shelf of finished work and my eye settles on a bonsai. At least, it was supposed to be a bonsai. It never looked quite right to me, so I set it aside. But it's beautiful--clear roots and branches tipped with blues and blacks. I decide it will make a fine token of my apology.

In the morning, I shower slowly after a long run, making sure to condition my beard, comb my hair. I decide an apology calls for extra attention to how I look. I even stick a blazer on over my t-shirt. Apparently I needed a wakeup call to remember my manners. I've decided to drive into the Post, find whichever reporter I mauled, and offer my most sincere apology.

The sweet thing at reception is putty in my hands when I turn on the charm. I offer her my best smile--the one I save for when I really have to work for it with the ladies. I lean across the counter and check out her nametag. "Hey there, Mindy." My voice is smooth. I know I look good, smell good, and sound good. "I'm Thatcher Stag. Last night I got interrupted when one of your reporters was interviewing me at my art show, and I never got her card. Do you know how I could find her? Just to see if she had any more questions?"

"Last night? Gosh. Hm. It could have been anyone..." Mindy crinkles her nose and looks at a computer screen. "It was an art show? What did she look like?"

"She had red hair and green eyes," I say. "Maybe...this tall?" I hold my hand about mid-chest.

"Oh. That's Emma." Mindy sits back in her chair and looks down the hall. "She got called in to talk to Phil, though. I actually think she will be glad you're here." She stands and walks around the desk, nodding toward the doorway. "Come on. I'll take you back."

I can hear shouting from halfway down the hall. Mindy points to the door that says EDITOR and heads back up front to the desk. I give her a wink and move closer to the editor's office, and I hear someone shouting my name from inside.

"Jesus, Cheswick. Did you even fucking Google him? I told you I wanted a puff piece. I absolutely cannot print a scathing defamation of his character."

Then I hear a familiar voice, sounding about as angry as she was last night. "Nothing I wrote there is untrue. He *is* a smarmy creep, and I did talk about how his delicate glass pieces brought light to the conservatory, in contrast to his awful personality."

I hear someone pound on the desk. "Damn it, Emma. Do you know who owns this paper?"

"Lash? What's that got to do with anything?"

The editor sighs. "Do you know who represents Lash, legally? Who is a major donor to our paper and likely funds the majority of your entry-level reporter salary?" He waits a beat. "Tim Stag. Older brother of Thatcher Stag, who I told you to write a fucking puff piece about."

"Phil, that feels inappropriate."

"It's not above the fold on the front page, Emma. It's Arts and Culture. If I wanted an exposé on Stag as a womanizer, I'd send you out to report the hell out of that story. But I want a nice, glowing review of the art show. Did you look at the art? Did you read the PR materials? Ok, then. Get the hell out of here and don't come back until you've got something I can work with. And get me a fucking quote!"

I can't help but smile, even if I am irritated that my brother's name gets evoked whenever I try to do anything. Emma's going to have to talk to me. When the office door flies open I lean back against the opposite wall, holding out my olive branch. She growls when she sees me standing there and her eyes fly wide open. "What the hell are you doing here?" She practically hisses at me.

"Sounds like I'm saving your ass, sweetheart."

66

EMMA

I drag Thatcher Stag through the office by the lapels of his blazer, only partially wondering why he's more dressed up today to come to the Post's headquarters than he was at his damn art opening. Once we reach the lobby, I let go of him and start laying into him. "Look, I don't know what you heard or what you are thinking, but you can't be here right now. I'd prefer if you left."

The asshole grins at me. "From what I heard, your boss wants you talking to me. Pronto. Asking me in depth questions. Sounds like it could take hours..."

I can only roll my eyes. Because of course he's right. I stomp my foot in frustration. I need to talk to this dickhead. *At least he smells amazing,* I think, immediately angry at myself for noticing. "Look," I say, "there's no place here to do an interview and I'd feel safer speaking with you in a public place. Can you meet me in the library on Federal in a half hour?"

"No." He smiles.

"What do you mean 'no'? I thought you just said you were here to talk to me."

"I've got conditions," he says.

I raise an eyebrow and cross my arms. "I'm absolutely not sleeping with you, so you can get that out of your head right the hell now."

He laughs. "Nothing like that, doll. I do need a favor, though."

I glance over at reception to see if Mindy is listening. Of course she is. Thatcher notices this, too, and says, "Walk me to my truck and I'll tell you what I have in mind."

I think about it for a few minutes, while watching him grow visibly uncomfortable. Before I open my mouth to talk again, he holds out a cardboard box. "I brought you something," he says. "By way of apology for my behavior last night."

Well, this is unexpected. "Thank you," I say. I crack open the box, peering past the lid, and then I gasp as I pull out a glass cluster of neurons. The work is exquisite, delicate. The bundle of nerve endings splays out blue and black from the stem in the middle. This is exactly how I always imagined things looked inside me. Exactly! How could he possibly know to give this to me? "Who told you about me?" My voice quivers more than I intended, and his face softens.

"Nobody said anything about you, Emma. I just thought you'd like this enough to accept my apology and hear me out. So will you walk with me a minute?" He rubs a hand through his beard, nervously.

I can only nod, tucking the glass back into the box. "Can I go stick this on my desk? I don't want to drop it and break it."

"So you like it then?" He raises his eyebrows, hopeful, and I can't help but smile. He looks like a kid who just made something for his parents. It's endearing to me that he cares whether I like his art.

My voice is a whisper when I tell him, "I love it, Thatcher." I rush off down the hall and slide the box across my desk. I grab my messenger bag and shove my laptop and digital recorder inside. I nod toward the doors and Thatcher walks with me.

Once we're outside, he leans against a battered old truck and says, "So here's the thing." He runs his hands through his beard again. "I'm in some deep shit with my family...and I'm just going to cut right to the chase. I need someone to pretend she's my fiancé until after my brother's wedding."

I wait a beat for him to laugh, tell me he's joking. Get to the real favor. He doesn't. "So...what now? You want me to *pretend* I'm going to marry you?"

He nods. "I promise I will give you unfettered access to me, and my studio, and I'll answer your questions without cracking jokes. You show up to, like, 2 family dinners with me and be my date for my brother's wedding and we'll call it even."

"Are you serious right now? That plan is absurd. And besides, a month of acting like I can tolerate you is way more effort than you answering my questions about glass in the gardens."

Now the mischievous grin returns and I feel myself wanting to slug him again. "It doesn't sound like your boss will like it very much if I clam up and refuse to talk to you."

Shit. He's right. I'm in deep trouble with Phil. He made that pretty clear in his office. I exhale slowly through my nose and Thatcher just stares at me, like he's studying me, and it makes me uncomfortable.

"I'll tell you what," he says. "I'll get you an in for another story that would be great for the Post, and I'll make sure you're the only reporter with access."

"What story is that," I ask, chewing on the inside of my cheek. He tells me that the woman his brother is going to marry is an Olympic gold medalist for rowing and that she has helped shift the mission of his *other* brother's law firm. "How many Stag brothers are there?" I ask, trying to keep it all straight. He grins and holds up 3 fingers.

"Tim is the oldest and runs Stag Law, which represents professional athletes *and* helps fight for equity for women in athletics, the arts...anywhere that gets federal Title 9 funds. And if you want to know more you'll have to agree to help me and talk with Juniper, because that is all I understand about what she does." He sticks his thumbs in his belt loops, looking like he's none too comfortable. What he's proposing sounds absolutely crazy...but he's right that I need this story. And it sounds like this pitch about his sister in law would be amazing to research and write.

I sigh, letting the air and frustration out of my entire body, and groan. "All right, Stag. I'll do it."

"Oh thank god," he says, visibly relaxing. He hands me his card with the address for his studio. We make a plan to meet there a bit later, and I text Phil that I'll have the revision for him tomorrow. Thatcher says we can hammer out the details for our pretend engagement over dinner later, and I agree to let him buy.

"But I am *not* sleeping with you. We need to clear that up right away."

He laughs. "I promise I will be on my best behavior." He opens the door to his truck and swings in, then rolls down the window and leans out halfway. "Unless you *want* me to misbehave." He winks, and I wish I had something to throw at him. But my imagination also flashes to images of Thatcher misbehaving with me, and I feel a flutter in my tummy.

"Get the hell out of here," I yell after him as he peals out, laughing. This is going to be a long month.

67

THATCHER

I make an attempt to clean up my studio a bit before Emma gets here. I know she's supposed to write about me in a positive light no matter what, but I've never had anyone from the press meet me in my space before. I really don't let anyone in here but staff. My work in progress is too important to me, too private. I hope Emma doesn't look too carefully at the things that aren't complete. She seemed to really like the bonsai, though, so that sets my mind at ease a bit.

I start to think about why it matters to me that she likes my art. *That's different.* I usually don't give a shit what people think of my glass...buy it or move over has always been my motto. I feel bad for hitting on her at the conservatory. I guess I have to re-classify her as someone I know professionally. For some reason I'm always able to rein it in with women in a professional context. I could kill Cody for making me think she was a groupie. This whole thing could have been avoided.

It would be nice if she wants to get wild with me, though. I remember the way her body looked in those slim pants and that breezy top that gave just a hint of her curves. And fuck me, a red head. Even her eyelashes are red. I noticed when I was staring at her in the parking lot, pleading with her to accept my crazy scheme. I wonder what it feels like to wrap that red hair around my fist, yank her head back...suck on her neck. *Knock it off, Thatcher.* This is going to be a long month.

I've got to not only *not* hit on Emma, but I can't go out and find anyone else to sleep with, either. If word gets back to my family that I'm cheating on my so-called fiancé, Tim would treat me like worse garbage than he is already. It fucking sucks having perfect brothers.

I hear a knock at the door, and walk over to answer it a little too quickly. I curse under my breath when I see that it's not Emma Cheswick, but my sister in law Alice, blowing on my nephew's cheeks. Fuck. I totally forgot I told them I'd babysit tonight.

"And there's Uncle Thatcher!" Alice coos to Peter, who claps his hand and reaches for my beard. Always with the damn beard. I hope he doesn't have anything sticky on his fingers.

"Come here, squirt." I pull him in and toss him up on my shoulders, where he moves his hands immediately to my hair.

"Thatcher, I really appreciate you watching him for us tonight. It means so much to us to be able to go to Dad's retirement dinner." Her eyes shine. I know she's proud of her dad, and also feeling a little blue that her mom can't be here for this. Alice's mom died of cancer when she was in high school, just a few years after our mom died.

"Dude-time with Petey is my pleasure, Alice." I lean down so she can reach me to kiss my cheek. Her hair is wild and curly as ever, but I notice Petey doesn't yank on it like he does mine.

"My brother isn't with you is he," I ask, not sure what I hope the answer will be.

She shakes her head, though, and I feel some relief. "He's still at the office reviewing notes with Juniper. They're trying to get things squared away before she and Ty leave for their honeymoon. Tim's meeting me at the restaurant."

I nod. "Well, I want you both to have a great time and not worry. Whatever I can't figure out, I'll just Google." She bites her lower lip and creases her brow. "Relax, Alice. I've watched Peter before." I don't tell her that Emma will be here soon helping me out. That's what a fiancé does, right? Helps with the nephews. As Alice pulls away I smile, thinking this month might not be so bad after all.

Peter and I head into my attached apartment and I turn some kids show on the TV. I sit on the floor next to him to watch and he crawls right into my lap. I don't get a lot of one on one time with him. It's nice just chilling with the little dude, even if he does yank on my hair. Twenty minutes later, the doorbell rings. Emma.

I answer the door carrying Petey in a football hold, and he drools and laughs as Emma's face registers shock at seeing me with a baby.

"You have a *child?*"

"Ha! No way, babe. Petey here is my nephew and I forgot that we are hanging out tonight. Hope it's ok if he sits in on the interview."

Emma looks uncertain, but I step back from the door and Petey starts clapping his hands. He's damn charming, like all the Stag men. She can't help but smile, and we all sit together on the rug. "Fire away, Ms. Cheswick," I say, pulling Petey back from her laptop as she tries to open up all her stuff.

"Maybe I should sit up higher," she says, climbing onto the couch. Peter pulls himself to standing and slaps at her laptop. I like this kid even more. He's pushing Emma's buttons, literally, and she's cute as hell when she's irritated. Her face flushes as red as her hair.

I lie on my back on the carpet and start to play airplane with Peter so he's out of reach of Emma. "Thanks," she says, and I catch her staring at my abs as my t-shirt rides up when I swoop Petey around. "So, um, why don't you tell me how you first got interested in glass."

68

EMMA

I am shocked at how good Thatcher is with his nephew. He's so comfortable tossing that baby around. It's damn sexy, and I almost forget the man is a sleaze just looking for sex. When he tells me about how he feels like the molten glass is part of his mind, malleable and able to bring his imagination to solid form...well. It's easy to see why women drop their undies for him. He orders takeout, and we pig out on Indian food while he holds his end of the bargain. Thatcher Stag tells me how the art teachers at his school were his saving grace after his mom died, how they arranged for him to do intensive programs and helped him apply for a scholarship when he decided to study glass blowing in college. "Only Stag to leave the state for college," he says, laughing at how the tiny town of Alfred in New York never stood a chance against his artistic vision...or his libido.

Thatcher talks to me about his work for a while and then he looks at his watch. "Hey," he says, handing Petey a pouch of some sort of food. "My sister in law will be back soon to grab Petey, so we better hash out our plan. Basically, you need to act believably in love with me when my family's around."

"Ok." I chew on my pen. "How did we meet?"

He grins one of those devilish smiles I've come to recognize. He saves those for women he's trying to hit on. "You interviewed me at an opening," he says, "and you were smitten immediately."

"I'd prefer if *you* were the smitten one and had to work for it a bit," I tell him, and he nods.

"That sounds more plausible. All right, I can just tell my family I was smitten and drove to your office to give you a glass bonsai in an attempt to woo you. Then, you were smitten."

"That was a bonsai?" I think back to the beautiful cluster of neurons I now have on the mantle of my apartment, where it catches the afternoon sun just right and sparkles.

"Well yeah," he looks insulted. "What the hell did you think it was?"

I flush, not meaning to. Of course I hadn't meant to insult his art, but I am taken aback. I thought the gift was so personal to me. That he somehow knew about me and was, I don't know, honoring that by giving me a symbolic artistic creation. "I, um..." I decide I'm just going to be honest. I'm going to have to spend a lot of time with him for the next month and I will be lying to enough people as it is. "I thought it was a bundle of neurons."

He scrunches up his face as if he's thinking about this. "I can see that. The trunk was sort of messed up."

"I really like it, Thatcher." My voice comes out as a whisper. "I like it very much. Thank you again."

"You're welcome, Chezz." We start to talk about the family dinner I will need to attend on Sunday. I'm not sure whether to believe him when he says it's casual. Just because he wears ripped jeans to fancy art openings doesn't mean people won't stare if I do it.

Just then, Petey toddles up to me and smiles. I get low and hold out my hand for a high five. He grasps my finger and scrunches up his face, loudly messing up his diaper. "Jesus, Thatcher." The smell hits the room in a cloud. Petey releases my finger, and he starts to cry. "We have to get him cleaned up," I yell.

"All right. Hm. I don't see the changing pad Alice usually sticks in the bag. Woo, Petey, you outdid yourself." Thatcher rummages through Petey's diaper bag, pulling out tubes of diaper cream and spare clothes. I fan the air, while Petey starts crying louder, so I pick him up, feeling that he's soggy all up his back. I start to bounce him and make shushing sounds.

"What if you put some of that down on the carpet?" I point with my toe at a box of bubble wrap Thatcher has sitting by the door. I guess he uses that to ship his art.

"Great idea! Ok, set him down here."

Together, we strip the soiled clothes off Petey's thrashing body to the chorus of crackles and pops as Petey wriggles around on the bubble wrap. We manage to get the diaper off and we use about 36 wipes scrubbing him from his neck to his knees. He lies on the bubble wrap smiling each time it crackles, while I gather up the messy clothes and the rancid diaper.

"Ok. I'm going to soak these clothes in your utility sink and throw this diaper away outside," I say. "Then I'll come back and it can be your turn to clean up."

"Got it. I'll find Petey some clothes."

I walk through the kitchen of Thatcher's house and open the basement door. I take note that the place is much tidier than I would have thought. Sure, there's wood paneling and 1970s-style wallpaper, but it's neat and it smells clean. The basement isn't even damp. I'm up to my elbows in suds and baby shorts when I hear Thatcher yelling, "No! No! Emma, help! Help!"

I fly up the stairs and into the living room, where Petey is smiling, half dressed, and a shirtless Thatcher Stag is holding an open tube of diaper cream. "Emma! He ate it! I turned away to take off my shirt because it had poop on it and when I looked back at him, he had this in his mouth!"

"Do you remember how full it was before?" I look at the tube. It's organic diaper cream, so I guess there can't be too many harmful ingredients.

Thatcher shakes his head and runs his hands through his hair. He looks panicked. "Go wash your hands, Thatcher. You're getting diaper cream everywhere." I pick up the baby. Thatcher looks down at his fingers and silently walks into the kitchen.

Petey is still laughing and clapping. His face is shiny and his breath smells a little like the cream. I sigh, remembering a story I researched not too long before. I dig out my phone and call up Poison Control.

"Yes, hi. My friend and I are babysitting and the little guy just ate some diaper cream." Thatcher walks back in the room and, seeing me on the phone, starts to panic all over again. I mouth "poison control" to him and he grips my arm while I bounce Petey. "No, I'm not sure-- hey Thatcher, how old is Petey and what does he weigh?" He snatches the phone from me and talks with the specialist. Within a few minutes Thatcher collapses to the ground in relief.

"He's going to be fine. Absolutely fine."

69

THATCHER

I rest my head against the wall until I feel my heart start to slow down. I seriously thought I had maybe killed my nephew, and now I'm more exhausted than I can ever remember feeling.

Emma, still holding Petey, starts rubbing her nose against his nose. Shit, she was ice cool during all of that. Didn't panic for a minute and she knew exactly what to do. She explained that she had just done a big research project about Poison Control and got to interview some of the people who work in the call center. Even now, she's calm. She says, "Why don't you go take a shower? Petey and I will clean up in here. When you get back I'll finish up down at the utility sink."

I look down at my chest, remembering that I had to take off my stained shirt. I think this might be the only time I've had my shirt off in front of a woman where I wasn't actively trying to take off hers, too. I don't totally get what's going on here, because Emma is seriously sexy, but all I'm feeling right now is gratitude for her. I nod and hurry upstairs. I have to scrub a lot to get all the oily diaper cream off. When I get out of the shower I hear Emma narrating. "We're taking this stinky pile out to the trash. Yes, we are! Yes, that is silly, isn't it? Do you feel better now that you got all that out?"

I walk downstairs and see her holding my nephew, smiling up at me, and I forget for a minute that we are about to start an illusion. This girl is the real deal. Just totally, honestly herself. Wide open. Willing to help me out, even with a baby shit storm. Only now I've roped her into this big lie, and it feels like she's off limits. I plunk a kiss on Petey's head and tell her, "You can go get cleaned up now. I'll try to keep this guy alive while you're down there."

She smiles. I notice that she's totally cleaned up the rug. I didn't even know I had carpet cleaner, but I can tell she scrubbed up some places where the bubble wrap wasn't sufficient barrier. I look at my baby nephew and wonder how such a small person can make such a huge mess. "Petey, man, what the hell did you eat?" He tugs my beard. Seems about right.

Eventually, I hear a car pull up outside. The three of us are sitting on the couch. Emma is coaching Petey through "braiding" my hair. I groan and lean my head on Emma's shoulder. "How the hell am I supposed to tell my brother I almost killed his kid?"

Emma pats my knee. "Petey was never in danger. Poison Control said that brand of cream is as harmless as cream cheese. Just tell Tim what happened."

"You forget that my brother is an asshole." I grit my teeth as the door opens. Alice comes rushing in to take Petey from me and doesn't notice Emma sitting there at first.

"Did you miss Mommy?" She purrs at him, shaking her head and her blonde curls wiggle all around. "Did you have fun here with your uncle and OH MY GOD! Is this her??"

Emma blushes, and Alice shoves Petey into Tim's arms. "I'm Alice Stag." She starts shaking Emma's hand and sits beside her on the couch. She pulls Emma in for a one-armed hug. "We didn't think you were real!! Thatcher, why didn't you say she'd be here tonight? Oh my gosh. You really *do* have a fiancé?"

Emma sort of waves and I clear my throat. "Tim, Alice, this is Emma Cheswick. My beloved." I grin.

Tim makes a sort of grunting sound. He's still pissed off from the other day, but whatever. Alice claps her hands. "Emma! Are you coming to dinner on Sunday? What's your favorite food? I'll make it for you. Did Thatcher tell you I'm a chef? Don't hold back. Tell me your favorite foods."

"Alice, slow your roll," I tell her, but Emma is smiling.

She says, "Thatcher didn't get around to telling me much about his family yet, although I did hear that his brother Tim is a bit of a big deal." Damn, this girl knows how to work a crowd. I wonder if this is how she gets interview subjects to open up to her. Within a few minutes, she's got Alice talking about her long journey to go to culinary school and how, thanks to Juniper's influence, they now have a daycare right in the office at Stag Law. Petey and their colleague Ben's new son are the only kids in there so far. Alice manages to get Emma to admit Nicky's Thai Kitchen is her absolute favorite place to eat in the city, while they talk about her living on the North Side. Soon, Alice has a whole Thai-themed meal planned out for Sunday and she and Emma look like they've been friends for years.

I sigh, exhaling deeply. I need to tell them about the diaper cream, and I figure it's better now while Alice is over the moon at meeting Emma. "Hey, so, Alice, Petey had quite a diaper incident earlier."

Tim grunts again. "That happens," he says, looking up the leg hole of Petey's new shorts, as if I wouldn't have wiped it all up.

"So anyway," I continue, "It was colossal. Emma had to go soak his clothes in the utility sink, and I looked away for just one second--one fucking second, I swear to you--and Petey ate a bunch of diaper cream." I blow out a breath, anticipating the onslaught.

My brother's face is stony. Irate. "What?"

"Luckily it was the non-toxic kind you had in your diaper bag," Emma pipes in, but Tim interrupts her.

"You need to stay out of this!"

"Tim!!" Alice stands up, looking like she wants to punch my brother.

Tim's face is purple with rage as he looks in Petey's mouth. "Why the fuck are we here and not at children's hospital getting his stomach pumped? Did you even call 911?"

"Hey, whoa, Tim. Take it easy, man. I'm trying to tell you. Emma called Poison Control."

"Take it easy? You called some sort of fucking answering service instead of calling medical professionals at--"

"Actually," Emma's own face is set now. Her voice is strong as she starts to correct Tim. "To work at Poison Control, you need to have a PhD in pharmacology or have at least worked in emergency medicine. These are highly skilled medical professionals, far more so than the paramedics who may or may not have only had a short training course, depending what the city has funding for that year."

Tim closes his mouth. He looks at Emma, waits a few beats, like he's trying to process being put in his place along with accepting that his kid is safe. He inhales slowly through his nose and rubs his hands on his temples. "Please tell me what they said at Poison Control."

He directs that question at Emma, and she answers, touching his arm reassuringly. "They said that brand of diaper cream is non-toxic-- basically just like cream cheese. For Peter's age and weight there is absolutely nothing to be worried about."

Tim nods and stoops to pick up the diaper bag. He starts walking out, but Alice says, "Timber Stag. I think you owe Emma an apology." She raises a brow and her violet eyes slice daggers at him. She's clutching Petey to her chest now and he has his head down, like he's about to fall asleep.

Tim sighs. "Emma, I apologize for my tone. I felt frightened for my son's safety and I was out of line to speak to you that way." I marvel at how Alice gets Tim to behave like a human. I've been the target of his snap panic more times than I can count, and I've never gotten an apology when he jumps to conclusions. No wonder he always said Alice drove him crazy when they first met. Marriage really suits him, I guess.

Tim raises his brows and looks back and forth between Emma and Alice. Alice smiles and kisses his cheek, and Emma says, "That's ok. I'd be scared, too, if I'd left my kid with Uncle Thatcher." She winks one of her green eyes and hot damn, if I don't get hard. I cough and adjust my pants, trying not to think about Emma that way.

The mood feels instantly lighter. We walk my family outside and they drive off in their super-safe Volvo. I look around, but I don't see Emma's car.

"Where's your car, Chezz?"

"I don't drive," she says. "I took a Lyft here."

"You don't drive? In Pittsburgh? How the hell does that work?"

She shrugs. "Plenty of people don't have cars. We have buses, you know."

I laugh a bit. "I guess. Well go on and get your stuff. I'll take you home. It's the least I can do for you."

She nods. "Oh I know," she says.

After I drop her off, I notice that my truck smells like her. Like jasmine and mint.

70

EMMA

"Cheswick!" Phil has stopped using his admin to summon me, instead just opening his office door to bellow my name across the farm of cubicles. I notice that I'm the only reporter who gets this treatment, and I can't decide if that means he likes me or if my neck is still on the chopping block. "Come on in here."

"Yep," I say, closing the lid to my laptop. I plunk into the seat across from Phil expectantly. I turned in my revised draft of the piece about Thatcher's opening. I stayed up most of the night to work on it, after the diaper incident.

"This is more like it," Phil says, tapping his monitor. "This isn't even a puff piece. You got him to really talk to you."

I smile. Phil never, ever hands out these sorts of compliments. I start to relax a little more, and then Phil says, "I want you to come to the editorial meeting later. Let's hear your ideas for the next few weeks."

My jaw drops. Junior reporters almost never get to go speak up in these meetings. We get whatever assignments nobody else wants. We work the beats, trudge into emergency rooms and interview operators at Poison Control, trying to sniff out our own angle on the assignments. The thought of sharing my idea about Juniper...well, Thatcher's idea...I squeeze my thighs to keep from clapping my hands in excitement.

"That'll be all, Cheswick," Phil says, already typing away on someone else's article submission.

"Thank you, Phil. This means a lot to me."

"Ungh." This time, I can tell his grunt is short for "you're welcome, now beat it and let me work."

I decide to take an early lunch. I text Nicole to see if she can meet me so I can tell her all about it. I practically skip across the bridge to our favorite Thai place--I could eat Thai every day--and I see her already sitting at our table on the back porch.

"Nick! You're not going to believe it!"

"Spill it," she says. She's dressed impeccably, as always, looking like she is off to kill it in the board room. "I've got 46 minutes before I have to pitch our software to an investor."

"Aha, so that's why you're dressed like a superhero today. Anyway!" I start to tell her the extended version of going to Thatcher's house last night, but she cuts me off.

"Wait. You went to that creep's house? Alone? After he practically molested you at the opening? What is wrong with you, Emma?"

"Oh, shit. I forgot I didn't fill you in." I grimace. I'm not supposed to tell anyone about Thatcher's and my plan to fool his family...but this is Nicole. I'm not going to be able to do this on my own. I need her advice, like always. "So I sort of made a deal with him where I'm pretending to be his fiancé and he's giving me open access to his studio and to his family--which is why I'm excited today and--"

"Hold on." She signals the server to bring her a Thai iced tea. "I need caffeine for this. Start at the beginning and leave nothing out."

ONCE I EXPLAIN the whole thing, Nicole has drunk two of those orange iced teas and she's tapping her fingers on the table rapidly, her nails clicking on the Formica. "I think it's weird," she says.

"That's fair," I respond, but explain that it's already paying off in my favor because I get to pitch at the meeting this afternoon. "I didn't even tell Thatcher that I'm going to pitch something his sister-in-law said about daycare in the office. That's, like, a whole third feature I could maybe get in exchange for pretending to like him for a few weeks."

Nicole has her phone out, tapping around, looking for something. "Oh," she says, sliding it across to me. "Is this him? Shit, he's hot."

I look at the picture. It must be an old one, where his beard is shorter and his hair isn't so...ratty. "He does look good there," I say. "He's more hipster, grungy caveman these days, I'd say. Not my type." *Liar,* I think, biting my lip.

"Ha! Girl, you don't have a type."

"I have a not-type," I tell her, diving into the noodles and sliced mango with coconut rice. "I will say, he's really sexy when he's taking care of his nephew, and he has amazing abs."

"Does he know about all your...stuff?" Nicole wipes her mouth and checks her watch. I can tell she's about to scurry off to her meeting.

I shake my head. "I don't see why he needs to know about that," I tell her. "I haven't felt a seizure aura for months. Really, Nick, I'm more worried that he will encounter my mother than I am about him finding out my health quirks." I finger the rose-gold medical alert bracelet that Nicole helped me find when we were in college. *"This one doesn't scream 'there's something wrong with me!'"* she'd said.

When I moved in with her she helped me find a new neurologist, and that was the first time I'd had control over my symptoms. The first time I felt like I could have a life outside of my mother's home, away from her oppressive care. I owe Nicole a lot more than just Pad Thai and friendship. She squeezes my hand. "Kick ass at your meeting, Em."

"You, too, friend." She winks, grabs her purse, and clicks out the door in her heels.

71

THATCHER

My phone buzzes on the metal table across the shop, but I'm holding a steel rod with molten glass on the end, so I can't answer. It buzzes persistently, distracting me from my work. I roll the rod, and the glass gloops off to the side. "Mother fucker!" I yell, tossing it into the bucket of cold water. I can't concentrate today. The phone keeps buzzing.

"What?" I yell into the phone, seeing that it's my brother Tim calling.

"Whoa, there, man."

"Tim. I'm working. What's up that you called twice?"

He coughs. "Sorry. Alice asked me to make sure Emma was still coming to family dinner this weekend. She's out buying special lime leaves, apparently."

"Alice has my cell. Why didn't she call herself?" I don't mean to be so snippy with my brother. Actually, maybe I do. He was a dick to me, and he was fucking rude to Emma after that incident with Petey. At least he apologized to *her*.

Tim exhales noisily. I can almost see the veins pulsing in his neck. "She wanted me to call you myself," he says. He doesn't say that Alice has been giving him shit for how he's been treating me and he doesn't apologize, so I keep my cold demeanor.

"Emma and I will be there. I promise." After a beat, I add, "Please thank Alice for buying special food for Emma."

"Will do. See you then." He hangs up.

My concentration is totally wrecked. I can't even remember what I had wanted to do with that piece of glass. I pull the rod from the bucket and tap off the ruined glob. I'm about to dip back into the furnace for more when I hear my phone buzz yet again.

"WHAT?" I roar into the phone without looking at the caller ID.

"Jesus, Stag. I think everyone on the bus just heard you."

"Emma? I'm sorry. I thought you were my brother again. What's up?"

She squeaks. Actually squeaks. I can tell she's excited as she tells me about her meeting with her editor. The guy loved the story she wrote about me after our evening with Petey--Emma wouldn't let me read it of course. Said I have to wait until it goes to print. But what's really got her excited is that she got to pitch the story about Juniper.

"The whole staff was so pumped about the idea of the feature story about Juniper *and* they love the idea of looking into childcare in the work place. I'm going to do a whole feature, where I look at what Stag Law is doing and talk to some other companies with unique approaches to being family friendly."

I smile, and forget that she can't see me. "That's great, Chezz. I'm really glad this is working out."

"I feel so invigorated!" she says, her voice buzzing. "I can't wait to dive in and write all these stories. SO I wanted to thank you. It's not so bad faking a relationship with you in exchange for this career boost."

"Gee, thanks." I laugh. "Hey, while I have you, my sister in law went and bought special lime juice or something today. She wants to make sure you'll be there Sunday."

"Holy shit! She found kefir lime leaves? Oh my god. This is going to be amazing. I wouldn't miss it."

I make plans to pick her up with enough time to stop at the flower store--she insists she wants to buy a gift for Alice, which is pretty damn cute. I feel really glad that she wants to impress my family. By the time we hang up, I forget that I'm angry and I dive back into my work, ready to create.

72

EMMA

"Oh, god." I wake up Sunday and I just know. I can feel an aura. I haven't been getting enough sleep lately--have been staying up too late doing research. Fuck. If I take my meds, I'll sleep for 12 hours and I absolutely cannot afford to lose an entire day to this, so I take half a dose. I try to go back to bed for just a few hours, but by the time Thatcher is due to pick me up, I'm still nauseated and feeling sluggish.

I can't miss this dinner, not after Alice went out of her way to go and get special ingredients, not when I'm supposed to be doing pre-interviews with Thatcher's relatives. My career depends on this next month. Fuck this *condition*. I close my eyes and press my fingers against my temples, trying to block out the ring of pearlescent light that bathes everything.

I catch a glimpse of the glass sculpture that Thatcher gave me. It reflects the sunlight in my apartment, and for some reason, when I'm staring at it, everything is clear. The light appears normal. *Huh.* Guess I'll just stare at that glass neuron until he gets here. I slip into some passable jeans and grab the nearest clean t-shirt. I decide I have to take Thatcher at his word that dinner will be casual.

I don't hear him knocking. I'm staring at the neurons, trying to hold it together, and suddenly I hear his booming voice. "Emma! Yo! What is going on? Can you let me in? Are you washing your fucking hair or what?"

I exhale deeply and walk to the door, keeping my head as still as possible.

"Oh," he says, seeing me. "You feeling ok?"

I start to shake my head no, which is a mistake, and I have to bite back bile. "Just a touch of a headache," I tell him. "I'll be ok once I eat something."

I hope that's true. I grab my purse and follow Thatcher down the stairs slowly, and I let him help me into the truck. This is why I don't tell people about my condition. I hate the way he's looking at me right now, with pity and like I'm some helpless child. He's not even teasing me or acting rude. I don't want him to act differently just because--oh shit.

"Hey, Stag, please tell me you have pineapple in here and I'm not losing my mind." When I'm about to have a seizure, sometimes I smell things that aren't really there. Thatcher's whole truck smells like tropical fruit right now.

He lifts a plastic bag from the floor near my feet. "I brought fruit. I knew Alice was doing Thai so I grabbed pineapple and mango from Whole Paycheck earlier. You've got a good nose."

Relief floods through me. If I'm not smelling things that aren't there, I might be ok. I might make it through without humiliating myself and ruining his family dinner. I lean my head back on the headrest just as Thatcher puts an arm around the back of my seat. I look over at him as he turns to look behind him to back out of the parking spot. *Shit, that's hot.* He's got one hand on the wheel and his grey eyes are tight with concentration. The way my aura is working right now, his head is sort of glowing. I notice how attractive he is, under all that hair and beard. I can see the strong bones of his face, the tight muscles in his shoulders and forearms.

He catches me staring and grins. "Are you undressing me with your eyes, Chezz?" He shifts the truck into gear and heads toward the highway.

"Don't flatter yourself." I close my eyes and say, "don't forget I want to stop and grab some flowers for Alice."

"Check the bag, Chezz," he says, merging onto Route 28. "I clipped some lilac from out back. Alice loves lilacs." Sure enough, he's got a mason jar with fat, white blooms, tied in twine. His thoughtfulness surprises me. He really knows his family well, cares about them. *Why does he need a fake fiancé?* I decide to press him about it later. For now, I need to close my eyes and pray I can keep my wits about me.

By the time we get to the Stag homestead, as I've been imagining it, the place is brimming with people. Thatcher leads me around to the back yard, where clusters of picnic tables and coolers dot the yard. I see kids blowing bubbles while adults stand chatting, animatedly. Everyone looks so comfortable, so happy to be there. My family "picnics" are loosely veiled political fundraisers where everyone wears suits and stands stiffly, drinking from real glasses.

This just feels like comfort. I even feel my aura ease up in the shaded yard that smells of honeysuckle and cooking food. This could be ok. Alice pops out of the back door carrying a tray of skewered meat and vegetables. When she sees Thatcher and me, she shoves the tray into someone's hands and comes running through the yard. "You made it! I'm so glad!"

She pulls me in for a hug and I have to quickly move the flowers out of the way. I flush, feeling badly at taking advantage of her kindness with our illusion, but I hand her the blooms. She buries her nose into the flowers and says, "I love them. I'm going to put them on the windowsill." She links her arm through mine. "Come with me into the kitchen and meet Juniper."

Alice passes me around to all the women inside the house--her sister, Amy, who is hugely pregnant with her third son but still making it through three 12-hour nursing shifts each week; Anna Stag, the brothers' grandmother who lives on the third floor of Tim and Alice's house; and Juniper Jones. The bride to be, focus of my next feature assignment. Her smile is warm as she greets me. "Thatcher hasn't told us a thing about you," she says, "So we're all dying to know everything."

"Everything," says Anna, shoving a drink toward me. "Drink up and spill, Emma."

"Oh," I say. "I don't drink alcohol, actually. Is there maybe some water?"

Amy raises an eyebrow at me and pats her stomach. "Any particular reason you're off the booze? Is this why Thatcher is suddenly engaged out of the blue?"

Alice claps her hands and Juniper's jaw drops. Their grandmother laughs and slaps the counter. They all stare at me. I flush, my body filled with heat. "No! Oh my god. No. I just...I can't...there's a medication I take and I..."

My voice trails off. I don't want to explain all of this. Anna actually looks disappointed, and starts chugging the drink she'd prepared for me. Thankfully, Amy walks over with another glass. "Try this," she says. "It's watermelon blended with coconut milk and mint. You *almost* won't miss the rum that's not in it."

I exhale and take a sip. It's delicious--refreshing enough that my nausea passes and the weird glow of my aura subsides a little further. I thank her and brace myself for the inquisition that follows. By the time Alice is ready to announce dinner, I've given them the full lie Thatcher and I had planned out about how we met, reinforced that we don't want to steal from Juniper and Ty's celebration by making a big deal of our engagement, and I even managed to get Juniper's work number to call her this week about an interview.

"My coach will be beside himself about the publicity," she says. Everything is going so well. I sit down by Thatcher, who drapes an arm over my shoulder and glares at me when I instinctively stiffen. I try to relax, and then I sink my teeth into Alice's Thai feast and I feel like I could stay here forever, eating myself into oblivion.

73

THATCHER

"Emma seems cool, bro," Ty whispers as she walks over to get more food. "She's real down to earth compared to...well. She's cool." Ty sighs. I know he's remembering some of the other women I've brought to his games. Flashy women who never dress appropriately for an ice rink, but who never mind because I'm always happy to whisk them away and warm them up.

Ty's right about Emma. She's nothing like any of those women. She's totally at home here in jeans and a well-loved t-shirt with a pair of Toms. And she's eating, right in front of my family. As a matter of fact, I feel like I need to lean over and protect my bowl of Tom Kha soup so Emma doesn't steal it from me. I see why she got so excited to learn Alice had driven all over the place for the ingredients. I need to make more requests from Alice, because this shit is delicious. I slurp the last of the broth and swallow, clapping Ty on the back. "Thanks, Ty. She's all right I guess."

He laughs at what he thinks is just a wry joke. "How come she doesn't have an engagement ring?"

Shit. He noticed. "Well..." I need to stall. Emma and I hadn't really talked about this, but she comes to my rescue.

"I don't need one. I told Thatcher I'd rather we spend the money on a down payment for a house." I could kiss her for thinking so fast, but I promised I'd be a gentleman, so I settle for stroking her cheek. I only touch her because my family has to buy that we're a couple in love, so I'm a little taken aback by the spark of heat I feel when I connect with her skin. Maybe she's just hot. She looks a little pale, come to think of it, but she smiles for an instant before her face drops back to a worried look. She seems off, but I can only concentrate on her scent as she leans against my arm. She smells nice, fruity and fresh but not overpowering. *Different from the last time,* I think, then feel unsettled that I'm remembering her different scents. This is unexpected.

The conversation around the table shifts and everyone starts helping with cleanup. I notice Emma seems to be struggling a little to stand up. "Hey," I whisper into her ear. "You ok?"

She nods slightly, but doesn't meet my eyes. "Just...maybe I need some water."

"Stay here. I'll grab some for you." I walk over to the cooler to grab a bottle of water but I hear someone scream.

"Thatcher!"

I look up and Emma is on the ground. Her body is stiff and Amy is crouched over her. I can't tell what's going on, so I rush over, then I see her face and I freeze in shock and fear.

"Thatcher," Amy's voice comes through my fog and I look at her, still not speaking. "What do we need to know about Emma? She said she takes medication?"

"I...I..." I struggle for words. I have no fucking clue what Amy is talking about. I barely know this girl and she's having some sort of convulsions on the lawn of my brother's house. Emma's face is stiff, her eyes unseeing. Her body twitches violently on the lawn. A minute passes and she turns her head sharply and vomits in the grass.

I notice Amy fumbling around with Emma's arm, tugging on the bracelet she always wears. I squint and notice that the rose-colored metal has one of those snake symbols on it. A Medic Alert bracelet. *Huh.* "Ok we need to get her to the emergency department," Amy says.

"Emma has epilepsy, but I don't know if she's had her rescue medications or how long she's been seizing."

I can't seem to move or concentrate. "Seizing?" None of this makes sense. Wouldn't I have been able to tell if she had epilepsy?

"Thatcher!" Alice's sister is yelling at me and shaking my shoulders. "Pick her up and carry her to the car. We're going to the hospital." I do as she says and climb in the back seat of Amy's minivan with Emma. I have no idea what to do.

Amy climbs in the drivers seat and Alice leans in the window to hand me a package of wet wipes. "So you can clean her up a little bit," Alice says, patting my hand. I look at Emma and nod. Her body is relaxed now, but she's totally zonked.

"Amy, what the hell is going on here?"

Amy looks at me in the rear view mirror. "Hasn't this happened before? How long have you been together?"

I try to dodge that question. "Never, Aim. I have never seen her like this."

Amy sighs. "Some people go months without a big seizure, especially if they're managing their medications. From what Emma said in the kitchen she must be pretty careful."

"She did say she wasn't feeling awesome, but I didn't know that meant...what should I do?"

I see Amy shrug as she pulls into the turn-around at the hospital. "At this point we probably just give her some benzos and let her sleep. But they'll probably have her info on file." Amy parks the van. "Carry her inside and I'll meet you in there after I park. Tell whoever's in triage that you're with me."

I carry Emma's sleeping form inside and drop Amy's name. They take me right back to a small room with a gurney, so I get Emma situated. Her clothes are a wreck. The nurse asks if I want help getting Emma into a gown, and it feels wrong for me to undress her in this state, so I nod and step back while she works. I turn away and see Amy bustling down the hallways as fast as a hugely pregnant person can shuffle.

She gives me the side eye and helps the nurse lift Emma's hips to take off her jeans. I feel myself flush at the sight of Emma's pink flow-ered panties, and I turn away, feeling super uncomfortable about this whole situation.

I hear a young, deep voice finishing a phone call and look up to see a man in scrubs, carrying an iPad. "Amy, didn't think I'd see you until Tuesday. What've we got here?"

"Oh, Jeremy. I'm glad it's you. Listen, this is my brother-in-law's fiancé. Wait. Are you my brother in law? This is my sister's brother in law...his brother is married to--"

"Amy, spare me the ancestry report. What's wrong?"

"Emma had a seizure. Her medic alert bracelet says she has epilepsy but I don't know what meds she takes, if she took her rescues, anything. Thatcher here has just been totally numb with worry, which is sweet, but useless."

I don't even bother to scowl at her, because I do feel sort of shell-shocked. I pretend I'm too upset to remember her birth date, but I manage to spell Emma's last name for the doctor, who clicks around in his iPad. "Cheswick, Cheswick...here we go. Hm." He looks down at Emma and starts to examine her. I hear him ask the nurse for some-thing that sounds like ox, which can't be right, but he lifts one of her eyelids and shines a light in her eye. They hook some machines up to Emma while I shift my weight uncomfortably.

"Listen," Dr. Jeremy says to me. "You're not listed on her chart, so I need to call what I assume are her parents. I can't say much more than that, even to a colleague who isn't on duty." I nod and he gives some info to another person in scrubs. I look over at Amy with a pained expression.

Amy scowls and says, "Hypothetically, Jeremy, if a patient presented unconscious after a tonic-clonic seizure, what would your treatment be?"

Jeremy smiles and squeezes my arm. "Hypothetically, I'd check out her heart rate and her oxygen levels, do some tests, but mostly give her some meds to help her sleep and discharge her after she woke up. I'd have this hypothetical patient follow up with her neurol-ogist on Monday...except I believe I saw this patient's hypothetical neurologist in the coffee shop a few minutes ago. If you'll excuse me, I feel the need for caffeine."

Amy smiles as he walks down the hallway.

"What the hell just happened here?" I ask her. I really feel like my head is spinning.

"She's going to be fine. They called her parents to fill them in, so you'll probably see them soon. Are they as nice as Emma?"

Oh shit, I think. Suddenly our innocuous plan is dragging us both deeper into the damn swamp. Why does everything have to be so fucking complicated?

74

EMMA

When I wake up, I have no idea where I am, but I know I've had a seizure. *Shit.* It's been months. Months! My head aches, but the aura is gone and I feel, above all, complete relief. My senses and awareness slowly catch up to me, and I hear a familiar, unwelcome voice.

"I just don't understand what's going on here at all. Edward, *who* are these people? Who is this *caveman* in Emma's room? Why is she still down here and not in a private room upstairs? Where is that doctor? Edward?" My mother is on one of her rants, and I start putting things together before I attempt to open my eyes.

I must be in the hospital, which means they called my damn parents. I remember feeling better, but then worse and asking Thatcher to get me some water after dinner. The rest is totally gone. *Caveman...*

I open my eyes and I see Thatcher sitting in a chair across the room. He looks worried. His legs are spread wide and he's hunched over on his elbows, his chin in his hands. Amy is here, too. She struggles to stand up and I hear her friendly voice talking to my mother. "You must be Mrs. Cheswick! I'm so glad to meet you. I'm Amy. Alice's sister."

My father scowls, adjusting his tie. "And just who is Alice?" His voice is toneless. I can see him classifying Thatcher and Amy as unimportant.

"Thatcher," Amy looks at him uncomfortably. "Introduce me to Emma's parents."

"I can assure you," my mom cuts in, "that I have never seen this man before in my life."

Amy opens her mouth to start saying something, and I decide now is a good time for a distraction. I groan and try to sit up.

"Oh, dear. You're awake." My mother bustles over to the bed and puts the back of her hand against my forehead. "I just knew this was bound to happen."

"Of course, Mom. I have seizures because I have epilepsy. Not because I moved into the city."

She clucks her tongue at me and starts asking a million questions about "this new aged neurologist" she doesn't approve of. Just because the guy she and dad sent me to for years couldn't control my symptoms and would never try any new medications...or even read about trials that might be helpful. "This is a research hospital, Mom. They know what they're doing here."

My father snorts and my mother looks over at Thatcher and Amy again. "Emma, shouldn't your *friends* be heading home now, dear?" I hate her tone. I hate everything about the way my parents judge anyone who doesn't seem like they're going to cut a huge campaign donation.

"Look," Amy's on her feet now, and a pregnant, frustrated Amy is apparently no one to be trifled with. "I don't know why you'd talk about Emma's fiancé this way, but I'm going to assume you're all just upset and in shock. So I'm going to go home and eat dessert. Thatcher, call me later."

Amy saunters out of the room just as the word "fiancé" registers with my mother.

"Fiancé?" she repeats it about six times, her voice increasing an octave each time. "Don't be *ridiculous,* Emma. You cannot marry someone like...you cannot marry this man. Do you even know this man? Where did you meet?"

"Look, Mrs. Cheswick," now Thatcher is on his feet. "You really don't get to talk about me this way. I don't give a shit who you are or how much your pearls cost. I'm here to support Emma and my guess is she has a pretty bad headache right now, so you're going to need to tone it down or I'm going to get someone to escort you out."

My face breaks into the biggest smile I can remember smiling. Nobody ever speaks to my mother this way. I want to watch as she sputters and tries to gather her wits, but even being awake this long has been difficult. My body needs to sleep.

"Emma Cheswick," she hisses at me. "Are you engaged to be *married* to this barbarian?"

"Mom, Dad, this is Thatcher Stag," I croak. "And he's right about the headache. I promise to tell you all about him when I wake up, but for now I need to go back to sleep." I feel the medication kicking in. They must have given me an IV. Yes, there. I can feel it in my hand now that I focus on it. I am vaguely aware of my mother and father arguing, then leaving the room. I drift off, sinking into sleep.

I WAKE UP AGAIN. I know I'm in the hospital, but I have no idea how much time has passed. I don't hear anyone in my room. I feel the urge to stretch, and find that I can, easily, though my muscles are aching. When I try to sit up, I see that Thatcher is still in my room. That's unexpected.

"Hey," he says. "You're up." He puts down a notebook where he'd been writing something. Sketching?

"What time is it?" There are no windows in my room. Am I still in the emergency department?

"Well, Chezz," he says, reaching for a cup of coffee. "It's about 9am."

I sit bolt upright. "It's Monday? Shit!" I start to get out of the bed, flinging the IV line, but Thatcher walks over and touches my arm.

"Hey," he says. "Don't be mad at me. But I called the receptionist at the Post and told her you were sick. I didn't say with what."

"You did that for me?" I look into his eyes. "That was very thoughtful, Thatcher. Thank you." I am definitely in no shape to go to work today. But I still feel desperate to get home. I hate that I've lost most of a day. I'm going to be so behind on work and--then I remember. I had a seizure at Thatcher's family dinner. "Your family. What must they think of me?" I bury my hands in my hair, tugging in frustration.

"Well, they've called here about 8 million times, worried sick and asking why I didn't tell them you have epilepsy."

I snort. "Because it's none of their damn business."

"Well I guess that's why you didn't tell *me* you have epilepsy, then." Thatcher scratches his beard. "So what does all this mean?" He gestures around the room.

I sigh. "It means I felt this coming on yesterday, but I didn't want to cancel on you...or Alice, so I didn't take the medication I should have. It was stupid. I haven't had a seizure in--well, it's been over a year."

"Emma, you don't have to put your health at risk for this...me. I--"

"This is why I don't tell people, Stag." I snap at him. "I don't want your pity or your deep concern or your fake, polite kindness. We both know that's not you. I don't tell people because I don't want to be treated differently or given a pass for family dinner. It's my business. I'm an adult."

"Ok, ok. Chill out, Chezz. Jesus."

"Oh, so I'm 'Chezz' now and not 'sweetheart?'"

Thatcher gives me an odd look and throws a plastic bag at me. "I got your keys from your purse and got you some fresh clothes from your apartment."

I look down at the bag. This is so totally unexpected that I have no idea how to respond. This is something Nicole would do. This is a friend move. I don't trust many people to know what I need without my having to ask them for help. I swallow.

He chugs the rest of his coffee and throws the cup in the trash.

"Why don't you get dressed and I'll drive you home. Your doctor said you were good to go whenever you woke up." I nod slowly and he steps into the hall, pulling the curtain closed around the doorway as he leaves the room.

75

THATCHER

I start pacing the halls of the emergency department, waiting for Emma to get dressed. This whole thing is getting really intense. After she fell asleep and her parents left, I drove around the city for a long time, just trying to calm down. No wonder she's secretive and private, if her parents are like that. I know I don't look like my brother Tim, between all my piercings and tattoos and facial hair. But who the fuck wants to look like that? Fuck Emma's dad for thinking that's the only way to hold value in the world.

I've got a piece of my glass in the damn MOMA for fuck's sake. I'm not sure why I care so much what this guy thinks of me. I see assholes like him all the time. Emma and I have 3 weeks of this left and then we're going to part ways. She and I are about as different as two people can be. I don't see us hanging out socially after this whole thing is said and done.

I'm about to turn around and walk back to her room, make sure she's safe to walk to the car, when I see something that makes my blood run cold. I feel my throat closing, my heart racing, the muscles in my limbs spasming as I clutch the wall.

My father is lying on one of the beds in the ER.

I stand opposite his room, staring at his form on the bed. I know it's him, even though I haven't laid eyes on him for over a decade. He sank into a depression and buried himself in a bottle when our mom died, leaving us home with only Tim to parent us. But you don't forget what your dad looks like. Momentarily breaking my trance, I huff out a laugh, noticing my father and I have the same hairdo and facial hair these days. I hope my fucking beard doesn't look like his, though. Christ, I can smell the urine on him from across the hall.

I'm clutching the wall, breathing heavy, staring at him, when a nurse comes walking down the hall. "Oh," she says. "Hello! Are you here to take Ted home?"

"Excuse me?" My eyes go wide. Take him home?

"You must be related to him," she says. "You look exactly like him." She sighs. "He's what we call a frequent flyer. We never see any family in here with him."

That shakes me back to consciousness. "Yeah, because he fucking walked out on his family and drank away our livelihood." I punch the wall, not caring that I'll have bruised knuckles and won't be able to shape glass today. Fuck. I haven't let myself feel angry at him for a long time.

"I'm sorry, sir." The nurse grits her teeth. She must see a lot of angry family members here in this department.

"I'm sorry...Robin, is it? You don't need to be hearing that from me."

She nods and makes her way down the hall. Lord. What am I supposed to do now? I can't just fucking walk out of here now that I know my fucking father is lying across the hall from Emma.

"FUCK!" I let myself scream just once. Hardly anyone is around at this time of day. Nobody even looks at me, except him.

He opens his eyes and turns his head my way, and our eyes lock. I stand, breathing through my nose, staring at the man who walked out on our family, who forced Tim into a role he shouldn't have had to worry about until his own son was born. I've thought about this moment, about what I would do if I ever saw my father again. In some versions of my fantasy, I beat the shit out of him. Sometimes I cuss him out, screaming in his face until my veins throb and my voice is raw. Most often, I make eye contact and then walk away.

Today, faced with the reality of seeing him, I stand frozen and silent. Staring.

"Son." His voice is hoarse, wavering. It snaps me back into full consciousness.

"It's Thatcher," I spit at him, still shouting from across the hallway.

His eyes flare for a moment. "You think I don't know which one you are?"

"I think you don't think about us at all," I shout back at him, and a passing employee shoots daggers at me with her eyes. I step closer to my father's room, hovering in the doorway. "I think you lost the right to speak to me casually when you walked the fuck out of our lives."

He closes his eyes. "I know I don't deserve your kindness right now."

"You're fucking right you don't." I make to walk back toward Emma's room, but his next words freeze me in my tracks again.

"I'm dying, son."

As I stand there breathing deeply, the thin metal frame of the dividing wall supporting my full weight, Emma emerges from down the hall. She gives me a watery smile and makes her way toward me, tentatively. "Sorry about earlier," she says. "Who's this?"

I don't look at him. I take Emma's elbow and guide her toward the exit. "Nobody," I tell her. "Let me take you home."

76

EMMA

Thatcher tries to lift me into his truck and I swat away his arm. "I can get in the damn truck by myself," I growl at him. But it's hard to climb up into the cab with my muscles aching. I'm exhausted, and realizing I need his help after all just pisses me off worse. My body feels like I got hit by this truck rather than lifted into it. "This is why I don't tell anyone," I say, resting my head against the glass. "Now you think of me as some victim."

I expect Thatcher to come back at me, for us to argue and fight about how he does or does not treat me, but he just stares ahead as he crosses the bridge to take me to my apartment. I close my eyes eventually, resting for the short trip, until he parks outside my door. I climb out of the truck and turn to thank him for giving me a ride, but he's already gotten out of the truck. He surprises me by following me up the steps and inside my duplex.

"I can...uh...take it from here, I'm pretty sure."

He sighs. "Cheswick, can I come in?"

I wrinkle my brow at him. "I guess so? You know I'm just going to go to bed, right?"

He nods and follows me up. I toss my stuff on the counter and stare at him. He leans against a column with his hands in his jeans pocket. "The guy at the hospital? That was my father."

"Your dad?"

He shakes his head adamantly. "Tim is my 'dad.' That guy was my biological father, who walked out on us, left us all for a bottle of booze when my mom died and he couldn't handle...all of it."

"What's wrong with him? Shouldn't you go back to the hospital and sit with him instead of me?"

Thatcher sinks into the couch and I join him, looking at him expectantly. He leans his head back against the wall with enough force that it rattles the pictures I have hung there. "He just told me he's dying. I haven't seen him in over ten years."

I don't really know what to say to this revelation from him, so I slide closer and grab his hand, giving him a squeeze. His skin is warm and smoother than I expected from someone who works with his hands all day. "Tell me more," I say.

Thatcher begins to talk, telling me about the car accident that killed his mother, how their grandmother moved in afterward to help with the needs of 3 young, motherless boys, and how Ted Stag drank more and more, helped less and less, until he lost his job. The boys were a handful, and Anna Stag wasn't always up to the work of parenting 3 angry Stags. Eventually Ted drifted away from their house, not to be heard from again. The Stag brothers lived on a life insurance payout and social security checks that Tim apparently had to cash using slightly-nefarious deception so nobody official became aware that the boys technically had no legal guardian at home.

"That's a really heavy burden your brother took on," I say. I hear echoes of my father's voice booming through my head about "lazy" people who "game the system" to receive handouts, who abuse safety net services. Then I remember what my mother said about Thatcher in the hospital.

"Holy shit, Thatcher. I'm sorry to interrupt you. I just need to apologize for what my mother said to you. My god, that was inexcusable." I pull his hand to my chest, pleading with him. I'm overcome with embarrassment. He's pouring his heart out to me, took care of me after I had a seizure at his family dinner party, and my mother called him a caveman.

He laughs, a bitter sound. "She's not wrong, is she? I'm the son of a deadbeat, I'm covered in ink, and I'm having inappropriate thoughts about her daughter."

I flush at this last bit, but choose to ignore it. "Thatcher, I can't tell you how sorry I am that you were put in a position where you had to endure someone speaking to you that way. I try and I try to distance myself from my parents, but sometimes..."

"They always come back to fuck with us, don't they?" He reaches out and tucks my hair behind my ear. The gesture surprises me as much as his words of understanding.

"Yes," I whisper. And then I just stare at him for a long time. We sit in quiet together, just feeling each other's heartache. Finally I can't stay awake any longer and I tell him, "I really need to go to bed now."

"I'll be here when you wake up," he says.

"Don't be ridiculous," I start to argue with him. He touches a finger to my lips to shush me. I bite my lip and my eyes go wide.

"My family has been blowing up my phone for hours," he reminds me. "They're never going to buy it if I don't stay here and take care of you. Alice is going to drop off some food later, in fact, after she serves lunch at Stag Law. Go on and sleep. Wait. Tell me your Wi-Fi password, and then go sleep."

77

THATCHER

While Emma sleeps, I pace her living room. I try to sketch out some ideas in my notebook, but I keep thinking back to my father in that bed. Dying, he said. How many times had I prayed for him to just go on and die? To be finally and definitely gone from our lives versus *choosing* to leave us for some other sort of life?

I'm itching to get back in my studio, but my family would give me endless shit if I left Emma here after having a seizure. When Alice texts me that she's outside with some food, I leap up and open the door so quickly, it startles her.

"Hey, sorry about that." I pull the takeout containers from her before she drops them. "Want to come in?" Should I be inviting Alice into Emma's house? I don't really know the etiquette for fake-fiancé personal space.

"Just for a minute," Alice says. "I want to write down info about the food for Emma."

Alice pulls out a notepad and starts taking notes on each container. She seems to have brought an entire week's worth of meals, all sorted and arranged. "Jesus, Alice. This is so much food!"

Alice nods. "Don't you eat a bite of it, either. It's not for you.

Hands off." Alice has baggies of herbs and toppings for tacos, fresh bread to go with soup, chicken parm with sauce in a separate container and..."Alice! Did you make pasta from scratch today?"

"Yes. I'm writing Emma a note that she should probably eat the noodles first. They'll be really good today. Let me tell you, Juniper really enjoyed those at lunch! The Stag Law staff all ate very well today." Alice finishes her manual of notes and sighs, smiling.

"Ok, I have to get back to the office. I want to give Petey a squeeze, but I wanted to talk with you about this weekend."

"This weekend?"

Alice rolls her eyes at me. "Do you ever open your computer? There was a whole email chain."

"Who was on the chain?"

Alice bites her lip. "Well, it was mostly me and Juniper and Ty. But you and Tim were included, I swear! And if you give me Emma's email I can loop her in."

"Loop her into what, Alice?"

"Ty and Juniper wanted a Stag Weekend. Instead of a bachelor party or bachelorette party? Get it--Stag? Thatcher, I absolutely know you were with us when we started planning...anyway! Obviously Emma is invited, but I wanted to find out from you if she would be feeling up to going."

I'm about to tell Alice Emma will, in fact, not feel up to a weekend away with the Stag clan, which means I should probably stay home with her to help her "recuperate," when a woman with voluminous blond waves, stiletto heels, and an impeccable manicure opens the door to Emma's apartment.

"Well, well, well," she says, looking at me. "So it is true." The woman tosses a cardigan over one of the stools at Emma's counter and then stands in a model pose in the middle of the room, crossing her arms and glaring at me. Alice looks back and forth between us, speechless for the first time since I met her.

"Can I help you?" I have to tread lightly here, because I have no idea who this woman is but can't let Alice know that Emma and I are basically strangers.

"When Mom called me hysterical crying because Emma is apparently engaged to a 'street fighter,' I had to come see for myself what all the commotion was. I am going to murder her just as soon as she gets her ass out here. She *knew* I was planning to announce my engagement to Logan this weekend! She just had to steal my thunder. As per usual."

Alice raises an eyebrow and opens her mouth to speak. I can tell she's about to launch into defense mode, so I place my hand on her shoulder. "Hey, Al, why don't you go back to work and hug your baby and let me handle this, ok? I'll call you when Emma wakes up and we will talk about the weekend." I usher Alice out the door. I'm pretty used to this sort of treatment from "upstanding" citizens. Sure, they all want a piece of my rogue artwork for their great room, because some critic called my glass "haunting and de rigueur." But none of them want to mingle with me outside of a gallery space. Which is fine with me, because these people drive me crazy.

I close the door behind my sister-in-law and stand opposite the intruder. "I assume you're the perfect sister?"

She snorts and flings her hair back over one shoulder. "I'm Veronica Cheswick, yes. And don't think I didn't Google you. I know you were seen last week, leaving a club with a woman who was not my sister, so don't feed me some bullshit line about being desperately in love with Emma. What's your game, Stag? Why is she set on spoiling my engagement announcement?"

I am taken aback to realize other people look at pictures of me online, leaving clubs with the women I fuck. What the hell else is out there about me in cyberspace? Alice is right--I need to open my computer more often. I pull it together, though, and retort to Veronica. "I can assure you Emma had no intention of spoiling your engagement announcement. She and I have kept our relationship on the D-L because, as I'm sure you saw during your research, my own brother is getting married and neither of us wanted to take away from his moment."

I can tell Veronica doesn't buy it entirely, but she starts tapping her foot and looks around. "Where is my sister, anyway?"

"She's in bed," I say, and then, feeling bold, I add, "where the hell does she usually go after a seizure?"

Veronica sighs, and a look of concern crosses her face. "She hasn't had a big one for awhile," she says, her voice quiet. "Mom is hysterical, and deflecting by freaking out about how it will look if Emma marries someone with tattoos and facial piercings."

"What the hell does anyone care how it looks if Emma's happy?"

This pulls a laugh from Veronica. "Oh, my. Thatcher Stag, you have a lot to learn about the Cheswick family." She picks up her sweater. "Tell Emma I stopped by and please have her call me when she's out of her fog." Veronica heads back out the door. At the last minute, she turns around and says, "She gets really, really sore after a big seizure. I brought her some Tiger Balm." She hands me the tiny tin of ointment and clacks out of Emma's apartment.

When Veronica leaves, I exhale deeply and sink into the couch. This tiny lie to get my brother off my back is becoming a huge, heavy web of confusion. I just want to get back to my life where I spend my afternoons creating amazing fucking artwork, my nights partying hard, and my mornings sleeping it all off. I am grateful to Veronica for at least distracting me from my father for a few minutes.

Thinking on what she said as she left, I text Juniper to ask if she knows any massage therapists who make house calls. I figure if I'm about to spring a weekend out of town with my family on Emma, the least I can do is butter her up first. I set up an appointment for tomorrow afternoon and then I decide it's been too long since I slept. I kick back onto Emma's couch and fall asleep in seconds.

78

EMMA

I feel so much better when I wake up. My muscles ache, my neck throbs in particular, but my head is clear. My relief is over-whelming, almost like I needed to have that seizure to feel normal again. I hadn't even realized I felt it building. I stretch and look at the clock. Five pm. I have basically been asleep for an entire day since having the seizure, which means my inbox will be full and I'll have about ten messages from my mother in my voicemail. I decide to shower, find food, and then tackle my phone.

After marinating in the hot water for much longer than usual, I wrap a towel around my head and walk into the kitchen. One of my favorite perks of living alone, I decide, is the ability to sit stark naked at my counter and eat without worrying about getting food on my shirt.

I whistle, marveling at how clear my head feels, and walk to the sink to fill the coffee pot. While I turn on the water, I happen to look toward the living room and I scream.

I drop the pot to the tile floor, and the glass shatters as I keep screaming.

Thatcher Stag sits up on my couch, rubbing the sleep from his eyes and then staring at me, open-mouthed. "Shit," he says.

"What the fuck are you doing here?" My voice is shrill and, having nothing in my hands, I move to cover my breasts and crotch.

"Don't move," he says, walking toward me.

"Don't come near me!! I'm naked."

He keeps approaching. "I can see that, Emma, and I'll try to look away, ok, but there's broken glass and you're barefoot."

I start looking around, wildly, unsure how to proceed here. Thatcher steps into his sneakers and walks toward me. "Woah," he says. "You have red pubes."

"Fuck you, Thatcher!" This is like a nightmare.

"I'm sorry, I'm sorry," he says, walking toward me and averting his eyes. "I just...the women I sleep with don't really ever have pubic hair. So..."

"Can you spare me the sexy storytime?"

He nods, keeping his head turned. As he approaches me in the kitchen, he reaches toward my head. I stiffen, but he's pulling the towel off my hair. "Here," he says, his voice surprisingly gentle. "You can cover up with this." He walks toward the fridge, where I have the dustpan and broom wedged between the appliance and the wall, and I hastily wrap the towel around my body. I stand stock still as he stoops to clean up the glass.

"What are you still doing here?" I whisper.

He pours the fragments into the trash and squints, looking around the kitchen. "I think I got it all," he says, "but just to be safe." He picks me up effortlessly and carries me over to the hall, placing me down as I stare at him with wide eyes. "I told you I'd be here when you woke up," he says, shrugging. "Go on and get dressed. I have to tell you what happened."

Five minutes later, when I'm safely dressed in sweats, Thatcher reminds me that my parents were rude, tells me how my sister stopped by to complain and maybe gloat, and he shows me the feast Alice left. Since there's no way I can eat all this before it goes bad, and since I've just about gotten over my humiliation at Thatcher seeing me naked, I decide to share the chicken parm and fresh pasta with him. He did, after all, hang out while I slept to make sure I was ok.

Twice.

He makes me laugh, impersonating my sister's hair toss while we wait for the water to boil for the noodles Alice hand rolled this morning. I fill him in on my family, avoiding eye contact. "My dad is a state senator," I tell him. "Our politics are polar opposites, Thatcher. I disagree with almost every measure he supports."

Thatcher tests a noodle and moans. "These are done," he says, shutting off the burner and draining the pasta. "Look, Emma. You can't help who your parents are and neither can I. Don't feel bad about that shit."

"Yeah, but it's not so easy figuring out how to navigate *seeing* your parents whose choices you hate, is it?" I know I've got him there. He's clearly thinking about seeing his father in the hospital as we go on to eat in silence. As soon as Thatcher finishes, he rinses his dishes and stands beside me.

"Don't make any plans after work tomorrow," he tells me. "I have a surprise for you." I raise an eyebrow, but he won't elaborate. "Call me when you get home from work, ok? We need to talk." He sidles out of the apartment, and I try not to stare at his ass as he leaves. Or the way his shoulder muscles move inside his t-shirt. *Shit,* I think. *He just saw me naked.* Thatcher Stag has probably seen a thousand women naked, and he basically admitted he was only taking a clinical interest in my bush. *Of course* the supermodels he fucks don't have pubic hair. There's no reason to think that he might still be thinking of this as anything but a mutually beneficial, non-sexual arrangement. I remind myself that he also saw me seizing on the ground at his brother's house, throwing up...but he didn't run away screaming.

Rather than think about why it would bother me so much if he had, I decide to read my emails and check my voicemails. After I call Nicole.

"Talk to me, Emma. You've been radio silent since the Reindeer party." I hit the major points of the disaster that was the past 24 hours while she runs on the treadmill in her office. "Do you need me to come over with tequila?" she asks.

"I know you're joking," I tell her. "But I appreciate the sentiment."

79

THATCHER

I can't get the image of Emma out of my head. She stood naked and gleaming in the sunlight in her kitchen. And even though her face was contorted in shock at me seeing her naked, I still have this memory of her bathed in light, glowing. She looked ephemeral. Supernatural. And so fucking perfect. Her body is everything, all curves and soft lines. Creamy skin. And Christ. That hair. Her red hair. Knowing I can't haul her into her bedroom and ravage her body, I settle for the next best thing to unleash all this energy. I drive as fast as I can and rush into my studio to work some glass.

I dip into the furnace and gather a ball of molten glass and sit to shape it at my work bench. Pulling long fragments, twisting, sprinkling on color, I work in a frenzy. I know hours pass. I sense the light shifting in the studio as the sun sets, but I don't want to stop even to turn on the overhead lights. I work by the light of the furnace as I sculpt the tendrils of glass just so, angle the reds and golden threads until I'm satisfied. This work is my lust, my anger, my fear. This is Emma, contorted with illness and rising in triumph. This piece is everything, passion and depth. So much color.

I haven't felt that inspired in months. I exhale and sit back, staring at what I've made. This is light and fury and fire. I shape a base so it will rest, stable, and then slide it into the kiln to slowly come down to room temperature, so the fragile material won't shatter.

Only then do I pause and breathe. I just sit in stillness. I feel so fucking calm after I've worked out all these ideas into the glass. It's a meditation for me, the way I find clarity. When I'm done, I can see what I need to do. I need to face my father, and find out just what the fuck he means when he says he is dying. I lock up the studio and drive back to the hospital.

I think the staff is starting to recognize me. I get a smile from the receptionist when I ask for Ted Stag's room. As she prints out my visitor badge, I realize that a week ago, I'd be slipping her my number, making plans to go fuck her in a utility closet before getting on with my day. *Huh,* I think. *I don't even feel like doing that.*

It's surprising--this lack of an urge to block out the world with some meaningless sex.

I take the elevator up to the floor where my father is staying. Apparently they usually release him when he sobers up, but this time they say they've found some things and need to keep an eye on him in-patient. He's asleep, his yellow-tinged skin practically glowing in the hospital lights. I wander over to the nurse's station to ask for the Cliff Notes version of what's wrong with him, and someone tells me they'll page the doctor.

While I'm waiting, my brother Ty texts me a few times, but I don't even feel like I can answer his questions about our cabin trip. I'm worried I'll give something away, somehow reveal that I'm standing a foot away from the man who abandoned us.

"Mr. Stag? Dr. Stone." An older man approaches me with his hand extended. "I must say, it's a pleasure to finally see a loved one here with Ted."

I try not to snort. "He said he's dying," I say, shaking the doctor's hand.

Stone exhales. "These conversations are never easy. Can I get you something? Coffee?"

I shake my head. "Just lay it on me. What's wrong with him? Specifically?"

I spend the next half hour learning about advanced liver failure, and how the only cure is liver transplant. They can't put my father on an organ list because he's still actively abusing alcohol. Dr. Stone is stern when he meets my eye and says, "if your father can remain sober for six months, we could not only assess whether his liver restores function on its own in the absence of alcohol, but it can prove to us that he is serious about staying sober if he were to receive a transplant operation."

There's really nothing I can think to say in response to that, so I just sit and stare at the bed until eventually Dr. Stone pats my shoulder and excuses himself. He leaves me with his card and some info about a rehab program they recommend. He also hands me a pamphlet about living organ donation.

80

EMMA

Tuesday, I wake up feeling energetic and sore as hell. I limp my way into work, hoping the walk will do me some good, but it's hard to concentrate. I'm thankful Phil doesn't have anything too complicated for me to work on. When I finally get home from work, I see a brown paper grocery bag on my stoop. My name is written on the bag in marker, with a note: *Hope this is the right size.*

I look inside and gasp to see a hand-blown coffee carafe. The bowl is clear with swirls of green and gold, and the thick, sturdy handle fits perfectly in my hand. I hurriedly unlock my apartment and, as fast as my aching, post-seizure body can move, hustle to the coffee machine, where I see that it is indeed the right size. I'm in the middle of fishing my phone from my bag to thank Thatcher for his surprise, when there's a knock at the door.

I peek through the window and see a sturdy-looking woman on my stoop, holding a folding table. "Can I help you?" I say, opening the door partially.

"Emma Cheswick? I'm Lucy, the massage therapist. Thatcher Stag sent me?"

Oh my god! This man not only makes me an artisanal coffee pot to replace the one I broke in nude shock, but he also sends me a massage therapist? The one thing in the world I really needed today but hadn't had an opportunity to arrange? *Is he for real?* I feel bad that my immediate thought is to wonder what he wants in exchange for all of this. I can't help but remember how he behaved when we first met, the sleazy, self-assured confidence that I was going to sleep with him in the greenhouse before his opening.

Lucy smiles at me expectantly, so I open the door for her. "I...don't know what to do. I haven't ever had...I didn't know Thatcher had hired you..."

"Don't worry about a thing!" she says, looking around. "I think I have plenty of room to set up in the living room. Give me five minutes and we can get started."

This gives me just enough time to fire off a text to the mysterious, ever-surprising Mr. Stag. **Are you for real with these gifts?**

You should make Lucy some coffee with your new, fragile *pot.*

Seriously, thank you, Thatcher. I don't know what to say here.

How about you let me come massage you instead?

Of course. Of course he wants to make this into some sex fantasy. **There it is. Pass.**

;) I'm kidding! But call me after.

I bite my lip as a thought forms. Before I can talk myself out of it, I type back **Just come over in an hour. We can eat the next meal from Alice.**

LUCY FINISHES SETTING up the table and soon, I am a blissed out puddle as her strong hands work out all the ache from my bones. We talk about my epilepsy, since it seems relevant, and it's so refreshing that she knows about seizures. Some of her clients suffer from them, too, and she knows just what to do to help me feel better. She pays special attention to my feet, which I hadn't even realized were bothering me until she starts to knead my arches. I could get used to this, for sure. When she's done, I pretty much roll onto the couch, guzzling water as per Lucy's instructions. I melt into the cushions, feeling my inhibitions slide away alongside my soreness. Thatcher knocks on the door and I holler at him to come in.

He laughs, seeing me sprawled out. "You look like you just smoked a bowl, Chezz."

"Mmm," I nod. "I actually have a meeting with my neurologist about that next week. There's a clinical trial at the medical school. For epilepsy."

"No shit?" His eyebrows fly up. He lifts my feet and sits down on the couch. My legs drape across his lap, and I feel the firm warmth of his thighs under my calves. He moves so casually that I hope he doesn't notice me squirm as heat floods my core. "I'd be down to help you with your research, Chezz. If you need someone to sample the goods and make sure they're safe, and all."

"Very funny," I tell him. I need to sit up and get my feet off his lap before I start stroking his crotch with my toes. I don't understand what's going on with my attraction to him right now. It's like my animal mind is attracted to his hot body and thoughtful favors, super-seding my rational brain who remembers that he's a screw-'em-and-leave-'em kind of guy. Maybe this is just him working hard to get in my pants.

Before I can decide if that would be a bad thing, I stand up to reheat the next layer of Alice delights. "Asian stir-fry today," I tell him, reading from the label. "With coconut Jasmine rice. God, she's amazing."

"She definitely is," he says. Thatcher walks over to the island and winds his long, muscular legs around one of my stools. As I wait for the microwave I stare at his jeans. His thigh must be two feet long. My cheeks flush as I think about how easy it would be to reach over and just give it a rub. When he starts to talk again, I yelp a little bit, drawn out of my fantasy. "So I was hoping Lucy would grease you up so you'd be more amenable for my next big ask for Operation Fake Fiancé," he says.

"Hm?" I slide him a dish of stir-fry.

"I forgot there's a bachelor/bachelorette thing this weekend. My brothers, their ladies, and us, holed up in a cabin in Deep Creek."

"This weekend?" I set down my fork and pull up my calendar app on my phone. "Oh. Shit. Fuck. That's why Veronica was so pissed." Everything comes back to me with my sister dropping hints about our family dinner this weekend. "Logan and Veronica are getting engaged." I reach for my fork, take a big bite, and look again at the calendar. "What are the details of this Deep Creek thing? My mom's going to want us to come pretend we're excited for Veronica and her country club friends."

"That sounds fun," Thatcher says, grinning. "I can put a hoop in my nose. Your mother will love it."

I almost spit out my food laughing. "You're terrible," I tell him, sort of hoping he's not joking. We map out the logistics. He's going to pick me up from work Friday with bags packed. We will duck out of the Stag party early on Sunday, leaving enough time to get to the country club for Veronica's perfect announcement. I'm actually looking forward to bringing him with me. There's never anyone I feel comfortable around when I'm out with my family, least of all my perfect sister and her perfect degree in political science and her perfect relationship with my father's chief of staff.

I feel sparks run down my spine when Thatcher's hand tucks a lock of hair behind my ear. "What's on your mind, Chezz?"

"Oh." I flush. His touch is really starting to affect me in ways I hadn't bargained for. "I was just thinking I am glad I will have an ally at this thing Sunday."

He smiles at me and his grey eyes are molten with...something. Can he be feeling this heat, too? I clear my throat and shift the conversation back to work, telling him about how excited everyone has been about his feature story and how much they're looking forward to reading about Juniper. "This weekend will really give me a chance to grill her," I tease.

Later, when he leaves and I sink back into the couch, I can smell traces of him. Spicy deodorant, the smoky smell of his workshop, and the lingering, wonderful scent of Thatcher Stag himself. **I think I'm in trouble, I** text Nicole. **I might be into this guy.**

81

THATCHER

I have no idea what the fuck I am doing lately. As I drive home from Emma's place, all I can think about is the feel of her ankles. I picked up her legs and put them in my lap without thinking, like I'd been doing it for years, but when my skin made contact with hers, I thought my dick was going to spring out of my pants.

Her legs felt like warm velvet, her peachy skin soft and silky from her massage. I could barely understand what she was saying as we talked, because all I was thinking about was how badly I wanted her to rub her foot just a few inches higher up my thigh as she squirmed around.

When I go to bed, I dream about Emma, her red hair sprawled over my sheets, her eyes closed in pleasure as I lick every inch of her skin. I wake up with my dick in my hand, so close to release. Panting, I close my eyes again, imagining holding my weight above her body, plunging into her depths. A few strokes of my fist are all it takes to send me over the edge. I can almost feel her body grip around my shaft as I pump once, twice. I groan as a fountain of white-hot cum hits me in the chest. I lie in bed breathing heavily, trying to figure out what to do about this. I don't even know how to go after a woman when it matters to me if she turns me down.

I remember when my brother Tim first met Alice, how he told me she distracted him, how thinking of her made him do things he'd never consider, otherwise. I realize I can't call him to ask for advice about it, though, because he thinks Emma is already engaged to marry me. How stupid would I sound telling him I need to figure out how to get her to like me when we're supposed to be in love?

I HAVE a meeting today with my agent about my next gallery show. I want to show her the new piece, but I feel suddenly private about it. Like I don't even want to display it. It's too personal, somehow. I'm still standing there staring at it on the shelf when I hear the studio door open. Cody walks in with Maria, my agent. He's looking scruffy as ever, dressed like me in jeans with an old t-shirt. Maria looks elegant in a blazer and slacks.

"Cody told me you have something new for the Warhol show," she says, practically jumping up and down.

"Cody should keep his fat mouth shut," I tell her with a sigh. I show her all the work I've finished since the opening at the conservatory, trying to avoid my private piece, but Maria sees it over my shoulder.

"My God, Thatcher. It's breathtaking." She reaches out a hand to touch it and I feel compelled to bat her arm away. I remember who I'm dealing with and catch myself in time, but Maria sees the movement. "Hm," she says, "Feeling protective of this one?"

She steps back a few feet and looks at my work. "Something happened here," she says, pointing to the things I finished since Sunday. "What happened?"

"What do you mean?"

"There's a shift," she says. She waves her hand around at the shelf. "The energy is different here. Something changed about your work. And then we have this." She points at my piece.

I blush, and I'm shocked to be blushing, which makes me blush harder, until Cody laughs. "Thatcher's been hanging out with a woman," he tells Maria, and I kick him.

Maria's jaw drops. "The *same* woman? More than once?"

I shake my head. "It's not like that," I tell her. "She's...we're friends."

This draws a laugh from my long-time agent. She's been chasing down my work since I displayed it at an art show in high school. "You don't have female friends, Thatcher Stag. I've seen you. Women, for you, are for sex and, in my case, for brokering art deals." When I don't say anything, she plunks her bag on the table and sits on a stool. "So. Tell me what you know about Alex Clemont."

"The architect?" Alex Clemont is hot stuff right now in Pittsburgh. His name turns up in the buzz alongside every new restaurant opening, every new boutique...his eye for design is putting Pittsburgh on the map.

Maria nods and slides me a proposal. "He's in the middle of styling his new bar, opening in Lawrenceville. It's going to be a gin joint in some refurbished firehouse. He saw your work at the conservatory and wants two things." Maria flips the pages to a snapshot of some of my work nestled among the plants at the conservatory. "He'd like you to do something similar to this, looking organic and I believe he said the word 'flamey.'" I nod. I can meet with this guy and pull something together in a few days, and it'll finance my creative side ideas for the rest of the year. Maria continues, though, and I frown. "And he wants you to do a series of glassware for the bar. Stag Glass exclusives for gimlets and gin mojitos. Sturdy, but with that Thatcher flare."

I recoil at this idea. "I'm not a fucking Ikea, Maria. I don't do tableware."

She pats my hand. "Sweetheart, Alex Clemont comes around with this kind of offer about as often as you find a woman you talk to more than once." She slides the folder toward me and rises, walking toward the door. "Read it over and call me by Friday."

As we listen to the gravel crunch under Maria's tires outside,

Cody snatches the folder from me. He scans the numbers and his jaw drops. "Jesus. Thatcher, come on, man. Look what he's offering."

I glance down, and then I sigh. I could have been making bowls and high balls for years if I wanted that. Hell, for awhile I made all my brothers beer steins every Christmas because it was easy and I could whip one up when I remembered at the last second. But that's not the direction I want for my work. Should I even consider this offer? Ever since all this...whatever this is with Emma, nothing makes sense.

I look back over at the shelves, trying to see what Maria saw about my work, how it's apparently shifted since last weekend. I realize, staring at a piece of dark green and black nodules inside a clear dome, that the day of Emma's seizure was also the day I saw my father again. I tell Cody I'll think about the Clemont offer, but now I have an idea for something bigger, something different. I chug a glass of water and get started.

82

EMMA

Nicole comes over after work on Thursday to "supervise" my packing for the weekend. I bubble on to her about my notes and outlines for the work I'm doing, and she pretends to be interested in my story ideas. Nicole always lets me talk at her while I'm in the brainstorming stage, and I never think she's listening, but she always has a comment that helps me move a story from blah to fantastic.

Today, she's definitely not listening, though. She's rummaging through my closet, grunting and huffing disapprovingly. "Emma," she cuts me off. "All you own are t-shirts and turtlenecks."

"Well, I have a cocktail dress for when my parents host events..."

Nicole rolls her eyes and looks at her watch. "Come on," she says, pulling my hand.

"Where are we going?"

"We have to get to the mall before it closes."

"Nick, stop. Come on. I don't need to go to the mall to go off into the woods with my fake fiancé and his brothers."

Nicole raises one eyebrow at me, marches over to my dresser, and pulls out a handful of cotton briefs, all a bit gray and saggy. "Ok," I say, "but so what if my undies are pathetic? It's not like anyone is looking."

"Did you not say he looked at you naked and commented on your pubes? Stop." She cuts me off before I can interject. "I am your best friend and I'm running an intervention on this saggy sports bra collection. Girl, not that I am trying to jinx this, but what if you have a seizure and pee your pants again? Do you want him to run into your suitcase and come out with a handful of Hanes?"

I mumble something incoherent, but follow her out to her car, and she drives to the mall. She grabs a giant shopping tote from the greeter in the department store and drags me to the lingerie department. We argue between the lacy, expensive selection and the practical, comfortable briefs, settling on some things that are functional, affordable, but sheer enough that Nicole stops rolling her eyes at me.

"Ok," she says, looking me up and down. "Now for a swimsuit."

"Oh, hell no," I protest. And it continues, but not for nothing is Nicole rising in the ranks at her company, landing investors and convincing top talent to come aboard. By the time she leaves my apartment that night, she has lightened my bank account, packed my bag for the weekend with the Stags, and left me more than a little nervous about what she's rolled into neat bundles in my duffel bag.

THATCHER SEEMS moody when he picks me up from work on Friday. His sullen demeanor leads me to chatter nervously about work, which feels weird to do with him since the subjects of my work lately are all related to him, or about to be. He pretty much just grunts periodically as he drives and I run out of things to say before we hit the state line.

"So," I say with a sigh. "What's on the agenda for this weekend? I should probably have asked before we were almost there..."

This he responds to, tossing an arm over the back of my seat and leaning his head against the glass of the driver's side window briefly. "Ty wants us to go for a run while you girls stay back and paint your toenails or whatever Juniper decides."

This makes me laugh. "I can't see Juniper choosing that particular activity..."

He finally smiles, and I feel the tension ease considerably. "No," he says. "She's not that type, is she, Chezz?" He tells me we will basically just be hanging out while Alice cooks her brains out without having to stop to take care of Petey. "He's back with Alice's dad and brother, having a man weekend."

The trip feels nice, familiar, comfortable, for a few minutes more, until Thatcher asks, "So, what if, you know, there's another seizure? This weekend? What do I do?"

My heart sinks. "I don't want to talk about seizures this weekend, Thatcher."

"Well," he protests, looking irritated, "I feel like I need to know what you can and can't do so you don't end up on the floor while we're in the woods far away from help or something."

"This is why I don't tell people. This. There is *nothing* I can't do, Thatcher Stag. You sound just like my mother, telling me I can't move away from home, can't attend classes in a brick and mortar school because of what *might* happen." He seems like he wants to interject, but now I'm pissed off. "I'm an adult, I take my medication, and the only reason I had a seizure the last time was because I didn't take my rescue meds. Because I didn't want to disappoint your damn sister and her special lime leaves."

He doesn't speak for a few minutes, but pulls his arm back to the steering wheel, holding it with two hands while we cross the border into Maryland. "Emma, I apologize for phrasing it that way. I know you're a very capable woman."

"Thank you."

He looks over at me and meets my eye, sweeping his long, dark hair back from those piercing grey eyes of his. In the fading light, in the shadows of his beard and long hair, he's all bright eyes and dark shadows. The tattoos on his arm blend together in the fading light until that looks dark, too. "Will you tell me if there's anything I should know?"

I sigh. "I take medications every day. I've told you--this is why I don't drink alcohol. If a seizure is coming, I can always tell, and then I should take my rescue medicine and sleep. I promise to tell you if that happens. Ok?"

He nods. "That's all I wanted to know."

"I'm just really sick of everyone in my life treating me like a baby," I say, looking out the window. Suddenly, I feel scorching heat on my thigh, and I look over to see him squeezing my leg through my jeans.

"I know you're no baby," he tells me.

I swallow, focusing on his hand on my leg, trying not to feel the pulsing heat, the burning desire for him to slide his hand a bit higher. "I just want someone to forget to be careful with me," I tell him in a quiet voice. When I meet his eye, there's no caution there. Instead, his hooded gaze is wild fire.

83

THATCHER

We are the first to arrive at the cabin, even though we stopped for snacks and supplies at the grocery store. I use the code Ty sent us to unlock, and step into the rustic space. There are high, vaulted ceilings with exposed wood beams, and the massive stone fireplace takes up one entire wall. I wasn't sure what to expect, but the cabin is furnished with deep leather couches, and the huge wooden table is set with candles.

Emma flicks a switch, and the whole place is aglow with twinkle lights inside and out. "Oh!" she gasps. "It's magical!" She wanders out through the sliding glass door onto the patio and I hear her exclaim, "There's a hot tub!" I laugh, knowing my brothers are going to drink too much and try to drown each other in there if we don't watch out.

I check my phone to read over the email from Ty, where he claimed the biggest bedroom for Juniper and him "because we're the fucking couple of honor," he wrote. Chuckling a bit, I peek into the next closest bedroom and toss my bag in the door. I feel Emma walk up behind me, and then she makes a small sound of surprise.

"There's one bed," she says.

I look over at her. I mean, I had assumed this, but I hadn't stopped to think that this would mean we'd be sharing. I suck air through my teeth for a minute and rub my beard, trying to think fast. I'm about to offer to sleep on the floor, but I see her collecting her wits. "Ok," she says. "We'll just build a pillow wall."

"A pillow wall?" I raise an eyebrow at her and grab her bag, placing it on the dresser.

"Yeah. A barricade. Because you can't keep your hands to yourself," she says, and without another word she starts unpacking her stuff.

Fuck, I think, seeing a glimpse of something black and sheer as she tucks her clothes into the top drawer. *I'm going to be in a bed with Emma.* I'm relieved when I hear my brothers pull up. They rode together because they came straight from the Stag Law offices where Tim and Alice and Juniper all work.

Soon, Alice is pulling out containers of dips and homemade pita chips, Juniper is mixing drinks, and Tim has even brought Emma a swing-top bottle of sparkling lemonade. When Alice plunks a sprig of fresh mint in her glass, they share a smile, and damn if I don't feel horny just looking at this woman fitting right in with my family.

Juniper brought a card game called Sushi Go, and soon, Emma and Tim are in a fierce battle for the win. Emma catches on really fast, and eventually, the rest of us stop really trying. We just want to watch Emma and Tim fight over sashimi and pudding cards. He starts yelling at her about tactics, and she doesn't miss a beat, dishing it right back to him, playing a defensive game. Emma isn't intimidated by Tim at all, and I love that. I catch Alice and Ty staring at her as Emma plays a card that causes Tim to throw his hand on the table and storm out the back door. Alice and Juniper burst out laughing while Emma tallies up the score. "Yes!" she says. "I beat him by 2 points."

I have to catch myself, because I want to kiss her for this, for beating my brother and pissing him off, but I know that would cross a line in our arrangement. Instead, I just smile at her silently, until I hear Ty and Juniper suggest that we help Tim cool off by throwing him into the lake.

Alice pretends to be worried at this idea, but everyone goes off to change into their swimsuits, leaving Emma and me sitting alone at the table. "You want to go change first?" I ask her. "I can clean up the cards."

She shakes her head and bites her lip. *Fuck*, I need to stop staring at Emma's lips. I want to lick them, and I really can't think that way. "I should tell you something," she says in a quiet voice.

"What's up, Chezz?" I put my arm around the back of her chair and turn sideways in mine, so I can lean close and hear what she's saying.

"So, I can swim, and I haven't had a seizure aura at all, but...it's risky for me to swim. Unless someone is watching out for me." She pauses. Her eyes are watery, like it's killing her to have to talk about this. "Can you make sure I don't drown?"

"Of course," I tell her. I wink, to try to ease up the mood a little. "I won't let you out of arm's reach." Emma smiles and goes off to change into her suit, leaving me to put away the cards and think about long division or come up with some other strategy to keep my cool while I'm in the water close to this red head in nothing but a swimsuit.

"Oh my god, Emma! Your suit is so stinking cute!" I hear Alice fawning over Emma in the hall and decide it's safe for me to go back and change. My breath catches in my throat when I see her in a blue and white polka-dot bikini top with matching little shorts. She is so fucking sexy, all curves and soft skin.

When I walk out the back door onto the deck, I'm grateful for the low light of the twinkle lights along the dock. My brothers are already in the water, Tim past his hissy fit at losing a card game. Alice and Juniper are floating in an inflatable swan. Then I see Emma. She's lounging on a raft, just her legs dangling into the water. The moonlight catches her pale skin and she seems to glow, her red hair shining like flames even in the dark. When she looks up and smiles at me, I'm gone. She has me totally under her spell and I don't fucking know what to do about it.

Then I see Ty swimming toward her while she looks at me, unaware. "No!" I scream, too late as I see him reach to tip her off the raft. Emma screams and flounders a bit. I know the lake isn't deep where she is, but I dive in and grab her.

I hold her against my body as she resurfaces, sputtering and panicking a bit. "My bad," Ty yells, treading water and looking sheepish. "I was just fooling around."

The lake water is slippery and warm, and Emma flails her legs looking for purchase. I keep one arm wrapped around her stomach while I move us toward her raft. I feel her body calm when she realizes I've got her, that she's safe. Ty keeps yelling his apologies while Juniper tries to dunk him and Alice rams him with the swan raft, scolding him for catching Emma off guard.

But all of that fades away for me as I realize that there's no hiding what I'm feeling right now. My body responds to Emma. I'm rock solid against her ass, even after she grabs the raft. She wriggles a bit in the water to stay afloat, but she stills, realizing that I'm hard as fuck. "Oh," she says, turning around to look me in the eye. "Oh."

"You ok?" my voice is low, my face close to hers. She nods. I feel her yearning for something, too, and I almost decide to lean in and kiss the hell out of her when my fucking brother cock-blocks me.

"Emma, are you mad?" His voice breaks the spell and Emma looks away, toward Ty. "I'm really sorry. I just wanted to treat you like one of the family."

"It's ok, Ty," Emma says, returning her gaze to mine. "But actually I'm pretty tired. I think I'm going to call it a night."

Her tone isn't one that invites me to join her in there, so I nod and stare at her as she climbs the metal ladder back up onto the dock. I don't even pretend I'm not looking at her ass as she reaches for a towel and then walks back up the ramp into the cabin. I float on my back in the lake, thinking about Emma rubbing up against me, Emma naked in the kitchen in the sunlight. I had sort of been turning off the part of me that goes right in for the fuck, knowing this thing with Emma has to hold together for at least a month. I really have no idea how to go about pursuing a woman slowly, maintaining a connection with her *and* fucking her. But shit. I want to fuck Emma

Cheswick, and that's bad news. I need to stay here, submerged in the icy lake water until my dick calms down.

Eventually I climb out. Emma is long gone into our room, and Alice and Juniper are bent over some magazines on the deck, talking about seating charts for the wedding.

I sit up with my brothers a bit longer, drinking a few beers and bullshitting with them. When I go into our bedroom later, I can barely see Emma asleep behind the barricade of pillows and blankets she's constructed in the middle of the bed.

84

EMMA

I wake up pinned under something heavy. I twist around in the blankets until I realize that my fortress of safety--every spare pillow I could find in the cabin--has all slid to the floor. The long, muscled, tattooed leg of Thatcher Stag is slung over my hip.

I roll over to look at him, trying to move his leg without waking him up. He's half on his side, sleeping in just a pair of shorts, and holy shit. I had forgotten the glorious sight that is his chest. His tattoos stop midway down his pecs, leaving his abs fresh and begging to be licked. *Stop it,* I tell myself. *This is a work weekend. You cannot mess up this arrangement with sex.*

The rational, journalist side of my brain who is just here to get information is struggling to overpower the aroused half of my brain who wants to run my nails down Thatcher's leg. My lizard brain keeps my eyes traveling straight down his abs to the huge bulge in his shorts. So it wasn't my imagination last night in the lake. Thatcher is packing a serious sword in his scabbard. I snort at my own joke, still trying to figure out what to do about being trapped under the long limb of this gorgeous, untouchable man.

Thankfully, I'm saved by the other Stags. Tim starts pounding on the door, yelling, "Thatcher! Get your ass up! We're going running in five minutes." He pounds a few more times for good measure, and I see Thatcher crack open one eye. He smiles at me, and I would probably fall over if I weren't already lying down. His grey eyes and dimples are dazzling, and I know he knows it. He looks damn good.

"Guess that's my cue," he says, rising from the bed and stretching. He faces away from me, so I'm forced to stare at his back muscles. The long hours of physical work shaping glass have done him a lot of favors--his body is exquisite. I'm staring, slack-jawed, until he bends over to put on his sneakers and socks, and walks out the door without looking back. "Coming, coming. You assholes better not leave without me!" he yells down the hall, and the Stag Brothers are gone.

I make my way to the kitchen, where Alice has set out an entire restaurant's worth of food. "Hey, Emma!" she sings, dancing her way between a griddle and a mixing bowl. "I'm making waffles. And eggs. And bacon."

"Gosh, Alice. Do you need help?" My eyes are wide, looking at the heaps of fresh herbs and vegetables, the little crock of fresh maple syrup she's set out on the table.

"Nope! Absolutely not," she says, sliding a mug of coffee down the counter toward me. "At work, I do all of this for about 50 people *and* I usually have Petey asking me 75 questions per minute while I'm trying to concentrate. You sit and tell me about working at the *Pittsburgh Post*."

It's so easy to talk to Alice. When she asks questions, she really cares about the answer. She'd make a great reporter, and she blushes when I tell her so. I start to wonder what's going to happen after Ty and Juniper's wedding, when Thatcher and I are supposed to break up. It hadn't occurred to me that I would enjoy spending time with his family, and then feel sad saying goodbye to them. When he first told me he was fighting with them and blurted the lie about a fiancé, I assumed they were all stuffy jerks like my parents.

I can see how Tim is uptight, but I decide to ask Alice if she knows more about the fight that led to the ultimate deception. "This coffee is amazing," I tell her, breaking the silence as she stirs and chops.

She nods. "The guys at Zeke's roast the beans right in the city. I get a delivery at the office once a week. Hey." She looks up at me and brushes some of her wild curls out of her face. "Let me know if I get boring talking about food and farmers. Tim says people don't want to hear allll the details, but I get excited!"

I laugh and assure her I'll let her know if I ever get bored. "I'm a curious person," I tell her. "I wouldn't be a good reporter if I cut people off when they're on a roll!" We talk a bit more about her work, and I start to jot some notes in my phone for the piece about the childcare they have on site. When we get to a natural pause in the conversation, I decide to just dive into the hard question. "What happened with Tim and Thatcher?"

Alice pauses and sighs. "You know," she says, "I'm not really sure. Tim was mighty angry that Thatcher was late to Petey's birthday party, and I think they just started to bring up a lot of years of held-in quarrels."

"I know Tim's opinion really, really matters to Thatcher. About everything," I tell her, looking out the window to make sure the guys aren't back yet. I see Juniper making her way up the steps to the back deck. She's wearing running tights and a sports bra and I nearly gasp when I see how fit she is. Her abs have abs.

She bursts into the kitchen and grabs a glass of water, chugging it down before she greets us. "Hey," she says, finally, heaving a bit. "I ran separately so the boys could bond and fight out all their shit."

Alice nods. "They really need to do that."

I look back and forth between them, puzzled. Juniper chugs some more water and continues, "They still haven't finished whatever they were getting into at the birthday party, and Ty thinks Thatcher is hiding something." She winks. "He hopes I'm going to get you to spill your guts today."

I frown, remembering that Thatcher had seen their father when he was waiting for me to change at the hospital. I guess he hasn't told his family about that yet. Well, I'm not going to be the one to bring that up. That's a hurt that runs years deeper than any of our involvement with this family. Then, of course, I realize that Thatcher is also hiding from them the fact that our relationship is pretend. I flush, realizing I'm part of this divide that's plaguing the Stag brothers.

"No worries, Emma," Juniper says, clapping me on the back. "Hey, anyone want to jump in the hot tub with me before the guys get back?" I tell her I'm going to stick to the house and Alice agrees to let me set the table at least. When the guys haven't returned an hour later, the three of us decide to dig in without them, and Juniper, fully at ease after her hot tub, really opens up to all of my questions.

85

THATCHER

Everything seems fine for about the first mile. My brothers give me shit about my new tattoos. I pretend that Tim is getting soft around the middle, and we all joke that Thatcher is starting to look like a shiny bodybuilder, his muscles are getting so big.

Then, Tim falls back beside me, letting Ty run on ahead, and I know it's all about to go down. "I read Emma's article about you," he says. "Why didn't you tell me you had a show at the Conservatory? I would have come."

I shake my head and keep running. "I did fucking tell you, Tim. I always tell you."

"When?" He seems genuinely shocked.

I just roll my eyes at him and speed up my pace. I'm not going to invite him to tell me I should really reach out to his admin if I want something to get on his master schedule. Somehow I doubt Alice has to do that, and my brother never misses one of Ty's hockey games. "I guess you don't remember shit unless it's earning your law firm money," I sneer at him.

By this point, Ty realizes we aren't in step with him and he pulls over beside a flat rock, panting a little bit. Tim stops running when we approach Ty and asks him, "Did Thatcher tell you about his art show at the Conservatory?"

Ty shrugs. "Probably? Was it in June? I can't be anywhere in June unless the team loses and--"

"I told both of you, like I always do. Neither of you assholes listens to me anymore because you've got babies and girlfriends. You've iced me out of your lives, but then you have the gall to get pissed off when I am late for one of *your* things. Fuck that."

I start running again, but Ty grabs my shoulder. "Don't run away, man. Let's talk about this."

"Fuck you," I snarl. "I liked you better when you just beat the shit out of anyone who pissed you off."

I take a step before I feel it. His fist is like a sledgehammer to my shoulder. *Finally,* I think. Then, I turn around swinging. Tim comes up to try to separate me and Tyrion, but years of scrapping have taught us both how to hit each other and how to avoid Tim's efforts to referee. I crouch low and aim for Ty's kidneys. He goes for my stomach every fucking time. Tim catches me in the eye with an elbow, so I hit him in the face, too. Eventually, exhausted, we all collapse onto the gravel path and just lie there, breathing heavy. I exhale long and slow through my nose and close my eyes. "Alex Clemont offered me a quarter million dollars to do a custom piece for his new gin joint and hand make all the glasses he'll need to serve."

"Is that the builder guy who did the fancy hot dog place downtown?" Ty asks, sitting up and stretching. I nod. "He does a lot of cool spaces."

Tim frowns and says, "Send your contract to Juniper. She's better at that kind of thing and can look at it for you."

A few minutes later, we turn around and head back for the cabin, the mood lighter. I know it's only temporary, though, because eventually I'm going to have to tell them I saw our father.

When we get back, the house smells amazing. I can tell Alice has outdone herself. She and Juniper are washing dishes and they both turn around, immediately swarming the three of us. Alice and Juniper see our cuts and bruises and get out the ice and soft hands, soothing Tim and Ty. I hear a lot of "poor baby" while they cluck their tongues. My blood is still pumping, and damn if I don't feel aroused after the adrenaline rush of fighting. I suck down some food until my brothers disappear into their bedrooms so their ladies can "check them out where there's better light."

I roll my eyes and grab a glass of ice water, clinking the cubes together in the glass while I slowly swallow. I walk softly down the hallway to the bedroom, looking for Emma, and I stop in the open doorway. Emma is perched on the bed, typing furiously. There's a far-off look in her eye while she writes and I can tell she's in the zone. Fully focused. Creating.

I chew on an ice cube, just watching her. She's so sexy, and I don't know if I'm just admitting it for the first time, or only letting myself concentrate on her while I'm agitated, but I want her. Badly. She's still wearing the too-big t-shirt she slept in, and it hangs low off one shoulder. Her red hair is piled on her head in a messy bun-thing, and I moan softly when I see that she's not wearing shorts. Just bare legs jutting out from beneath the laptop.

My cock springs to life as I watch her work, the way she nods her head and smiles when she must have found just the right word. Eventually, she clicks a few keys triumphantly and then clasps her hands under her chin, smiling. She looks so fucking happy right now, and I realize this is how I feel when I finish a piece in the studio. When I take an idea and form it into something solid, something real. Emma's words are her art, and it's hot watching her creative process. *Shit,* I think, watching her stretch, seeing her heavy breasts move inside the baggy shirt. *Fuck it.*

I crunch another ice cube, and she looks up at me, startled. "Oh," she says. "I didn't know you were back."

I close the door behind me and walk toward the bed, sinking down beside her. "Can I see what you wrote?" I set the glass on the night stand and lean toward her laptop, but she slams the lid shut and clutches it to her chest.

"NO!" she yells, surprising me with her ferocity. Then, she shakes her head slightly. "I never show anyone my drafts."

I raise an eyebrow at her, confused. "Why not?" But if I'm honest, I can guess why. Probably the same reason I don't discuss my designs or let anyone in the studio with me when I'm working. Hell, half the time I send Cody away if I'm deep into an important piece.

"It's like...it's too personal," she says. "It's private. It would be like seeing me naked."

I smile, remembering the sight of her in her kitchen. "I've already seen you naked, Chezz." I remember the feel of her body last night in the lake, the way she wriggled against my aching cock. I'm bursting with need for her. I slide the laptop out of her hands and set it gently on the floor beside the bed.

She sits sort of frozen, and I can see her chest rising and falling as she breathes, anticipating. She wants this, too. Her nipples are hard and I can see them jutting out through the thin material of her shirt. *Fuck me, she's perfect,* I think. "Come here," I say, huskily, and she closes her eyes for a moment, swallowing. When she opens them, her pupils are dilated until there's just a tiny ring of green around a sea of dark, wet black.

I lean back against the headboard and gently ease Emma onto my lap. She straddles me with those thick, bare legs of hers, and I groan as the weight of her settles against my throbbing hard-on. "I was watching you write," I say, moving her hips along my length. "You're so fucking sexy, Chezz. Do you know that?"

Emma emits a tiny moan and I know I can't stop until I hear her make that sound again, until I make her come and get to watch her face transformed by pleasure. I lean in to kiss her, pulling her close against me. I have one hand on her neck and the other on her ass, digging my fingers into the soft flesh, slowly inching that shirt up until I have a hand on her panties.

"Oh!" she exclaims, pulling back from my lips. "Your tongue is so cold."

86

EMMA

"You like that, Emma?" he asks, sliding his frozen tongue along my lips. Holy shit, do I like it. The heat of his body, the ice-cold of his tongue. The mix of sensations is like nothing I've ever felt before. My skin has been buzzing since last night in the lake, and now I'm finally connecting with Thatcher, touching him, feeling him touch me. It's sexy enough to be sitting on Thatcher's lap with his hands on my ass, but when he kisses me? I'm gone.

"Thatcher," I breathe, "I can't...work..." Alarm bells are ringing in my head. The ethics of what we're doing are already pretty terrible without me giving into some wave of lust. But then, I think about how long it's been since I've been with a man, and none of them ever touched me like this. None of them ever left me shaking with need.

I can't seem to find any words, and I just start moving my hips along his rock-hard dick. Last night in the lake, I thought he was maybe he got hard because he was embarrassed to have to rescue me or something, but now, his grey eyes are intense as he looks at me and thrusts his tongue into the far reaches of my mouth. He explores my mouth and his lips suck and nibble at mine. He's shirtless from his run, and I finally get to feel every firm inch of him. My nipples, achingly hard, brush against his through the material of my shirt. This is far and away the sexiest kiss of my life.

"I fucking burn for you, Chezz," Thatcher breathes, and I want to tell him I'm scorching, too. That I've been hot for him since he first pressed against me in that hallway, but I'm still reeling from the kiss, so I just sit there, panting. "Are you hot, too, Emma?" he asks, and then he looks at me, a devilish grin spreading across his sweaty face. He reaches onto the night stand and plucks an ice cube from his water glass. I gasp, nervous about what he's planning. His free hand slips down the back of my panties, his long fingers rubbing the sensitive skin of my backside. He lifts the ice cube slowly with his other hand, and I start panting when he presses it to my collarbone.

Slowly, deliberately, he drags the ice along my chest, up my throat, and along my jaw. He follows behind with his mouth, now searing hot, leaving a trail of opposite sensations that have my entire core on fire. I'm circling my hips, desperate for stimulation on my clit. He's torturing me with how good this feels. Thatcher puts the ice cube between his teeth, freeing his hand, and his cold, cold fingers slip down the front of my panties.

My shivers give way to frantic moans when I feel his icy fingers fluttering on my clit. "Jesus, Emma, you're soaked," he says, crunching the ice between his teeth before kissing me again. His tone is so casual, but there is urgency in his touch. His fingers start to circle my nub inside my panties and I drop my head back, exposing my throat to him. Thatcher takes the opportunity to suck on the taut skin. "This feels so good, Thatcher," I moan. I am out of my mind, drunk on the sensations.

"Do you like this?" he asks me, sliding a cold finger inside me.

"Fuck, yes, Thatcher. Please."

"Please what?" he whispers in my ear, flicking his cold tongue along the shell. He never stops moving his hand on my center, teasing apart my wet folds. I can't even form thoughts right now and I struggle to answer him, but abruptly, he stops his movements. "Tell me, Chezz. What do you want?"

My mouth hangs open. I pant, my chest rising and falling. I reach behind me to strip off the shirt, baring myself to Thatcher, and I gasp, "Please make me come, Thatcher."

He laughs again and cups my breasts, the sensitive, soft globes filling his rough hands. His thumbs flick my nipples and I moan again as he says, "I thought you'd never ask."

I start sliding my palms up and down his chest, over the stag tattoo that matches the ones his brothers both have. I love the feel of his muscles shifting beneath my hands and I hunch down to lick one of his tiny nipples, enjoying the rumble in his chest when my tongue connects. I lick a salty path all the way up to his chin. And then I'm lost when I feel Thatcher's mouth close over one nipple, sucking deeply, as he circles the other with another ice cube from his glass.

I drop my head back and groan in pleasure, no longer able to think when he switches sides, sucking deep pulls on the frozen nipple. He eases the melting ice back into his mouth and begins to slide his lips up and down my stomach, tilting me back, his hands under my shoulders supporting my weight, until his mouth has the access it needs to my belly.

He shifts his weight abruptly. Pulling me back against his chest, Thatcher kisses me again. I suck his tongue hungrily into my mouth, kiss his cheeks, frenzied in my need to connect with him physically.

His busy hands move to the waistband of my sheer panties, giving them a tug. "Can I see inside, Chezz?" I nod, and then yelp when he tugs them with both hands. I hear a rip as Thatcher yanks the ruined material off my body. "Holy fuck, Emma. Fuck, that's so hot," he says, running his fingers through the soft curls. "You're red *everywhere*."

My arms jerk and my back arches when he finds my slit. I might come if he touches me just once more. I'm trembling now as he takes his time exploring. "So wet, Emma," he breathes, sliding a fingertip just where I need the friction. Suddenly, Thatcher tips me backwards so I'm lying sprawled on the bed between his legs, looking up into his grey eyes. He grins his lopsided, devilish smile and reaches for the last ice cube. I gasp. He purrs, "You look flushed, Chezz. I want to cool you off." I'm frightened for a moment. Surely the ice on my most sensitive skin will burn? But then I feel the sting of contact paired with his scalding touch and I know I'm ruined for all other men. Forever.

"Oooh, ooh, shit, Thatcher. Yes. Oh my god," I start rambling and mumbling, fisting the sheets into my hands when he starts the agonizing, slow tease, sliding the ice cube up one thigh, then the other. He never takes a hand from my seam, and his fingers are cool from passing the ice between his hands. I feel my hips jerking involuntarily, a building sensation throbbing throughout my body.

Thatcher slides me back a bit further on the bed and bends forward. "Oh, god," I moan when he slides the ice inside me. There's just a small chip remaining, and the heat of my core melts it in seconds, but not before I come, hard, screaming his name and burying my fingers in his long hair.

I think he will stop when the sensation subsides, but he doesn't. He sticks out his tongue and licks me, over and over again while his long fingers massage my ass. His thumbs reach around my legs to stroke the skin of my upper thighs and his tongue thrusts inside me. "I can't, Thatcher," I yell, pulling his hair. My thighs slam shut against his ears when he starts to chuckle.

He sucks my clit between his teeth, lets go of my ass, and spreads my pussy open with his fingers. He dives back into me, fucking me with his tongue. Before the first orgasm wanes, I come again, so hard that I can't tell where my body stops and his begins, and I lose track of the world. All that exists is this wave of pleasure that crashes again and again. Slowly, it subsides and I become aware that Thatcher has moved his head and hands away from my body.

"Emma," I hear him say. I open my eyes to see him kneeling above me. He reaches into his waistband, stroking his cock inside his shorts, and stares at me. "That was the hottest thing I've ever seen in my life."

87

THATCHER

"Emma," I say, looking down at the goddess on the bed, all curves and softness and cream. She opens a green eye, her blissed-out expression gorgeous as fuck. Knowing I put that look on her face has me hard as glass, but I want more. "I have to make you come again."

"I need a few minutes," she says, reaching for my leg, one hand lazily exploring up and down my shorts. And then I remember something really fucking unfortunate.

"I didn't bring any condoms," I tell her, sinking down to the sheets so I'm lying beside her. Fuck, I'm so hard it hurts. It actually hurts. "Are you on birth control?"

"Of *course* I'm on the pill," she says, sharply. "But..." Emma looks at me, concerned. "Have you ever been...tested for anything? I know I'm safe..."

I lean in to kiss her, moaning when I taste those soft, full lips again. "I always use condoms, 100% of the time. And I got tested, really recently, actually." I kiss her again. "I'm clean."

She melts a bit in relief and closes her eyes again. "I trust you," she says, and with that I climb on top of her. I have to feel her against me. This is different from every other time. I've never even considered sleeping with a woman without protection, but suddenly I cannot imagine sex with Emma with any kind of barrier. Fuck me, I *have* to see her come again, have to feel it with nothing between us. I can't keep my hands off her pussy, the feel of that tight, wet tunnel capped with those amazing red curls. This is all new for me. Sure, the ladies have a good time when I'm with them, but it's never turned me on this much to make someone come. Taking Emma over the edge like that--twice!--was the sexiest thing I've ever done.

It's Emma's turn for busy hands, though, and I nibble at her neck while she searches my body, tracing the muscles along my spine and then yanking down my shorts. It kills me to separate from her body, even for a minute, but I draw back to get my shorts and my boxers down, kicking them across the room before I ease myself back on top of her.

I hiss when she grabs hold of my shaft, her small hand wrapped fully around me at the root. Christ, I fit perfectly into her hot little hand. She starts to stroke me just right and I'm worried I'm going to cum in her hand. "Chezz," I tell her. "You feel so fucking good right now. Your hands are amaz--"

"Thatcher," she says. I look her in the eye and she seems impatient.

"Huh?"

"Shut up and fuck me." Emma lines me up with her opening and she doesn't have to tell me twice. I sink inside her, letting out a deep groan as I fill her up. This is bliss. Emma is hot and tight, slick with need, against the bare, sensitive skin of my cock. She moans and moves with me as I slide, slowly, in and out. I think back to her words from my truck. *I want someone to forget to be careful with me.* I know now that she doesn't want slow and gentle. She wants fire, hot enough to melt ice. I look into her eyes, touching my forehead to hers, and I slam into her.

"Ahhh! Yes!" she says, bucking her hips to meet mine. "Yes. Harder."

You got it, I think, pounding her body, but I can't even find words to talk. Emma is so wet, so tight. I can feel her squeezing my dick and she feels like home. Emma starts moaning into my mouth as I slam her mercilessly. I brace my heels against the headboard for leverage and redouble my efforts. My dick rams into her and each time I think I've gone too far, she claws at my shoulders and yells, "More, Thatcher! Fuck me just like this. Now!"

I start sweating, my weight balanced on my forearms. I look down and watch her tits jiggle with each thrust, and I feel savage. But Emma looks me in the eye with a fierce expression, and she's just as wild as I am. Her nails dig into my shoulders as she tries to pull me closer. She tilts her hips up against me, finding the friction she needs, until she starts pulsing against my cock. I can feel it before she even starts moaning that she's coming for me. Fuck, her face is beautiful when she comes.

"I'm going to cum, Emma," I pant out, and then it happens. I see sparks. My balls draw up tight and I explode inside of her, hot jets spurting out endlessly until I collapse on top of her. I feel Emma still throbbing around me and I kiss her. She holds my face with both hands, moaning into my mouth until her waves of pleasure die down. This is so different, being with a woman I know and, well, someone I care about, even as a friend.

"Holy shit, Stag," she says, breathing heavily. "I've waited my whole life for that."

Exhausted, I lower my upper body to the side of her, stroking her hair and letting her hold me. "For what, Chezz?" I don't want to move. Ever.

"For someone to fuck my brains out." Her eyes close. She's still breathing pretty heavy and I like looking down at the way her body moves as she breathes.

"You had sex before me, though? That didn't seem like your first time..." Panic surges through me at the thought that I was just rough and rowdy with a virgin, but Emma shakes her head.

"No. You misunderstand me. I've 'made love' before and had slow, gentle, boring-ass sex with men who asked me things like whether they should stop before I have an orgasm, because they were worried I'd have a seizure."

"Hmmm," I just sort of make a sound of displeasure. That hadn't occurred to me, but from the tone of her voice she didn't really like that level of caution during sex.

She wriggles out from under me and I feel a sense of loss when I slide out from her body. Emma props up on one elbow and traces a finger along the ink on my chest. "I'm saying thank you, Thatcher." She kisses my skin and the wet heat of her mouth makes my cock spring back to life. "Thank you for unleashing your inner beast."

I laugh as she runs her hands along my body. I take her hand in mine and guide it toward my dick, now standing straight up against my stomach again. "Chezz," I whisper into her hair, "I'll get wild with you any time that you want."

88

EMMA

After a blistering round two of riding Thatcher's cock while grabbing the wrought-iron bed frame for dear life, I feel both thoroughly exhausted and utterly embarrassed that his family likely heard me shrieking and screaming. "They're all going to know we were fucking in here," I whisper, hiding under the sheet once the sex-drunk euphoria begins to fade.

"Chezz," he says, tugging my hair, "They already assumed we've been fucking. We're engaged, remember?" I roll my eyes at him. Sex was never supposed to be part of our arrangement. I rub my fists on my temples, trying to figure out how to get back on track to professionalism. If that's even possible. Shit.

I rise from the bed, rummaging around the drawers for some clothes, and almost don't hear Thatcher ask, "What did you mean when you said *of course* you were on the pill?"

"Hm?"

"The way you said it, like I should know already. It's not like we had a lot of contraception chats when we got fake engaged..."

"Oh," I say, plunking back down beside him on the mattress. "To be fair I was a little distracted by all the orgasms you were handing out at the time." He laughs, pulling my hand to his mouth and kissing my palm. I'm stunned by the gesture, by the gentle feel of his lips beside the scratchier sensation of his beard along my skin. I pause and enjoy what he's doing. *So much for not mixing work and pleasure, I guess,* I think, before continuing. "The tone was me feeling like I have no choices about being on the pill. There's a correlation between seizure activity and hormone levels in a woman's cycle," I tell him, waiting for him to cringe, but he just looks at me, listening. "So I take a pill that keeps the hormones steady all month long. It helps, along with my other medications."

"I think all that shit is fascinating," he says, standing to put on his swim trunks. "The way they can know what might work to make your brain stop freaking out. Or whatever it's doing."

I nod, and then remember my own question. "While we're talking, can I ask you something?" He looks up from his duffel bag, where he'd been rooting around searching for something. "When did you get tested?"

"Oh," he says, biting his lip and looking out the window. "That was just last week actually."

I frown, assuming he'd gone to the clinic with the intention of sleeping with me this weekend. "So you just thought I'd jump into bed with you? What ever happened to your best behavior, Thatcher?"

He puts his palms up in surrender, saying, "Easy there, Chezz. Testing had nothing to do with you, although I never once let up hope that I'd convince you to sleep with me. Let's be perfectly clear about that." I make to leave the room, but he tugs on my arm. "I got tested because of my father," he says.

Wow, I think, sitting back down. "Ok, tell me more about that."

He flops next to me on the bed. "This whole fucking week, Emma. This whole fucking week has been so crazy. You had a seizure, I saw my fucking father, my agent got me a quarter million dollar project offer and--"

"Holy shit, Thatcher! You didn't say anything!" I slap his chest. "We should celebrate!"

He grabs my wrist mid-smack and pins my hand against his skin, and I can feel his heart racing. He's quiet for a minute, but says, "My father is dying. He won't get sober, so they won't put him on a transplant list. I started talking to the hospital about their living donor program." He looks at me, his grey eyes hard as steel right now. "That's when I got tested. For basically every disease that exists."

"Thatcher," I whisper, struggling to adjust my body so I can reach out to him, offer some sort of comforting gesture. He seems almost startled by that, so I extract my hand from his and pull his head onto my lap, running my fingers through his hair. "That's a hell of a week." He nods, silent, pondering, but relaxes into my touch. I take a deep breath, feeling way out of my element with this. Things have certainly moved beyond our little quid-pro-quo contract. "I think you should tell your brothers you saw your father."

I feel his body stiffen and I can literally feel him constructing an emotional wall between us. "I think you should stay out of my family business, Emma," he says, his voice cold. He rises from the bed and grabs a towel from the top of the dresser. "I'm going wash the sweat and sex off myself and then soak in the hot tub." And, in a few sharp strides, he's gone from the room.

THATCHER AVOIDS me most of the day. Not obviously, but I can tell by his subtle shifts away from me or the way he abruptly tosses in a joke to steer the conversation away from anything related to his family. I don't know why I feel like I should meddle on this issue. I guess I feel partially responsible for him even being in this position. He wouldn't have seen his father at the hospital if I had done what I needed to and slept rather than go to his brother's house. *But then he'd never know about his father,* a small part of my consciousness reminds me. Surely questions are worse than working through a painful truth.

I bring my concentration back to the room, where everyone is hanging out and talking. Juniper and Ty picked up their marriage license. She starts telling a story about not having had parents and how that affects her when she's giving a health history, whether she's at the courthouse or registering for the Olympic team. I think about the tradeoffs for having parents that were involved in every, single aspect of my life. My mom was always so worried about my health that she never let me do anything. Always chaperoned every trip, said no to every slumber party invite until those faded away, and told me I was too fragile for every single after school activity, saying they'd all either stress me out until I had a seizure or else risk me getting hit in the head, triggering a seizure.

Over dinner of grilled steaks and roasted potatoes with corn on the cob, Tim startles the room by asking me about my medications. "I'm sorry," I tell him, looking up from my food. "Can you ask again?"

He dabs at his mouth with a napkin. "I was wondering who your neurologist is and whether you're participating in any new trials for epilepsy." Everyone stares at him, because Tim has never casually asked me a question. He shrugs. "My college alumni magazine had an article about some new research for seizures."

I nod. "My doctor is Dr. Khalsa and yes. Everything I'm on now has been part of his research, since I started college." I tell them how my big act of defiance against my parents was applying for a room and board scholarship so I could live on campus and finally get out from under their thumb. Once I moved into the dorms, my roommate, Nicole, learned about my epilepsy and dragged me to the student health center. She'd read a case report for one of her intro classes, studying Dr. Khalsa and the business angle of the medications he developed. I look around at all the Stags and Juniper and they're fascinated by what I'm saying. Not concerned or pitying--interested.

It's been so long since I've told anyone about my condition--not since human resources when I got my job. I'm really not used to people who don't flip out and treat me like I'm some fragile flower about to wilt.

So I keep talking, blushing a little bit as I explain that after my seizure at Alice's barbecue, Dr. Khalsa invited me to try a study for medical marijuana. Thatcher perks right up at that. "I forgot about that, Chezz." He waggles his eyebrows at his family. "Now you really know why I'm marrying this girl."

I shake my head. "I can't share with you. That'd be unethical--and illegal. I haven't decided if I'm going to do it, anyway."

Tim nods, contemplating. "I wonder what the ramifications are for medical marijuana use for, say, professional athletes...I mean it's legal in this state for certain conditions..." Alice swats his hand and tells him to stop thinking about work while we're on vacation.

As she rises to clear the table, Tim stands to help her. I meet Thatcher's eye and try to signal that I think he should tell his family. "Tell them," I whisper. "They deserve to know."

Thatcher's gaze turns dark and he shakes his head, his eyes holding me to silence.

89

THATCHER

We all swim in the lake again after dinner, but Emma keeps her sexy ass as far away from me as she can. I know she's pissed that I'm not telling my family about finding Ted Stag on his deathbed, but fuck if I'm going to bring that up two weeks from my brother's wedding. He should be focused on his bride, on starting a life and a new family with this woman.

I sigh and think back to fucking Emma this morning. I'm not used to the idea of sticking around--I do *not* do relationships with women-- but I definitely want to go at it again with her. I need to get her to stop being mad at me first. Maybe knowing we have an expiration date makes sex with Emma feel more comfortable. Not comfortable. Explosive. Searing. Addictive. *Fuck.* I'm forced to float on my back in the water and stare at her, remembering the look on her face earlier when I made her come with my tongue and, later, my cock.

Juniper wants a Sushi Go rematch after the sun sets, but I try to send signals to Emma to wrap things up early so we can go to pound town again. She seems oblivious, and kicks my foot away when I try to stroke her calf with my bare toes. I was kind of a dick to her all day, but I know I can make up for it. I make a point of rattling the ice in my glass, making eyes at her over the top, but she scowls. All right, enough of this shit.

"Emma, can I talk to you for a second?" I rise from the table and head toward our room.

"I'll be back in just a few minutes," she says, not moving her eyes from her hand of cards. "I'm about to kick Tim's ass again."

I feel myself getting angry, and that just pisses me off further. This is why I don't get into relationships, damn it. I don't understand what's pissing her off right now, but I know it all definitely changed since we had sex. I kick the bedpost in our room, yelping when my bare foot connects with the iron. I'm hopping around howling in pain when Emma comes in, crossing her arms and looking pissed off.

"What the hell is with you, Emma?" I hiss, sitting down to rub my foot.

"What the hell is with *you*, Stag? You give me the silent treatment all day, refuse to tell your family that you're thinking of giving a major *organ* to your father, and expect me to keep this secret from them all?"

"You have no problem keeping the fact that we barely know each other and are pretending to be engaged a secret," I whisper-yell at her. "I gave you the scoop you needed to keep your job, and now you have the access you need to my family for these other articles, so mind your fucking business. Play your part."

Her eyes flare at me and she puffs out her cheeks. I can tell she wants to deliver an earful, but is trying to contain herself. We stare at each other for a few minutes until she says, "I'd prefer it if you slept on the floor tonight."

"Fine!" I throw all the pillows from the bed down onto the braided rug on the floor. I yank off my shirt, grab the quilt from the trunk at the foot of the bed, and flop my ass on the carpet. She huffs out of the room, I guess to finish her card game, and I pretend to be asleep when she comes back a few minutes later.

I close my eyes and listen as Emma gets herself ready for bed. She turns off the light and we listen to each other breathe until I eventually fall asleep.

. . .

IN THE MORNING, Alice sends us off with a huge cooler of snacks and sandwiches, as if it's a six-hour drive to Emma's parents house instead of an hour and a half. Tim tells me to give Senator Cheswick his best and I grit my teeth when he asks if I can slip him Tim's card. Emma looks fucking amazing in her fancy dress for this country club party. She's even wearing pearls. She looks me up and down--I told her dark jeans and a button down with wingtips is the most I'll nod toward that square lifestyle--and I can't tell if she approves or not, but she sniffs and hugs Alice and Juniper.

Ty gives her a high-five, then pulls her into a hug. I stand leaning against my truck with my arms crossed while the five of them act like they've known each other a lifetime, and are parting ways forever more. "Emma," I say, "We don't want to be late for your sister's thing."

She waves and climbs into the truck, her good mood fading as the door slams shut. After a few minutes of driving, she says, "Ok, we need to make a plan for today."

"I plan to deflect every question to you, Chezz," I tell her, shifting into fourth gear and letting the sound of the tires on the highway drown out her voice. By the time we pull into the party and I toss my keys to the valet, I think there can't possibly be anything colder than Emma's mood. And then, of course, we encounter her parents.

90

EMMA

"I accept your apology, Veronica." After the nightmare at the country club, Thatcher dumped me and my things on the curb and peeled off in a snit. All I want to do now is sink into a hot bath and then go to bed. "Yes, I understand that you had planned this announcement with Logan a long time ago. I never intended to upstage you. Thatcher and I were trying to keep things quiet until after his brother's wedding, like I said."

From the second we arrived today, my family picked at Thatcher. To his credit, he smiled and politely deflected every barb. I flush with pleasure again remembering my mother asking him where she might have seen his "little creations," since he's an artist. Thatcher smoothly asked her if she'd ever heard of the Museum of Modern Art. Did it with a straight face, too. She fluttered her hands around and promised to look him up later.

But Veronica threw an absolute fit. She grew louder and louder, hissing and screaming that I sprung some edgy, artist fiancé on the family on purpose just to detract from her big moment with Logan. And my father chimed in that he didn't think my "engagement" was a good tactical move for his re-election campaign. The wait staff actually had to come to our table and ask Veronica to keep her volume down.

"Veronica," I interrupt her asking me if it's absolutely necessary for Thatcher to wear a nose ring to her wedding. "I have a meeting with my neurologist in the morning, so I need to get some rest." Talking about my neurologist always gets my family to shut up immediately. They hate that they didn't select this doctor for me from their approved list of big names, but they do begrudgingly recognize that his help has improved my life dramatically. We hang up the phone after she offers another half-assed apology for letting her manners slip away in public. Because, of course, in private the other Cheswicks think it's fine for my family to judge people and make decisions about my love life based on how it looks for my father's campaign. I set an early alarm and flop angrily into bed, wondering how I'll smooth things over with Thatcher.

I SPEND the morning writing from home and submit a draft to my editor, who is giving me comp time for the afternoon since I "worked" this weekend. Around 3, I take the bus to the hospital and run into Dr. Khalsa in the lobby, which surprises me. He must be really excited about this medication trial. "Ah! Emma! There you are." He takes my arm and introduces me to his colleagues. We walk to one of the conference rooms rather than his office, where he sets up a presentation and starts to explain their new clinical trial on medical marijuana.

There are tons of questions from the International Review Board and a hell of a lot more paperwork than I signed when I started taking my other medications. Those actually alter my brain function. Isn't this a bit much hoopla for some pot? After about an hour of this, Dr. Khalsa asks me if I'd like him to go with me to the dispensary to pick up my "medication" for the trial.

"Um, sure?" This is hands down the most bizarre experience of my life, up to and including the time I covered the Furry Convention for the *Post* and had to interview guys who get their rocks off dressing like foxes and squirrels. We walk a few blocks to a standard-looking office building and take the elevator to the Wellness Center. When we walk inside, the space looks like a spa, with potted orchids and sleek, modern furniture.

I thought it would be skeezy, reminiscent of the pot dealers I visited with Nicole in college. There's not a Bob Marley poster or tie-dyed tapestry in sight. There are tablet devices on the wall for people to go "shopping," and Dr. Khalsa explains that we don't need to use those because I need to use very specific products for the clinical research. An employee greets Dr. Khalsa warmly and takes us back to a small, private office. Instead of chairs, we sit on yoga balls while the staff explains that I'll be using a vaporizer and cartridges that come pre-filled.

They slide me a slim device that looks like a compact mirror...but Dr. Khalsa explains that I simply slide the cartridge inside, press a button, and inhale the vapor. Eventually, the goal is for me to no longer need my standard medications, but Dr. Khalsa has me on a graduated plan for his clinical trial. All the cartridges are pre-filled, ready to go. "Just follow the schedule, and I will see you in two weeks for some testing," he says.

I feel my jaw drop when the cashier asks me if I saw the discount for Shark Week, but Dr. Khalsa explains that I'll be using the hospital's account. I am assigned a number, and everything is taken care of by the researchers. Dr. Khalsa even arranges for a car service to take me home, so I don't have to sit on the bus with my medication. I know he's just feeling antsy about me getting pick-pocketed, but I'll take a ride where I can get it.

I ease into the back seat of the sedan, enjoying the leather interior and air conditioning on full blast, and I pull out my phone to a series of missed calls and texts. Nicole, of course, is eager for details from this weekend.

A text from Phil: **This draft is tolerable, Cheswick.** Definitely nicer than when I submitted my last draft. I think I'm really solidifying my spot on the staff. I squirm in my seat a bit, anxious to get to work tomorrow and see his comments for revision on my article about Juniper.

Then a text from Thatcher. **Can we talk?**

I chew on my fingernail. I know I need to see him. We left things...tense. I tap back *Want to come over? I'll be home in ten.*

C u soon. Will bring sandwiches.

One thing I am really coming to like about the Stag family is they always have food. *Door will be unlocked. Just come in,* I write back.

When we get to my apartment, I tip the driver and settle into my couch to re-read the instructions on the "vape" pen. Because of my condition, and how much it sucks to have seizures, I never experimented with drugs or alcohol. Once I found out what works to keep me healthy, that's always felt more important than a temporary buzz. If I'm honest, I'm glad Thatcher is coming over later to be here after I use these cartridges. I have no idea how my body is going to respond. I finger the medic alert bracelet that's always with me.

Reading through the information sheet one last time, I decide I'm ready. I slide the cartridge into the pen, press the button, and breathe deeply. I feel the cool vapor swirling into me, and I slowly exhale. Not bad. I try again. *Hm.* Now I guess I just wait. I whip out the log from Dr. Khalsa and record two puffs, 4pm, Monday. No seizure aura today. Feeling great.

I set the supplies on the coffee table and wait to feel...different. Nothing happens except I have to pee, so I make my way into the bathroom, slightly disappointed.

91

THATCHER

"Knock-knock," I yell, feeling weird just walking into Emma's house, even though she told me to. I hear water running somewhere in the apartment, so I walk in and sit down on the couch. I drop my messenger bag filled with takeout sandwiches, and look around. I love that Emma keeps the glass I gave her in a prime spot where it gets the sun. It's the focal piece of her entire apartment, and I smile, knowing she's thinking of me basically any time she's looking around her living room. I also definitely see now how she thought I made her a neuron.

The afternoon light catches the sculpture, and I follow the line of reflected light to the coffee table. "Hey now," I say to myself, seeing what Emma's got: an entire bag full of cartridges from the dispensary and...yep. A loaded vape pen just sitting on the table, begging me to try. *I brought this girl sandwiches,* I think. *She can spare a hit.*

I breathe in the smooth vapor, realizing Emma has acquired some seriously high quality THC. I'm just exhaling it all through my nose when Emma opens her bathroom door and sees me using her shit. She looks pissed.

"What the fuck, Thatcher," she shrieks. "I told you that's from my doctor. I'm not allowed to fucking share that!" She throws a shoe at me. Honest to god, reaches down, takes off her shoe, and throws it at me. I duck. "It's illegal and..." she grunts and throws the other shoe, "It's going to mess with Dr. Khalsa's results."

I set the vape pen down on her table and stand. "Emma, Jesus, I'm sorry. I took one hit." I pick up one of her shoes and hold it out to her, and she stares at it, laughing hysterically. *Oh, so she's already stoned.* I meet her eye and draw back, like I'm going to throw the shoe back at her. She squeals and fumbles around, reaching for the bookshelf.

"Thatcher Stag, don't you dare!" Emma yells.

"How do you like it, Chezz?" I toss the shoe at her, not hard, and both of us laugh when it hits her in the boob.

She gets closer and nails me with a book. "Will you knock it off? Fuck!" She hits me in the head with a hard back, and I stride across the living room to block her. When I get close, Emma yelps and starts running away with a copy of Harry Potter book 7. "Oh no. You're not throwing that at me. That's the heaviest one." I catch up to her in the hall and reach for the book. She's holding it up high as if I'm not almost a foot taller than her. But rather than snatch it easily from her hand, I decide to tickle her armpit.

She shrieks and tries to run again. *It's on now.* I can definitely feel a buzz, which makes this whole thing even more hilarious as I chase her. We're both laughing now. She tries to slam her bedroom door in my face, but I block her with my foot, wiggling my fingers like a tickle monster. Emma trips on a pair of shoes and goes to the ground. I drop on top of her, dodging a spike heel, and start to tickle the fuck out of her.

"Damn you, Stag," she grunts, kicking at me, but then she starts laughing a deep belly laugh when I find a sweet spot on her sides. She keeps on laughing and I pin her arms above her head with one hand, using the other to lift the hem of her shirt. I meet her eye, and then drop my head to blow raspberries on her stomach.

The sound of Emma laughing is probably the most magical thing I've ever heard, or maybe the vape cartridge was just that good. Soon I'm lying on top of her and Emma stops laughing when she feels me grow hard against her stomach. She breathes heavily for a minute, searching my face, for what I'm not sure.

I smile at her. "You ever fuck someone while you're high, Chezz?" She shakes her head. I drop one hand to her tits and squeeze. "You want to try it out?"

She lifts her head to take my mouth in a fierce, possessive kiss. I respond in kind, thrusting my tongue in and out of her mouth, hard, while I reach up inside her shirt to find her nipples. I fucking love how she feels under my hands, helpless with her arms pinned above her head, and loving it.

She moans as I circle one rosy nipple with my thumb, so I release her arms and get both hands on her sensitive tips. There's no finesse to how she's moving now. She's desperate, needy. I can tell her nerve endings are firing like crazy and I love seeing Emma unhinged like this. "Thatcher," she breathes, the sound of my name on her lips the biggest turn-on since I saw her naked for the first time.

Her hands fumble with my t-shirt and waistband, like she can't figure out which to take off first. I sit up to help her out, reaching behind my neck to strip off my shirt with one hand. "Ahhhh, shit," I hiss, as Emma dives into my jeans. She pulls out my shaft and gives my balls a squeeze. I look down as Emma climbs to her knees and drops her head into my lap. "Oh, fuck," I moan, as that pink tongue darts out and circles the tip of my cock. "Emma, holy shit. That feels so good."

I kneel on the floor of her room while Emma sits in front of me, sliding her perfect mouth along the length of my shaft. She's got one hand at the root of my cock and the other massaging my balls. This is an art form, a fucking thing of beauty. She looks up at me with those big, green eyes, her red hair tumbling all over her face, sticking to her sweaty cheek, and then she slides me so far into her mouth I can feel the back of her throat on my tip. I groan and drop one hand to her back, gently rubbing her, while the other rests on her head. I don't ever want this to stop...until I realize that I might blow my load in her mouth, and I haven't gotten to fuck her yet. "Emma, sweetheart, you gotta stop," I say, and she pulls off my dick with a wet-sounding pop.

"Or what, Stag?" she says. "What will happen if I don't?" She teases me like she's going to dive right back on to my dick, but I can tell she's playing with me now. I grab hold of her waist and spin her around until she's on her hands and knees on the floor.

"I'll fuck you from behind until you scream, Emma," I whisper into her ear as she moans. "That's what." I yank down her slacks and panties, pulling them just past her knees. I haul her up so she's on all fours and reach down to her center. I find her wet and hot, swollen and ready for me to slam inside her. "You want me to fuck you now?"

She nods, and I slide a finger inside her. "You're soaked, Emma. What's got you so wet?" I tease her, withdrawing my finger as I kick off my jeans and boxers. I kneel behind her, massaging her round ass, giving it a shake.

"Thatcher," she groans. "Please. Fuck me, Thatcher."

And there it is. With that permission I grab hold of her hip and drive inside her. Emma screams, delighted, and I wrap my other hand into her ponytail. I love how my fingers look entwined with the fire of Emma's hair. She bucks her hips back against me as I pound into her. I can feel my knees scraping on the floor and I know I'm going to have brush burns later, but I don't give a fuck. I've got an incredible woman wrapped around me right now and I don't ever want to let her go. The realization of that scares me for a minute, and I slow down.

Emma looks over at her shoulder, her eyes hot with lust, her mouth hanging open until she bites her lower lip. I meet her eye and redouble my efforts. She starts breathing heavier and lifts one hand, moving it to her clit so she can get herself off. "No," I growl, surprising us both as I push her hand out of the way. "I'm going to make you come, Emma. Me. I fucking love to make you come, Chezz," I say as I bury my hand in her red hair. One above and one below. I rub one of my thumbs along the back of her neck, and I rub the other in slow circles along her throbbing clit.

As Emma starts to moan, I drop back onto my heels, pulling her onto my lap so she's bouncing up and down on my cock. Lowering my hand from her neck to her chest, I feel her tits shake in my hand while she rides me. "I'm so close, Emma." I'm panting as I pull her against my chest. "I need you to come for me." And for probably the first time, she does what I tell her to. Emma starts to moan and I feel her pulsing around me, milking my dick until I blast off inside her.

"Emma!" I shout her name, pulling her in tight until the lightning stops, until the thunder of my orgasm quiets down and I can see again. Together, both of us gasping and slick with the sweat of exertion, we tumble to the floor in a knot of red hair, Emma's jeans, and wet pleasure from both our bodies.

92

EMMA

"Is this what drunk feels like," I ask, one hundred years later, entwined in Thatcher Stag so tightly I can't quite figure out where each of my limbs is located.

"No, Chezz," he says, laughing at me. "This is what stoned feels like."

"Hmmmm," I sigh. "I like this." I think I drift off to sleep, but eventually I open my eyes to see Thatcher kneeling beside me with the hand towel from my bathroom. I hear it dripping on the floor. "Did you just soak my towel?"

He starts to giggle. "I couldn't find a wash cloth, but I wanted to clean you up," he says. And the gesture is so sweet, that I try to let go of my frustration. I spread my legs a little and let him wipe me, slowly and gently. The warm cloth feels good along my thighs, along my center. "Mmmmm, that's nice," I say.

"Do you know how hot you are, Emma Cheswick?" he asks, and I shake my head. "You're the most amazing woman I've ever seen." He drops to his knees between my legs and plans a kiss on my clit. Suddenly, I'm wide awake as he shows me just how much he likes what he sees in me.

My skin feels like it's been electrified. Every inch of me is tuned in to what Thatcher is doing in a totally unique way. I feel laser-focused on his tongue and the way it slowly laps at my folds, the way his thick fingers slide inside my body. This is what it feels like to be worshipped, and I am loving it. I come quickly, taking me by surprise, and I groan his name, pulling him up by the shoulders until his head is close to mine.

I reach out a hand to touch his beard. He's glistening with moisture. *Me,* I realize, touching the hair beneath his lower lip. "Mmm," he moans as I slide my thumb along his lip. "That's right, Emma. You're dripping wet for me." He kisses my neck and slides a finger inside me. "So." Another kiss. "Wet." Another. "Just for me," and he slides inside me, fully sheathed. Our hips touch and I open my mouth wide.

"I'm so full, Thatcher. So full of your cock." And then I can't think, can't form words as he thrusts, hard. I have no idea what I'm doing with my limbs, but I see myself wrap my legs around his waist, dig my fingers into his shoulder. I cling to him, not wanting any separation from our bodies, as he grunts and, just as I shatter into another orgasm, he fills me with his own sticky release.

BY THE TIME Thatcher brings the sandwiches into my bedroom and we tuck in, breaking all my rules about food on my sheets, it's dark outside. He hands me a huge glass of water and tells me it will help with my dry mouth.

"How did you know it was so dry???"

He laughs. "This isn't my first time getting high, Chezz." I tell him I'm glad he's here, since I have no idea what to expect, and he says, "I'm like your weed doula."

"What the hell is a doula?"

He talks with his mouth full, wiping his wrist over his lips, explaining, "Alice and Amy hire these ladies who help them out when they're in labor. So it's like...someone who helps you do hard things. Anyway, it was a joke."

Weed doula. "I like it, Thatcher. There's not a lot of people I trust to help me do hard things." And damn if Thatcher Stag doesn't blush a little bit when I tell him that.

He finishes his sandwich and rolls on his side, looking at me. "We need to talk about the thing with my father," he says, his expression stern. I nod. "I'm going to tell my family. All of it. But I'm not going to tell them before Ty's wedding," he says. "I don't want to give Ty the burden of having to decide if he wants him there or not."

I furrow my brow. "Wouldn't he want his father at his wedding? I mean, doesn't he want that now, regardless of whether you found him?"

Thatcher shakes his head. "He wants a dad at his wedding, someone who raised him and cared about him and wants to see him happy. That's Tim. Ted Stag walked out on us when we needed him most."

"And...so you're just going to give him an organ? Undergo an invasive, risky surgery? Because why?"

He flops back on the bed. "Jesus, Emma, I wish I hadn't told you. I didn't say I was going to do it, ok? I said I asked about it. I got some testing. I still don't even know if I'd be eligible, but--" he drifts off.

"But what, Thatcher?"

"But it has to be me if it's going to be one of us. Tim has kids and Ty is a professional athlete. It matters more if something happens to them."

"Thatcher!" I sit bolt upright. "Do you mean to say you don't think it *matters* if something happens to you during surgery?"

He exhales long and slowly. "Look," he says. "I just got a huge fucking contract. I can live off that money for a few years, at least! The way I see it, I can complete the work for Clemont, have the surgery, and take my sweet ass time recovering. I'll even be able to float Cody's salary while I'm laid up."

I stare at him with my mouth hanging open. "You were going to just go through with that entire plan and not involve your family? How would you feel if they did the same thing," I ask.

He closes his eyes. "I'm going to tell them. After the wedding. I promise." And he rolls over, snoring in my bed before I can even decide if I want him to spend the night.

93

EMMA

I can't muster up the energy to leave my room, but I'm also not ready to fall asleep yet, so I stretch, reach for my phone in the heap of clothes on the floor, and call Nicole.

She picks up immediately. "Listen, my so-called friend. You have kept me waiting for like 36 hours to hear about your weekend with the Reindeer. This better be good." I can tell Nicole is still at work. If she's at home, her voice echoes off her nearly empty apartment walls.

"You know it's Stag. And anyway, you can't yell so loud your co-workers hear, Nicole." I hear her chair creak as she adjusts her seat.

"Yeah, yeah. Spill it, Ems." I sigh. "A sigh like that? Shit, I should get some ice water."

"Funny you should mention ice," I tell her, and proceed to fill her in on the wild, mind-blowing sex I had with Thatcher.

"So he gave you an orgasm before your first orgasm was done...orgasming?"

"Pretty much."

"Jesus, Emma. Can I have a ride when you're done with him?" I know Nicole is kidding, but it doesn't sit right with me. I don't like the thought of Thatcher with someone else. I frown. "Your silence is very telling, friend. Want to tell me more about that?"

I look over to Thatcher's sleeping form. He's rolled onto his stomach and one long arm dangles off the edge of my bed. He's so tall that his toes peep out from the bottom of my blankets, suspended in the air, making me giggle. "He's here right now, Nick. I, like, texted him for sex and he brought sandwiches, and I thought he'd leave after, but now he's asleep." I blurt it all out so fast that I don't have time to hold anything back.

"Hmm," she says. "I'm going to have to meet him. I need to see how he acts around you."

Usually, I don't move ahead with a guy until Nicole gives him at least a thumbs sideways, but I feel sheepish at the idea of asking Thatcher to meet my best friend. "I don't know..."

"Let me know the next time you're going to see him and I'll at least give you a ride. Before he gives you a ride." She bursts out laughing so loudly I look at Thatcher, making sure he doesn't stir. "Seriously, though, Emma, I'm really glad you found someone who gives you hot sex. You deserve some hot sex. Never settle for mediocre sex."

I sigh. "I see that *now*. I really had no idea. Did I tell you Dr. Khalsa has me doing a trial of medical marijuana?"

"Jesus! I'm coming over. Wait. You have a naked man in your bed. Shit. When am I supposed to hear all about this??"

Once I get Nicole to calm down I am able to tell her how Thatcher stole a hit from my "science weed" as she calls it. "I still can't believe some dude got to see you for your first high. I've known you for years! Can I watch you get high tomorrow?"

"Of course, Nick." We share a laugh and plan for her to come to my apartment tomorrow evening. Once we hang up, I realize there's nothing left to do but crawl under the covers with naked Thatcher, and try to sleep. I try to ignore my sense of longing for him to drape that inked-up arm over my shoulders.

94

THATCHER

I open my eyes to see what's tickling my face. I know I have long hair and a beard, but I don't usually half choke myself on my own locks. Then I remember. I fell asleep at Emma's after two rounds of, frankly, the best sex of my life. When I turn my head, she's there next to me in the bed. Her red hair is sprawled everywhere. Thick and straight, it has strands of gold, brown, and umber. I can't help myself--I reach out and start to run my fingers through the silk, stroking it and watching the colors shift in the light. I look at the contented smile on her face and, rather than feel eager to get the fuck out of here, I feel so damn glad to wake up beside her. I was supposed to be talking with her about our exit plan for this contract. I need it to be her who breaks things off, or else the whole thing was pointless. But right now, ending things with Emma is the farthest thing from my mind.

My stomach growls and I decide to comb Emma's cupboards and make us some food. That's what a real fiancé would do, right? Might as well play the part since I'm here anyway. I slip on my boxers and dig through the fridge. She doesn't have much, but I figure I can make French toast at least. I get to work and am just sliding the first slices on to a plate when I see Emma padding down the hall wearing my t-shirt. I freeze as a huge, unidentifiable emotion seizes my chest. It's not arousal, although I definitely feel turned on looking at her with no bra, imagining her pink, tight nipples pressed against the fabric of my shirt. I frown, realizing that I'm feeling some combination of possession and pride and, well, joy at seeing her like this in the morning. Limping a little, smiling a lot, looking content.

"You cook?" her smile is dazzling. I'm glad I decided to do something nice for her, if it means I get to see that look on her face.

I shrug. "When I'm hungry." I drop a piece of toast onto another plate and then slide it down the counter toward Emma. "You've got a hitch in your giddy-up, Chezz," I say, grinning when she winces climbing onto the stool.

"Well, whose fault is that?" She takes a bite of toast. "Mmm, this is really good, Thatcher. Did you add cinnamon?"

I nod, turn off the burner, and sit in the stool next to her. I nudge her with my shoulder playfully. *What the hell am I doing?* I haven't flirted like this in years. I don't need to. Women are usually throwing themselves at me, and I always know I'm going to go back to their place. Emma is different. I care what she thinks about me, and she calls me out on my bullshit if I act like a jerk. I made her breakfast, for fuck's sake. I clear my throat and get to the matter at hand. "So, Emma, like I said, I think we need to make a plan for, you know, after Ty's wedding."

She frowns and puts down her fork. "How am I supposed to break up with you? I'm not doing it in public or causing a scene at the wedding, let's be clear about that."

"Jesus. No. You don't even have to actually do anything. We just need to agree about what we're going to *say* you did. Will do. Whatever." I finish my toast, thinking. "You know it has to be you ending it, right? We talked about that."

She nods, pushing her fork around in the puddle of maple syrup on her plate. I think for a bit, sigh, and tell her, "I think it can work if we just tell my brothers your parents don't approve of me. Which is true anyway."

Her jaw drops. "Thatcher Stag, I would never end a relationship with someone because of what my parents think! No. Absolutely not!"

"Emma," I put my hand over her hand. "This isn't about what you would *really* do. Remember? This is about convincing my family that I'm not an oversexed playboy."

"They're going to think I'm some frivolous child who does whatever her parents want her to do!"

"Well who cares what they think of you?"

She recoils from me, staring. "Are you serious? This whole thing is about you caring what they think of you, Thatcher." She sighs and stomps off to the bedroom.

"Hey," I chase after her. "Come on, Emma." She throws my jeans at me.

"I have to go to work, so you should probably get dressed and take off. That's your M.O. isn't it? Morning meeting? Busy day ahead?" She yanks on a pair of jeans and a black t-shirt, throwing my shirt back to me before she slides her feet into a pair of Toms. "Look, Thatcher, thank you for the great sex and the breakfast. I don't accept your proposal for this ending to our illusion, but I'll think on it and get back to you in a few days."

"My proposal?" I fish around under her bed for my shoes. Shit, this gives me a sense of déjà vu.

"Yes. This is a business transaction, right? I'm negotiating our exit clause. But first I'm going to go meet with my editor and you're going to leave my apartment and do whatever it is that you do."

I'm used to women being angry when I leave the morning after sex, but I'm not used to feeling like I want to make things right. This shit with Emma is screwing with my head, because she's supposed to just be someone I'm making a deal with, and now everything is complicated and layered. I shake my head and rest a hand on her shoulder for a minute since I feel like kissing her, but know that she'd probably slap me.

When I get in my truck I pound the steering wheel a few times. "Fuck!" I shout in the empty cab. This is why I don't do relationships. Even when it seems like it's just fun, it always gets intense.

Before I can check myself, I aim my truck toward downtown and pull into the visitors lot at the hospital. I'm in a foul mood, and I feel like telling my father a few things about how fucked up it is to leave your family when they need you. They moved him to a private room on a different floor. The nurse in the hallway tells me he's getting released soon and they're hoping someone can convince him to check into a rehab center now that he's been safely detoxed.

I don't greet him, just walk in and sit in the chair beside his bed. He drops the newspaper he's holding and turns to look at me. "Didn't think I'd see you back again."

"Yeah, well you were asleep the last time I came. So now I've been a better son to you than you deserve. Twice."

He closes his eyes, then looks at me. "I want them to let me die, Thatcher. I can't do this without Laurel."

I want to feel bad for him, that he's so wrecked about this, but it's not like my brothers and I weren't wrecked, too. "Fuck you," I spit out. "You had responsibilities. To us. You think she'd want you to treat us this way?"

He just shakes his head. I feel depleted now, so I stand up and shove the chair away and walk out of the room.

95

EMMA

Phil calls me into his office first thing to talk about my draft. I submitted a profile of Juniper, highlighting her journey to Olympic gold while also transforming the law office where she works. Stag Law used to just focus on *male* professional athlete contracts, but Juniper helped them expand to represent women's sports and other equity issues. Now Stag Law has a huge, national reputation as the go-to firm for equal rights or equal pay cases. They even handle cases for people who need legal protection based on their sexuality. I closed the article by describing Juniper sitting for the bar exam in various states, years after she finished law school and initially took the exam, so she'd be able to serve clients wherever they need.

Phil, of course, wants more. "Needs more grab," he tells me, sliding the marked up copy across the desk. That's it. The extent of his commentary. I interpret this brief speech as him sending me back into the field, which is how I find myself riding the elevator up to Stag Law to shadow Juniper at work for the day.

She greets me with a hug at the elevator and ushers me directly to the kitchen, where Alice is getting ready for lunch. "Can't talk now," she says, stirring a giant cauldron of something delicious-smelling.

"I'll ring the bell in an hour and you can sit with me and Juniper and dish!"

I feel awkward accepting their friendship after Thatcher and I just tried finalizing plans to end things. But I had agreed to play the part for two more weeks. I wonder if there's a way to break up with Thatcher but still hang out with his family? I follow Juniper to her office, where the walls are decorated with pictures of her on the podium in Tokyo. I pause in front of a picture of her with Ty. She's got a gold medal around her neck and is beaming straight at the camera. Ty just looks at her, his face utterly transformed by love and pride. He's got an arm around her shoulder, squeezing like he never wants to let go. *I want someone to look at me like that,* I think, drawing a ragged breath.

"So," I ask her, sitting down opposite her desk. "What are you working on this morning?"

Juniper smiles and spins her laptop around. "I know I shouldn't," she says, "But I'm looking at wedding stuff." She's got a Pinterest board open with different ideas for favors and programs. She bites her lip, waiting for my response. I'm touched that she'd show me something so personal, so obviously important to her.

"You're quite a complex person," I tell her, scanning the different pictures.

Juniper says, "I want to do something that celebrates hockey and rowing...I mean those are really the things that are important to Tyrion and me...none of these templates have quite what I want."

"You know," I tell her, digging into my bag for a card. "Some of the graphic designers at work do this kind of thing on the side for spare cash." I find what I'm looking for. "I bet if you hit up Hillary she could lay out a program for you in a few hours."

"Really??" Juniper claps her hands. "This is the very last thing we have to really do before the wedding. That would be amazing." She snaps up the card and closes her laptop. "Ok, whew. Enough about that. Now we're going to drive over to the football stadium and yell at some offensive linemen who got a drunk and disorderly the other night."

.   .   .

A FEW HOURS LATER, and I know for sure I have Juniper's story rounded out. I can't wait to get back to my revision. I want to show everyone this amazing woman I've met, who can man-handle 300-pound football players and, in the next breath, navigate a settlement with a university who refused to offer equal scholarship funds to the women's varsity rifle team. By the end of the day, Phil agrees they can run the piece a few days before Juniper's wedding. He claps a hand on my shoulder. "Nice work, Cheswick," he says with a smile. "This will generate the kind of buzz we need, and it's writing that's got meat to it." He stands up from his desk, grabbing his bag. "I'd offer you a drink, but you don't do that. So I'm sending you home early to cele-brate...however you do that sober."

I can't believe my boss said "nice work" to me. I'm doing really creative writing, interviewing interesting people and getting feature-length assignments in the biggest newspaper in the city. It's like a dream come true! I immediately text Nicole to see if she can get away for a bit.

When I get to her office, she's in the middle of an intense game of foosball with a group of colleagues. I lean against the wall, watching. I love how Nicole takes no shit from anyone, elbowing some guy out of the way when he tries to offer advice on how she can get more leverage. She sinks a goal and pumps her fist. "Yes! All right. Now, I'm taking a break for two hours. I expect that proposal on my desk when I get back, guys. I'm serious."

She drapes an arm over my shoulder and we walk out into the warm July sunshine. "Friend," she tells me. "We are going to get ice cream, and then buy you a dress for this celebrity wedding, and then you promised I could watch you get stoned." I laugh, relieved I can trust Nicole to help me find a dress my mother would hate, but will make me feel comfortable in a room full of lawyers and professional hockey players. "Do you think you can hook me up with any of those Fury hockey players?" she asks while we wait for our waffle cones. "I need to have some sex that has me limping like you, girl."

96

THATCHER

Emma doesn't call for a few days, and then texts me out of nowhere, demanding a ride to family dinner on Sunday. Ok, she didn't demand. But I don't even know how the hell she found out about the dinner, unless she's been texting with Alice and Juniper. If that's the case, then I am well and truly screwed when it comes to ending this whole thing. Sure, sex with Emma is amazing. But then we always end up in a fight and it's too much work to make peace. Now she's hanging out with my sisters in law. They're getting way too friendly. It's starting to feel like an actual relationship with Emma, and that's a lot of work I'm not interested in doing.

I'm cold and distant when I pick her up, and I can see by her face that she's pissed at that. I'm not even sure why, but I really dig into her and say, "You didn't have a seizure aura today did you?"

She whips her head around to glare at me. "No. What makes you ask that?"

"You're acting like something crawled up your ass and bit you," I sneer at her, knowing full well she's just responding to my bad attitude. I don't even know why the fuck I am picking at Emma. Probably because I had a shit week after seeing my father, a shit meeting with my agent, and now I don't feel like playing pretend at my family dinner.

Emma just sighs and stares out the window. I must be acting like a dick if Emma Cheswick doesn't even feel like fighting with me. Fuck it.

We get to the house and Emma disappears with Alice and her sister. Amy looks a little bit like she's going to explode, but I hear her tell Alice she still has 3 weeks left at least. I try to remember what Alice looked like pregnant with my nephew, but that draws up a memory of my mother, swollen and round, pregnant with Ty. I don't have the space to be thinking about my mother today so I head out back to the cooler where Tim keeps the good beer.

I don't even pause to appreciate how it tastes. I work on drinking it quickly until I hear my younger brother coming toward me. "What's eating you, Thatch?" Ty is Mr. Good Mood, sauntering shirtless into the back yard.

"Why the fuck do you look like that?" I gesture at his mesh shorts and sweaty hair.

He shrugs and cracks open a beer. "Juniper and I ran here."

"From Washington's Landing? What's that, like 3 miles uphill?" I chug the beer even faster now. Literally everything is pissing me off today.

Ty sips his beer. "Four and a half. We went around the zoo. Hey, man, take it easy." He sticks out an arm to slow me as I open a second beer, but I shove him out of the way. I down it and grab a third. Used to be, the three of us went running together every Sunday and then ate pancakes with our grandma. Now Ty runs with Juniper. Who even knows if Tim leaves the house anymore. I've been running alone.

When I get back inside, Alice's brothers are watching baseball on the couch, so I sink in next to them and try to ignore everyone until it's time to eat. I'm feeling just about buzzed enough to calm down after 3 beers, but everyone definitely stares at me when I take a seat opposite Emma instead of next to her.

The table creaks under the weight of 12 sets of elbows, and I focus on the scratched wood, precariously heaped with corn, tomatoes, and grilled chicken. Eventually I become aware that someone is talking to me when there's a lull. "What?"

Emma clears her throat. "I was just telling them that I got a new assignment to interview the director at the Center for Organ Research. The national headquarters is here in Pittsburgh, and they're going to talk to me all about organ donation."

"That's fucking morbid, Emma." I shove a forkful of chicken into my mouth. I know I've hurt her. She's so interested in everything, always wants to research different things and learn more until all her damn questions are answered.

She narrows her eyes at me. "Well, some things are morbid, Thatcher."

Tim makes a face and puts down his fork. "Our mother was an organ donor," he says. We all stare at him, and Emma, sitting beside him, puts a hand on his shoulder. What the fuck is going on here? She has no right to be comforting my brother about our dead mom.

"Nobody wants to talk about organs and dead bodies over family dinner," I grunt, emphasizing family and glaring at Emma. She pulls her hand back into her lap and raises an eyebrow at me. "Why don't you ever write about anything pleasant?"

"Oh, like a smarmy ladies man who sticks glass in the gardens?" Emma tosses her napkin down on her plate. Ty and Tim stare at us, but I don't say anything. Fucking Emma keeps going, though. "Thatcher might be an interesting source for this piece about organ donation," she says to the room at large.

Ty pipes up, "Why would anyone care about Thatcher for a story about that?"

I shake my head and kick her under the table. *Oh fuck. Please, shut up, Emma. Fuck. No.* But I'm not fast enough. She blurts, "Because he's looking into the living donor program." I guess this is how she responds to me being rude on purpose. By airing out my shit to my nosy family.

I breathe slowly through my nose, trying to hold my shit together. I want to throttle her right now. "I can't fucking believe you, Emma."

She stares at me and I glare back at her.

"What's all this?" Tim is in full dad-mode now, leaning forward past Amy, who starts to interject about all the living kidney donors she treats at work and how great that is.

Amy looks at me. "Are you donating a kidney to someone?" She looks back at Emma, who is red in the face and shifting in her chair uncomfortably. I hope she feels bad now that she's stirred up the Stag family drama.

"I think you should leave now, Emma," I say, my voice cold. My family all stares at me. I'm going to have to hash it out with them now. They won't fucking ease up until I tell them everything, and I am furious.

Emma just nods and stands up. She stumbles a little walking toward the door, and Alice runs over to her. "Emma, wait. How are you going to get home? Tim will drive you."

"Alice," Tim says, his eyes on me, his voice flat. "Call Emma a car service. I think my brothers and I need to have a talk." He stands from the table, throwing down his napkin and gesturing toward the garage out back. The Petersons all cough uncomfortably and Alice's brothers keep eating, but Ty stands up. Sighing, I follow them out back. Might as well face the music.

Ty shoves me against the wall. "The fuck is wrong with you, talking to Emma like that? And why the hell would you get angry-drunk at family dinner?"

"Enough," Tim says, crossing his arms, staring at me like he used to when I came in at 2am on a school night. "Tell me what the hell is going on. Leave nothing out."

AN HOUR LATER, Tim screams at Ty to put a shirt on and he drags us all into his Volvo. "Where the hell are we going?" I sneer at him from the back seat. He just grits his teeth. I know full well he's driving us to the hospital.

"We're going to confront him," Tim says, "and tell him we hope he dies a slow and painful death, and that he is absolutely not risking your life to take one of your fucking organs, Thatcher."

"It wasn't his idea," I say. "He doesn't even know I met with the counselor about it." I had gotten my results back earlier in the week and I am a perfect match for my father, in perfect health.

"Tell me again what your plan was here, bro?" Ty grabbed another plate of food from the house and is eating in Tim's car, swatting his hand away when he tries to take the messy food. "You were going to get the money for your project and then, like, get your body parts chopped out and rest up for a year?"

"Something like that."

"At what point were you going to inform us of this master plan," Tim spits out. "Did you think we would just not notice when you showed up with a cane and a giant scar?"

"Do you really think you would notice, Timber?"

"Fuck you, Thatcher." He slams the car into park and starts walking toward the entrance. We follow him, the three of us slowing down as we approach the room where Ted Stag is fully unprepared to see us en masse, for the first time in 15 years.

He drops the book he was holding as the three of us stand in the doorway. Tim grinds his teeth, seeping fury and pent up rage. Ty looks like he's going to cry, taking deep, heaving breaths. Our father looks back and forth at the three of us, our mother's grey eyes staring coldly back at him. I know we look intimidating. Hell, we were intimidating as kids. We're grown ass men now, all over 6 feet tall, and pissed as hell. Our father speaks first. "Good to see you again, Timber. Should I kick *you* out of *my* space this time?"

"What is he talking about," Ty asks, shoving his hands in his pockets.

"This asshole tried to crash your party," Tim says, not breaking his stare at our father. "After your first game with the Fury. I had him ejected."

"What?" It's my turn to feel shocked. Our sanctimonious brother saw our dad and never fucking told us? And somehow I'm a dick for keeping secrets?

"If he can't be there when we need him most," Tim grits out, "he doesn't get to be present when we celebrate."

Ted Stag swallows and his head flops back against the bed. "I suppose that's fair." He looks out the window. "Thatcher told you this is it for me?"

Now it's Ty's turn to speak up. "He fucking told us you have an opportunity to get sober."

Dad scoffs. "You think I want someone's liver? You think I'd take that? Would you want your mother's liver to go to me?" Tim recoils like he'd been shot. God, now I'm thinking about who got our mother's organs, who got to use her final gifts.

"Ok," Ty says, his voice shaking. "So you don't get a second chance at life. But don't you want to spend your final days sober? You only get one fucking life, Dad. You think Mom wouldn't fight like hell to enjoy every second of this?"

"Your mother was always better than me," he says. "In every way." A tear rolls down his cheek, but I can't drum up the energy to feel bad for him.

A few minutes of tense silence pass before I place a hand on each of my brothers' shoulders. I lead them into the hallway and, as soon as we're in the elevator, I pull them in for a group hug. For a long time, we just hold each other, not speaking, communicating everything and nothing all at once.

97

EMMA

I tell Tim's driver to take me to Nicole's office, where I collapse on her couch in a heap of tears. Nicole shouts for an intern to bring me soup from their kitchen and I marvel through my sobs at how different life is inside a tech startup.

"I blurted his secret," I moan to Nicole. "And now he's so angry at me!"

She furrows her brow. "Weren't you scheduled to break up with him in a week anyway? Sounds like fate took that out of your hands..."

My eyebrows rise. "But...it wasn't supposed to be this way."

"What way, Em? Did you think you'd become fuck buddies and then make your silent exit and never see each other again with no hard feelings from either side?"

"Yes!" I shout, burying my head in my hands. My nose is running but I'm too upset to wipe it up. "No! I don't know."

Nicole slides onto the couch next to me and puts her arm around my shoulders. "Honey," she says. "It's ok to have feelings for him."

I shake my head. "He doesn't do feelings," I insist. "Have you seen him on the Internet? He's a cold-hearted snake."

She pets my hair, speaking softly and comforting me. "It sounds like he's just defensive because the people he cares about keep dying or walking out on him."

Nicole urges me to go home and take an extra puff on my vape pen before climbing into bed. I notice she's got a copy of the Post on her desk and I sob again when I see that my story on Juniper is on the front page of the Sunday edition.

OVER THE NEXT FEW DAYS, I leave Thatcher five texts and two voicemails, trying to apologize for blurting his secret to his family. I've stopped crying as hard about it and start remembering how he was such a dick from the moment he picked me up that day. In fact, he had been rude to me since the morning after we last slept together, so maybe it's not me who needs to be in apology mode. Well. Anyway we both messed up sort of equally.

What would a relationship with him be like? Constant fighting probably, his moody outbursts. Me always worried about blurting the wrong thing to his family members...*Or maybe he'd always bring you just the right food and make you come until your eardrums burst,* I think.

I spend the week trying as hard as I can to get over Thatcher Stag and our fake, amazing-sex "relationship." I'm on the verge of getting there when my mother shows up at my apartment Wednesday evening. After I let her in, she stands in the doorway, sniffing uncomfortably as she looks around my home. She's only been here once before and it's better for both of us if she doesn't stay long. "Emma," she says, lifting one eyebrow at me while I microwave the dinner she interrupted. "You know your sister has *such* a lovely little home in the southern suburbs. There's a direct train line to downtown..."

"My office is on the North Side, mom," I say, trying to keep emotion out of my voice and focus on the facts. "I'd have to transfer."

She sighs. "Well, anyway, I've come to make sure you have an appropriate dress to wear tomorrow evening." When I look at her, confused, she points to a stack of mail on the coffee table. "Your father's fundraising event is tomorrow. I made certain to inform you via email and by post, as this one takes place in your...neck of the woods." Because of the weird way that voting districts are mapped out, my father's constituents mostly live in the wealthy suburbs south of the city, but there's one small panhandle that reaches the north side of the city. I'm actually surprised he hasn't hit me up to do more campaign propaganda for him before this.

"I've been busy with work, since the hospital and all..." I wave a hand at the stack of mail. It's a total lie. Work has been amazing. At home I'm just wallowing in sadness that I messed things up with Thatcher.

My mother frowns. "I hope you haven't been giving too much of your time to that man you're calling a fiancé."

I sniff. Then I sigh and roll my eyes. "Give me the breakdown about dad's thing."

She smiles. "It's in an art gallery! Andy something."

"Dad's having a fundraiser at the Andy Warhol museum? I'm impressed. He must really be courting edgy voters." I start to slurp at the frozen soup I nuked for dinner. I don't invite my mother to sit, and she doesn't.

"Yes! Well, voters are voters, dear. There are a number of artists whose work is being displayed, and they'll be present, mingling with donors. It's going to be a very impressive evening."

I make a face at my mother. "You know artists do things like pierce their noses and grow long hair, right?"

She clucks her tongue. "I'm certain that's only the low level artists who aren't *used to* the notoriety that can come with pricing their work at this level." She sniffs and her nostrils flare. "This will be a *sophisticated* event. I'll expect you there at 6pm. Dress is cocktail attire, Emma."

She swirls out the door just as my phone vibrates with an incoming message. I snatch it up eagerly, hoping it's Thatcher, but my heart sinks when I see it's from Juniper. **The programs turned out just perfect! Can't wait to show you Friday night at rehearsal!**

I feel like I shouldn't even respond until I hear back from Thatcher. I don't even know if I'm still supposed to be going to the wedding with him. Maybe the explosive Sunday dinner was the ending to this whole charade after all.

98

THATCHER

Maria paces around my workshop with me, helping to select the final piece to stick in the new showing at the Andy Warhol museum. It's a big fucking deal to have a piece in that museum, and I know that, but I'm so wrecked emotionally that I can't get it together to micromanage my display. Thankfully Maria knows her way around my work and the look I am shooting for. She's got Cody boxing up my new series of green glass. I'd been melting down old beer bottles and adding in bits of cobalt, sculpting ephemeral looking shapes. Lots of swirls. People are into swirls these days. I like them, but Maria frowns, walking past, tapping her fingers against a clipboard.

She walks over to the shelf where I keep my Emma. I'd been calling the piece she inspired my Emma. I stare at it for hours each day, trying not to think about her, but unable to look away. I know I need to call her, talk to her. I haven't seen my brothers since Sunday, either. Just been holed up in my studio working at the furnace nonstop.

"This one," she tells Cody, reaching for Emma.

"No. That's not for sale." I fly off my stool.

"Thatcher," Maria looks at me, puts her hands on her hips, and scowls. "You don't need to sell it. You just need to *display* it. This is the fucking Andy Warhol museum."

I shake my head vehemently. "Not that one. That one's private, Maria. I told you that last time."

"I remember. And I disagree with you." She turns to Cody and insists he box up the piece. "We'll display it in the center of the green glass swirls. I like how they go together."

"If you so much as chip it, Cody, I'm going to pull out your teeth one by one." I start pulling my hair, which reminds me that I promised Ty I would trim my hair and my beard before his wedding. *Just make it so it looks deliberate,* he'd said. He really did ask nicely, and I make a mental note to visit the barber. Anything to keep my mind off all this shit with Emma and my family.

When Maria and Cody take off with my glass, I feel unsettled. I don't like being in the studio without my Emma. I think back to how I was feeling the day I made that piece, how I'd just come from sitting with her in the hospital and then taken care of her like it was noth-ing. And it was nothing--it felt as effortless as taking care of my nephew. I do that for family. Not anyone else, though. It's too risky. Safer to just keep everyone distant before they get a chance to walk away from me when I'm an asshole. The thing is, Emma isn't going away. She left me a bunch of messages this week. I'm the one who isn't calling back. It's me not letting her in. I keep telling myself if I ignore her, she will go away and I can focus on my art in peace. Just how I like it.

Only today I can't find any fucking calm. My refuge is buzzing. The empty space on the shelf makes me uneasy, and I don't want to be in here anymore. I close up shop and drive over to find my broth-ers. I can be near them even if we're all mad at each other.

Tim's office is closest, and I'm surprised when I run into Ty at the reception desk. Then I realize he's probably there to fuck Juniper on her lunch hour. I'm not sure why that pisses me off, but it seems like everything irritates me this month. "Thatcher," Ty yells. "Good. You saved us a trip. Come on."

"Where are we going? What's going on?" Tim walks into the hallway, adjusting his tie as I see Alice slink out of his office, smoothing out her work coat.

I snort. "Jesus, Tim. Can't you guys do that at home?"

He coughs and mutters something about the childcare at work, and then turns on Ty. "What was so important I had to leave my meeting early?"

"Your meeting? Come on, man."

We ride down the elevator and pile into Ty's new Range Rover. "You like?" he asks. "Juniper bought it for me as a wedding present."

"You two are ridiculous," I mutter, punching Tim's shoulder since he made me sit in the back seat. "Where are we going?"

Ty sighs. "I don't want to get married and start a new life with JJ until we hash shit out with dad."

"Nope," I say, pulling on the door, which unfortunately locked when Ty put the car in gear. "Not going with you for that." I jiggle the handle to no avail.

"Fuck you--I have it on child lock in case Petey rides with us," Ty says. "This is what I want from my best men. I want us to go together and tell our father to go to hell, but also I want us to invite him to clean his shit up and maybe stick around. Meet his daughters in law and grandkids someday."

For the next hour, I remain silent. When we get to the hospital, Ty tells him exactly what he said in the car. Ted asks questions about Tim's wedding band, waves around Emma's article from the Post, asking about Ty's wedding this weekend. I roll my eyes. "You don't get to know any of those details," I tell him, pressing Tim back into his seat before he has an aneurism. "You didn't show up for Ty's junior league games, you didn't pay the bills while Tim was in college working full time to support us, so you don't get to know about the ways we turned out happy despite all that." I'm just getting started now. "I fucking know you've read about me in the paper, too, and I don't care. Do you know I looked into giving you my liver? What the fuck was I thinking? You don't care enough about your own sons to get healthy, work on your grief, and be part of this family. Let me give you some parting comfort: we turned out ok. All of us. And it had nothing to do with you."

Tim and Ty just stare at me, and our father starts crying then. He buries his head in his hands and sobs and Tim pulls us all out into the hallway. "Enough," Tim says. "Let's get out of here. We've said our piece. Now let's let it lie." I exhale, feeling the weight of the years lifting a little bit. We start walking toward the elevator, but a nurse comes jogging down, calling out, "Stags? Are you Ted Stag's sons?"

99

EMMA

I call Thatcher one last time before getting ready for my father's fundraiser. The call goes directly to voicemail, so he either has had his phone off for four days or he's declining my calls. I sigh. This was supposed to be simple. Hang out with him and his family a few times to get an interview. Get some great clips for my portfolio, and maybe earn some credibility at work. Why does it feel so shitty now that all of that has happened? I wonder what his family thinks about our apparent breakup. He must have told them he can't trust me...

I slide into my cocktail dress. It's a black shift, so it's more form-fitting than I prefer, but I like how the boat neck shows off my collar bones. Nicole insists the dress makes my boobs look hot, and I turn sideways, observing that they do look pretty high and front with this bra she made me buy. I fasten a string of pearls around my neck, but refuse to put on nylons in the middle of July.

As I pull my hair from the hot rollers, I think about how my end of the bargain worked out. Work has been amazing. Phil praised me during the staff meeting today, and my in-depth piece about the organ donors is going to be phenomenal. None of that feels as good as Thatcher making me a new coffee pot when I broke mine, or letting me have the ham sandwich even though it's both of our favorite.

I can't even look around my bedroom without remembering the feel of him taking me from behind. Every other man I've ever been with has treated me so cautiously, I felt like they didn't even respect that I'm a whole person. Thatcher managed to be wild, all the while focusing on what made me feel good. "He made you a neuron before he knew that mattered," I say to myself in the mirror. I try not to cry because I've put a touch of brown mascara on my auburn lashes and I don't want it to smudge.

I decide this is as good as I'm going to look, and I slip into a pair of heels, grab my bag, and begin my walk to the museum a few blocks away.

When I get there, I see Veronica first, sipping white wine and clinging to Logan's shoulder in such a way that her diamond ring is visible to everyone. "You're going to cut me with that," I tell her as she pulls me in for a fake hug and a fake cheek kiss. "Since when are we French?"

Veronica pouts at me and says, "Jesus, Emma, can you just behave one time for Dad?" Logan smirks and I roll my eyes, looking around for our mother.

I hear her before I see her. She's bellowing, "Oh *there's* our other daughter, Emma! Emma, you simply must meet Tristan Cummings!" I turn around just in time to be thrust toward a smarmy-looking guy who is escorting my mother across the room. *Shit, she's trying to set me up,* I think, realizing this is how she is responding to her horror at learning I am engaged to Thatcher Stag. Was engaged? Anyway, there's no way I'm hanging out with this guy. She makes a face at me and I stick out a hand for Tristan to shake. "Tristan just made partner at his law firm," she says, fanning herself. "He's not even 30!"

"Congratulations," I say, smiling my fakest smile.

"What do you say we grab a drink to celebrate?" He asks and he honest-to-God winks at me.

"Hm, you know, I haven't said hello to my father yet," I tell him. "Won't you please excuse me?"

I never thought I'd be using my father as an excuse for, well, anything, but to escape Winky Lawyer, I slip toward the center of the gallery space. "Daddy," I say, coolly. "This is a lovely event."

"Emma!" He kisses my cheek. "You remember Mayor Gil."

I nod. I've actually interviewed him more than a few times, and printed critical articles about his proposed referendums. His smile is strained and he looks for something to say, so he gestures to the art I haven't had a chance to take in yet. "Interesting stuff, this."

As soon as I look up I know it's Thatcher's work. There's a glass woman in the middle of the room, the focal point of the entire gallery. She's made from orange and red glass, twisting up, lit from within. She's reaching toward the heavens, rays of red and orange and yellow shooting from her hands. The display is stunning. She's set on a pedestal, surrounded by low sculptures blown in vibrant greens and blues. She looks like the sun, rising from the sea. Triumphant. I nearly cry, the piece is so moving. I can't believe how the light and the space all work together to transform the work from what I saw on the shelves in his studio. I hear my father saying, "Yes, it's quite dramatic. Evidently the artist will be here tonight."

I gasp. *Thatcher will be here.* I start to look around, and I feel my mother come up and put her arm around me. "Emma, do you see what I meant about quality artwork? This piece here--this is the work of someone refined and elegant. Passionate and bold!"

I stare at her, not believing that she hasn't bothered to read the plaque bearing Thatcher's name. I don't really get time to ponder this for long, because Tristan glides back over holding two flutes of champagne. "Emma, darling," he says, his voice slick as an oil spill. "How about we take that drink now?"

I sense Thatcher arriving behind me and my body yearns for him. Then I hear his deep voice, smooth and certain, with an edge of danger. "The lady doesn't drink alcohol." I smell him, the familiar, wonderful scent of *him* above the evergreen soap. I feel his big, strong hand wrap around my waist and he pulls me close. I exhale, feeling like I haven't drawn a breath since our fight Sunday. When I look up at him, I'm stunned. Thatcher has trimmed his beard short and neat.

He's cut his long hair underneath, buzzed it into a tight undercut and kept the top long. In his dark, fitted button-down shirt and black slacks, he looks so fucking sexy I nearly swoon. I let myself lean back against him, savoring the close warmth of his touch.

Tristan's expression darkens and he asks, "And just who might you be?"

I can feel Thatcher smile behind me. "Thatcher Stag," he says, sticking out one hand for a shake and keeping the other possessively on my stomach. "Emma's fiancé."

My mother giggles, a high-pitched, nervous sound, as my father's eyes start to bulge from his head. "How silly of me to forget to make introductions. This is just all so *new* that we aren't yet used to Emma's...betrothal."

My father clears his throat. "Yes, we're all quite excited. But if you'll excuse us, we are due to meet with the artist before things kick off this evening, so..." He drifts off and looks back and forth between Thatcher and the Mayor. I blush and bite my lower lip.

Thatcher clears his throat and keeps his hand out. "So glad you're enjoying my art, Mr. Cheswick. Pleased to meet you in person, Mr. Mayor. When I did a piece for the lobby of the city council building last spring, I only met with your staff."

The mayor pumps Thatcher's hand. "Stag! Yes! Of course! I see the similarity in style with this work here. You did that black and gold bridge for us. We get so many compliments." He gestures toward my father with his drink. "Cheswick, you didn't tell me your daughter was marrying a *Stag.*"

My mother's skin has gone grey and she starts fanning herself with her program. Veronica floats over with Logan and tries to ease the tension. "Can you tell us what inspired this piece here?" She leans in to read the plaque. "Emma? Oh! It's called Emma! That's you!"

Thatcher grins. He leans forward and beckons for my family and the mayor to lean in. He whispers as my father takes a sip of his gin. "I made this one the first time I saw your daughter naked."

100

THATCHER

Emma's dad spits gin all over the mayor and her mother screams. Chaos erupts, with staff members rushing over to dab up the mayor and wait staff offering everyone ice water. I just stand there, holding Emma against my body, enjoying the feel of her shaking gently, trying not to laugh. I found out who this event was for, and knew she would be here. Hell, I wanted to just skip the whole thing rather than deal with any drama. Maria, of course, practically dragged me here. I had intended to avoid Emma all night, but when I saw her walk in wearing that dress I just about came in my pants.

Then I saw her talking to that douchebag and I realized something huge. I don't want anyone else to be with Emma, because I want to be with Emma. I don't just want to sleep with her. I want to make her smile, and watch her get excited about researching weird, morbid articles. I don't want her going to fundraisers with uptight men who use too much gel. I want her with me, even if that means figuring out how to talk about my feelings and being in a fucking relationship. And realizing that makes my dick even harder than it was before.

I thrust my hips against Emma's back, letting her know just what's going on with me, and she inhales sharply. "Yes, Chezz," I whisper into her ear. "I want you right fucking now."

She looks over her shoulder, and then back to her family. Her mother and sister are dabbing the mayor with napkins and apologizing while her father puts on a fake smile and tries talking to the guests who have pulled in closer to see what's going on. Nobody is going to notice our absence for a long time, and I grab Emma's hand, pulling her down the hall to the bathroom.

Outside the door, she grabs the wall. "Wait," she says, shaking her head. "No."

"Chezz," I say, nuzzling her neck, "I need you."

She flicks my chest and backs away from me. "You were such a dick the last time we talked, Thatcher, and now I haven't heard a word from you all week."

I sigh. "I know, Emma. I know. Please understand that this whole week? This whole month, really, has been so hard for me." I try to close the distance between us, needing to be close to her. "I don't know how to do all this," I say, waving my hand between us as she scowls at me. "But I'd love it if you could give me a chance to try."

Her face softens. "What do you mean? Try what, Thatcher?"

I pull her pale wrist to my lips and kiss her softly, stalling while I try to think of what I need to say. It all sounds so lame when I think about telling her everything on my mind. I look into her green eyes and see trust there, behind her frustration. I shrug. "Just try to be better at talking to you. I don't want to push you away anymore. I want to be right by your side, even if you're puking in my brother's yard. I want to fight with you and bring you sandwiches. Be with you."

She crosses her arms and frowns. "You want to be with me? Like for 3 more days?"

I shake my head. "No. I mean yes, but I don't want to stop on Saturday. Emma." I touch her cheek. "I want all of you." I gesture over to her family. "All of that."

Emma licks her lips and runs her fingers along my collar. I breathe a sigh of relief, because I think I have won her back over. "All of this?" she asks, stretching up on tiptoes and biting my lower lip. I grin at her and kick open the bathroom door, tugging her in alongside me.

Once we're inside, I twist the lock and pull her in, sinking my lips against hers. I moan because it feels so god-damned good to taste her again. I delve into the corners of her mouth with my tongue, needing to claim her, to show her all the things I can't find words to say. She emits a tiny moan and I'm done for. I spin her around, looking over her shoulder at our reflection in the mirror as I pull her in to my chest. My hands splay over her tits, feeling her nipples spring to life under that tight-ass dress, and I slide one hand up to fist her hair. She has it all curly and draped over one shoulder and it looks hot as fuck.

I tug on her hair, tilting her face up toward mine. "Emma," I whisper, my lips against her mouth. "Look how good we look together." She moans as I move my hand to her skirt, inching up the hem until I can slide a hand around to her wet heat. "You're so wet, Chezz," I say, nipping at her ear, watching her reflection in the mirror.

Emma leans forward, supporting her weight on the counter as I yank down her panties. She bites her lower lip and turns to look at me directly. "I can't believe we're doing this, Thatcher! In the bathroom at the Warhol..."

"Believe it, Emma." I drop a kiss on her mouth and pull one of her hands to my crotch. I help her ease down my fly and when she hoists my dick out of my pants I grunt like a wild animal. That's how she makes me feel--feral. I suck on Emma's neck and nudge her thighs apart with my knee as I palm my shaft. She's panting for me, and when I slide a finger along her pussy, I feel that she's swollen and wet. "You ready, Em?"

I line my tip up to her opening, teasing her folds and sliding along her wet seam. "Mmm, Thatcher, please. Now," she says, jutting her hips back against me, drawing me inside. I grin into the mirror and thrust inside, sliding home. Something snaps inside me, and I think about how this is the only place I want to be. The only woman I want by my side, around my cock...everything. "Thatcher," she says, her voice snapping me back to the present.

Emma is slamming her hips back against me, bracing her arms

against the sink and moaning. I match her rhythm and the sound of our skin slapping together echoes off the bathroom walls. I'm not going to last. It's been too long since I was with her, and I got too worked up seeing her talk to that asshole. "Chezz," I pant.

She nods. "I'm close, Thatcher. Oh! God, yes. Just like that." Her head drops back against my chest and I pull her tight, wrapping both arms around her body and rocking into her.

"Emma!" Her name is a plea, a prayer, a release, and I feel her contracting around me, coming right with me as I pour into her until I'm spent and replenished, empty and somehow bursting all at once.

101

EMMA

I grasp the edge of the sink with both hands, trying to catch my breath as Thatcher pulls out. He sinks to his knees and, looking at me in the mirror, slowly eases my panties back up my legs, then adjusts my skirt.

He stands and washes his hands while I'm still trying to breathe slowly. Once I feel ready to adjust my hair and my bra, I notice that he's all tucked in and looking perfect. "When did you cut your hair," is all I can think to say. Every single time with that man leaves me dizzy, literally seeing stars and weak in the knees.

Thatcher runs a hand up the dark stubble of his under-cut. "You like it? I only went this short for Ty's wedding, because he asked nicely." He grins. And then I'm so overcome, I just start to cry. "Hey," he says, "Chezz, don't cry." He pulls me in and holds me. And he just feels so warm and safe that I actually do stop crying, believing for a moment that things can be ok.

"Can I tell you something?" he breathes into my hair and I nod against his chest. We always seem to communicate better when we're either naked or not looking at one another. He takes a deep breath and tells me, "My dad agreed to go to rehab."

I draw back so I can see his face, feeling like I have to look into his eyes for something like this. "He did? Truly?"

Thatcher nods, and tells me that the three of them had gone to see Ted in the hospital, spewed decades of angry words, and then made to leave until a nurse flagged them down. "He's going to give it a shot. His doctor said they can prescribe an antidepressant for him..."

He drifts off, and a tear leaks from my eye, because I know what it means for him to be telling me this, for him to finally be finding some closure in this area of his life. "Thatcher," I whisper. "I'm so glad for your family." And then I bury my face in his chest again, not wanting to let him go.

He holds me, murmuring into my hair about how he and his brothers are going to sign up for a group at the hospital. They have programs there for grieving lost parents, and the Stag brothers never really worked on their feelings about losing their mom.

"Hey," I tell him, reaching up to cup his face. I smile and look into his eyes, wanting so badly for his return smile to be mine for always. "I'm really proud of you."

He shakes his head. "No, Emma. It's because of you. You led me to find him, and you pressed me to be honest with my brothers. This never would have happened without you. So thank you, Chezz." He kisses my palm. "Thank you." And then his lips are on mine and nothing else matters.

Until I hear someone pounding on the bathroom door.

"Emma Cheswick, you open that door this instant." It's my mother. "I know you're in there."

I sigh and look up at Thatcher, who adjusts his collar and runs a hand through what's left of his long hair. "You ready for this?" I ask him, and he nods.

When I open the door, my mother digs her nails into my arm and pulls me into the hall. "How. Could. You. Humiliate. Us. Like. This?" She jabs an index finger into my chest with each word.

Ordinarily I would be super stressed out to see her freaking out like this, but I'm still high on a Stag orgasm, and I'm strangely calm.

So I tell her, "Excuse me, mother, but I think I am the one who should be embarrassed." She recoils. "You've been nothing but rude to Thatcher since you met him in the hospital. You treat him like garbage and make assumptions on him based on his appearance, which I love by the way, and then you don't even do your diligence to look at the fucking name of the artist in the space where Dad's having a fundraiser."

Thatcher squeezes my shoulder supportively while my mother flares her nostrils. I keep going. "And further, I should be embarrassed that you're so hung up on appearances that you kept me with a useless doctor for years of uncontrolled seizures. Thatcher has been super supportive, helping me with my new medications from Dr. Khalsa. You haven't even asked about my visit from last week."

I want to walk away. I'm feeling absolutely done with her. But I'm not expecting her to start crying.

Tears roll down her face, smearing her foundation. "Emma," she whispers as Veronica approaches. "I was so scared." She sinks into a folding chair that's been stashed in the hallway. "Do you know what it's like when your baby has something wrong? I don't mean what other people think, although I worried about that, too." She dabs at her face with a tissue. "I mean the feeling of utter helplessness. I couldn't help you. I took you to the doctor everyone talked about. I didn't know there were other ideas, newer treatments. I just thought that was going to be it for you, and I needed to keep you isolated and safe."

She looks up between me and Thatcher and Veronica, now. Everyone is silent as she pleads with us. "I thought I was doing my best by you, and then when I realized how out-dated it all was, how much *better* you were doing with a doctor you'd found on your own..." She drifts off and swallows. I can see her struggling to breathe in between sobs and I just stand there, my hand on Thatcher's on my shoulder. I need the warm touch of his skin to keep me grounded.

"I was dreadfully ashamed, Emma. Of the years I cost you. I'm so terribly sorry, and I don't know how to begin to make amends for that."

The hallway is silent for a long time until Veronica sniffles. I bite my lip. "I accept your apology," I whisper, and then, for the first time in a very long time, I lean forward and willingly embrace my mother.

102

THATCHER

S hit got really real there at the Andy Warhol museum tonight, and I feel like I need a good, stiff drink. Except I'm leaving with Emma on my arm, and she doesn't drink alcohol. She and the other Cheswicks cried and hugged for awhile. Eventually her dad shook my hand and told me my sculpture was nice. I try to imagine how I'd react if some asshole told me he made art from my naked daughter, and I decide Mr. Chezz isn't all that bad.

Emma wants to walk home, so I take her high heels from her, draping an arm over her shoulders while she walks barefoot along the sidewalk. "Did you really make that sculpture based on me?" she says, the street light reflecting off her green eyes and looking amazing. It gives me ideas. She's always inspiring my work, and I love that.

I nod. "You looked like the dawn after a long darkness, naked and glowing. Aurora," I tell her. "I don't ever want to forget that moment." We walk in silence a bit more until I gather up the nerve to tell her what I really need to say. "Emma," I say, squeezing her hand. "I want to talk about us."

"Hm?" she looks down, stepping over a pothole as we cross the street. I squeeze her shoulder and stop walking.

"Chezz, I don't want to end things with you after the wedding this weekend."

Her eyes dance back and forth, her gaze searching mine. "I need you in my life to keep calm in emergencies. You inspire me, Emma. Christ, do you know what you do for my work?" I gesture around. "All of that back there, that's you. That's all you. You are my muse." She starts crying now, and I rub my thumb on her cheeks, brushing away the tears. "Be with me, Chezz. Give us a shot." There's an eternity where my heart stops and she doesn't respond, and I think I've put myself fully on the line, raw and exposed, and she's going to turn me down. But then she closes her eyes and stretches up, grabs hold of my face with both hands, and sinks into the sweetest, best kiss of my life. Then I know she's mine.

103

EMMA

Nicole insists on giving me a ride to Ty and Juniper's wedding. Thatcher had to be there super early to deal with flowers and tuxes and stuff, but promised he'd come outside to see if Nicole approves of him.

She spends an hour setting my hair in hot rollers in the morning, spraying my red locks into a cascading fountain of curls. "You look hot as fuck," she tells me as I slip into a pair of jade green strappy heels. They match the dress perfectly, and I twirl around, watching the skirt billow out. I definitely look ready for a celebrity wedding.

Ty and Juniper are getting married in the conservatory, surrounded by Thatcher's glass of course, and because Ty and his teammates will all be there, security is heightened for the whole area. Nicole beams as we pull up to the guard blocking the street from through traffic. "I feel like I'm chauffeur for the rich and famous," she tells me. Then she leans out the window and tells the guard, "I'm delivering Emma fucking Cheswick to Thatcher Stag."

He looks through the window over the top of his sunglasses and waves Nicole on. She squeals. "Nick, you're being ridiculous," I tell her. "They're just *people.*"

But I feel giddy when I spy Thatcher up ahead, waiting for me on the sidewalk. Nicole whistles and I don't blame her. Thatcher in a tux is pure elegance, pure sex, and all mine. He grins as we pull up, running a hand through his neatly-trimmed beard. He opens a door for me and whistles as I climb out. Nicole laughs, but Thatcher looks awestruck. "Chezz," he says. "You look so beautiful right now." His words are so earnest that I blush and squeeze his hand. "You ready for all this," he asks, gesturing toward the photographers swarming around the Escalades and Range Rovers bearing Fury players and their dates.

Nicole sighs and clutches her hands under her chin. Then she leans over and sticks out her hand toward Thatcher. "Nicole Thomas, best friend. Damn glad to meet you, Thatcher Stag." He grins at her, shaking her hand. "You take care of our girl, now."

He pulls me against his side and kisses the top of my head. "She doesn't need taking care of, Nicole. I need her to take care of *me*."

When Thatcher says that, Nicole punches her horn and gives me a double thumbs up. "Emma, he's a keeper. Go mingle with the hockey stars, get me someone's number, and then go have hot sex and beautiful babies." I laugh as she peels out.

Thatcher escorts me inside, where the entire conservatory seems to be in bloom to celebrate Juniper and Tyrion. Thatcher kisses my hand and leaves me with some other guests while he takes his place up front just as Tim and Ty enter the room. The trio of brothers standing tall, dressed to kill, is quite a sight to behold. I hear a sniffle beside me and see Anna Stag taking pictures of her grandsons, then dabbing her eyes with a hanky.

I give her leg a squeeze just as the violins start playing and Juniper makes her way toward her beloved. Tall and sleek in a simple, elegant white dress, Juniper has eyes only for Ty. They make their way through the ceremony, holding hands. Ordinarily I find this kind of thing cheesy, but I can't help but smile during the vows when Juniper blurts out, "I'm keeping my name!"

Ty smiles at her and squeezes her hands. He says, "I sort of thought you might, Junebug." When he leans in to kiss her, Thatcher pulls him back, scolding him for jumping the gun.

After they are pronounced married, there's a loud commotion from the crowd of well-wishers. I bite my hand in glee when I see all Juniper's rowing friends line one side of the aisle holding oars. Ty's teammates line the other side of the aisle holding hockey sticks. The two sides form an unlikely arch, and Ty and Juniper walk through their friends, laughing. Smiling. Happy and in love. I catch Thatcher's eye and we share a moment until he walks forward.

He kisses his grandmother's cheek and then, with a lustful look, squeezes my shoulder and asks, "Gram, can you excuse Emma for a minute? I need her." Anna Stag smiles and pats my hand as Thatcher tugs me into the hall.

"Where are we going," I ask, looking around, until I realize we are in the hall where we first met. Where he took me for nefarious purposes. Things have certainly changed in the past month. "Oh," I say, running my hands down his chest. Ty picked out stunning grey tuxes to match his brothers' eyes and I let my fingers trail down the long tie, wrapping it in my fist and pulling Thatcher in for a kiss.

He growls and boxes me in against the wall like he did that first night, nibbling my neck, and this time, I let him. Eagerly. "Emma," he breathes, "Do you want to know what I was thinking about during that ceremony?"

I roll my head to the side as he kisses a trail up to my ear, down along my chin. He smells so good and I love these gentle touches. "How much your brother loves your new sister-in-law?" I ask him, playfully.

He shakes his head and looks into my eyes. "No, Emma. I was thinking about you. How right you look sitting with my family, being here for my family's important days. I love you, Emma Cheswick."

I feel a whoosh as my breath leaves my body. Oh, to hear these words from this man! Since he asked me to be with him the other night, he's been so present. We've barely spent a moment apart in all that time, and now, as I lean against the glass wall of the conservatory where we met, I know I feel the same. "I love you, too, Thatcher."

EPILOGUE: THATCHER

SIX MONTHS LATER

"Just try your best to relax," Emma says, standing behind the couch and rubbing my shoulders. I have restless legs and can't settle my hands. This day is so intense. I look around the industrial loft we just renovated so Emma and I could finally move in together. I found a fantastic building in Emma's neighborhood that met all our needs--she can still walk to work, I have a studio for my furnace and kilns, and we have lots of space for her to set up a home office.

Emma slides open one of the glass panels I made to separate different areas of the loft. In doing so, she lets in more light and I can see how hard she's worked to set things up for today. "You bought more chairs?" I ask, noticing that she's arranging comfortable seats around small tables with fresh flowers. Emma nods and dusts off her hands.

"I think we're ready. Alice should be here soon with all the food." I nod and Emma kisses my cheek just as we hear the groaning sound of the old elevator bringing up my siblings. Tim and Ty look about as relaxed as me, which is to say they're stiff and sort of grey.

Today, we're going to introduce our father to our families.

Throughout his time in rehab, he leveled out his antidepressant medication and went through intensive therapy to both face his grief and begin atoning for his choices. We all started receiving packages-- birthday and Christmas cards to symbolize all those holidays he missed since our mother died. Letters expressing his regret that he missed all of our important milestones by allowing his grief be more important than our needs. We don't know if his liver has recovered enough to keep him healthy, but he's been sober for six months and we all agreed to have him over after we met with him a few times at his rehab. It's been hard emotionally, but I've had Emma by my side the whole time.

Living with her really feels as seamless as breathing. Suddenly I had someone to come home to every night, an inspiration for my work, someone to collaborate with for ideas and challenges. I always thought it would be so much work for little reward to give myself to a woman, but Emma is my partner in every way. Hell, she's in the middle of a huge investigative story, but she set aside time this weekend to support me and my family. She reminds me every day that she's not going anywhere, and I trust her. I love the hell out of her, and I can see that she loves me right back.

Petey squirms out of Tim's arms and runs over and climbs in my lap. I hold him tight, rubbing his warm, sticky cheek against my own. Normally we have all our family dinners at Tim and Alice's place, but everyone agreed it was better to have this first meeting at a more neutral space. I sigh and stand, slinging Petey up onto my shoulders. I hear the elevator start to move again, and my breath catches in my chest.

Emma reaches up on tip-toe to kiss my cheek and squeezes my hand. "You can do hard things, Thatcher Stag," she says, looking into my eyes with those emerald orbs of hers. "I'm right here by your side and I love you."

"I love you, too, Chezz," I say. And knowing that helps me feel strong.

When she opens the door to my father, she isn't awkward or

timid. She pulls him in for a quick hug and says, "Ted, hi. I'm Emma Cheswick, Thatcher's fiancé. We're so glad to have you here in our home."

WANT TO CATCH UP WITH THE STAGS?

Check out A Stag Family Christmas and Beautiful Game
to close out the series.

Want to see Nicole get her happily ever after?
She stars in Foundation: A Grouchy Geek Romance.

If you loved this series,
you can subscribe to my newsletter
for bonus scenes, book bargains and more.
Visit laineydavis.com